THE DESIRE OF A LADY

LINDA RAE SANDE

Twisted Teacup
PUBLISHING

The Desire of a Lady

V1.6

ISBN: 978-0-9915075-7-3

Cover photograph © PeriodImages.com and © DepositPhotos.com

https://www.lindaraesande.com

ALSO BY LINDA RAE SANDE

The Daughters of the Aristocracy
The Kiss of a Viscount
The Grace of a Duke
The Seduction of an Earl
The Sons of the Aristocracy
Tuesday Nights
The Widowed Countess
My Fair Groom
The Sisters of the Aristocracy
The Story of a Baron
The Passion of a Marquess
The Desire of a Lady
The Brothers of the Aristocracy
The Love of a Rake
The Caress of a Commander
The Epiphany of an Explorer
The Widows of the Aristocracy
The Gossip of an Earl
The Enigma of a Widow
The Secrets of a Viscount
The Widowers of the Aristocracy
The Dream of a Duchess
The Vision of a Viscountess
The Conundrum of a Clerk
The Charity of a Viscount
The Cousins of the Aristocracy

CHAPTER 1

A LADY PONDERS A TALE

June 1817

Lily Wellingham sighed as she read the last word on the last page of *The Story of a Baron*. She closed the leather-bound book, relieved the fictional characters Lady Geraldine and Lord Ballantine were finally together and about to embark on their happily ever after. She wondered if the author, Anonymous, had experienced such a union and used it as the inspiration for the tale. Several characters bore a remarkable resemblance to some Lady Lily knew in real life, which meant if those characters were based on members of the peerage, then the author was certainly amongst them, either as a peer or as a servant privy to *ton* gossip.

Lily smiled at the thought of a lowly servant writing such a tale, quietly earning royalties that might be used to pay for a fashionable townhouse in Mayfair when said servant was ready to retire from service. After all, she had imagined such a life for herself if only because that's what maids did—imagined lives much like those found in fairy tales.

A charming prince, besotted, sweeps the maid off her feet and rides off into the sunset... a handsome prince kisses the sleeping maiden to wake her from a spell, lifts her to his horse, and rides off into the sunset...

A lowly frog requests a kiss from a princess, transforms into a prince, and they ride off into the sunset.

Well, that last one was quite impossible, Lily decided. She rather doubted there was a princess on the planet willing to kiss a frog.

Except, as unlikely as the events of the book were to have happened, Lily knew from her own years in service that when it came to members of the *ton*, anything was possible. Just as in *The Story of a Baron*, an earl's sister could end up happily married to a baron—Evangeline Everly and Jeffrey Sommers were a perfect example. And truth be told, her own situation certainly qualified as unlikely. Illegitimate daughter of a maid, happily working as a lady's maid in a viscount's household until one day—just the year before, in fact—an earl appears to inform her he is her half-brother and wishes to acknowledge her as such.

Lily looked up from the book, realizing she was sitting in the very chair in which she had been sitting that fateful day when Gabriel Wellingham, Earl of Trenton, introduced himself as her brother and said he would see to it she was settled with a suitable dowry and all manner of clothes and frippery appropriate for her new station. Thank goodness Lady Samantha Fitzsimmons had volunteered to see to it Lily was transformed into a lady, her efforts resulting in a successful introduction to the *ton* at the Earl of Mayfield's ball. Lily had also ended up with a number of suitors.

There were too many suitors, in fact.

Lily set the book on the tea table and slumped in her chair. One or two suitors would have been welcomed. The first two had been such a surprise, she remembered feeling rather special, remembered feeling *wanted*. But then another appeared and still another so that she found herself the subject of too much attention, both by the men who claimed to want her hand in marriage as well as by the gossip mongers. As well as those who wrote the gossip for the daily papers. Goodness! The articles made it sound as if she were being courted by half the eligible men in the peerage!

Well, four suitors weren't exactly unmanageable, but by now she had hoped one of them would be the man she thought of every night before she fell asleep. The man who appeared in her dreams. The man she thought of first thing in the morning. The man featured in her daydreams.

But none of those men were that man.

For the man she thought of nearly every day wasn't a member of the peerage. He wasn't even a well-to-do cit. In fact, she wasn't quite sure what he did for a living. Or where he was living. Or if he even remembered what he had done for her all those years ago.

Was it normal to hold a candle for a man who had saved her from certain ruination? Who turned on a friend to make sure said friend didn't extend his licentious behavior onto a defenseless maid?

Probably not, but Lily remembered how the young man had saved her. She wished he could have been one of her suitors. Instead, she had four aristocrats claiming they wanted her hand in marriage.

She was a former maid, half-sister of an earl, and an illegitimate daughter of an earl. With four suitors and none she was particularly keen to marry.

Some stories were just too unbelievable. And she found herself right in the middle of this one.

CHAPTER 2

ON THE TOPIC OF A POPULAR
SISTER

Sarah Wellingham, Countess of Trenton, speared her fingers through her husband's butter blond curls. "Why, give me a glance with those beautiful blue eyes and toss me a sovereign and I'll give you a tumble right here and now."

Gabriel Wellingham, Earl of Trenton, straightened at his desk and regarded his wife with widened eyes. "What?" he replied in shock. "It didn't cost me anything last night!" he claimed in mock dismay.

Grinning in delight, Sarah shrugged. "It's those blue eyes and that blond hair," she whispered as she ruffled up his hair with her long fingers. A gold filigree bracelet dotted with sapphires encircled the wrist at the base of her hand. Although the piece of jewelry was more appropriately worn at balls and the opera, Gabriel had insisted she wear it everyday. "You'll need a reminder you're a countess now, and no longer a commoner," he had said when he first wrapped it around her wrist.

Sarah tore her eyes away from the winking blue jewels and settled them back on her husband's blue eyes. "And speaking of your very best trait, you must know your sister is receiving a good deal of attention, and not all of it because of those blue eyes and blond curls of hers," she said with an arched eyebrow. "She was mentioned again in *The Morning Chronicle*."

The earl rolled his eyes and sighed. "I am a bit concerned

about that," he admitted, "Which is why I'm considering sending the coach to London for her. It would do her some good to spend some time in the country."

Sarah nodded her understanding, not about to tell him she had already sent a letter to her sister-in-law with the invitation to visit Trenton Manor.

Although Sarah was still the manager of the Spread Eagle in Stretton, she had arranged for Margery Higgins, her eventual replacement, to see to the operation of the coaching inn while she prepared for her sister-in-law's arrival. At some point, probably sooner than later, Margery would simply take over and run the inn, but Sarah had promised the owner she would continue her involvement until Margery was truly ready to assume command. With a toddler hanging onto her skirts and what she was sure was another baby on the way, Sarah hoped it would be sooner.

"I fear those who pay her such attendance don't necessarily have her best interests at heart," Sarah said as she took the chair across from her husband's desk. Although she had only been his countess a bit more than a year, Sarah had settled into her role much like she had when she agreed to manage the Spread Eagle.

An earldom, as it turned out, was very much like a business.

Gabriel frowned. "You think they mean to ruin her and... what?" he asked in alarm.

Allowing a sigh, Sarah leaned forward and lowered her voice. "Ruin her and *marry* her," she clarified. "She's a very pretty chit, but there is another reason all the young bucks, and some not so young ones, are interested in taking her as their wife."

His blue eyes widening in alarm, Gabriel shook his head. "Her dowry, do you suppose?" he asked finally.

It took everything Sarah had not to roll her eyes. Although Gabriel was usually a smart man—he hadn't always been, but that had more to do with blind ambition and youth than brains —he sometimes seemed a bit dense when it came to matters of finance. "I suppose," she replied with a hint of derision. "Gabriel, every man vying for her hand may only be doing so because they expect their wedding day to be the means to pay off their gambling debts, hire another mistress, buy a yellow phaeton, and enjoy an auction or two at Tattersall's," she admonished him.

Visibly wincing, Gabriel slumped in his chair. He had been guilty of everything she mentioned and more when he inherited the Trenton earldom three years ago. At least he didn't have to marry for a dowry. His inheritance was quite substantial. "Don't you think she'll be able to discern the fortune hunters from the *legitimate* suitors?" he countered, hoping his half-sister was smarter than Sarah implied with her comment.

Just fifteen months ago, Lily Harkins had been a lady's maid for Lady Samantha Fitzsimmons. The illegitimate daughter of a house maid, Lily knew the identity of her real father, but given the Earl of Trenton never acknowledged her as his daughter, she never expected any consideration from him— nor from his estate. So imagine her surprise when Gabriel showed up at Fitzsimmons Manor and announced he was recognizing her as his sister! Gabriel made it clear he intended for her to enjoy all the comforts afforded to one who was a relation of a rich earldom.

The fact that Lady Samantha had stepped forward and volunteered to take Lily under her wing and see her through her first Season was a testament to his sister's pleasant demeanor and willingness to learn everything she needed to know to succeed among the fickle *ton*. Gabriel often wondered if Lily did it simply to prove to him she could. She certainly hadn't seemed very pleased to learn that she was being acknowledged as a Wellingham at the time.

Sarah considered her husband's question for a long time.

"I cannot speak for Lady Lily when I say this," she hedged carefully, "But I do not believe sincerity is always so easy to determine."

Gabriel leaned back in his chair and rested his head against the soft leather back. "I suppose you are right," he replied. "And given the Fitzsimmons' plan to spend the summer in Europe looking for a suitor for Lady Samantha, I'm going to suggest she spend the rest of the summer with us."

Sarah blinked, rather surprised her husband had thought of such an arrangement. The idea of having another woman in the house for a couple of months was rather intriguing. "An excellent idea," she said. "She can regale us with stories of her time in the *ton*. Tell us a bit about the men who may have asked to court her or who have made it clear they wish to marry her," she continued, her excitement building. When she noticed Gabriel's increasing frown, though, she added, "And you can decide if any of them are suitable prospects."

The earl took his wife's hand and brought it to his lips. "That, my dear, is a capital idea. I'll send word to her of our plan on the morrow."

Sarah gave her husband a nod, hoping Lady Lily would agree to the arrangement. *But, of course she will. What else is there to do in London in the summer?*

CHAPTER 3

A CLERK MEETS A LADY

The very next day William Overby made his way toward Puddle Dock, his destination the large brick building that housed Wellingham Imports. Having been employed as a caddie for owner Thomas Wellingham since before he was six years old, William had worked his way up in the company and now held a position as an inventory clerk. His responsibilities included keeping track of the goods delivered by incoming ships and matching them with customer orders. With a ship due into one of the Wellingham docks later that day, he expected to work later than his usual seven o'clock end time.

Not having anything better to do, mostly because he didn't wish to spend his hard-earned funds to gamble or employ a mistress or take in many plays on Drury Lane, he didn't mind the late nights at work.

As he neared the side of the building facing the River Thames, he was suddenly aware of a coach coming up from behind him. Stepping toward the front entrance of the import company, he dared a glance over his shoulder and paused. The ancient coach, painted a glossy black but with no markings indicating the identity of its owner, had come to a halt. The driver jumped down from his perch to open the door.

"Thank you, Farley. I don't expect I shall be long."

William stilled himself at the sound of the feminine voice. Familiar, but not quite the same, it reminded him of his mother's voice—his real mother's voice—with its lilt and pleasant tone, its promise of a stern admonishment coupled with a loving hug.

All at once, he was back in the one-room hovel he shared with her and his sister in the Seven Dials, a barely habitable space that his mother, Madeline Overby, had kept as clean as she could until illness prevented her from doing more than her seamstress skills could manage. Death had taken her, he hoped to someplace better.

Turning, William watched as a young woman made her way around the matched Cleveland Bays and headed in his direction. *Of all the times to need a haircut,* he thought in dismay, realizing he had probably needed a trim for over a month.

But the thought of a haircut was gone with the rest of his reasoning ability when he was suddenly aware of her eyes— cornflower blue eyes—for when they caught sight of him, William felt as if he couldn't move. He was also quite sure that his mouth was hanging open in awe, but for some reason he was unable to close it. He knew those eyes, he was sure, knew he had been held captive by their gaze sometime in the past. *Blue eyes.*

He blinked, not quite wanting to remember that night when he had first been caught by those eyes. But the woman who approached him was far better dressed, far more refined than the girl whose eyes had him so mesmerized all those years ago.

How could that be? Was she a sister? Perhaps a relative?

He was about to give the thought some more consideration, but a smile appeared beneath the blue eyes and seemed to brighten the day even more than it already was.

"Good morning," the young lady said with a nod in his direction. A yellow parasol floated above her head, although sunlight still bathed her porcelain complexion and reflected in golden glints from her blond curls. A golden yellow pelisse edged in delicate ruffles and embroidered flutterbies topped a yellow muslin gown embroidered with the same flutterbies.

Blinking, William was about to look around to discover the identify of whomever it was she addressed with her greeting when he realized *he* was the beneficiary of her attention. "Good morning, my lady," he was finally able to say, his voice nearly cracking, its hint of Cockney marking him as a commoner. He remembered to bow and then reached for her hand, thinking he rather wished he was one of the flutterbies that decorated her ensemble.

His adoptive mother, Livia Bingham, had taught him how to greet a lady, and he put the lessons to good use as he brushed his lips over the back of her white kid-gloved hand. "William Overby, at your service," he managed to get out.

A blush colored the porcelain complexion, and the blue eyes widened in surprise. *Or was it recognition?* "It's very nice to meet you, Mr. Overby. I am Lily Harkins, and I am in search of the proprietor of this establishment. Could you tell me where I might find him?" she asked as she executed a perfect curtsy.

William was quite sure he heard a hint of Cockney in her query despite her highborn manner and otherwise refined speech. "Thomas Wellingham. Yes, I... I can take you to him, in fact," he replied with a nod, completely forgetting what he had been about to do when he stopped to regard the coach. Whatever it had been couldn't be as important as escorting the young lady to the owner of Wellingham Imports.

William was about to turn and lead her to the front door, but something about the way she stared at him gave him pause. Good God! *If eyes really are the windows to one's soul, then she has the most beautiful soul imaginable,* he thought as he was momentarily mesmerized by their cornflower blue irises and dark lashes. *I could get lost in those eyes,* he considered, swallowing hard. And, indeed, for a moment, he was lost, for now he was quite sure he had seen those eyes before. It was several years ago, in fact, whilst in the company of a young woman at Vauxhall Gardens.

He had never forgotten that night, mostly because that was the night he ended his friendship with Zachary Hayer, his best mate from his youth. They had gone to the pleasure gardens for an evening of what he thought would be fireworks and a stroll through the gardens. Instead, his friend had used the opportunity to take advantage of a young lady, claiming he would be making his own fireworks on the lawn.

At the moment, William rather wished he hadn't been reminded of that night, for it hadn't been nearly as enjoyable an evening as it should have been, especially when he had been forced to send one of the young women fleeing lest she be Zachary's next victim.

William shook his head as if to clear the unwelcome memory. Concentrating on the woman who stood before him, he simply stared at the chit with what was probably the same look a stableboy displayed when seeing an Arabian stallion for the very first time.

Although Lily Harkins was well aware the young man was staring at her, she couldn't tear her eyes away from his. Not until she had determined their color. *Hazel? Or are they golden brown?* she wondered. *They're golden brown. Which suits him perfectly, given the golden brown color of his hair.* The slight waves in his hair suggested it might be curly if it weren't so long. His hair certainly didn't follow the current conventions for a man of his age—cropped short and combed forward to look like a senator from Rome's earlier age. Goodness, it reached beyond his collar! A rather nice collar. Not made of worsted wool, but rather of superfine, as was the rest of his top coat. His breeches were Nankeen, she thought, and although she didn't dare break her gaze to take in his boots, she was quite sure they were made by a decent cobbler. They would have to be, given how finely tailored the rest of his clothing appeared.

He had no doubt been dressed by a valet who prided himself on keeping his master looking his very best, as this man was certainly looking rather fine. Rather rich, despite his age. He couldn't be much older than five-and-twenty.

Is he an aristocrat? But if he were, she didn't recognize him from any of the events she had attended the past two Seasons. And wasn't there just a hint of a Cockney accent to his otherwise perfect diction? She dared a glance at his hands, surprised to find he wasn't wearing gloves, and his fingers were stained with ink.

He looked familiar, and yet, Lily couldn't quite place where she had seen him before. *Was it in the park?* Or perhaps in a shop? His voice sounded familiar, but where had she heard it before?

She would have given herself more time to contemplate the young man, but she was suddenly aware he was staring at her. Staring, and not even trying to hide the fact that he was staring at her!

"Do I have something on my face?" Lily asked as she lifted a gloved hand to her cheek and attempted to wipe away whatever it was that held Mr. Overby's attention.

William sighed as he gave his head a shake. "Only the most beautiful blush I have ever seen," he said in wonder.

Lily blinked. And she blinked again. Well, there was something to be said for a man who came right out and said what he was thinking. But, of course, the man would come to his senses at any moment and realize what he had said, apologize profusely, beg her forgiveness, and take his leave of her with his proverbial tail betwixt his legs.

Except that he didn't. He continued to stare at her.

"Why, thank you," was all Lily could manage, momentarily wondering why she was there.

Why am I here?

Cousin Thomas!

She was about to finally meet the man who owned Wellingham Imports. He was the man who was the son of her late uncle, Graham. Graydon Wellingham's brother. Although Graham had been the black sheep of the Trenton earldom, eschewing a life of privilege to build his own import business, she had heard his son, Thomas, was more accepting of his family's origins. Apparently the man was as comfortable in a room full of gentlemen as he was in a warehouse full of laborers.

She wondered how he would greet her. Would he afford her the welcome of a relative? Or give her the cut direct for being the illegitimate daughter of his uncle? Well, she was about to find out. At least, she would if the young man who was staring at her would provide an escort into the huge building that stood behind him. "Could you take me to Mr. Wellingham now?"

William blinked, the spell cast over him suddenly broken. *Good grief! I've been staring at the poor chit like a damned puppy in love!* he realized. He was sure he recognized her, but since she hadn't shown the least hint of recognition toward him, William wondered if she just looked like the young maid he remembered from all those years ago. Back at Vauxhall Gardens, at dusk. Just before the fireworks and that nasty business with his best friend at the time.

But he had promised himself he wouldn't revisit that night. Promised himself he would keep the events of that evening tucked away in the back of his brain, never to be thought of again. Well, the events anyway. There was no forgetting her. No forgetting the maid.

Suddenly all business, William gave her a nod. "Yes, of course, my lady. Right this way." He offered her his arm and Lily took it, rather liking the idea of being escorted by such a nice gentleman to meet her cousin for the very first time.

CHAPTER 4

A LADY MEETS HER COUSIN

Thomas Wellingham regarded the stack of manifests on one corner of his desk, the stack of orders on another, and an invoice that one of the clerks claimed required his immediate attention. He sighed. "Remind me again why I allowed Mr. Vandermeer to take off an entire month?"

His wife, Emma Fitzsimmons Wellingham, set down her quill and turned from her desk that was located beyond the door and at the back of his office, a grin replacing the grimace she had been displaying only the moment before. "Because he's worked here far too long without a holiday, and his wife threatened to leave him if he didn't take her and the children to Derbyshire," she replied with a sigh. "A tactic I am considering using on you if we don't have a chance to take a holiday this fall," she added before turning her attention back to the ledger spread out before her.

The ledger had been a source of concern the entire morning, not because the numbers were poor, but rather because they proved that business was booming. Their import business, a trade Thomas had inherited from his father and built up to its current status as one of London's premier import and transportation concerns, might become a victim of its own success if they didn't see to adding more employees—and another broker along the lines of Todd Vandermeer.

A bit alarmed, Thomas rose from his desk and joined his wife. Although she had awakened him that morning with a kiss on the temple and a body ripe and ready for his arousal, he had sensed something was wrong by the time they had mounted their horses for the ride to London from their manor house, Woodscastle, near Chiswick.

Thomas reached down and wrapped his arms around Emma's middle, lifting her from her chair. He spun his surprised wife around so he could pull her into a hard hug.

"I was merely teasing," she managed to get out when he released his hold on her.

"No," he whispered, his head shaking against her forehead. "I promise we'll take off, perhaps when Todd returns next week," he murmured. "'Bout time we took up Gregory's offer of a stay at Cherrywood."

At the mention of the Grandby estate home in Derbyshire, Emma relaxed into Thomas' hold. "Sounds divine," she whispered, her lips meeting his for a brief kiss.

The sound of footsteps—and the slight vibrations in the floor—indicated someone was climbing the stairs to the office level of Wellingham Imports. Given the unevenness of the thumps—*thump-thump thump thump-thump*—and the occasional slighter *tap-tap tap-tap* in between, Thomas realized it was two persons on their way up. Reluctantly, he gave up his hold on Emma. "Are you expecting anyone?" he asked.

Emma shook her head. "No, but given the time of day, it's probably someone for you," she said as she returned to her seat.

Thomas frowned, hoping it wasn't another merchant in need of an almost impossible-to-get product. London's appetite for unusual goods was becoming a bit of a bother.

"Perhaps it's that young lad from the warehouse, asking if he can take tomorrow off because he's finally mustered the courage to ask his gel to marry him," he said as he returned to his desk. "'Bout time I had some success at matchmaking," he added to no one in particular, his comment ending just as a familiar knock sounded at the door. *This must be William Overby.* "Come, he called out as he lowered himself into his chair. He was back up to his feet in a second, though, when he took in the sight of the rather attractive young woman William escorted through the door.

"Mr. Wellingham, you've a visitor," William said as he indicated the comely blonde with her kid gloved hand resting on his arm. "Miss Lily Harkins, this is Thomas Wellingham," William said by way of introduction, his manner rather nervous. Finding he didn't have anything else to say, he suddenly gave Lily a bow and took his leave of the office.

Lily managed a quick curtsy as she watched the clerk depart. A bit disappointed he didn't stay for what she imagined would be an awkward first meeting, Lily turned her attention back to Thomas. She then nodded to Emma when she noticed the tall woman standing in a doorway at the back of the office.

Before she could say anything, Thomas moved from behind his desk to give her a deep bow. He reached for her hand, brushing a kiss over the back of it before he angled his head. "You really must be a cousin on my father's side," he said, the corners of his mouth turning up. "In fact, you look as if you could be Trenton's sister."

Her eyes widening in surprise, Lily nodded. "I am, indeed," she agreed. At Thomas' sudden frown, she added, "Half-sister, actually."

"Welcome, Miss Harkins," Emma said as she moved to stand next to Thomas. She dipped a curtsy. "Emma Wellingham. This is quite a nice surprise," she said, giving her husband a quelling glance. "I must apologize for my husband's reaction. Despite my having told him several times of your existence, he seems to have forgotten he has another cousin," Emma explained with a slight shrug of her shoulders.

"You're Lady Lily," Thomas said suddenly, his eyes widening. "Of course. Oh, I apologize for not realizing the connection," he said. "Please, have a seat, won't you." He waved to the leather chair across the desk from his own.

"I'll get the tea," Emma offered as she disappeared through the door at the back of the office.

"Thank you," Lily replied. The blush that had colored her

face was finally fading as she took the proffered chair. "May I ask about the young man who brought me here?"

His eyebrows arching up, Thomas allowed a grin. "That was William Overby. He's one of our inventory clerks here. Been an employee since he was..." He held out a hand to indicate the height of a very young boy. "... Yay high. He's in desperate need of a haircut. I do hope he was polite," he said with some concern.

"Oh, very," Lily said quickly. "He was most helpful, in fact. Married, I suppose?" she asked, wincing when she realized she sounded a bit obvious with her query. These days, thoughts of marriage seemed far more important than they should.

Emma returned with a tea tray and set it on the one corner of Thomas' desk where there wasn't a stack of papers threatening to spill over. "Still a bachelor and probably will remain so until he feels he can support a wife in fine style," Emma said as she poured a cup of tea, wondering at Lily's interest in William.

Although he was in his early-twenties and had grown up in the slums, Emma knew William was determined to earn a living that allowed him a decent place to live and money for all the essentials. His mother, a seamstress, had died in their Seven Dials apartment, leaving William and his younger sister, Katie, orphans. Stephen Bingham, Wellingham Imports' warehouse manager, had taken in the two waifs upon the death of their mother. Stephen's wife, Livia, took on the role of their surrogate mother, a role she played to perfection. "Sugar? Milk?"

Lily nodded. "Please. It's so nice of you to make me feel welcome when I haven't made an appointment. Samantha and Lady Chamberlain have left for Italy, you see, and Lord Chamberlain will be on his way to join them next week."

At the mention of Samantha Fitzsimmons, Emma suppressed the urge to gasp. "Italy?" she repeated. "And they didn't take you along?" she added, her brows furrowing.

Lily felt a bit of satisfaction in hearing the concern in Emma's voice. Of course, she could have gone with them, but under the circumstances, she thought it better Samantha and her aunt make the trip without her. "I was invited, of course, but I have reason to believe I would have been a bit of a distraction," she said with some hesitance. "And my brother has plans for me."

"Distraction?" Thomas repeated, taking the cup of tea Emma had prepared for him.

The blush reappeared on Lily's face. "Lady Chamberlain is determined to find a husband for Lady Samantha. I seem to have more than my fair share of suitors, so I am staying here in London until my brother sends for me," she explained. "I expect a Trenton coach to arrive any day from Staffordshire. I'll be staying with him for most of the summer, you see."

Emma took the other chair in front of Thomas' desk, eager to hear what the girl had to say. "In the meantime, you're staying at Fitzsimmons Manor all by yourself?" Emma asked, an eyebrow arching in surprise.

Lily shook her head. "Hardly, given the number of servants there," she replied. "My mother used to be a servant there as well, but she died a couple of years ago."

Lily's mother, Beatrice, had been a maid in the late Earl of Trenton's London townhouse. Once Beatrice's pregnancy with Lily became apparent, though, Charity Fitzsimmons Wellingham, Countess of Trenton, took action in an effort to deter gossip. She saw to it the maid's employment at the townhouse was terminated. Charity then arranged for Beatrice to work for her brother, Matthew, Viscount Chamberlain. Fitzsimmons Manor had been Lily's home from the time she was born.

"What's this about your brother sending for you?" Thomas asked as his brows furrowed. At one time, Thomas hadn't thought much of his cousin, Gabriel. The son of Graydon Wellingham, a somewhat cruel man who used his privilege to take advantage of others, Gabriel might have followed in his father's footsteps. His first few months in Parliament and a disastrous Little Season seemed to humble the man, however. Now that he was married and the father of a toddler, Gabriel was nothing like his late father.

Lily gave a shrug. "I've been expecting a summons, I suppose you could say. Now that I've been out for two Seasons,

I have been the subject of several news sheet articles suggesting I am about to accept an offer of marriage. A recent letter from his countess has me believing it won't be long. Apparently, the earl is curious as to who will claim my dowry," she added with a wave of her hand.

Emma exchanged a worried glance with Thomas. "You seem to have settled well amongst the *ton*," Emma offered as she took the last tea cup. "And have you been made an offer? Or two or three?" she asked carefully.

Taking a breath as if she intended to answer in the affirmative, Lily slowly exhaled. "Or four, I suppose," she finally admitted. "Although, only one was what I would call a true marriage proposal," she hedged.

Emma stirred her tea, wondering at the young woman's words. Sensing the talk of marriage was uncomfortable for Lily, she changed the subject. "You could not have had a finer sponsor than Lady Samantha for your come-out."

Truth be told, Emma had felt a bit of jealousy when she learned the illegitimate sister of Gabriel Wellingham was spending so much time with her own half-sister, Samantha. Since she hadn't yet been allowed to introduce herself to Samantha as her sister—she had agreed to Caroline Fitzsimmons' suggestion that she wait until the viscountess had a chance to tell Samantha about her real father—Emma wasn't at liberty to mention her relationship to Samantha.

"She has been ever so helpful," Lily agreed with an enthusiastic nod. "And I would have come to meet you sooner, but..." She stopped and finally shrugged.

"Trenton probably should have made the introductions when he was last in town," Thomas said with his own shrug, referring to Gabriel. "But, I must admit, Gabriel barely knows me. My father, Graham, was the black sheep in the family, after all," He glanced over at Emma before returning his attention to Lily. "You really must come to the house for dinner tonight," he insisted. "Meet my sister, Christiana, and her husband and their brood."

"The Grandbys?" Lily clarified, hoping she had kept all the

names straight. The only reason she had learned about Gregory Grandby was because, unless Lady Torrington gave birth to a boy in a few months, Gregory would probably inherit the Torrington earldom.

"And you can meet our son, Graham, when he returns from Eton for the summer," Emma added, her face splitting into a huge grin.

Lily's eyes widened. "Another relative?" she murmured. "I must admit to a bit of surprise at how welcoming everyone has been, considering I was born on the wrong side of the blanket."

Thomas exchanged a quick glance with Emma. "Wrong side or not, you're family," he said with conviction. "And whilst Lady Samantha is away, and until Trenton's coach comes for you, we can see to whatever you might need."

Lily's face brightened. "Truly?" she replied. "I have been a bit concerned about... well, a proper escort. Samantha insists I should have a man with me whilst I'm out of the house— for safety's sake—and said I could always request a footman accompany my maid and me. But having been a servant, I know I would be taking a footman from his duties. I would feel just awful at being an inconvenience. Do you know of someone who wouldn't mind squiring me about? Someone who knows their way around London?" she asked hopefully.

Emma arched an eyebrow as she gave her husband a knowing look. Having seen the expression on William's face when he introduced Lily to Thomas, Emma wondered if the young man wouldn't mind spending more time in the lady's presence. "The clerk who escorted you to the office knows his way around town quite well," she offered.

"Quite well, indeed," Thomas chimed in. "Mr. Overby used to be my caddie."

Lily's eyes widened as she allowed a nod. "Oh? Do you suppose Mr. Overby could be... compelled to escort me on occasion?"

Emma had to suppress a snort. "Why, I think Mr. Overby would be grateful for the opportunity to escort you anywhere you would wish to go," she said, a bit of mischief in her voice.

Thomas straightened in his chair. "Well, that is, if he's not at work—"

"I can see to it that Mr. Overby's responsibilities are covered should his presence be required by you," Emma interrupted, quite aware her husband was glaring at her in surprise. She ignored him as she continued. "Yes, within reason, of course. How often is it you require an escort?" she asked then.

Lily blinked as she considered the question. Now that Caroline and Samantha were gone on their trip to Italy and the summer season meant fewer invitations for soirées and balls, her only wish was to continue her daily walks in the park.

She dared a glance at Thomas before turning her attention to Emma. "Once a day. I know I should probably go to the park during the fashionable hour, but I prefer to go in the early morning. Before the nurses arrive with their charges."

Emma's eyes widened, not sure what time the general populace invaded Hyde Park for the day. She rarely had the opportunity to visit the park given the long days of work at the warehouse. "And that would be …?" she questioned.

"At half-past six o'clock," Lily responded with a nod. "I try to be at the gates around seven so that I'm leaving the park by eight."

Well aware of the hours most aristocrats kept, Thomas' jaw dropped. "You must get up at dawn!" he said in surprise.

Her own eyes widening, Lily appeared almost embarrassed as she gave a shrug. "Habit, I suppose. From my days as a maid. I've tried to sleep until ten, but I just cannot," she replied. "I awaken that early even after an evening at a ball."

Emma suppressed a chuckle, understanding the young lady's comment. She and Thomas tried to be at Wellingham Imports by nine every morning, but to do so meant rising before the sun. "Should I have Mr. Overby call on you at Fitzsimmons Manor at say six-thirty, tomorrow morning?"

Thomas was about to protest on the clerk's behalf—what if William Overby wasn't interested in escorting Lady Lily through the park at an ungodly hour of the morning?—when his cousin suddenly shook her head.

"I couldn't impose on Mr. Overby like that!" she said in alarm. When Emma gave a small shake of her head, Lily added, "He doesn't even know me."

Emma ignored the look of surprise she knew was on Thomas' face. "I should think that won't be an issue after a day or two," she replied.

Lily considered the offer and finally nodded her head. "If you're sure he won't mind —"

"Of course he won't. He'll be at your door at half-past six. And we'll see you at Woodscastle for dinner tonight."

Nodding her agreement, Lily gave her thanks and took her leave of Wellingham Imports, all the while wondering why she had been so worried about meeting her cousins.

CHAPTER 5

A CLERK RECONSIDERS BACHELORHOOD

William Overby entered his bachelor's quarters in Golden Square and sighed, happy to be home and surrounded by the familiar accoutrements he had carefully assembled in the four rooms that made up his apartment. The parlor, bedchamber, bath and study were beautifully appointed, and his wardrobe was extensive, although not varied—and it wasn't because William had spent his hard-earned annual salary of two-hundred-and-twenty pounds to make them so.

As an inventory clerk at Wellingham Imports, William benefited from situations considered unfortunate to others. When a ship arrived in port carrying goods that might have suffered damage en-route, William simply salvaged what he could.

For example, when a single bolt of snowy white silk in a shipment of one hundred from India arrived having been soaked in seawater whilst in a ship's hold, William accepted the ninety-nine good bolts, arranged for the payment of the shipment, and took the ruined bolt off the hands of the sea captain.

His housekeeper and laundress, Mrs. Greenleaf, was quite adept at restoring sea-soaked fabrics, and his tailor, Mark Woolgemuth, was equally talented in making neck cloths out of silk —hence his extensive collection of starched white cravats.

When a shipment of blue superfine arrived from the Continent, one bolt exhibiting a snag from the wooden crate in which it had been packed, Woolgemuth managed to work around the snag to create topcoats in the latest designs. As a result, William had a different topcoat for every day of the week. A similar situation had occurred with Nankeen from the Orient, which meant he had plenty of pairs of breeches.

Every piece of upholstered furniture in his parlor was because of similar circumstances for lengths of tapestry and brocade, since Margaret Greenleaf 's talents didn't end with silk. His employers were friends of an upholsterer in Leadenhall, so William was able to employ the tradesman to turn what had been cast-offs from an aristocrat's London townhouse—a settee and several chairs—into new-looking furnishings.

His bed's headboard had been one of ten carefully crafted by a woodworker in the United States, but when one arrived with a damaged foot, William merely paid a fraction of the total price and employed a local woodworker to make the necessary repairs.

Even the accessories—a slightly chipped vase in the parlor, a barely cracked hurricane lamp in the bedchamber, a figurine missing its mate in the study—gave William's apartment the air of quarters belonging to a rich aristocrat. Having begun his life in the slums of London, he had decided years ago he would live better than he did as a child—promised himself he would.

But what value did beautiful rooms and comfortable furnishings hold if William didn't have someone with whom to share them? After over ten hours a day, six days a week at Wellingham Imports, William rather hoped that one day he would arrive home to find a comely blonde chit waiting for him in his bedchamber, preferably naked and anxious to make his acquaintance.

He could dream, couldn't he?

He was doing just that when he pulled a note from his waistcoat pocket. Mrs. Wellingham had given him the missive just as he took his leave of his desk in the clerk's office. "I do hope you won't be too inconvenienced," she had said before bidding him farewell. In a hurry to meet a friend at a nearby public house for supper, William had forgotten about the note.

Unfolding the small sheet of parchment, William read the script and frowned.

Be at Fitzsimmons Manor at 6:30 in the morning to escort Lily Harkins to the park. You're welcome. E.W.

William's head snapped up. He blinked. He glanced back down at the note and reread it.

Six-thirty? In the morning?

Lily Harkins?

The park?

"Thank you, Mrs. Wellingham," he murmured aloud, wondering if he really did feel gratitude for the arrangement.

Although he was usually up that early in the morning—he had to be in order to arrive at the warehouse by seven o'clock—he would certainly have to wake up much earlier in order to arrive at Lady Lily's house by half-past six. She lived at...

He returned his attention to the note.

Fitzsimmons Manor.

William sat down—hard—into the nearest chair, the fingers of one hand raking through his long hair as he reread the note again. *I need a haircut.*

What if Lily Harkins really was the young woman from that night in Vauxhall Gardens? The comely blonde with eyes so blue he thought he might drown in them? The woman he found he couldn't live without so he simply conjured her image every time he felt lonely.

William settled back into the chair, remembering how beautiful she looked in the morning sun, how her smile seemed to brighten his day. Indeed, every time he thought of her for the rest of the day, his heart seemed lighter.

Was this how other men felt when they noticed a woman like Miss Harkins? Did they think of her all day? Did they imagine escorting her on their arm as they window shopped along New Bond Street, as they sat across from her in their favorite public house whilst eating their supper? Did they imagine sitting in comfortable chairs next to the fire whilst reading or enjoying a quiet conversation? Imagine undoing the buttons down the back of her gown so that she might undress without the help of a maid? Help her get ready for bed by pulling a night rail onto her svelte body, warm fingers caressing her as they gently smoothed the fine lawn over her silken skin?

Well, he rather doubted he would bother with the night rail. He would simply lift her into his arms and carry her, naked, to his bed. Settle her onto the feather mattress and slowly cover her with the bed linens before stripping off his own clothes so that he might join her in the bed. Draw one hand down the length of her body whilst his thumb caressed the side of her breast, her belly, then lightly touch her thighs and back up the other side. He would delight in hearing her soft gasps, in feeling her body's shivers of delight, in seeing her nipples swell and harden into ruched buds begging for his tongue and teeth.

He imagined her urgent whispers, pleading for surcease, pleading for him to take her. And he would. He had no plans to make her beg, to make her wait for his turgid manhood, wait for a release that would bring her the ultimate pleasure and send her into ecstasy. How could he? It would be cruel to tease and then withhold such pleasure. To fondle and caress and kiss without finishing what he had started by simply sitting with her by the fire.

William jerked upright.

Is this what married men did during their evenings? What wealthy men did with their mistresses on their appointed nights? What rakes did at brothels nearly every night?

No wonder nearly every clerk at Wellingham Imports was married! A *woman* awaited his arrival at home. A woman who enjoyed his company by a fire, his kisses by candlelight, and his caresses in the dark. One who enjoyed the feel of his touch on her bare skin, of his lips on hers, of his tongue as it explored her mouth and plundered every inch of her body, including the swollen nub at the base of her thighs, flicking and tasting and teasing until she came apart into a billion tiny pieces of pure pleasure.

William sighed as he closed his eyes and imagined doing such things to Lily Harkins. Bringing her to ecstasy seemed so easy to achieve, so desirable, so...

Necessary.

William blinked. And then he blinked again.

Where had that last thought come from? From where had he determined he needed to see to Lily Harkins' *pleasure?* To her ultimate ecstasy? For he couldn't do so unless he was married to the chit. He was quite sure she wouldn't allow such intimacies outside of the promise of marriage. Probably even outside of marriage at all.

Which would mean he had no other choice but to take the poor girl as his wife.

One hand covered his face as he groaned with his realization. Making her his wife meant he would have to become a husband. Which would mean he would be taking on all the expenses of another person, of being responsible for her, of providing her protection and paying for all the fripperies and finery she required, of seeing to her daily needs, her wants, and her desires.

The costs would be considerable!

Could he *afford* her as a wife?

William closed his eyes and ran the numbers in his head, adding up the expenses, guessing when he wasn't sure what things cost and wincing when he was, for to take Lily Harkins as his wife meant he would soon be a very poor man. So poor, in fact, he might end up in debtor's prison.

Shaking his head, William sighed.

Should he truly want Lily Harkins in his life—and he did— he could no longer imagine a life without her—he would have to make her his wife. There didn't seem to be another alternative. But to do so meant a life of work. Late nights at the office and perhaps a second job.

Was she worth it?

Was Lily Harkins worth the extra effort, the extra cost?

Well, until he met her at the front door of Fitzsimmons Manor—he still wasn't sure she was who he thought she was—he wouldn't allow his imagination to run away with him. He would find out who she was and then how much she would cost—or wouldn't—soon enough.

At half-past six in the morning, in fact.

CHAPTER 6

A DINNER WITH THE
COUSINS

L *ater that day*

The Fitzsimmons' ancient coach pulled into the drive to Woodscastle and lumbered along a paved path to the stone manor off Burlington Lane near Chiswick. Lights filled the windows both at the ground level as well as the second story, making the house of Thomas Wellingham and Gregory Grandby appear most welcoming.

Lily wondered what it might look like at Christmastime. She imagined brilliant lights and swags of greenery wrapping the stone façade, festive music and the sounds of excited children coming from the residence. Even now, youngsters bounced about outside the front door of the large home, their high-pitched voices sounding ever so excited. Delighted, in fact, for at the sight of the Fitzsimmons coach, their cries increased in volume and merriment. They congregated as a constantly moving group at the base of the stairs to the front double doors, their eyes all fixed on the carriage.

Oh, my, Lily thought as she took in the sight of the boisterous children. There were so many! And all appeared clean and dressed in rather expensive gowns and britches, their feet covered with stockings and shoes. Were they about to leave for an evening in London? A special night on the town? Dinner at one of the fine hotels?

The coach suddenly halted, and a sideways jerk told Lily a footman had stepped off the driver's seat. The door opened and, with an assisting hand from the footman, Lily made her way down the two steps to the pavement. Although it was dusk and the colors were fading to gray, she could easily make out the faces of the children as they suddenly broke apart and rushed towards her. She was startled when she found herself surrounded by a chorus of children's voices welcoming her, of young boys bowing and even younger girls giving her curtsies.

"Goodness!" she said as she returned the courtesy.

The tallest of the boys—he had to be at least thirteen—stepped forward and offered his arm. "You'll have to excuse my brothers and sisters. They've been waiting for your arrival all day," he said as he turned to lead her and the brood into Wood-scastle.

"I can't imagine a more welcoming welcome," she replied, reaching down to give a tow-headed boy a quick pat and to shake hands with a tyke who couldn't have been much more than a year old. The youngster displayed a happy countenance as well as a mouth containing only a few teeth.

The young man chuckled. "They're a bit mad, but they are my siblings," he said. "I'm Roger, by the way," he offered.

"Lily," she replied, deciding not to add her last name just then. Seeing this bunch made her wish she had adopted the name 'Wellingham' instead of her mother's maiden name.

As if the brief introductions were a cue, every child surrounding them began reciting their names, and Lily was forced to giggle as she tried to make out the monikers through the cacophony of voices that vied for her attention.

When the front doors suddenly opened and a rather tall man—a very tall man—nearly filled the vertical opening, the children were suddenly silent. While they stared at the hulk silhouetted on the threshold, Lily wondered if the man was the butler. If so, he must have ruled the household with an iron fist, for the children seemed to wait with baited breath for him to say something.

"Well, don't just stand there, you wild little bairns, get in the house and wash up for dinner!" the man called out, his voice filled with humor.

Lily couldn't help but giggle as the mass of youth poured through the front door and seemed to move en masse toward whatever room it was where they washed up for dinner. She had a momentary thought about the poor maid who would have to clean up after the bunch once they finished washing their hands.

"You must be Lady Lily," the man said as he reached for Lily's gloved hand and brought it to his lips. "Gregory Grandby," he said with a bow.

Grandby? Lily blinked before she afforded him a curtsy. "Lily Harkins," she responded. "A pleasure to meet the heir to the Torrington earldom," she added, wanting the man to know she was well aware of his standing in the peerage.

"Oh, not if my cousin's wife bears a boy in the next couple of months or so," he replied. "Which I'm rather hoping Lady Torrington does," he added. "I can't imagine taking on an earldom at this point in my life." He made the comment as he waved towards the group of children who were making their way up the stairs at the west end of the large hallway past the vestibule. *Thump-thump-thump. Thump-thump, thump-thump-thump* until the sound faded to just a *tap-tap, tap-tap, tap-tap.* "Your cousin is around here somewhere. Probably in the library," he said as he motioned off in the same direction the children had disappeared.

A butler did suddenly appear, ready to take her pelisse and reticule. "My lady," he said as he gave her a bow. He gave a glance in Gregory's direction, as if he wondered whether he should escort her to the library or if Gregory would do the honors.

"You'll have to excuse me. I need to finish dressing for dinner," Gregory said by way of an apology. "My wife, Christiana, will be down in a moment. When I last left her, she was quite vexed as to what she will wear for dinner this evening."

Lily gasped. "Oh, I do hope she's not going to extra effort on my behalf," she said as one of her hands went to her chest.

Gregory shook his head. "Not especially. She usually has a difficult time deciding, mostly because she has to find a gown with the least amount of baby vomit on it," he claimed, an arched eyebrow indicating he was teasing.

"*Gregory!*" a feminine voice scolded from the base of the west wing stairs.

Lily turned to see a well dressed and rather petite woman making her way toward them, her strides rather hurried.

"Ignore him," the small woman said with a nod in Gregory's direction. "He's being cheeky."

Lily had to suppress the urge to giggle at the red-headed woman who stood barely five feet tall. Goodness. The poor woman seemed half the size of her husband!

"Lady Lily, may I introduce the love of my life and the mother of all of my hellions, Christiana. My dear, this is Thomas' cousin..." He paused a moment and frowned. "And your cousin, Lily Harkins," Gregory stated, his manner suggesting he was rather familiar with formal introductions but eschewed them in favor of informality in his own home.

"I'm very pleased to make your acquaintance," Lily said as she nodded to Christiana.

"Me more than you. I'm afraid my brother has been regaling my children with tall tales of you all day, and they have been impossible to deal with as a result. Prepare for an assault after dinner," she warned with a roll of her eyes. "And in the meantime, let us have a drink in the library. I could certainly use one."

Lily nodded as she joined Mrs. Grandby. "They're actually rather delightful," she said as she walked alongside the woman who might one day be a countess. "And they seem ever so polite."

Christiana beamed despite her response. "Devils, they are. Every last one of them. But I love them. Dearly. Truly." This last word was said as if she were trying to convince herself of the truth of her own words.

"How many are yours?" Lily asked, thinking there were

enough children for several families. Christiana couldn't be more than five-and-thirty.

"All ten of them," Christiana replied. "Oh, there's a nephew, too, but he's off to school right now, so I can't even use him to help lessen the blow," she replied with a shrug. She led them into a large library, the odors of vellum and vanilla forcing Lily to pause and take a deep breath.

"I dearly love the smell of books," she murmured, just as she realized Thomas and Emma were sitting together on a large leather clad sofa. The two stood up upon her entry, though, and afforded her a bow and curtsy.

"Lady Lily, it's so good of you to join us this evening," Emma said as she waved to an upholstered chair. "It's our custom to have drinks before dinner. Would you like a glass of claret or something stronger, perhaps?" she asked. "Or there's coffee, of course."

Thomas had moved to the sideboard where an array of crystal decanters were displayed along with matching tumblers.

Used to the Fitzsimmons Manor butler, Porter, pouring the drinks, she watched wide-eyed as her cousin seemed poised to do the honors. "Claret will do fine," she said with a nod.

"For me, too, brother," Christiana murmured as she made her way to a chair and dropped into it.

Thomas proceeded to empty a decanter of wine at the very moment the butler appeared with another bottle and a plate of walnuts. "I've opened another, sir," he said as he set it down on the sideboard. "Cook informs me dinner will be served momentarily."

Nodding to Frederick, Thomas took the wine glasses to Lily and Christiana. "Ladies," he said. "I believe a toast is in order."

Thinking they should wait for Mr. Grandby, Lily's eyes went to the open door to the library. But Thomas was already raising his glass.

"To family," he said with a nod to Lily.

The three women raised their glasses and murmured the toast, each taking a sip of wine before the sound of ten children could be heard coming down the stairs. *Thump-thump thump*

thump-thump thump-thump-thump. Lily had to suppress a giggle as she imagined the youngest one making his way down backwards, carefully pushing out a foot and backing himself up until his toes could take purchase on the next stair below so he could lower himself onto it. *Bump*. And then he would do the same with the other leg until he was down another step. *Bump*.

So it was a bit of a puzzle when the sounds of the children faded—they had apparently made it down the stairs and gone into a nearby room—and she heard a slight *bump-bump-bump-bump*.

Curious, she moved to the threshold and dared a glance toward the west stairs. The youngest boy—the one who didn't yet have many teeth—was on his bottom and bouncing his way down the stairs. If his momentum didn't take him far enough to bounce down onto the next step, he kicked a foot and pushed with his pudgy hands until he was moving again.

Farther up the stairs, Gregory stood watching his youngest son until the boy was safely at the bottom and working his way to his feet. "Milton, you'll be the death of me yet," the man called out as he struggled to secure a cuff link at his wrist. When he noticed Lily watching the boy, he gave her a nod and a mischievous grin. "Named him after my oldest cousin," he called out. "He used to go down the stairs the very same way when we were children."

Lily took a moment to figure out he was referring to Milton Grandby, Earl of Torrington. "I don't suppose he says the same about you," she responded.

Gregory made it to the bottom of the stairs and gave a nod. "Of course, he does. We used to race to see who could make it to the bottom first. It had worked well for me until he was old enough to slide down the bannister." He scooped up his son, the babe settling himself into his father's arm as if he did it everyday. "If his wife delivers a boy, I'll bet you a hundred pounds he names him Gregory."

The sound of a throat clearing had Lily turning around to find her cousin giving Gregory a quelling glance. "There will be no wagering in this household," Thomas stated with a rather serious expression. "However, if there were, I'd take that bet," he added with a smirk.

When Lily dared a glance at Emma, she found the woman barely able to suppress a grin while Christiana simply rolled her eyes. "Ignore those two," she said. "They're the best of friends, and no one can figure out exactly why."

Lily wondered what Christiana meant by her comment and was about to ask, but the butler appeared to announce dinner was served. Gregory repositioned Milton so the poor boy hung head first over his shoulder. The boy giggled in delight as the adults made their way to the dining room.

On the way down the hall, Lily dared a glance at the decor. The unmistakable marks of children were in evidence—she knew to look for the tell-tale fingerprints on the painted wood-work—but for a house with ten children, she was rather impressed the place looked as clean and as elegant as it did. She noticed the lighting overhead was gas-fed, which meant the house had been recently renovated to add the necessary lines. She figured the plumbing had also been installed to provide running water and toilets in the bathing chambers. From what she knew of Gregory Grandby, the man was wealthy enough to own his own manor house, and probably one much larger than Woodscastle.

So why did the Grandbys and Wellinghams decide to share this estate house? She made a mental note to ask should there be an opportunity.

"You're probably wondering why my brother would allow my brood to live here," Christiana said as they made their way down the wide hall.

Lily wondered if the woman could read her mind. "I did, in fact, but the two seem the best of friends, so..."

"Gregory bought half of Woodscastle for me. As a wedding gift," Christiana said. "The bad half. So that I might remain close to my brother and to my best friend." She gave a nod in Emma's direction. "We shared a room at Warwick's," she added, referring to the grammar and finishing school so many of the daughters of the *ton* attended.

The bad half? The entire house looked well maintained, its appointments nearly new. There didn't seem to be a bad half. But before Lily could ask what Christiana meant by her comment, they entered the dining room to find all the children already seated and waiting patiently for the adults to join them.

"She's here!" one of the young girls called out, which resulted in most of the other children giving her a quick "shush". The girl's face suddenly pinked up and seemed to disappear into her shoulders.

Lily grinned, realizing she was the subject of the comment. "Look at all of you," she said with a sweep of her hand. She turned to Christiana, who was directing her to a chair on the other side of the table. "They're so well behaved!"

Christiana angled her head and allowed her gaze to take in all of her children. "On the threat of not being allowed in the parlor with us after dinner if they should misbehave, of course," she explained. "So that means we'll have a rather civil dinner this evening."

Emma leaned over and whispered, "I rather wish you could come every night," a look of humor lighting her face.

Thomas waited for Lily and the other ladies to be seated before he took one of the carvers. Gregory, at the other end of the table, deposited Milton into a high chair and took the other carver.

"I rather like being dressed for dinner this evening," he said, giving Christiana a nod. "Thank you, Lady Lily, for joining us," he said as several footmen appeared with wine and bowls of soup.

"Thank you for inviting me," Lily replied, blushing when she realized all the eyes at the table were on her.

A chorus of "You're welcome" came from around the table, the children beaming before turning their attentions to their soup. Lily secretly cringed at the thought of the thick, creamy lobster bisque dripping onto their clothes, probably the same clothes they wore to church.

She was about to ask Christiana if the children were always

present for dinner when Emma asked about Lady Samantha. "Have you heard any word from her?" she asked.

Lily shook her head. "Not yet, but she and Lady Chamberlain only left five days ago. I don't expect news until they reach Italy," she said, noticing how Emma seemed a bit deflated by the answer. "Is she a relation of yours, perhaps?" she asked, thinking Emma looked like she could be Samantha's sister.

Emma's eyes widened in surprise. "Why ever do you ask?" she countered, aware her cheeks had taken on a pink blush.

Before Lily could reply, several footmen appeared to clear away the soup bowls and refill wine glasses. Thomas deftly took up the conversation, steering it away from the Fitzsimmons to a variety of topics even the children could participate in if they were addressed directly.

By the end of the dinner, Lily knew the names of every child at the table, but was left wondering why Emma seemed so surprised by her query. *What is she trying to hide?* she thought as they took their leave of the dining room and made their way to the parlor. Thomas and Gregory split off for the library, intending to enjoy a cheroot and a glass of port before rejoining the ladies and children in the parlor.

"Will it be acceptable for me to play with the children?" Lily whispered, her question directed to Christiana.

"*Expected* is more like it," the red-head said with a grin. "You're a doll to do it. But don't think you have to get down on the floor with them..." She broke off when she realized Lily had already joined a cluster of the youngsters on the Axminster carpet. "... Unless you really wish to," she added with a questioning grin aimed at Emma.

"Only child," Emma whispered with a nod in Lily's direction. Their conversation was easily covered by the sounds of giggling children and by the music provided by the oldest daughter, Ariel, who had taken a seat before the piano-forté.

"I couldn't help but notice you didn't answer her question about being related to Samantha," Christiana murmured, keeping her attention on her brood.

"I hardly think it appropriate for me to tell Lily before I

have a chance to tell my own sister we're related," Emma replied, taking a three-year-old into her arms when the girl tugged on her skirts.

Christiana turned her attention to Emma. "When she returns from Europe—"

"I'll tell her, whether I have Caroline's permission or not," Emma assured her. "Besides, she'll no doubt come home a betrothed woman and will be married not long after." As a result, they wouldn't have much of a chance to get to know one another. Samantha was already twenty-three years old!

A few minutes later, Thomas and Gregory appeared at the parlor door, pausing to take in the site of Lily on the floor, surrounded by eight children who were listening intently to her recitation of a story.

"Reminds me of Christiana when she was younger," Thomas said with a sigh.

"I was going to say Emma," Gregory countered, giving Thomas a look of surprise. The two each took a deep breath and made their way into the room.

A chorus of squeals erupted as the two men reached down to tickle the young ones. "Time for bed," Gregory announced, a hand coming up as one of the young boys almost... almost responded with a protest. "Say good-bye to Lady Lily."

Although several children did as they were told, the youngest three took turns hugging Lily around the neck and kissing her on the cheek.

"It's very good to meet you," Lily replied. "I look forward to seeing you again." Her words elicited more hugs before the children had all departed.

Suddenly quiet, the parlor seemed to have lost its life with the departure of the children. "You were a very good sport to put up with them as you did," Christiana said as she helped Lily to her feet.

"Oh, it was no trouble," Lily replied, surprised the woman would think she hadn't had as much fun as the children. "Truth be told, I rather enjoyed myself," she said, shaking out her skirts.

Emma offered her arm and the two walked out of the parlor, Thomas on her other side. "Thank you for joining us. Truly," Emma said as the butler held out her pelisse. "I cannot tell you how happy Thomas and I were to finally meet you."

Lily angled her head. "Me more than you, I am sure. I truly wish I could see you again soon, but I am expecting to spend the summer in Staffordshire with the earl."

Thomas nodded. "You'll be back in town for the Little Season, then," he said. "And you'll probably be married not long after."

Lily blinked at his simple comment. She hardly knew how to respond. "Possibly," she allowed with a nod. She turned her attention to Emma. "Did you have a chance to ask Mr. Overby if he will be available to escort me in the park tomorrow?" she asked, her head leaned in so only Emma could hear the query.

Emma allowed a knowing grin. "I've given him all the details. I'm quite sure you can expect him at Fitzsimmons Manor in the morning," she whispered back, hoping William would have the good sense to check his pockets when he retired that night.

Lily's eyes widened with an expression of gratitude showing. "I understand. Thank you again for the invitation. I will pay a call on you when I return to London."

With a round of "good-byes", some of them coming from the top of the west wing stairs, Lily took her leave of Woodscastle.

For the entire trip back to Fitzsimmons Manor, she thought about the words she had overheard in the parlor, words she was keen to hear for she had wondered why it was that Emma Wellingham bore such a striking resemblance to Samantha Fitzsimmons.

Lady Samantha is Emma's sister.
And she doesn't even know it.

CHAPTER 7

TEA WITH WILLIAM AND LILY

William regarded Fitzsimmons Manor from where he stood across the street. The sun had barely come up, fog still swirled around his boots, and the smell of rain was in the air. *This is madness,* he thought as he waited for a hackney to pass by before making his way across Park Lane. But given his sleepless night and the images that haunted him throughout the dark hours, he had to know if Lily was the same girl he had sent running from the darkest part of Vauxhall Gardens all those years ago.

He was about to reach for the brass lion-head knocker on the front door when it suddenly opened. A very old butler, tall but with stooped shoulders, peered at him.

"Good day," William spoke with a nod. "William Overby to see Miss Harkins," he stated evenly, hoping his voice didn't betray his nervousness.

The butler stepped back and to the side. "One moment whilst I see if Lady Lily is in residence," he said, waving William into the small vestibule.

"Thank you," William replied as he stepped over the threshold, realizing the butler had referred to Lily as *Lady Lily. She wasn't a maid, then, but a member of the peerage. So she's not the same chit,* he thought with a bit of disappointment.

Then he remembered the rest of the butler's response. *How*

inane! Of course Lady Lily would be in residence. It was half-past six in the morning! If she wasn't in residence, he rather hoped a Bow Street Runner had been dispatched to find her.

The butler headed into the hall beyond and climbed the stairs, his quick steps belying his age.

Realizing it might be some time before the man returned—would the man have to search every room, or did he already know the whereabouts of Miss Harkins?—William studied the only painting featured in the vestibule, a landscape secured in a rather elaborate gilt frame.

The style of the painting was much like the one in Emma's office at Wellingham Imports. Locating the signature in the lower right corner, William expected to find a famous artist's name and instead found *S. Fitzsimmons* in a simple, even script. He straightened, surprised it was exactly the same as the signature on Emma's painting.

Who is S. Fitzsimmons? he wondered as he clasped his hands behind his back. Emma Wellingham had been Emma Fitzsimmons before she married Thomas, he remembered, which had him wondering if she was related to the artist.

He moved his attention to another part of the painting. The brushwork was fine, the strokes almost tiny. As a result, the most minute details were rendered realistically. Although the brushwork on the sky was larger, the clouds in the distances and the varying shades of the setting sun made the painting appear as if it were lit from within.

"Lady Lily will see you in the parlor," the butler stated.

William nearly jumped off the floor. *How had the man managed to return to the vestibule without making any noise? Or was I so absorbed in the painting, I didn't hear him?* "Very good," he responded, rather surprised the young woman hadn't just come to the front door so they could be on their way to the park. "By the way, who is the artist of this painting?" he asked as the butler turned to lead him up to the parlor.

The ancient butler paused and angled the top half of his body to one side. "That would be Lady Samantha Fitzsimmons," he intoned. "One of her early works, I believe."

William blinked. *Early works?* From what he knew of Lady Samantha, she was still a rather young woman. Unless there was another Lady Samantha or this one had been a child prodigy, the painting couldn't be more than five or ten years old.

He made a mental note to ask Emma about her painting as he followed the butler to the second floor parlor. Perhaps Lady Samantha and Emma were related, he considered. That would certainly explain how Emma had a Fitzsimmons painting on her office wall.

The double-doors of the parlor were both wide open as the butler stepped just over the threshold and stopped. William noticed a maid mending clothes near one of the windows.

"William Overby, my lady," the butler said with a bow. He stepped back and disappeared from William's view. It was then William noticed Lily. She was seated in a floral-patterned upholstered chair, her yellow sprigged muslin gown a perfect complement to her blue eyes. A silver tea set on the low table in front of her looked as if it had just been delivered, tendrils of steam rising from the teapot's spout. Lily stood and made her way toward him, her face brightening as she did so.

"Mr. Overby, 'tis so good of you to come," she said as she held out her ungloved hand.

William gave her a bow and took her hand, kissing the back of it. Perhaps he held onto it a bit longer than he should have with his own gloved hand, but Lily didn't seem to mind.

"Mrs. Wellingham said you wished to have an escort for your walk in the park this morning," he said with a nod. "Have I come at the wrong time?" he asked as he indicated the tea tray. "It looks as if you're expecting a caller."

Lily spread her skirts and lowered herself into the chair with a sigh. "As it happens, I haven't had any callers since Lady Chamberlain and Lady Samantha left for Italy. But your timing is perfect. I was about to have a cup of tea all by myself," she said with a hint of a pout. "You will join me in one, I hope? Then, if it no longer smells as if it's going to rain out there, we can take our leave for a walk in the park."

William swallowed in an attempt to control his nervousness.

"Of course, my lady," he replied, remembering the butler's use of the honorific.

Lady Lily?

Oh, dear. This wasn't just Lady Lily, acquaintance of some kind to Thomas Wellingham. This was *the* Lady Lily featured in the gossip rags, the one who was the darling of the *ton* at the moment. The one who was said to have a half-dozen marriage proposals to consider.

But if she were a lady, then she couldn't possibly be the young woman he saved from certain ruination that night in Vauxhall Gardens.

William took a steadying breath, remembering the rest of Lady Lily's story. She was a former maid to Lady Samantha and the half-sister of the Earl of Trenton.

How could I have been so dense not to have realized the chit was the earl's sister? he wondered, wishing he had been more formally introduced to her when he escorted her to Thomas' office. The Wellinghams might be in trade, but Thomas had been a nephew to the late Earl of Trenton. And Emma was a Fitzsimmons.

Is Emma a relation to these Fitzsimmons? he thought again, thinking of the painting in the vestibule and the painting in Emma's office.

William was about to excuse himself, realizing he had no business escorting an earl's sister through the park even if it wasn't during the fashionable hour, and remembering he was in desperate need of a haircut, when Lily asked, "Sugar or milk?"

His breath caught at how eager she seemed. "Milk, please," he responded with a nod as he took a seat in the settee directly across from Lily.

Lily leaned over the table and offered him his cup, the circle of milk slowly swirling in a perfect white spiral on the surface of the tea.

"How did you manage that?" he asked in wonder, a smile finally erasing his look of nervousness.

Pouring her own cup, Lily displayed a grin of embarrassment. "If you pour the tea at just the right angle to the edge of the cup, it sends it into a circle, so when you add the milk the same way, it follows the same path. Doesn't always work, though," she added, as she poured milk into her own cup. The dollop reformed into a swirling blob before she used her spoon to mix it into the tea.

She let out a sigh. "You must have thought me the biggest fool yesterday, the way I was staring at you," Lily spoke as she sat up straight, her teacup resting on its saucer.

William's eyebrows furrowed. "Hardly, my lady," he said. "In fact, I was a bit concerned you might think the same of me. Your eyes are just so... *blue,*" he said, resisting the urge to roll his own eyes at his insipid response. "They are quite a pretty blue, in fact."

Even as a blush covered her face, Lily suppressed the urge to giggle at the young man's comment. Truth be told, she had noticed him staring, although not until she had been staring at him for some time, concentrating on his eyes. She was quite sure she had seen those eyes before, although not as she had seen them yesterday. She certainly didn't remember anyone of his age with such long hair. "I must admit, I thought you seemed familiar," Lily said as she brought her teacup to her lips. "I still do. Have we met before yesterday?"

Shifting on the uncomfortable settee, William considered how much to admit. "Aye, we have, m'lady." He was quite sure —no, he was quite positive—she was one of the young women his friend had threatened to ruin that fateful night in Vauxhall Gardens, the night he realized he could no longer consider Zachary Hayer a friend.

The rake had sidled up to two young women who, from their modest clothing, were no doubt servants. Their arms were linked together as they walked the crushed granite paths in the pleasure garden. "Ah, two lovely ladies," he had said as he pulled his hat from his head and gave a leg. "Who look as if they are in need of escorts," he added, an eyebrow arching up.

The young women—William thought them no older than fourteen or fifteen—gave a start, but the one with dark hair quickly recovered, giving up her hold on the blonde to take

Zachary's arm. "Why, thank you," she replied with a nod, giving her friend a brilliant smile that suggested she had planned such an encounter.

Embarrassed by his friend's behavior, William stepped up to the blonde and introduced himself. "I would be honored to escort you about the grounds," he had said as he gave a bow.

Without a word, the blonde girl placed her hand on his arm, her gaze indicating her nervousness. The four of them strolled about the crowded grounds, Zachary leading them farther away from the populated areas as the sky grew darker. Although William couldn't hear Zachary's conversation with the maid, he was fairly sure the rake was working toward a kiss.

Soon, they were stopped next to a tree and Zachary had his girl up against the trunk, his body moving in front of her as he whispered something. The girl giggled, obviously pleased with the attention her escort was providing.

Perhaps she was the one to initiate the kiss or perhaps it was Zachary, but it mattered not. In a moment, the two were engaged in rather scandalous behavior against the tree.

William dared a glance at the girl on his arm. She was staring at the kissing couple, her expression indicating she was a bit horrified.

"I apologize. My friend is usually not such a rake," William murmured. The hand on his arm gripped a bit harder, and he felt it tremble.

"Really, Zack. That's quite enough," William said, his attention turning back in the direction from whence they had come when a firework sizzled and then exploded into streamers of light off in the distance.

The dark haired girl pulled herself away from Zachary. "Fireworks!" she said happily. "It's why we came tonight," she said, attempting to extract herself from Zachary's hold.

He kept his arm around her waist, though, and pulled her back. "Lie down, my lady, and you can see them at their finest. No need to strain your neck," he commented as he moved to pull her down to the lawn. Although the girl protested at first, she was soon on her back watching the colorful bursts of light,

Zachary pressed along the length of her. "Come join us, Lil," the brunette called out. "They're beautiful when you can look up at them like this."

William placed a hand over the hand that held onto his arm, and he felt the maid flinch. "Can you see them all right like this?" he whispered, worried she would join her friend on the ground.

"This is fine," the blonde answered, occasionally stealing a glance in her friend's direction between the bursts of light brightening the sky above them. The muted sounds of the appreciative crowd in the distance reached them, their 'oohs' joining the night sounds of crickets and frogs but never quite drowning out the sounds of kissing and fondling originating near their feet.

William realized Zachary's intentions when he found the rake suddenly over the dark-haired girl, kissing her again as one hand kneaded one of her breasts. Although the girl should have protested, should have struggled and pushed Zachary off of her body, she instead giggled a bit and continued to kiss Zachary. Her sounds soon changed, though, when Zachary slowly pushed her skirts up her legs.

"You've got me all excited," he murmured. "As are you," he added, one of his hands at the apex of her thighs.

William glanced back again to see his friend attempting to spread open the girl's legs. Although she wore half boots and stockings, her legs were otherwise bare. "Zack, no," he said, "She's rather too young for..."

The girl let out a cry as Zach tried to hold down one of her wrists. "Nonsense. When I'm finished with her, we can have a tumble with your pretty chit."

Shaking his head in the blonde's direction, William realized Zachary wasn't about to give up his hold on the dark-haired girl. He took a deep breath, hoping he was wrong about his friend. He leaned toward the blonde, keeping his voice low as he said, "Go. Run." He glanced back at Zack, appalled at what he was seeing. "I'll see to getting your friend out from under him," he said in urgent tones.

"I shouldn't leave her," the blonde protested just as another firework exploded above them. In the bright light that followed, William found himself staring into the most beautiful blue eyes he had ever seen. And he would have continued to stare except for the scream that accompanied the next fireworks explosion. "Go!" he yelled.

Those blue eyes widened and took one last look at her companion before turning away.

After seeing to it that the blonde was running toward the crowd watching the fireworks, William hurried to pull Zack off of the other maid. The poor girl's skirts were rucked up past her hips, and Zack had the placket of his breeches open. He was already settling himself between her legs when William reached them.

He wasn't sure where the strength had come from to lift the larger man from atop the girl and toss him to the crushed granite path, but somehow he had managed it. And then he pulled the poor girl to her feet and tried to send her off with the same one-word command—"Run!"—he had used with the other maid.

However, the dark-haired girl shook her head and instead moved to kneel next to Zachary. Angry, blood dripping from the side of his face, Zack stared at William as the girl attempted to cradle his head in her lap and wipe away the blood with her skirts.

"What the devil?" he shouted. "I was about to enjoy a tumble with this gorgeous woman. And you could have been doing the same with the blonde!"

William shook a finger at Zack. "She doesn't *want* a tumble, you fool!" he countered. Truth be told, he couldn't say what she wanted other than maybe a kiss, and he wasn't even sure the blonde wanted that.

Now that he gave the evening some more thought, William realized that, although Lily had been nervous, the other maid had been rather forward, almost teasing Zack into kissing her. The brunette had glared at him as if she welcomed Zack's advances.

Perhaps she did.

When Zack suddenly got to his feet and balled his fist, moving it to use on William's face, William shook his head before landing another punch directly across Zachary's nose. Blood spurted and then flowed from the rake's nose as Zack howled in pain. The dark-haired servant girl rushed to wrap her arms around her man. "You brute!" she cried out as she buried her face into the small of Zack's shoulder.

"We're through," William said as he aimed a warning finger at Zachary. *"Done."* And following the path back toward the crowd still watching the fireworks, William hurried off in the hopes of finding the blonde maid.

He spent nearly an hour looking for her, hoping he could see to her safe return to wherever it was she lived. She was gone, though, as was his friend.

He never saw either one again.

"I was quite afraid that night," Lily said before taking a sip of her tea.

William glanced up, stunned at her simple words. *She is the blonde maid from that night!*

"I was especially afraid for Mary. She was such a fool. She talked me into going to the gardens that night. Said we would just have an ice and watch the fireworks." She paused a moment, her gaze suggesting she was still back at Vauxhall Gardens. "But I think she went looking for a boy. Looking to be kissed. Perhaps more," she murmured, her attention on the plate of scones on the tea tray.

"I worried about you the entire night and all of the next day," William said quietly. "And her, too, although I thought perhaps she was a bit peeved at me for having interrupted her... tryst... with Zack."

"Zack?" Lily repeated, one brow furrowing. "You knew him? Before that night?" she asked. She straightened in her chair, color suffusing her face again. But this time, the color was due to anger and not embarrassment.

William realized he had to be careful. "We went there as friends, but I assure you, my lady, we did not leave as such. I may have broken his nose in my effort to save your Mary," he explained carefully. "Although I knew he wasn't a saint, I did not think him capable of taking a woman's virtue against her will," he added quietly, hoping the maid sitting near the window couldn't hear their quiet conversation.

Lily relaxed again, her empty teacup resting in the palms of her hands. "She was rather angry with me that evening. I returned here shortly after I left you," she explained. "Or rather, as soon as I realized Mary wasn't planning to come home with me. She obviously stayed for the rest of the fireworks display, or for the opportunity she nearly missed as a result of your good intentions."

William's eyes had widened in alarm. "She *wanted* to be ruined?" he whispered. Had he misinterpreted what he saw that night? But, no, he was quite sure Lily was frightened—for herself and for her friend. He had no idea how the other girl felt.

Lily swallowed and considered how to respond. "I rather think she already was," she whispered, "And was hoping I might join her that night."

His eyes still wide, William shook his head. "I would not have allowed it, I assure you," he said in a hoarse whisper. "Had he touched you, I do believe I would have been capable of..." He didn't say the word that came to mind, but he also hadn't put any thought to spending the rest of his life in Newgate. But he doubted he would have regretted whatever he would have had to do to protect the defenseless maid. To protect Lily.

"Thank you," Lily said quietly. "I can't imagine anyone wanting to defend an illegitimate maid from a rake." The words were out of her mouth before she realized to what she admitted. But then, every newspaper in town had written something about her being the illegitimate sister of Gabriel Wellingham. She allowed an audible sigh. "And now you know my sordid story," she said with an expression of disappointment.

William leaned forward, his empty teacup held out. Without asking if he wanted more, Lily filled the cup and added the milk, allowing a wan smile when it landed in a round circle in the middle of the brew. "I hardly think I know your story, m'lady. But I should like to know more."

Lily stilled herself, realizing she had talked of things long put away. "What of you? You must tell me your story," she insisted, refilling her own teacup.

William regarded her for a moment and realized he would eventually have to tell her where he started life in London. The truth would come out sooner or later. "I was born in the Seven Dials." He heard Lily's hiss before he caught the look of shock on her face. "My real mother, God rest her soul, was a seamstress for a modiste. I started working for Mr. Wellingham as a caddie when I was five or six. My mother died in our apartment when I was eight, so I took my sister—"

"You have a sister?" Lily had interrupted, her eyes wide.

William nodded. "Katie is at Warwick's Grammar and Finishing School. This is her last year. I expect she'll be married before long since she's a rather beautiful chit," he explained with some pride. "I'll have to provide protection until then, of course, although our adoptive father is rather good at it," he added, remembering Stephen Bingham's comment about what he would do to the unfortunate man who showed any interest in Katie before her come-out. "Which is why I would like to see her settled soon. I would like to know she is being looked after by someone who... who deserves her."

Does that make me sound unworthy? He had no intention of breaking off ties with his sister, but she did benefit from a real education and opportunities he never had due to his age when the Binghams took them in.

"And your father?" Lily asked, leaning forward as if she were truly interested in his life story.

Taking a shallow breath, William shook his head. "I barely remember him. I'm not sure if he died or if he simply left us, but I remember he was there until after Katie was born."

Lily sighed, suggesting she felt pity for him. "What did you do then? When your mother died?"

For a moment, William wondered how to respond. "I gathered up everything we owned and took my sister to Wellingham

Imports. I was naïve enough to think we could simply live in the warehouse," he said with a chuckle. "For a few minutes after we were discovered by the warehouse manager, I thought the Wellinghams were going to take us in, but Mr. Bingham said his wife wanted bairns, and so we moved into their house that very evening."

Lily blinked. "They took you in? Just like that?"

Grinning, William nodded. "Well, there were some concessions we had to make. Baths, for one." He could swear he heard Lily snort, and he nearly laughed at her expense. "I despised bathing, as did my sister. But once we had several years of London dirt and soot washed off us, we were deemed acceptable children."

"They adopted you then?"

"In a manner of speaking," William said with a nod. "I've worked at Wellingham Imports almost my entire life and cannot imagine working anywhere else."

Lily allowed a grin of her own. The young man was settled then. He had an orderly life. He had a future. Even if he did need a haircut. "Do you still live with the Binghams?" she asked, hoping beyond hope he did not, and then thinking he wouldn't simply because he was old enough to have his own apartment and would have been a burden on his adoptive parents if he still remained with them.

William shook his head. "Not for several years now. I'm in bachelor quarters near Golden Square."

A combination of awe and disappointment passed through Lily just then. Awe, because a man who couldn't be more than three-and-twenty was living on his own, supporting himself in fine style, given his clothing, and was apparently rather pleased with his orderly life. Disappointment, for at no time during his recitation did he indicate a desire for a wife and children. "You sound... happy," she said quietly.

William was about to agree when he realized he wasn't. Not really. He hadn't realized he felt lonely until the day before, when he had stared into her cornflower blue eyes and was suddenly lost, or drowned.

I will be when you agree to be my wife.

The thought had him blinking. *Where the hell had that come from?*

The butler suddenly appeared on the threshold of the parlor. "Pardon me, my lady."

Lily tore her gaze from William's, wishing she could spend the rest of the morning with him. He was so easy to converse with! They had spent their entire lives in London, living lives of quiet desperation, and doing so without one another. *He saved me once. Perhaps he will again,* she considered before saying, "What is it, Porter?"

The butler bowed. "The Trenton coach has just pulled into the drive, my lady."

Lily swallowed upon hearing the proclamation. Although she had been expecting word of its arrival all week, it was still a bit of a shock that she was expected to simply take her leave of Fitzsimmons Manor and spend several days on the North Road to Staffordshire.

She had never before been outside of London!

As her sister-in-law had warned, Gabriel Wellingham, Earl of Trenton, had sent his coach and expected her presence at Trenton Manor in a few days. "Thank you, Porter." She turned her attention to her guest. "My brother is expecting me in Staffordshire." Contrary to her words, she remained seated and allowed a sigh. "I can't say his timing is particularly good," she murmured, "Seeing as how I was just starting my volunteer work."

William straightened. "And where might that be, my lady?" he asked, curious as to what charity might be of interest to the young woman.

"Lady E's Finding Work for the Wounded," she responded in a lowered voice, leaning forward as if she were sharing a secret.

Remembering having seen a shingle with the name, William tried to recall just where in London he had seen the sign. "In Oxford Street?" he guessed, fairly sure it was next door to a solicitor's office.

"Indeed," Lily confirmed. "Number thirty. I haven't yet told my brother, given its founder was Lady Bostwick," she added, a look of guilt crossing her face. At William's slight shake of his head—he was attempting to remember how he should know the woman in question—Lily explained. "She was Lady Elizabeth Carlington. I am to understand my brother at one time thought to ask for her hand in marriage, but the lady opted to marry George Bennett-Jones instead. Which was for the best, given who my brother has since married."

William nodded his understanding. "And what is it you do there? At Lady E's?" he asked, a bit concerned the chit would be working amongst men who had at one time been soldiers or seamen. He rather hoped the men knew to treat her with respect.

"Well, it's hardly work, and really rather simple to do. I merely read newspapers looking for listings of open positions. When I find one that might be appropriate for a former soldier, I simply use a scissors and cut out the advertisement. Then a man in the office, Mr. Barnaby, attempts to match an applicant with the position," she explained. "Lady E... I mean, Lady *Bostwick* does as well, when she's in the office. But these days, she's rather busy with a baby and another on the way, so she can only spend a few hours in the office every week."

Surprised to learn a lady of the *ton* was so involved with her own charity—most merely provided financial support or held soirées or benefits to help fund their favorite charities—William shook his head. "Is it... *safe* for you to be there? Without a chaperone, I mean."

Lily grinned, secretly pleased William would be so concerned for her welfare. "Oh, yes. Absolutely. Mr. Overby and Mr. Barnaby are quite the gentlemen."

At the mention of 'Mr. Overby', William's head jerked up. "Mr. Overby?" he repeated.

Her grin widening to a smile, Lily nodded. "Oh, yes. In fact, I meant to ask you yesterday if perhaps Mr. Overby is a relation of yours. He's been with the charity since its beginning.

Two years now, I believe," she said, helping herself to another cup of tea.

"What do you know of him?" William asked, holding out his own cup. Surely the man wasn't a relation, but... but what if he was?

Lily poured tea into his cup and then added a dollop of milk, watching as the white merged with the dark in a perfect swirl. William's eyes met hers and he smiled. "Well done," he murmured.

"Thank you," she replied, setting down the creamer. She took a deep breath and let it out. "Augustus Overby was one of the unfortunate men to have been at Talavera," she said then, using a spoon to mix her tea. "He's a bit older. I think he said he was three-and-forty. And he has an awful limp. Seems his leg was damaged by mortar during the war," she went on, her mouth closing when she realized William was staring at her, his teacup held aloft, as if he was about to take a drink and then had stopped suddenly.

"Augustus?" he repeated. He blinked. Afraid he would spill the tea, he lowered his cup to its saucer and stared into space for a moment.

He didn't remember much about his father and even less about his uncle. He couldn't even conjure an image of the men, for he had been far too young when the two Overby men had taken their leave of their lodgings in the Seven Dials and never returned. But the name had him remembering his mother's voice saying that particular name.

Auggie.

Jesus! Could he be the same man? Could this Augustus Overby be his uncle? But if so, why hadn't he come back to their one-room apartment when he returned from the war?

Or had he?

Had Augustus Overby returned to discover his sister-in-law had perished and his niece and nephew were long gone? The man would have had no idea where William had taken his sister, would have had no way to know where to begin to look for them.

When William's eyes cleared, he found Lily staring at him, her eyes wide. "He is a relation. Isn't he?" she whispered, studying William's facial features for clues. The golden brown eyes were an exact match, she was sure.

William nodded, not sure how else to respond. "Yes, possibly. Probably," he amended with a nod. "I'll... I'll go to Lady E's later today. After we've taken our walk in the park," he stammered.

Lily shook her head. "I do hope you have a covered conveyance, Mr. Overby, for I am quite sure it will be raining before long."

Shrugging off the idea of getting a bit wet, William felt a stab of disappointment to learn they wouldn't be walking in the park. Even if it poured the entire trip, he wanted any excuse to spend time in the company of Lady Lily. The idea of her leaving London for the rest of the summer had his chest compressing in a manner he had never experienced before. "Not to worry, my lady. I shall simply hire a hackney." He drained his teacup. "Now, I am rather sorry you must leave London," he said sadly. "I was rather hoping you might accompany me for an ice at Gunter's. Your maid would have to join us, of course," he said with a nod toward the girl who sat near the window. Without turning, he knew she had overheard his comment when he was aware of her head jerking up.

Lily inhaled sharply. "You would take me there?" she replied, her face indicating surprise. *And my maid?*

William gave a shrug with one shoulder. "Yes, of course. What's your favorite flavor?" he asked, thinking she probably liked the lemon or strawberry.

"I've only ever been once. With Lady Samantha," she said. "I had the bergamot pear. It was... sweet and tart and rather delightful."

William allowed a wan smile. "Perhaps we can go when you return from Staffordshire," he said with a nod. "Do you expect to be gone long?" he asked carefully.

Lily gave a sigh. "I've really no idea. I'll be gone at least most of the summer. I am being summoned, you see," she explained, leaning forward as if she were sharing another secret with him.

"Summoned?" he repeated, his eyes rounding with concern. "But, why?"

Lily angled her head. "I have reason to believe my brother is... curious about my suitors, seeing as how the newspapers seem rather intent on printing whatever they please in that regard."

William nodded in sympathy. "Have you made a decision as to whom you will marry then?" he asked, knowing his question was wholly inappropriate. Seeing Lily's surprised reaction had him wishing he hadn't put voice to his query.

"Your question assumes I have received offers of marriage," she replied, her chin suddenly set at a defiant angle.

Straightening in his chair, William stared at Lily. "And you have not?" he asked in surprise.

Lily seemed to deflate before him, her sigh almost audible. "I... I'm not really sure," she finally admitted. She stood up suddenly, forcing William to get to his feet.

"My lady, I... I apologize," he stammered. "It's none of my business, of course, but..."

Lily watched as William's face changed from the friendly visage he had been displaying only moments before to one laced with pain. "But?" she whispered, hoping he would finish his thought.

The man seemed so forthright only moments ago, speaking his mind rather than making her guess what he might be thinking, like so many of the young bucks who paid attendance on her at balls.

"I came today because I had intended to escort you on your walk in the park. And to... to ask if I might be allowed to court you. Until the butler addressed you as a lady, I was unaware of your station in the peerage. I am not worthy of you, of course, so please forgive me for having taken so much of your time..." His voice trailed off.

He had come with a list of reasons why she should consider him a worthy husband—he had memorized them the night before, gone over them a hundred times as he lay awake—but now he couldn't put voice to a single one of them.

Lily stared at her guest for several moments, stunned at his words. "Worthiness has little to do with courting, I have found," she said, her hands clasping in front of her. "Whilst honor and intent and integrity carry far more meaning."

William regarded Lily for a moment, wondering if he should take hope in her words. Honor and integrity, he could understand. But intent? *What had her other suitors done or said to cause her to question their intent?*

"I am an honest man, and I live my life the best way I can," he stated suddenly. "I do not cheat or steal or gamble, nor do I employ whores," he said, the last word causing him to wince when he realized too late his poor choice of words. When he saw that Lady Lily didn't appear offended by his words, he continued. "I would honor you, my lady, every morning and every night, with proof of my affection." He set his mouth in a straight line as he watched Lily's eyes widen, whether with alarm or with surprise or with shock, he knew not. "As for intent, I would wish to make you as happy and content as I am able given my modest income as a clerk."

Lily blinked. And blinked again when she realized nothing had been said about her dowry.

Didn't he realize her brother intended to settle some amount on whomever she married? If they lived in a modest home and were careful with the funds, she rather doubted her husband would need to be concerned about money. "Income?" she repeated, her blue eyes gazing into his golden brown irises. Warmth, she thought suddenly. *Warmth and adoration and,* dare she hope? *Love?*

"Two-hundred and twenty pounds a year. Plus a bonus should my ships deliver a premium shipment," he added, hoping she would understand that last bit. Once again, he secretly chided himself. *Good God! We're discussing money!*

Lily's gasp was audible. As a maid, she could never have hoped to make anything close to two-hundred pounds! Not even in ten years! But as a sister to the Earl of Trenton, her gowns and frippery probably cost half of that every Season. "You must feel... *rich,*" she finally commented.

William finally nodded, not exactly agreeing with her assessment. "Do you suppose your brother would even read my missive if I sent a note asking his permission to court you?" he asked.

Lily's eyes widened again. "My *brother?*" she repeated. "But... But what has he got to do with this?" she asked with some degree of surprise.

William blinked. Then he blinked again. Didn't the chit realize she wouldn't be allowed to marry just anyone? Her brother was her protector. "Given he's your brother and an earl, I am quite sure he wants to see you settled with someone suitable, my lady. I rather doubt he will allow you to wed a... rake or... or an aristocrat looking to profit from your dowry... or a tradesman bent on gaining a higher position in Society through marriage," he explained, hoping he was making his intent clear. These were the very points he had covered the night before when he had argued with himself over his own suitability.

"But what if I don't like his choice?" Lily countered, her ire apparent in her high color.

Damn! Now I've gone and made a cake of it, William thought as he considered how to respond. "I am merely suggesting he may not agree with your choice, my lady. On the other hand, I rather doubt Trenton will *force* you to marry someone you don't find acceptable," he tried to assure her.

Lily stared at the clerk for several moments, inwardly cringing when she realized she sounded like a shrew with her question. William was merely trying to warn her, she realized.

Don't shoot the messenger.

"You are right, of course," she said suddenly. "I hardly know the man."

William stepped up to stand directly in front of Lily, one of his hands reaching for hers. "Tell him of your concerns, my lady. Tell him what you want. *Who* you want, and I'm quite sure he'll be reasonable," he said in a whisper, hoping beyond hope she hadn't already decided on someone else.

Lily allowed a look of disappointment to show on her face. *Goodness, the man certainly doesn't mince words,* she thought sadly. But the way he gazed at her had her suddenly mesmerized, had her wondering if he would dare kiss her.

A frisson passed through her as she imagined his lips coming down onto hers, of one of his hands wrapping around her waist to pull her body hard against the front of his, of the other hand cradling her face and then the back of her head, of that same hand working its way down her neck, along her collarbone to her shoulder, down her arm to gently graze along the side of her breast. Another frisson, this one far more intense, seemed to shake her entire body.

How could the mere thought of him kissing her have her nearly trembling?

"Speaking of the earl," William said softly. "It sounds as if his carriage awaits."

Earl who? she nearly responded. Lily sighed. Rather loudly. "You needn't remind me," she replied, angling her head. "Would you like more tea?" she suddenly asked, thinking they could simply sit back down and resume the rather pleasant conversation they were having over hot tea and swirling milk. Certainly the driver would like a bit of breakfast before they departed. And maybe luncheon, too.

William allowed a grin. "I would like nothing better, my lady, but I fear your butler would not allow me entrance into Fitzsimmons Manor ever again should I accept your hospitality."

"I've a mind to curse you," Lily replied in a hoarse whisper.

William allowed a wan smile. "Something I am most sure you would do frequently if given the chance." He reached over and lifted her hand to his lips. Kissing the back of her knuckles, he allowed his lips to linger as he did so. "Safe travels, my lady," he murmured, his forehead tilted down so it nearly touched hers. He imagined asking her if he might be allowed a kiss. Imagined how his lips might settle onto hers, how she might taste, how long she might allow him to suckle her lush lower lip...

"Kiss me," Lily murmured, rather stunned when she realized she had said the words aloud.

A look of doubt crossed William's face, but it was gone in an instant. *Did she just tell me to kiss her?* he thought in alarm, his heart suddenly racing. Bullocks! Could she read his mind?

He didn't wait for her to change hers, but leaned down and cupped the side of her face in one hand. He touched his lips to hers, unsure of how hard to press, of how close he could stand before her, of how long he could inhale the scent of citrus and honey and spice and not go mad with his desire for her.

But before he could decide if it had been long enough, Lily's lips responded, moving slightly beneath his, opening a bit wider as her free hand moved to rest on his shoulder. And then it was as if he had been awakened from a stupor, for his entire being had come alive with awareness. Her skin beneath his fingers was so smooth, like velvet. He felt her soft breaths, felt her pulse beneath his thumb as his hand moved to the base of her neck. He deepened the kiss, heard her moan in what he hoped was encouragement, he felt her fingers tighten their hold on his shoulder. His other hand moved to her waist, for he was quite sure she was about to lose her balance and fall against him. And although he would have welcomed her body pressed against his, he was quite aware—too aware—there was someone else in the parlor with them and what they were doing was wholly inappropriate.

The sound of a throat clearing made William end the kiss, his eyes squeezed shut. *Christ!* He had been caught with his hand in the biscuit jar!

When he opened his eyes, he realized the maid who had been sewing near the window was suddenly standing beside them.

"Porter's coming!" she whispered in warning.

Relieved the maid wasn't going to report his behavior to the ancient man, William gave her an appreciative nod and stepped back. Turning his attention back to Lily, who appeared a bit dazed and ever so beautiful with her blue eyes glazed over and her bee-stung lips looking ever so pink, he nodded. "I trust your brother will let you know if he has granted me permission to court you, my lady," he said as he gave her a bow. "I fear I shall worry about your fate until you arrive safely at the earl's residence."

Not sure she could trust her voice just then, Lily gave him a nod. "I'll have a footman and a groom, of course," she whispered, taking some satisfaction in learning he was concerned for her safety.

"Good day, then," William replied, giving her another nod as well as the maid who stood with a bemused expression on her face. "I look forward to your return."

With that, William took his leave of Fitzsimmons Manor.

Lily stared at William as he departed the parlor, the back of her hand still tingling from the kiss he had left there, her lips still throbbing from the kiss he had left there, her cheek and neck still warm from where he had held them as if they were made of fine porcelain. Indeed, her entire body thrummed from where he had touched her, all warmth and tenderness and intimacy. Her entire body shivered at the thought of what it would be like to have his lips kissing her everywhere with the kind of reverence he spoke of when he mentioned honoring her.

Every morning and every night.

Except that he wouldn't.

Not if what he claimed was true. If her brother didn't allow her to marry whom she wanted to marry, she would end up in a marriage of convenience, a marriage most likely arranged because some rake needed funds to pay off his gambling debts or to pay for a townhouse for his mistress or to prop up a property that bled red ink every year.

"Are you... all right, my lady?" the maid asked as she watched Lily recover from the guest's brief kiss. From Lily's reaction, the maid thought perhaps her mistress had never been kissed before. And if anyone asked her if she had witnessed the kiss, she would have to say she had not, for the kiss had been so brief, she thought it merely a friendly peck.

Lily finally turned her attention to her lady's maid and shook her head. "I am not, actually," she whispered.

Frustrated, she stomped a slippered foot on the Aubusson carpet and crossed her arms. *Men!* she thought in dismay. Even the honorable ones were a conundrum. For despite William Overby's claim that he wished to court her, at no point in their conversation had the man actually proposed! Or said anything about intending to ask for her hand in marriage!

Of all the men who had indicated an interest in procuring her as a wife, William Overby was the only one who seemed to require her brother's permission.

But the worst of it was the manner in which he had made the comment about going to Gunter's Tea Shop—*Perhaps when you return from Staffordshire*—for Lily was left with the distinct impression that, despite his words, they would not be going.

Damnation!

CHAPTER 8

A REUNION

*D*espite the warmth of the rain that fell when he took his leave of Fitzsimmons Manor, William felt a bit chilled when he settled into the squabs of the hackney that was now bounding along Oxford Street. Once he learned he wouldn't be accompanying Lady Lily into the park for her early morning walk, William thought he would merely make his way to Wellingham Imports for a normal day of work. He would arrive later than normal, of course, but he could stay later to make up the time. He *would* stay later to make up the time. He had no idea how long he would be away now that he thought his uncle might be an employee of 'Lady E and Associates' Finding Work for the Wounded.' He also had no idea when the charity opened its doors for business each day. He might be arriving hours before its scheduled opening.

When the hackney reached Number Thirty, the coach came to an abrupt halt in the middle of the damp street. William tossed a coin up to the driver and tipped his hat, grateful for the ride. Although it had rained the entire time he was in the conveyance, the clouds had suddenly parted and the sun looked as if it might make an appearance.

Buoyed by the better weather, William made his way to the office of Lady E's charity and paused before pushing on the front door. He could see through the window in the door. He also could see that at least two gentlemen were seated within. He took a deep breath and finally entered the office, removing his top hat as he did so. "Good morning, gentlemen," he announced as he entered.

The two men both looked up from their work and gave him accessing glances. The taller of the two stood up. "I am Nicholas Barnaby. May I be of assistance?" he asked, giving William another examination. "You don't look as if you need our services."

But William's attention was on the other man. On the man whose graying brown hair was long and pulled back into a queue, whose cheekbones and lips were a match for his own, whose eyes were the same golden brown color. "My business is with this gentleman," he murmured in response to Mr. Barnaby's query. "Are you Mr. Overby?" he asked of the gentleman still seated at a desk piled with papers. His pulse pounded in his ears. "I just came from having tea with Lady Lily," he added as he made his way toward the older man.

At the mention of Lady Lily, Augustus Overby's eyes widened. "Is she all right?" he asked in alarm, attempting to come to his feet.

William waved him down. "She is fine. She is... she's about to leave for Staffordshire," he stammered. "The Earl of Trenton's coach arrived earlier this morning."

The man's expression showed a combination of relief and disappointment. "She'll be missed," he commented. "A rather pleasant young lady, that one is."

William couldn't agree more. "You must be Augustus Overby," he said, his voice pitched low.

The older man angled his head, studying William for a moment. "I am," he replied with a nod. "And you are ...?"

Dipping his head, William said, "William Overby. My mother was Madeline, God rest her soul, and my sister's name is Katie. Lady Lily..." Before he could say another word, the man was up and out of his chair and making his way toward William with a limping gait.

"Jesus!" the taller man whispered as his arms went around

William's shoulders. "William! I'd given up on ever finding you," he said as he pulled away. "I thought I'd lost all of you," he whispered as he studied his nephew's face.

About to be seated at his desk, Nicholas Barnaby quickly stood up again and made his way towards them. "Auggie?" he managed to get out before his eyes suddenly widened. "Good grief! He's you, only twenty years younger!" he exclaimed as he stared at William.

"Aye," Augustus agreed. "Come. Sit. Tell me everything," he ordered as he pointed to a chair next to the desk he occupied.

William considered the time, but decided the opportunity to spend time with his uncle outweighed any need to get to work just then.

The two Overbys spent the rest of the morning in quiet conversation until hunger demanded a break for luncheon. It wasn't until they had finished their meal that the two took their leave of one another, Augustus returning to the charity office and William finally reporting to Wellingham Imports.

He would have some explaining to do.

"Have you seen Mr. Overby this morning?" Thomas Wellingham asked as he took a seat at his desk. He added several papers to the stack on the far corner of the desk, wincing as he did so.

Emma raised her quill from where she was about to write a number and frowned. "I have not, but—"

"The *Constellation* is about to dock. He needs to be on board to help with the inventory," Thomas stated, his voice sounding with annoyance.

Lowering her pen to her desk, Emma pushed herself away from the small desk she used in the office behind her husband's. "I can do it," she offered, secretly hoping the young man was still in Lady Lily's company and not off on some fool's errand.

"You most certainly will not," Thomas replied, rising from his chair almost as quickly as he had fallen into it. At Emma's look of surprise, he added, "That crew is worse than a band of pirates and probably just as horny. I'll not have you on board hearing their cat-calls," he claimed.

Emma had to suppress a grin. She often wondered if her husband knew half of what happened on board a cargo ship. "All right. But you should know I sent Mr. Overby on an errand this morning."

Thomas frowned as he regarded his wife. "Errand?" he repeated, one eyebrow cocking up with the query.

Emma sighed and had the good sense to at least appear a bit sorry for what she had done. "Your cousin, Lily," she started to say.

"Yes?" he replied rather carefully.

"She required an escort for her morning walk in the park. She likes to go early—at half-past-six, but she doesn't care to bother the servants to be chaperoned, so I insisted Mr. Overby join her. I expect he'll return at any time." She glanced at the clock in her office, rather surprised it was nearly time for luncheon.

Thomas stared at his wife for a few moments. "Are you ...?" he paused, not quite sure if he should ask what immediately came to mind upon hearing what she had done.

"Playing matchmaker?" she finished for him. "Yes, I suppose I am," she admitted.

Thomas' eyes widened. "Emma!" he countered. "She's a lady! You can hardly think my cousin the earl will allow her to marry a... *a clerk!*" he managed to get out without his voice being heard beyond the office door.

Sighing loudly, Emma angled her head. "She was a maid, Thomas. She's illegitimate. You can hardly think the aristocracy will accept her as one of their own," she whispered, her opinion of the peerage having suffered over the years given her very own sister couldn't know of their relationship. At some point, Emma was sure she would be allowed to introduce herself to Lady Samantha as her sister—they shared the same father, after all. She promised herself she would do so just as soon as Lady Chamberlain gave her permission, although she was beginning to wonder if the viscountess would ever give her that permission. If the information ever became public, the *ton* would realize Lady Samantha was illegitimate, that Caroline

Harrington had given birth to the child everyone believed was born to her late sister—before her marriage to Matthew Fitzsimmons.

Emma rather doubted Lord and Lady Chamberlain could abide the gossip, and given Lord Chamberlain's position with the Foreign Office, he couldn't afford such a scandal.

Emma had to feel sorry for her uncle. Matthew had accepted Samantha into his home when he married Caroline. He had helped raise her, thinking the entire time Samantha was Caroline's niece, when in fact, she was his niece.

Oh, the tangled webs we weave, Emma thought with a shake of her head. And all because Caroline, as a young war widow, had fallen in love with the older George Fitzsimmons, a hat maker.

The entire time she had worked with her father in his hat shop, Emma never understood why George and his brother, Matthew, seemed at odds. Even now, it seemed rather silly that the second son of a viscount could be so vilified for wanting to build his own business. And now that Matthew had been at the Foreign Office for so many years—certainly what he did could be considered work—she wondered if perhaps he didn't regret their estrangement. What would the man think, though, if he learned his wife's first love was his brother George?

Or was that the reason for the estrangement?

She shook her head. It couldn't be. The two brothers had apparently come to blows long before George and Caroline had their *affaire*. This could only mean that if Matthew ever discovered the truth about Samantha, he would have that much more reason to hate his late brother.

At least George Fitzsimmons' legacy continued. His hat shop, now 'Fitzsimmons and Smith', had expanded into the real estate on either side of the original location and the owner, Ambrose Smith, continued to pay Emma for the use of her father's name and tag line, 'Hats That Make the Gentleman'.

Once the man started exporting hats to the Continent, the royalties from his top hats proved more lucrative than her meager earnings as a payroll clerk at Wellingham Imports. But she wasn't about to share that information with Thomas. Better that it buy a five percenter and be available should something awful happen to the business.

Emma sighed and shook head. She was barely aware of her husband's arms wrapping around her shoulders, of how he pulled her hard against the front of his body and held her as tears pricked the corners of her eyes.

"I hardly think you need to cry over a lost cause," Thomas murmured as he held her.

Blinking back the tears, Emma frowned. *Lost cause?* Then she remembered what they had been discussing when her thoughts wandered to Samantha. "I hardly think William is a lost cause. Even when it comes to Lily," she countered, lifting her head from his shoulder. "In fact, I think we should be doing whatever we can to see to it those two do end up together."

Thomas gave her an assessing glance, a bit suspicious of her motives. What did she know of Lily—of William—to be so sure the two would even suit? "I'll agree with you, but on one condition," he said, angling his head to one side. "We're not going to piss off my cousin in the process," he warned, not bothering to apologize for his coarse language.

Arching an eyebrow, Emma regarded her husband for a moment.

Men. Why did they have to be so vexing?

"Agreed," she finally said with a sniffle.

CHAPTER 9

WAITING FOR A SISTER'S ARRIVAL

Gabriel Wellingham paced his study, his nervousness apparent in how he held his body taut. "When she arrives, the first thing I'll have her do is provide a list of every suitor—"

"The first thing you're going to do is greet her," Sarah interrupted, one finger extended into the air. "And then you're going to kiss her on the cheek and allow her to go to her suite so that she may refresh herself and perhaps take a nap—"

"And have a spot of tea and biscuits," Gabriel chimed in with a roll of his eyes as he took a seat in the leather chair behind his desk.

"And *then* you can ask about her suitors," Sarah finished with a nod from where she sat next to his desk. Seeing her husband so nervous about his sister's impending visit had her rather amused. He was usually quite confident—cocky, even— when it came to how he dealt with matters of the earldom.

Lady Lily wasn't a typical matter, however. Lily had the man quite out of his element.

"I love you," Gabriel stated as he leaned forward and reached over the desk for one of Sarah's hands.

"Of course, you do," Sarah replied with a wink. "You wouldn't put up with me otherwise," she added as Gabriel kissed the back of the hand he held. "Oh, and against my better judgement, I suppose I love you, too," she added gleefully.

Gabriel was about to feign offense, but he was interrupted by a knock at the door to the study. "Come!" he called out.

Fitzroy, the butler, appeared at the threshold. "Your carriage just pulled into the drive, my lord," he stated in a baritone worthy of an opera singer.

Both Sarah and Gabriel were out of their chairs in an instant. "She must not have required the coach to stop very often," Gabriel murmured with a hint of awe.

"She's not as spoiled as you," Sarah countered with a playful grin, hurrying to the vestibule with her husband at her side. When she suddenly stopped, Gabriel took another step or two before realizing he needed to stop. He whirled around to face his wife. Before he could ask as to why she had halted in the grand hall with no warning, Sarah's lips were suddenly on his, and one of her arms had circled his neck.

Rather surprised by Sarah's assault of affection, Gabriel returned the brief kiss before slowly pulling away, apparently unaware of the stares of the footmen poised to meet the coach. "I must ask why you would afford me such a sudden and rather public display of affection," he whispered, his forehead pressed against hers.

"I do love you," Sarah whispered in reply. "Please, do not be offended by my teasing," she added with a slight shake of her head against his.

Gabriel kissed her nose. "I would be offended if you did not occasionally remind me I am a mortal," he replied with a wink.

"I spent the entire carriage ride here thinking I might be better off *not* marrying," a feminine voice called out from the vestibule, "But then I pay witness to you two lovebirds and think perhaps I should become a wife post-haste!"

The earl and countess whirled around to find Lady Lily standing at the end of the great hall with one hand on her hip and a huge grin on her face.

"Lily!" Sarah called out as she hurried to join her sister-in-law. The two hugged before leaning back to regard one another.

"Marriage certainly agrees with you," Lily stated as her brother joined them. "And you," she added as she gave her brother a thorough look. She reached up and kissed his cheek, not sure what was acceptable when greeting an earl who was also a brother.

A bit startled at his sister's comment, Gabriel gave Lily a kiss on the cheek and regarded her for a moment. "It's my sincerest wish it will agree with you as well, although I have learned the choice of a spouse is paramount..." Gabriel stopped when he realized his wife was giving him a quelling glance. He suddenly sobered. "You must be exhausted from your trip. Allow me to escort you to your bedchamber so you can take a nap and freshen up before dinner," he suggested, remembering Sarah's edict.

Lily grinned and turned to Sarah. "My, how well you've trained my brother," she whispered with an arched brow.

Sarah nodded. "A bit of work, but well worth the effort," she whispered back.

"I heard that," Gabriel said with feigned offense, one open hand pressed against his chest. "How I'll manage the two of you whilst you join forces against me is beyond my comprehension."

The two women exchanged innocent glances before Lily shook her head. "Dear brother, you should know by now that you cannot manage a woman," she said in a whisper filled with delight. "It's the woman who manages the man."

And with that, Lady Lily and Lady Trenton made their way up the steps and to the guest bedchamber.

CHAPTER 10

A CLERK GETS CALLED INTO THE BOSS' OFFICE

illiam Overby regarded the last entry he had written in the ledger and frowned. The numbers didn't seem to add up despite his having done the math on a separate sheet. He double-checked the numbers again and whispered a curse.

"Is something wrong, Mr. Overby?"

The clerk gave a start, obviously surprised by the question, and found Emma Wellingham standing next to his desk. "Numbers just aren't adding up the same, is all," he replied. And they hadn't done so for the entire day, but he didn't mention it to the woman who was essentially his boss at Wellingham Imports.

Emma leaned over so she couldn't be overheard by any of the other clerks that shared the large office. "Could I have a moment of your time?" she whispered.

William swallowed. Except for the day she had offered him a position as an inventory clerk—a promotion from the warehouse job he had held for nearly ten years—Mrs. Wellingham had never requested his presence in her office. "Of course," he replied, placing his pen next to the ink pot.

He followed the owner's wife out of the large clerking office, their departure causing a few of the other accomptants to lift their heads at the interruption. When the door shut behind him, he put voice to his main concern. "Have I done something wrong?"

Emma turned her head in his direction as they made their way along the rail-lined walkway overlooking the warehouse space. "Probably not," she replied, a quirk lifting one side of her mouth as she waited for him to open the door to the office she shared with her husband. They moved past his desk— Thomas was down on the warehouse floor and wouldn't be back for some time—and through the doorway that led to the small office in the back. "Take a seat, Mr. Overby. We just need to go over a couple of ledgers."

Bracing for the worst, William took the seat adjacent to hers at the long desk and watched as she arranged two open ledgers in front of them.

"But first, do tell me her name," Emma said as she lifted a pen from the inkwell.

William blinked. "Beg pardon?" he replied, his eyebrows furrowing.

Emma allowed a mischievous grin. "Mr. Overby, I have never found you to be as distracted nor as troubled as you have been these past few days. With any of the other clerks, I would think there might be a problem with their wives or children, but you are not married. So..." She gave a shrug.

His hands clutching the bottom of his waistcoat, William stared at Emma. He hadn't considered his inability to add numbers could be due to a chit! It was true, though, that he was distracted and had been ever since the day the young lady with the blonde curls had paid a visit to Wellingham Imports. Since the day he had shared tea with her at Fitzsimmons before the Trenton coach arrived to take her away. She probably wasn't yet in Staffordshire, which meant his note to her brother, requesting permission to court her, probably hadn't arrived yet, either.

"Lily," he blurted, a red stain suddenly covering his throat and face. "I don't recall the rest of her name," he added, which wasn't entirely true, but he didn't think it necessary to share that with his boss just then. Besides, was she really still 'Harkins' or was her proper name now 'Wellingham'?

Stunned that William would give her a name and even more pleased by the name he spoke, Emma stared at the clerk for several seconds. "Harkins," she finally managed to say. "Lily Harkins. Sister to Gabriel Wellingham, Earl of Trenton," she added with an arched eyebrow. She remembered having given him the note requesting he escort her in the park during her morning walks. "So, your walks in the park have been agreeable?" Emma asked gently. "You've been left with a favorable impression?"

More than the one time, William thought to himself. "We actually never made it to the park," he replied. "I mean, we were going to go for a walk a few mornings ago, but it smelled like rain, so we stayed at Fitzsimmons Manor and had tea instead."

It was Emma's turn to blink. "Oh. And what about the mornings since?" she asked carefully, thinking the opportunity to have tea with the young woman was certainly a good start to a courtship. That is, if William was seeking a courtship.

William shook his head. "The Trenton coach arrived to take her to Staffordshire. She left later that day." He paused and angled his head. "I know you read all the papers. She's not yet married, but is there a bookmaker's favorite? A likely match?"

Emma sighed. Poor boy. He was obviously smitten with the young lady. "Not yet, but from what I've read in *The Morning Chronicle*, she certainly has a number of suitors," she admitted. She couldn't help but notice how deflated the young man seemed by the news. "Despite being illegitimate," she added, just to see how the young clerk would react.

She wasn't disappointed.

At this reminder of Lily's situation, William suddenly brightened. "She told me. Do you suppose there's a chance for someone like me, then?" he replied as he sat up straighter.

Emma had no idea how to respond to such a query. *Did he have a chance? A chance at what? A walk in the park? Courting? Matrimony?*

Although Lily Harkins seemed to have adopted the ways of the *ton* in the manner in which she dressed and spoke and carried herself, Emma couldn't help but think the young lady seemed a bit like a fish out of water, even after over a year and two Seasons of balls and soirées. "When it comes to matters of the heart, Mr. Overby, there's always a chance," she finally replied. "Perhaps you should pay a call on Lady Lily when she returns and discover for yourself if you have a chance."

Although her first reaction to William's comment might have been to discourage the young man, she found she wanted to play matchmaker. Trenton might have thought he was doing his half-sister a favor by recognizing her as his sibling and seeing to it she had a worthy sponsor in Lady Samantha, but Emma wondered if his intentions had been welcomed by the former maid.

When Lily had paid a call on them only a few days ago, she seemed relieved to discover her cousin was affable. *I was so worried. I thought you might find me abhorrent, given I was born on the wrong side of the blanket.*

Of course, Thomas had quickly abused her of the notion, reminding her that she had no choice in the matter of her father and shouldn't have to suffer on his account. Emma took a great deal of pride in how her husband had managed that bit of discomfort.

An evening of dinner and conversation at their house in Chiswick three nights ago, and Lady Lily was soon at ease with everyone in the household, including all the Grandby children. The younger tykes had taken a liking to their cousin when she joined them on the floor in the parlor and played with them, laughing and giggling as if she had known them her entire life. The oldest, Ariel, was already a beautiful young lady at fifteen, her skills on the piano-forté already surpassing her mother's at that age.

"I plan to," William stated with a nod.

Pulled out of her reverie, Emma stared at William. "And?" she pressed, rather impressed the clerk hadn't given up on the idea of courting the young woman. He had even located Fitzsimmons Manor without help from her. But then, William had been a caddie in his younger years and certainly knew his way around London. Goodness, he probably had the nose of a hound dog and could follow Lily's delicate scent all the way back to Fitzsimmons Manor! But it was rather disappointing the chit was off to Staffordshire just now. Just when William had been made aware of her existence.

However, given the Fitzsimmons' recent departure for the Continent, Emma thought perhaps it was a good idea Lily was on a trip of her own.

"The timing couldn't be worse," William replied. "When that coach showed up, it was as if someone was spying on us and decided she had to be rescued from me or something," he complained. He didn't mention thinking the butler might have had something to do with it. The ancient man didn't seem the least bit pleased to have to admit him into Fitzsimmons Manor, especially with the Fitzsimmons away on some trip to the Mediterranean.

Shaking her head, Emma said, "A coincidence, I am quite sure. Lady Lily has been receiving a bit too much attention by the newspapers of late, and I rather imagine her brother is a bit... *concerned* for her welfare, is all," she added carefully. "How was your tea with the lady?" she asked, curious as to how he got along with Lily.

The red stain reappeared on William's face. "Good, I thought," he offered before turning away to stare at the floor. "She seemed to genuinely *like* me," he said with a nod. "We spoke of many things, including our past, and we laughed a bit, and..." He stopped, his eyes lifting to meet Emma's. "I think I may..." He stopped again, not sure if he should admit he thought himself in love with the comely blonde.

He had been through this before with her. Lily had consumed his thoughts nearly every waking moment since he had met her that night in Vauxhall Gardens. For months after that night, he had thought of her, wondered about her, hoped she was safe. The memory had finally faded, and then, out of nowhere, she reappeared so that he was once again forced to think of her nearly every waking moment since the day she had arrived at Wellingham Imports.

He thought of her nearly every sleeping moment, as well.

Dreaming of Lily was like dreaming of an angel, only this one looked like Cupid's sister. And he was learning her aim with a bow and arrow was just as deadly.

"Perhaps a letter is called for," Emma offered. "I can see to its delivery to Trenton Manor on one of the northbound coaches," she added. "There's one leaving in the middle of the night." Wellingham Imports could boast of a rather extensive network of coaches that travelled throughout England, delivering products to various clients and picking up products from other port cities to bring back to London on their return trips.

"A letter?" William questioned, his brows furrowing.

"Yes," Emma replied. "If you send a letter telling her how much you appreciated the time you spent with her, she'll be more likely to put in a good word for you with the earl," she explained. "The other suitors probably don't know she's gone to Staffordshire, and I rather doubt the butler will inform them of her location should they pay a call at Fitzsimmons Manor."

William nodded, understanding how his missive might be the only one Lily would receive whilst at Trenton Manor. "I shall write a letter tonight," he said, his spirit rising.

"You shall do so right now!" Emma countered, handing him a pen and a sheet of parchment. "I have spent the past three days correcting your mistakes on these ledgers," she said as she motioned to the two that lay open on her desk, "And I refuse to continue doing so, Mr. Overby," she admonished him. "Either profess your love for her, or let her know you have moved on." She took a breath. "While you're at it, write one to her brother, as well."

William's eyes widened. "Whatever for?" he replied.

Emma shrugged. "Ask his permission to court his sister," she ordered. "Then you'll know where you stand with her other suitors."

William stared at Emma for several seconds, his attention finally going to the pen he held. *Should I admit to her I already did?*

The note had been simple, short and to the point.

Dear Lord Trenton, I have had the pleasure of knowing your sister for over five years. Despite my lowly position as a clerk at Wellingham Imports, I want nothing but the best for your sister. I wish to see her happy and, if given the opportunity, will honor her for the rest of her days. I seek your permission to court Lady Lily. I look forward to your favourable reply. William Overby.

The second to the last sentence had made him pause.

I seek your permission to court Lady Lily.

That implied he wanted to court her, which he did, he supposed. Which meant he wanted to marry her, which he supposed... *Good grief!* Did he want to marry the girl?

Well, actually, he *did* want to, he decided. *I do want to marry her.*

"I already sent the note to the earl," he replied with a nod, which had Emma's eyes widening in surprise. She had the decency to blink, at least, William noticed, so she certainly didn't expect his comment.

"I must admit, I am rather impressed, Mr. Overby," she said. "Now take it one step further and make your intentions known to the lady."

It was William's turn to blink. "Yes, ma'am," he replied with a nod. "But before I do, may I ask you a question about the painting?" He pointed to the landscape above her desk, a painting exactly the same size and done with the same tiny brush strokes as the one in the Fitzsimmons Manor vestibule.

Emma's brow furrowed. "Of course," she replied as her attention went to the landscape.

"Are you related to the painter?"

Emma blinked. She turned to regard William. "Why would you think that?" she finally responded, her gaze moving back to the artwork. *How much does he know?*

"I saw a similar painting done by the same artist in Fitzsimmons Manor," William said, his voice rather quiet. "The butler said it was one of Lady Samantha's early works. I just thought since you had one of her paintings that you might be... related."

Emma had to blink back the tears that collected in the corners of her eyes. "I wish that I could tell you we are, but I cannot," she finally whispered. "Now, do get to your letter writing, won't you?"

With that last directive, Emma quickly left the office, leaving William wondering at her odd response. *Why couldn't she acknowledge her relationship to Samantha Fitzsimmons?*

Before he gave it another thought, he regarded the parchment before him and realized he had no time to waste. Taking a deep breath, he began to write, a bit relieved when Emma took her leave of the office and allowed him to write the note in the privacy of an empty office.

Dear Lady Lily, London has not been the same since your departure. The sun hasn't come out from behind the clouds. The rain continues to pour. And I've just been admonished by your cousin, Mrs. Wellingham, for having made a cake of my inventory books this past week. I blame you, of course, since I can think of nothing but you. I think of you day and night. It's my fault, of course, for having allowed myself to drown in your beautiful blue eyes. I've yet to come up for air and don't know that I will. Or that I want to. Needless to say, I look forward to your return. I've a hankering for an ice at Gunter's, and I should like you with me when next I go. Yours very truly, William Overby.

Taking a deep breath and letting it out slowly, William reread his heartfelt words, frowning as he did so.

Such dreck!

Lily would no doubt read his note and begin laughing in that delightful way she had of expressing her mirth.

Slowly, he wadded up the missive and tossed it into the wastebasket next to the desk. Taking out another sheet of parchment, he paused before putting pen to paper.

Dear Lady Lily, I miss you. Terribly. Yours truly, William Overby.

When he finished, he folded the missive and carefully addressed it. *Lady Lily, Trenton Manor, Bilston, Staffordshire.* Finding a stick of sealing wax on Emma's desk, he held it over the nearest candle lamp and allowed it to melt a puddle of red over the seams of his letter. When it was dry, he left the note on Emma's desk and returned to his own desk in the clerks' office.

With his mind entirely on inventory and numbers, he corrected all his errors before the end of the work day and took his leave of Wellingham Imports only an hour later than normal.

CHAPTER 11

MATCHMAKERS AT WORK

*E*mma Wellingham watched her favorite clerk take his leave of the office she shared with her husband and wondered if the young man would soon be taking his leave of Wellingham Imports.

William had worked for Thomas since he was a small child, delivering missives to ship captains and shipping clerks and bankers and even the headmistress of Warwick's Grammar and Finishing School where she and Thomas' sister, Christiana, had lived before their marriages. She couldn't imagine Wellingham Imports without William. But if he succeeded in winning the hand of an earl's sister—her cousin by marriage— he might never need to work again. Lady Lily's dowry might provide them enough income to live on for the rest of their lives.

Or not.

If Gabriel Wellingham did give William permission to court his sister, the young man would still have a good deal of competition when it came to winning Lady Lily's hand. And all of them were members of the *ton*. They were gentlemen who held lands, had incredible wealth or who owed money to every gaming hell east of the park.

Sighing, Emma entered her office and found the folded missive William had sealed so completely with wax. She was about to add it to her other correspondence when she noticed the rumpled sheet of parchment in the wastebasket next to her desk. Reaching down, she captured a corner between her thumb and forefinger and lifted it. She read the heartfelt words, a smile forming as her head tilted to one side.

"I rather wish I had written whatever it is you're reading there," Thomas said from the doorway to her office.

No longer surprised at being spied on by her husband whilst at work, Emma gave him a quelling glance. "I rather wish you had, too," she replied, finally grinning.

Thomas joined her, taking the note from her fingers and holding it up to the light from the window at the back of the office. He read in silence, a long sigh finally escaping as he handed it back to Emma. "Me, too," he said before giving her a kiss on the temple. "It might have saved myself some courting time."

A giggle erupted from Emma. *Courting* wasn't exactly how she would have described the time she had spent with Thomas prior to their wedding. "Should we be worried?" she asked in a whisper.

Thomas glanced from the wrinkled parchment to the neatly folded missive Emma held in her hand. "Depends on what's in the one he decided to send her," he replied, one eyebrow arching up.

Emma gasped, realizing the note they had read was without errors, without smears or any signs that it was unacceptable to send.

So what had William decided to send instead?

Dropping the missive to the desk, she used the edge of a fingernail to lift the wax from the edges.

"What are you doing?" Thomas asked in alarm.

"Spying," Emma responded, carefully unfolding William's final missive to Lily, her businesslike manner suggesting she felt no qualms in reading the clerk's private mail. She read the simple words and straightened. "*Really?*" she exclaimed, obviously disappointed.

Thomas had moved to read the note from over one of her

shoulders and let out a huff. "Come now. You cannot blame him for—"

"For his lack of backbone? For failing to claim what he has every right to?" Emma interrupted, her ire quite evident in her posture and tone of voice.

Thomas stiffened. "Right to?" he repeated, stunned by her words. "He's a *clerk*, Emma. He has no right to court a lady. If Lily decides—"

"She was a *maid*, Thomas," Emma stated as she turned to face him. "She was an illegitimate maid. Don't you think our William has every right to court her? More of a right, in fact, than one of those pompous aristocrats?" she asked then, her eyes brightening with tears.

Thomas frowned, one hand moving to cup his wife's cheek. "You make a good point," he whispered with a nod. "But I beg you to be careful. You are speaking of my cousin," he chided gently.

Emma inhaled sharply, as if she might be about to argue. Instead, she rested her head against his shoulder. "I apologize, Thomas," she whispered.

Thomas moved his hands down her sides and pulled her body so she was fully pressed against the front of his. "No need, my love. You do make a good point," he said, leaving a kiss on her forehead. "And these things tend to work themselves out somehow," he added absently. "Remember how blind I was when everyone else knew we should end up together? And I was trying to match you with Mr. Vandermeer," he murmured with a hint of disgust.

"It's a good thing women know better about these things," Emma replied with an impish grin. At one point, she had actually imagined a life with Todd Vandermeer, had thought for a few moments about how life might be with a man who was too tall and too innocent and perfectly suited to her best friend, Deborah. Thank the gods she realized she and Todd would make a poor match, even if Todd claimed Emma was his first love. If something happened to Thomas, Emma would have

Todd as a protector—he had made that promise many years ago, before he had married Deborah White and sired two children and been the primary reason Wellingham Imports had nearly doubled in size in only a few years after his joining the firm.

"Are you about to call an end to your workday?" she asked.

Thomas nodded. "I am thinking we should take our leave of this place in another half-hour. Maybe spend the night at the townhouse instead of riding back to Chiswick. Let's have a quiet night. Agreed?" With Gregory and Christiana's children taking over the parlor every night after dinner, Woodscastle was a lively house these days. But some nights required peace and quiet.

Emma lifted her head from his shoulder, deciding she rather liked the idea of spending the night at the townhouse she had let after her years at Warwick's. "Agreed."

She moved to take her seat at her desk, pulling a ledger into place so that she might continue her work. Meanwhile, Thomas carefully tucked William's rumpled missive under his arm and disappeared through the door to his side of the office. Once at this desk, he took great pains to smooth out the wrinkled parchment before folding it to match the one in Emma's office. He addressed the finished envelope, adding the necessary numbers so that it might arrive at its destination a day or two ahead of the other, and placed it atop the pile of outgoing correspondence.

If William Overby wanted to marry his cousin, and if her earl-of-a-brother could find it acceptable for him to do so, then why shouldn't William be allowed the same chance as any pompous ass of an aristocrat?

Playing matchmaker was rather fun, Thomas decided. He grinned as he completed the rest of his work for the day.

CHAPTER 12

AN ICE AT GUNTER'S

June 7, 1817

William regarded the festive storefront of Gunter's Tea Shop and took a deep breath. The scents of sweets and Earl Grey and chamomile touched his nose. Although it was the middle of the day and not particularly warm, the inside of the shop was bustling with customers. Nearly every table was occupied by nattily dressed gentlemen and their lovely ladies.

Moving to a small round table near the back, William glanced around the shop before taking a seat and opening that day's edition of *The Times*. Although the table could host a party of two, one of the chairs had been pulled to a nearby table for four, around which was clustered a group of young matrons. William knew this because several had already removed their gloves, and gold rings, some topped with sapphires or diamonds, adorned their left hands. Their chatter had subsided somewhat with the delivery of their ices, the colorful confections served in pretty glass dishes.

Although he couldn't really afford an ice, William allowed himself the luxury on this day, the occasion of his twenty-third birthday. At least, he was fairly sure he had the correct date. Not having proof in the form of a certificate or a Bible in which the date might have been recorded for posterity, he simply took his mother's word for it when she had said he was born on June 7th. Had his younger sister, Katie, not been otherwise engaged with classes at Warwick's Grammar and Finishing School, he would have invited her to join him.

"Lemon ice," he said with a nod when the waiter appeared to take his order.

The portly man nodded in return and hurried off through the crowded room.

Inhaling the wonderful scents drifting about, William nearly closed his eyes. The young matrons were back to their chattering, though, and he couldn't help but overhear their conversation as he pretended to read.

"They say she has a half-dozen suitors, but I rather doubt that can be true," said one who was dressed in a deep blue walking dress topped by a lighter blue pelisse.

"Oh, but I think it is," countered another, one whose hat sported one of the largest feathers William had ever seen. *Could feathers really be that color of pink?* he thought absently, thinking it probably glowed in the dark.

"I hear her dowry is quite substantial, which can be the only reason anyone would wish to marry the chit," said another, her spoon waving about so light reflected from the shiny silver. Or perhaps it reflected from the gemstones embedded in the bracelet she wore. *Good God!* The bauble was probably worth more than William made in six months at his clerking position!

"Lady Pettigrew says she has so many men paying her attendance because of those blue eyes of hers, which I must admit, are rather striking," a more charitable woman put forth.

"Striking?" the one wearing blue repeated. "They look positively demonic!"

"Jane!" the feather woman gasped.

A chorus of gasps had the table quieting before a round of titters replaced the uncomfortable silence. "It's true!" the one apparently named Jane claimed. "And then there's that hair. Can those blonde curls truly be *natural?*" she asked rhetorically. "She probably has some poor maid using the iron on her hair for an hour every morning and then again before dinner. No wonder it's short. The rest has probably been burned off!"

William had to suppress a wince at the harpy's comments. What poor blonde-haired, blue-eyed lady could they be discussing? Blonde-haired, blue-eyed ladies probably made up over half the *ton*!

His curiosity piqued, William was tempted to lean over and ask as to the identity of the poor girl, but thought better of it. To ask implied he had been eavesdropping. And there was probably some obscure rule of manners that covered just such an occasion.

The one wearing a butter yellow pelisse shook her head. "Well, I think she's rather pretty. And she's rather sweet. I spoke with her at Lord Weatherstone's ball, before all the gentlemen were lining up to sign her dance card. And her eyes aren't..." She stopped, apparently unable to say the word 'demonic'. "They're simply the color of cornflowers."

The feather woman angled her head to one side, causing the feather to dip dangerously close to another patron's cup of tea. "Something tells me Jane's husband must have been caught ogling the chit," she teased.

Jane's eyes had widened in alarm. "How dare you?" she said with a good deal of mock ire. "Brougham has been nothing but attentive to me since our wedding day," she claimed before softening her voice. "It's true he used to stare at the blondes, but I've been quite effective at changing his preference to brunettes," she said, her cheeky comment and exaggerated wink eliciting a round of giggles.

The waiter appeared with William's ice. "Thank you," William murmured as he moved his paper to the side and took a spoonful of the lemon ice to his lips. He closed his eyes as the cold confection reached his tongue. Although he could claim a liking for lemon biscuits, lemon meringue and lemonade, lemon ices were his favorite food.

Thankfully, the topic of discussion at the next table had moved on to someone's ball and a countess who was expecting a baby.

"She's as a big as a house," Jane claimed as one hand pantomimed a rather large, round protrusion at the level of the table. "Her words, not mine," she added when the other ladies all gasped as her description.

"It's her first, poor dear," the charitable one said.

"And probably her last," feather woman commented. "If she doesn't have a boy, why, whatever will happen to the earldom?" she asked in dismay.

"Torrington's cousin will inherit, of course," the one wearing yellow said with some authority. "If you believe Grandby, the cousin is apparently better suited to the task."

"And he already has an heir and several spares," Jane put in.

William straightened, realizing the women were speaking of the Earl of Torrington and of his cousin, Gregory Grandby. Thomas Wellingham's sister, Christiana, was married to Gregory, and she was the mother of all those heir apparents.

Taking another bite of his confection, William turned the page on his newspaper. His gaze settled on a column featuring news of aristocrats. Scanning the article, his eyes stopped when he caught the words, 'Lady L'.

"I suppose Torrington's heir is married to a commoner," one of the ladies said with a good deal of condescension.

Yellow lady shook her head. "Mrs. Grandby is actually a cousin to Trenton, so she's not entirely a commoner," she explained before touching the tip of her napkin to the corner of her mouth. "She's really rather a sweet thing," she added, "Despite the fact that she's mother to all those children. Goodness. You think she could have a lock installed on her bedchamber door."

There was an uncomfortable silence for a moment before the nicer woman said, "But she *wanted* all those children, as did her husband."

Feather lady angled her head to one side. "So, if Mrs. Grandby is a Wellingham—"

"She is," the yellow-garbed lady affirmed.

"—then she's related to this Lady Lily as well," she said as a sour expression crossed her face.

"Indeed. She's a cousin, in fact," the charitable one said with a nod.

Jane tittered, and a couple of the others joined in. "We cannot choose our relatives," she sniffed. "And with that, let's pay a visit to Lady Torrington, shall we?"

William's gaze rested on the words in the article referring to Lady L. *Good grief!* They were talking about Lady Lily. The woman he had decided he wanted to marry. She was the comely blonde who could double for Cupid's sister, the beautiful chit who had visited his dreams only the night before and had done so on many earlier occasions.

Those eyes!

The image of the cornflower blue eyes faded and was replaced by the text of the newspaper. He stared at the words before him.

Now we're not sure which suitor Lady L will choose to marry, but marry she will and probably by Christmastime. Lord T may insist on it. We admit to being a bit surprised at how many seem to be vying for her hand, but apparently a man in need of a dowry is willing to abide a former maid for a wife—even if she is illegitimate.

William swallowed, suddenly understanding the catty behavior at the neighboring table.

How could they be so cruel with their comments? Well, the charitable woman wasn't so bad, he realized, but the others seemed delighted over the poor girl's situation.

What had Lady Lily done to deserve such gossip? He was vaguely aware of the ladies standing up, of gloves being pulled onto dainty hands, of bonnets being adjusted and of reticules being opened and closed. A moment later, and the cruel women were gone from the tea shop.

William felt a pang of sadness grip his heart. His lemon ice, half melted, no longer seemed appealing. If Lily had been sitting across from him, it would have been long gone.

Lady Lily would never be accepted in the *ton*, no matter

who she married, he realized with a sigh. Although, as he gave it some more thought, it meant his suit might put him ahead of the aristocrats.

It might, but then it may not. He wondered how she was getting along in Staffordshire. Wondered what her brother was saying, what she was saying. She certainly had some stories to tell about those who were courting her, he knew. He could only hope one of those stories would put him in a good light.

Allowing a sigh, he fished some coins from his pocket, placed them next to his dish, and took his leave of Gunter's.

CHAPTER 13

A COUNTESS LEARNS IN THE LIBRARY

*H*aving toured Wellingham Manor after her arrival that afternoon, Lily knew exactly how to get to the library for her pre-dinner meeting with her sister-in-law.

"I merely wish to have a few moments alone with you so that we might speak freely," Sarah had said when she left Lily in her bedchamber earlier that afternoon.

Lily had readily agreed. She had questions and concerns, not the least of which was how she was going to tell her brother about the various suitors who had either already asked for her hand or who had indicated they intended to do so during the Little Season.

Sarah was already in the library, her son sound asleep in her arms. "There's no need to whisper. He sleeps through everything," Sarah said as Lily approached, a grin forming as she studied the toddler. With his blond curls and dimpled cheeks, Gabe looked like Cupid's little brother. The older version was apparently dressing for dinner upstairs somewhere.

"He's adorable," Lily said with a sigh.

"Thank you. With any luck, the next one will be just as handsome," she said, one hand smoothing over her middle as she arched an eyebrow.

Lily's eyes widened when she realized what the gesture meant. Another nephew, or perhaps a niece!

"Yours will no doubt look similar," Sarah replied, giving Lily a brilliant smile. The girl was dressed in a deep purple silk de Naples gown, the bodice edged in a tiny ruffle. Her white gloves fit as if they had been specially made for her arms. Which they probably were, Sarah realized, remembering how Gabriel insisted his sister be outfitted in the finest clothes.

Lily's eyebrows arched up in surprise. "Perhaps," she said as she took the chair adjacent to Sarah's. "Especially if I end up with Sir Tristan."

Sarah regarded the younger woman for a moment. "You don't seem happy with that prospect," she offered, wondering at Lily's mention of the young baron.

Lily gave a shrug. "He has his merits. And his faults, not the least of which is gambling to excess."

Her eyes widening with concern, Sarah shook her head. "Scratch him off the list. He'll use the dowry to pay off gambling debts and then run up some more. Probably end up in debtor's prison or worse."

It was Lily's turn to look surprised. "Oh, well that one's easy, at least."

"How many more are there?" Sarah asked as she moved Gabe to a Grecian lounge.

"Four," Lily answered.

"Four?" Sarah repeated as she returned to stand next to her chair. She shook out the skirts of her peach satin dinner gown, secretly glad her son hadn't wet his nappy whilst she held him on her lap. Free of ruffles and furbelows, the gown was elegant in its simplicity. Besides the ever present sapphire bracelet and her gold wedding band, hidden beneath her gloves, a pair of diamond ear bobs and a tiara encrusted with diamonds were the only jewelry in evidence.

"Five in all, actually," Lily said with some hesitation.

Sarah blinked. Then she blinked again and sat down. "Oh, dear. I knew you were popular..."

It was Lily's turn to blink. "Pardon?"

Shrugging, Sarah nodded. "I read *The Morning Chronicle* and a few of the gossip rags when I can get them from

Margery," she explained. "Sometimes your whole name is mentioned and sometimes it's merely 'Lady L'."

Lily rolled her eyes. "And the entire time, I was hoping one or two of those gentlemen might transfer their attentions to Samantha. It's such a shame she has to go to Europe in search of a husband." She heard Sarah's gasp and gave the countess a shrug. "She claims she would be happy as a spinster, and I rather think she would be, but I do wish she could be settled before I am. I feel rather guilty at attracting all the attention, especially when I know most of it is probably due to my dowry, rather than *me*," she explained.

Sarah allowed a sound that was almost a snort. "Do not sell yourself short, sister. I rather imagine at least one of those gentlemen wants you for *you* and not just the money," she replied. Lily seemed genuinely agreeable, and given her beauty and youth, she deserved the number of suitors she claimed to have.

As Sarah studied Lily's reaction, she realized her words were true. "And something tells me you know which one."

Giving Sarah a guilty glance, Lily nodded. "But I rather doubt my brother will allow me to marry a man who is not of the *ton*," she countered in a quiet voice.

Placing a hand on Lily's knee, Sarah leaned closer to her sister-in-law. "May I remind you he married *me*, and I haven't a drop of blue blood in me?" she whispered, one eyebrow arching up to emphasize her point.

Lily's eyes had widened in surprise. "Oh," she managed as she regarded the countess. "It's true then?" she replied, remembering when she had met Sarah at the Mayfield ball the year before. They hadn't had much time to get acquainted that evening. "I thought... I mean, when I heard talk after the Mayfield ball, I just sorted someone hadn't connected the right... dots, is all," she stammered. Of course there had been talk in the parlors of Mayfair as to whom the Earl of Trenton had selected as his countess. No one had heard of Sarah Cumberbatch, but many thought she was perhaps a baronet's sister or the daughter of a knight or the granddaughter of a viscount.

Sarah gave her a brilliant smile. "I'm sure there's some ancestor way back when, who was a brother or sister to some king or some such, but if there was, I don't know who it was or when it was."

"I'm rather glad you agreed to marry him," Lily said then, her eyes bright. "I cannot imagine him married to one of those insipid waifs I see at all the balls and soirées. Other than ensuring they're dressed in the latest fashions, they seem utterly helpless. None of them could manage a household let alone an earldom," she insisted.

Stunned by Lily's words, Samantha regarded her sister-in-law for a few moments. While Sarah had been spared from having to face a close examination by the *ton* simply due to having stayed in Bilston and Stretton, she knew Lily hadn't. By remaining in London, the poor girl was constantly under scrutiny by the gossips and a target for scandal should she so much as use the wrong fork at a dinner party. "Thank you," Sarah murmured with a nod. She glanced up at the mantel clock. "The dinner gong will sound at any moment. Is there anything else you want to ask before we join the earl?"

Lily shrugged. "How will I know which one to choose? I want to make the right decision," she whispered as she leaned toward Sarah.

Sarah took the younger girl's hands in hers. "Trust your heart, no matter how loudly your head might scream at you," she said.

Her eyes widening in shock, Lily finally nodded.

Gabriel relaxed against the wall outside the library, his eyes closing as he considered the snippets of conversation he had overheard between Lily and his wife.

From the sounds of it, he wondered if he had done Lily any favors by recognizing her as his sister. Perhaps it was unrealistic to expect she would be accepted by the *ton*. Unrealistic to expect she would have better luck than he'd had in London's Marriage Mart.

Guilt by association. *To me.*

She had suitors, though. And she had promised to tell him all about them. With any luck, he would know enough about each to determine their suitability without having to hire a man to investigate them.

As for Lily, at least she seemed to be taking it all in stride. She probably had Lady Samantha to thank for that, he considered. Although the chit still wasn't betrothed, she seemed to take everything in stride. Someone out there would recognize the trait as valuable in a wife, if not in England, then perhaps in Italy.

In the meantime, he wondered at Sarah's last recommendation.

Trust your heart.

He hoped that's what she had done. He certainly had, and he couldn't imagine his life without her in it.

At the sound of the dinner gong, he straightened and made his way into the library, greeting his wife and sister with kisses and waking his son with a peck on his forehead. He lifted the toddler from the couch and held him against his shoulder. "I've come to escort my lovely ladies and handsome son to dinner," he said as he crooked his free arm.

Lily exchanged a nervous glance with Sarah and joined her hosts as they took their leave of the library.

CHAPTER 14

DINNER NUMBER ONE

"How was your trip, sister?" Gabriel asked as a footman poured white wine. "Have you been this far north before?"

Lily thanked the footman who poured her wine before turning her attention to her brother. Despite having been instructed by Lady Samantha not to thank the servants— "It's their job to serve, so you needn't thank them every time they do something for you"—Lily found she couldn't break a habit her mother had instilled in her. "It was diverting," she answered, giving Sarah a quick glance. She knew there wasn't any reason to be nervous, but she hadn't spent any appreciable time in the company of Gabriel Wellingham, and she wasn't yet sure how to speak to him. "I've never been outside of London before," she added, just then remembering the rest of what he had asked her.

Gabriel took a drink from his wine glass. He noticed his wife's subtle hand wave, at first wondering if it was intended for him before he realized it was directed at the head footman. As a result of that gesture, the first course appeared, as three footmen delivered the oyster soup so the bowls were set down in front of the diners at precisely the same time. "I hadn't considered this might be your first trip in a coach," Gabriel replied, his manner suggesting he may have made a mistake in sending his equipage.

But the thought of Lily riding in a mail coach didn't seem right, either. "I do hope you found it... comfortable."

Lily nodded. "Oh, it was, Gabriel. I spent most of the trip staring out the windows." Napping, really, but she wasn't about to tell him that. "The scenery was beautiful." The scenery on the back of her eyelids, actually, for sleep had allowed her time to imagine a life with each and every one of the men who had put voice to their intentions to ask for her hand. The four aristocrats and the clerk.

That time in the coach had also given her time to consider what she might say to her brother when he asked her the very questions she was sure he was about to ask. *This will be interesting*, she thought.

"The landscapes can be quite diverting," Gabriel agreed. "As can a Season in London." He ignored his wife's silent sigh and roll of her eyes, thinking his segue rather ingenious. "It was your second, wasn't it?" he asked before taking a spoonful of his soup.

Oh, he is clever, Lily considered, dabbing the corner of her mouth with her napkin. The soup was excellent—probably the best she had ever tasted. "Yes, and it was so much more enjoyable than the first. I was far too nervous that first year," she said, her comment aimed first to her brother and then to Sarah at the other end of the table. By the end of the night, she was sure she would have done the equivalent of watching a lawn tennis match if she continued to direct her comments to both ends of the table.

"As was I," Sarah chimed in, her simple nod to a footman near the door a cue to serve the next course. "But seeing as how you spent most of your time at balls surrounded by adoring young men, I can hardly believe you found time to be nervous."

Lily's eyes widened, surprised Sarah would say such a thing. Then she recognized Sarah's tactic for what it was and said, "True. I was rather flattered by all the attention, even if all the newest debutantes were beneficiaries. Thank goodness I didn't have to consider any proposals of marriage," she said before finishing her soup.

The comment had Gabriel frowning. "You didn't have any offers of marriage last year?" he asked in dismay.

Lily shook her head. "Marriage was not discussed until this past Season," she clarified, relieved when a footman set a plate of fish in front of her. She couldn't help but notice Sarah's plate held a different course, however, and she was about to ask if a mistake had been made when she remembered Sarah's motion indicating another Trenton baby was on the way.

"And how many young bucks discussed matrimony with you?" Gabriel asked, relieved his sister was giving him all the verbal cues he needed. After his discussion with Sarah, he had been worried about how he would coax the information from his sister.

"Five," Lily replied, her attention on her fish, especially as it related to the tiny bones that might be found therein.

Gabriel's eyes widened. "*Five?*" he repeated. "You have *five* suitors?" he asked, apparently in dismay.

Sarah gave her husband a quelling glance, and Gabriel struggled to calm himself.

Lily wondered if he thought five were too many or too few. "Well, one of them isn't of the *ton*," she offered.

Blinking, Gabriel leaned forward. "But four are?" he clarified, still rather stunned his younger sister had managed to gain offers of marriage from so many. But as Sarah had warned him, some of those were no doubt in search of dowries to pay off gambling debts or otherwise shore up depleted bank accounts.

"Yes," Lily replied with a nod, still not quite sure if the number was good or bad.

Gabriel sat back and regarded his sister with new-found respect. "Well, then I suppose you need to apprise me of each one," he said, his arms crossing over his chest.

Lily blinked. *Goodness!* If she told her brother about all five suitors tonight, they might not be able to leave the dinner table until breakfast was served! "Perhaps if I just start with the first one this evening," she suggested, realizing the stories she had to go with each suitor were timed to last the length of a typical dinner. "And then tell you about the others in subsequent conversations."

Angling his head to one side, Gabriel was curious as to what—and how much—Lily planned to tell him about the men who had indicated an interest in matrimony. "Surely there can't be that much to tell," he countered, thinking a few words about each man would give him enough information to decide if they were suitable matches for his sister.

Lily gave a slight shrug. "Oh, there's much to tell, brother," she replied. *Too much.* "Let me start with a baron."

Gabriel wondered at her comment, but gave a nod of permission. "Then let us hear about your baron."

CHAPTER 15

A SOIRÉE WITH SIR TRISTAN

Sir Tristan Nisbet, a baron, regarded his reflection in the cheval mirror and cocked an eyebrow. "You don't think this looks a bit... pretentious?" he asked. His valet, Peters, had wrapped a new cravat about the baron's neck and was working the ends into a mail coach knot.

"Pretentious?" the Irishman replied, his own eyebrow arching in question. He stepped back and gave his master a shake of his head. "I should think it looks appropriate for a ball," he responded, rather pleased he had managed to dress Sir Tristan in evening clothes at all. Tristan rarely attended *ton* events, opting instead to play faro or attend the horse races.

"I'll trust you, then," Tristan replied, his nervousness increasing. Had anyone told him going to a soirée at Lord Morganfield's Mayfair residence, Carlington House, would be this... *frightening*, Tristan might have declined the invitation.

He couldn't though. Not any longer.

In fact, he would need to accept each and every invitation from here on out until he found a wife. His bank account was in desperate need of funds.

Although he didn't gamble to excess—he was, in fact, rather careful with his bets at faro—he had agreed to his mother's request for a larger townhouse near Berkeley Square. Had his solicitor explained it would take nearly all of his funds to pay for said townhouse, Tristan was quite sure he would have spoken with his mother, explained the limited funds available for such an indulgence, and managed to talk her out of the whim.

She had probably been in another dowager's London townhouse and been envious of the abode, prompting her to make what she thought was a reasonable request of her only son. And Tristan, in his haste to rid himself of her company on a night he planned to spend at Miss Penelope's faro table at The Jack of Spades, had agreed to buy her the townhouse. He chided himself that he would allow thoughts of Penelope to drive him to such distraction.

What was he thinking?

It wasn't as if the proprietor, Frank O'Laughlin, would allow him a formal introduction to Penelope. The chit was one of Frank's dealers, after all. A girl he had informally adopted and trained to be a dealer who no doubt brought in more clients than all the other male dealers combined. She was certainly a draw for Tristan. And no matter what feelings he might have developed toward her outside of how successful he was when he played at her table, he knew deep down he couldn't consider her as a potential wife. For one thing, she was a commoner. For another, she was a faro dealer! Even if she had saved up every pence she ever earned in tips, he rather doubted her dowry would improve his financial situation. And he also doubted Frank would ever approve of the match. The man knew she was responsible for his continued success as a gaming hell owner. Frank wasn't about to allow his golden goose to leave the farmyard.

That left Tristan with the need to find another chit to marry. He could hope for an amiable young thing who lacked brains but made up for it with beauty and a good fortune, but he was quite sure chits meeting that criteria had already been snatched up by would-be earls and viscounts.

That left less desirable chits, although he hardly knew who they might be. It wasn't as if there was a list he could consult— at least, he didn't think there was such a list.

Perhaps someone kept a list of all the eligibles at White's.

In the meantime, his solicitor assured him there would be some monies available once the old townhouse was sold. Until then, Tristan limited his expenditures and read every invitation Peters brought to him.

"Have the coach brought 'round," Tristan said as he straightened his cuffs. "I need to leave before I change my mind."

Peters nodded. "Very good, my lord."

I could have walked, Tristan thought as he stepped into the dark interior of his town coach. Nearly as old as he was, the coach featured dark leather squabs and walls lined with scarlet velvet. His mother had referred to it as his father's second bedchamber, claiming the man had hosted all manner of light-skirts therein. Tristan wondered how that would have been possible in the cramped confines, trying but failing to imagine how two people could engage in intercourse without bumping their heads, bumping their bottoms, bruising their knees and squishing important body parts.

Except... he shook his head, almost succeeding in putting aside the sudden image of his favorite Cyprian in a pose she couldn't possibly manage.

Neither could he.

Once the old baron had died, Tristan saw to it the coach was thoroughly cleaned and the fabrics replaced. No need to feel as if he were riding in a brothel when he ventured somewhere.

The coach had travelled only a few streets when it came to a sudden stop, nearly tossing him from the squabs. His driver, Hemsworth, called out something and a feminine voice—a not so polite feminine voice—replied. Tristan wasn't quite sure what the chit said, but he was quite sure he would have colored up had he heard the words spoken in a parlor.

After a few more seconds, the coach jerked forward. Tristan dared a glance out the window, surprised to see a well-dressed woman hurrying onto the opposite walkway. She stopped, turned around, and stared directly at him! Her stare was most fierce, as if she were determining how he would come to his end on the planet.

Tristan froze, his gaze taking in the sight of a rather pretty young woman. Although she sported a small hat mounted at a jaunty angle, he could tell her hair was blonde and dressed into a mass of curls that surrounded the short brim of the hat. Her carriage gown might have been green, although given the effect of twilight, he couldn't be sure. She had to be a lady, though, so she couldn't possibly be the chit who had turned his driver's ears blue with her curses.

Could she?

Only a few moments later, Hemsworth pulled the coach into the half-circle drive in front of the Morganfield residence.

The Palladian house, with its white exterior and dark green front doors, appeared recently painted. The shrubs along the drive had been trimmed, and the pots on either side of the entry bloomed with summer flowers. "If I'm not out in ten minutes, come back in two hours," Tristan said to the driver, thinking he would make his escape if the gathering were deadly dull. Two hours would give him an opportunity to play cards should the amusement be offered as part of the soirée.

"Very good, my lord," Hemsworth replied as he shut the coach door and made his way back up to the box. Once he had the coach moved to the end of the drive, another took its place. Tristan considered waiting so that he might accompany whoever had just arrived, but in the event it wasn't someone he knew, he turned to make his way to the front door.

"Pardon me," a voice called out.

Tristan paused and glanced around, wondering if the woman who spoke was in the carriage behind him. Two men were stepping down, though, and no women followed them to the pavers. He was about to resume his trek to the front doors when he became aware of quick steps—*tap-clunk-tap tap-clunk-tap*—coming up from behind him.

"I say, could you please hold up?"

Turning to his left, Tristan stopped to regard the young woman who was suddenly right next to him. "Oh, I apologize. I didn't see you there," he said, giving the young lady a bow.

The very lady he had seen after the kerfuffle earlier!

"Neither did your driver," she replied with a huff.

About to reach for her hand, Tristan paused and considered how to respond. "I beg your pardon?" he managed, not sure what else to say.

The blonde angled her head to one side, the hat following suit. "Your driver nearly ran me over," she claimed. "Now I can barely walk."

With those words, Tristan was quite sure he heard a hint of Cockney in her voice, but her manner of dress, indeed, everything about her suggested she was a lady of quality. "Are you injured, my lady?" he asked with enough concern to seem sincere.

Suddenly bathed in light from the open front doors—the two gentlemen who had arrived after him were just going in—he could see the chit's eyes under delicate brows. Combined with the curly blonde hair and pale complexion, she looked like Cupid's sister. Or mother, perhaps, since her cheeks were no longer round. Her lips were certainly kissable. She had perfect bows, looking all delicious given their fresh berry coloring. Tristan was tempted to lean over and help himself to a taste.

Large blue eyes, once angry but now suddenly not, blinked and then lowered to her foot. "I am uninjured, my lord, but, unfortunately," she exposed her slippered foot from beneath her skirts, "my shoe has lost its heel," she said with a hint of disgust.

Tristan's attention turned to the chit's foot. Her ankle, actually, as it was on display as much as the broken dance slipper. A rather well-turned ankle, Tristan thought as he was forced to swallow before returning his attention to her face. "Sir Tristan Nisbet, at your service," he said as he offered her his arm. He wasn't about to offer recompense for the broken heel. He rather doubted his driver had anything to do with her having broken it, although perhaps she had been trying to retrieve it when Hemsworth nearly ran her over.

The young woman's blue eyes widened, as if she were seeing him for the first time. "Lady Lily," she replied with a curtsy, apparently unsure if she should add her new last name.

Before her brother had paid her a visit the year before, Lily had never used the Wellingham name as her last name, opting instead for her mother's last name. She was merely a lady's maid back then, after all. She was an illegitimate daughter of an earl and a house maid.

Lily took the proffered arm and allowed the baron to escort her to the front door, limping a bit given her heel was either loose or missing.

"May I ask why you were on foot this evening, and not in a carriage or coach?" Sir Tristan asked before they reached the front door. He decided not to ask about her rather vocal tirade, although he found himself rather amused she knew so many curse words. He wondered where she had learned them. "Have you no escort?"

*L*ily allowed the footman to take her dark green mantle, its removal revealing her white tulle and satin gown over a rather pleasing figure. Surrendering the hat revealed more blonde curls woven with baby's breath.

She turned to the baron, whose cape coat was removed by a footman to reveal black evening clothes and a bright red waistcoat embroidered with gold threads. Under the lights of the vestibule, the baron appeared rather regal, his blonde hair cut and combed in the Titus style, and his angular face and aquiline nose betraying his aristocratic lineage.

His dark blue eyes were piercing in a manner that was more friendly than fierce, and his lips were... Lily had to take a breath just then, thinking it would be rather interesting to kiss those lips. Not that she had any experience in kissing, but those lips would certainly be a good place to start.

"I just came from Fitzsimmons Manor," she replied with a shrug, hoping the man hadn't noticed her perusal of his features. "I hardly think it necessary to inconvenience a footman when I only had to cross the street and walk in front of a few houses."

Usually she would have been in the company of Lady Samantha Fitzsimmons, the niece of Matthew, Viscount Fitzsimmons, and his viscountess, Caroline. But Samantha and

Caroline had just departed for Rome and wouldn't be back in London until the Little Season started.

Tristan appearance took on that of guilt. He probably had come about the same distance, and yet he had done so in a coach-and-four requiring a driver and who-knew-how-many groomsmen to prepare the equipage and horses.

But then, that was their job.

What would they have done instead on this pleasant, warm evening had he not provided them with an errand?

"A link boy should have been employed," he countered. "Without a moon, it's rather dark out there," he argued, once again offering her his arm.

Lily angled her head in agreement. "I suppose," she replied, allowing the baron to lead her into the large parlor. Most of the furnishings had been pushed to the sides of the room so that the middle was open. The Aubusson carpet, apparently recently replaced, was welcome beneath her slippered feet, especially the foot that was missing its heel. Although she tried hard not to limp, she knew it appeared as if she had turned her ankle.

"How is it I haven't seen you at one of these events before?" she asked as she glanced around the parlor, hoping to see a familiar face. A friendly, familiar face. She had already experienced the stares of women who found her lineage abhorrent and didn't care to see them here tonight.

Tristan sighed, his hopes that she hadn't attended many of these events dashed. "I only recently inherited the barony," he replied, "And I admit to a certain fondness for pursuits not nearly as worthy as *soirées*."

The blue eyes widened as a smile appeared on Lady Lily's porcelain face. "You're a gambler, aren't you?" she accused, her tone of voice suggesting she was rather amused by his admission.

Not surprised the young woman had guessed his vice, Tristan nodded and said, "Faro, although not to excess and only for as long as my funds for the night will allow." He watched her face as he made the statement, wondering if she were bright enough to catch his meaning.

"Allow?" Lily replied, an eyebrow arching up in question.

Tristan found himself rather intrigued by the young woman. She was unlike any aristocrat's daughter he had ever met, although he had to admit to not having met many of them. "I set a limit for myself when I gamble," he explained, giving a nod to a passing acquaintance. "Even if I win, I promise myself I will stop when I have reached that limit. And I do."

Lily inhaled slowly, apparently surprised to hear a man—an aristocrat, even—admit to gambling and then give such a logical response to her question. "And when you win?" she pressed, hoping he would divulge what he experienced on a good night.

"Ecstasy, my lady," he said, his eyelids lowering as if he were imagining that very event.

Lily inhaled sharply, the sound loud enough for the baron to overhear. A frisson passed through her at the thought of the baron in ecstasy, at what it would be like to be right next to the man as he experienced a win at the gaming tables. She felt joy and excitement and a thrill unlike anything she had ever imagined. "I should like to be there when you win," she whispered, not meaning for her words to be overheard by the baron.

Tristan swallowed. Hard. The look on Lady Lily's face had been so sensuous, as if she had experienced the sort of ecstasy his last mistress claimed to have felt when he had pleasured her.

He missed the sight of Dahlia beneath him, writhing and moaning with his every thrust. With every lick of his tongue across her ruched nipples. His every kiss on her belly and between her thighs. God, he missed Dahlia. But mistresses cost money, and he could no longer afford the luxury.

Too bad the Cyprian was warming his best friend's bed now.

Damn her. And damn his best friend.

"I rather think it unlikely you would be allowed in The Jack of Spades," he finally replied. Although many women gambled at the gaming hell he preferred for faro, they were mostly widows or older spinsters who no longer cared about the opinions of the *ton*. Nor did they care for the opinion of their relatives.

Lily nodded. "I suppose you are right," she agreed with a

hint of sadness. A footman appeared with a tray of champagne. Before Lily could help herself to one of the flutes, Tristan took two and offered her one.

"I do hope you're allowed," he said just as she took the flute from him.

A brilliant smile had appeared on her face, one Tristan found himself wishing he could see every day. And every night.

"I am," Lily replied with a nod. "And more than one."

CHAPTER 16

A BARON'S TALE,
INTERRUPTED

Gabriel stared at his sister, his eyes wide with shock. "How is it you know such *intimate* details of Sir Tristan?" he asked in dismay, his stemmed wine glass nearly tipping over after he slammed it onto the table.

Lily nearly jumped out of her skin, rather surprised her brother would react with such violence over her tale of meeting Lord Tristan Nisbet. "I asked him, after he had several drinks, of course. It's amazing what you can find out from a man who is deep in his cups," she replied with a shrug.

Despite her husband's anger, Sarah found Lily's tale amusing. She knew from the girl's first words she had probably made up some if not all of the story, for if she had presented Sir Tristan in a more fair light, Gabriel would find him agreeable. This way, he would question everything about Sir Tristan until he would decide he wasn't a suitable match for his sister.

"No doubt," Gabriel said with a roll of his eyes. "I do hope you didn't spend the entire soirée in his company."

Lily finished her wine and gave a shake of her head. "No, of course not. I made the company of several people that evening, including the host and hostess," she said.

Gabriel visibly slumped in his carver. Although he had been in Lord Morganfield's presence several times since that fateful day he had nearly asked for Elizabeth Carlington's hand in marriage, he felt ever the fool for having thought he could get away with using the chit to embarrass the marquess. And now that he had another year of Parliament behind him and another year of learning the politics of his fellow aristocrats, Gabriel found himself siding with Morganfield more often than not on matters of state.

Who could have ever guessed such a strange turn of events?

"What did you think of Lord and Lady Morganfield?" Sarah asked, giving a nod to the butler. Several footmen had appeared to take away plates and pour more wine.

Lily regarded her glass of wine for a moment. "They were very obliging, I thought. When I was alone with the marchioness, she claimed she was pleasantly surprised I accepted the invitation."

Adele Carlington was Italian by birth but had been in England for nearly thirty years, her relocation due to David Carlington having discovered the beauty whilst on his Grand Tour. The two were married before he even returned from his trip.

"And why was that, do you suppose?" Gabriel asked, an eyebrow arching with concern. He knew his sister would suffer from the reputation he gained during his first year in the *ton*, but he could always hope it wouldn't be held against her. She had enough to overcome being a bastard daughter of an earl.

Allowing a sigh, Lily said, "I think she felt sorry for me. Lady Samantha and Lady Chamberlain were on their way to Italy, and I had no companions with whom to spend the evening."

Gabriel relaxed a bit. "So, she didn't pity you for being my sister," he clarified.

It was Lily's turn to appear shocked. "No, not at all, Gabriel. I have only ever thought she approved of you." She paused a moment, remembering the marchioness' comment about Gabriel's kissing. "Except for when she heard you kissed like Harold MacDuff. Then she apparently fainted and had to be carried to her bedchamber. Although, I distinctly remember thinking when she told the tale that she wasn't truly unconscious but merely acting as such so that she might have the company of the marquess..." Lily stopped speaking suddenly, her face taking on the unmistakable reddish cast of embarrassment. "I do apologize. Lady Morganfield is Italian, you see," she said before downing the rest of her wine. "She is a bit forthcoming with her comments."

Sarah lifted her napkin to her mouth, attempting to hide her sudden smile as Gabriel slumped further into his chair. "I fear I will forever be compared to a dog," he said with a roll of his eyes.

"Only your kissing, my darling. Not you," Sarah said. "And we both know your kisses are no longer like those of Harold McDuff." She ended the comment with an arched eyebrow, her expression suggesting she meant far more than her words implied.

Gabriel suddenly straightened in his carver, one of his eyebrows matching his wife's.

Despite his large purse and handsomeness, there wasn't a single woman in London who would have agreed to marry him for his ability to kiss. His reputation as a poor kisser was renowned. "It's always heartening to hear you say it, though," he countered, a bit embarrassed his sister knew some of his humiliation from his first year in London. He turned his attention back to Lily. "Sister, I do believe you were telling us about Sir Tristan. I take it you have more of the sordid tale to tell?" he hinted.

Lily exchanged glances with Sarah. "I do," she replied. "But I fear you won't find this part of the story nearly as amusing as I did."

Tristan downed his fourth glass of champagne, wishing there was something else offered by way of refreshment, and not the ratafia in the punch bowl. Although he had lost the company of Lady Lily to the hostess only a few minutes after arriving at Carlington House, Tristan found himself smiling when she once again appeared before him.

"Paid your respects to the hostess, I see," he managed to get out, a bit surprised at how the words sounded muddled in his ears.

Perhaps he had drunk more than four glasses of champagne.

"I did," Lily acknowledged. "A rather gracious woman, given her station," she said as she leaned in. "I'm rather surprised you're not in the card room. Do the games not interest you this evening?"

At the news there was a card room, Tristan thought to simply take his leave of Lily and move to the card room. A game of whist was certainly preferable to standing about and guzzling who-knew-how-many glasses of French champagne. Probably illegally imported French champagne, but then their host was a marquess and probably had access to every form of illegal liquor through somewhat legal means.

On the subject of cards, however, Tristan had promised himself he would pursue possible wives at this *soirée*. "I can play cards any evening, my lady," he answered smoothly. "However, I cannot be in the company of a lovely lady every evening."

Lily regarded the baron with raised brows. "And who might that be, my lord?" she asked, hoping to learn a bit of gossip she could use when next she visited Lady Torrington's parlor at tea time. She always felt a little left out at never having any news to share with the ladies in attendance.

Tristan blinked. Then he blinked again. *Am I so foxed that I've misunderstood her question?* What lovely lady could she think he was in the company of if not her? "Why, the woman standing in front of me, of course," he answered with a shrug of one shoulder.

And bullocks, if Lady Lily didn't turn around to look behind her! When she returned her attention to him, her eyes were wide. "Why, Sir Tristan, are you *flirting?*" she asked in a whisper suggesting she was rather delighted by the thought.

One of Tristan's blonde eyebrows arched up so high, it nearly reached his hairline.

Am I flirting with her?

Well, he hadn't intended to flirt with her when he made his

comment, but the champagne had obviously loosened his tongue.

Did he want to flirt with her? She had practically accused him of running her over with his coach, even though he wasn't driving it at the time!

Come to think of it, he never actually drove the coach, leaving the spirited matched foursome of Cleveland Bays to the expertise of his driver.

Now, his phaeton—that was a fine example of equipage he could drive. His grey practically pranced with joy when pulling the bright red conveyance. He wondered if perhaps a yellow one might look more sporty behind Samson, but decided he didn't wish to own the same color phaeton as the one the Earl of Trenton had been seen driving in Hyde Park during the fashionable hour. *When had that been? Was it this past Season? Last Season?*

No, it was two Seasons ago, by Jove! he realized, thinking time certainly flew by. And the thought of Gabriel Wellingham had him thinking the chit who stood before him looked an awful lot like the earl. She looked like she could be the cherubic girl in a Gainesborough painting, all pink and lace and dimples and blonde curls. Of course, in the painting, she wouldn't look like she did just now, her expression screwed up in a look of confusion that made him think she was regarding him with a bit of puzzlement.

A good deal of puzzlement.

Tristan blinked, realizing the full-grown cherub was waiting for a response.

What was the question?

"I beg pardon, my lady. I..."

*L*ily blinked and lowered her eyes. Of course the man wasn't flirting with her. A moment ago, she found herself rather incensed with the peacock, and now she found herself disappointed that his query hadn't been a form of flirting. "Please, excuse me. I seem to have left my manners with my shoe heel in the middle of Park Lane," she said in a voice only he could hear.

Tristan shook his head. So, it was back to that. Her broken shoe. "If my lady will allow, I would be more than happy to replace the shoe," he offered, secretly hoping it wasn't some ridiculously expensive footwear she had obtained in some faraway locale. Like St. Petersburg or Bombay or, *good God*, Boston!

Lily's eyes widened at the suggestion he would replace the poorly made footwear. Goodness, the slipper was merely one of a pair she had found on a cobbler's shelf in Oxford Street, easily repaired or replaced.

Had he misunderstood her earlier rant? Her anger hadn't been due to the loss of the shoe so much as to the way in which his driver had nearly run her over as she crossed Park Lane. "My lord, I assure you, there's no need to trouble yourself with the replacement of my poorly made shoe," she finally replied, thinking the baron was about to fall onto the floor. His body seemed to be listing a bit too far to the left, as if a strong wind was blowing him over. She glanced about, wondering if someone had opened a window. The room could certainly use some fresh air.

Tristan knew he was about to fall over and took measures to right himself. At least, to the level he thought he would be vertical. When Lady Lily's hand reached out and gripped his arm, though, he realized he had over-corrected and was about to fall over to his left. "My lady, I..." And before he could complete his sentence, Tristan fell forward, his eyes rolling up into his head as his body fell entirely onto Lily.

Having foreseen the inevitable, Lily had braced herself for Sir Tristan's fall. However, she had misjudged just how tall the baron was, for his sudden weight against the front of her body had her stepping back on the foot with the good heel while her hands attempted to take purchase on some part of the aristocrat's body that wouldn't seem inappropriate.

The foot with the missing heel slipped, though, and she

knew she wouldn't be able to stop the baron from ending up with his face in the middle of her bosom.

Although her gown wasn't cut too low in the bodice, she wore no fichu or other garment to cover the exposed flesh above her pert breasts. She wore nothing to cover the very place where Sir Tristan's face was suddenly and very firmly planted.

She glanced about, allowing a look of alarm to appear on her own face. "A bit of help, please," she called out, hoping beyond hope Lady Jersey or one of the other dragon ladies of Almack's wasn't in attendance. She rather liked the waltz and looked forward to the day she could obtain a voucher allowing her to do so.

"*G*ood God!" a masculine voice cried out.

CHAPTER 17

A LADY EXPLAINS HERSELF

*P*ulled out of her tale by the exclamation, Lily found her brother staring at her with what could only be described as an expression of horror. She thought for a moment that the man had seen a ghost behind her. Lord Norwick, perhaps. She had heard tales in Lady Torrington's parlor about the late earl's ghost haunting his twin brother and his widow, Clarinda.

Lily turned around and dared a glance behind her, much like she had done when Tristan had made the comment about being in the company of a lovely woman.

When she didn't see any evidence of a ghost—not that she would have known what such an apparition would look like since she had no experience with the paranormal—she turned around to find her brother staring at her.

"Did anyone *see* him with his face on your chest?" Gabriel asked in alarm.

Lily blinked, not quite sure how much she should admit just then. "Well, yes," she replied, her head nodding. "Yes, but only those in the same room at the time."

Sarah had to suppress a giggle as one hand moved to cover her mouth. But her husband's look of alarm merely intensified.

"Who? How many had seen?" Gabriel asked, leaning so far

over his plate, his waistcoat was in danger of landing on his beef Wellington.

Lily sighed. "Twelve, I think. I do not know all their names, although I assure you Lady Morganfield was quite helpful in having her husband remove Sir Tristan from atop me."

Gabriel's eyes widened. "He was *atop* you?"

Blinking again before stealing a glance in Sarah's direction, Lily shrugged meekly. "Sir Tristan was quite heavy. I couldn't continue to stand there with his entire body leaning on me, so I sort of crumpled a bit," she explained. She sighed again. "Lord Morganfield is very strong, though, and managed to get the baron up and off of me whilst Lady Morganfield helped me to my feet. Or foot, rather. The slipper missing the heel seems to have disappeared in the fray and..."

Sarah could no longer help herself and burst into a fit of giggles, much to the dismay of her husband, who could only continue to stare at his sister with a look suggesting he was still seeing the ghost.

"Adele Carlington is such a doll. She assumed my shoe had broken when Sir Tristan fell on me, and she offered to find me a pair of slippers from her daughter's collection. Apparently Lady Elizabeth... or rather, Lady Bostwick, since she's married to Viscount Bostwick now, has a rather large collection of dance slippers—"

"No doubt," Gabriel murmured, his eyes rolling about. To think, he might have been married to Elizabeth Carlington had the young lady not been averse to his multiple mistresses and his fashionable mode of dress. A mode of dress that was probably more appropriate for a molly.

Thank the gods he had remembered Sarah and knew to marry her instead of some insipid aristocrat's daughter! Although, to be fair to Lady Bostwick, the viscountess did have one of the most celebrated charities in London and had bestowed her husband with an heir almost exactly nine months to the day after their wedding. Even if she had been the one to describe Gabriel's kiss as like that of her best friend's dog, Harold MacDuff, Elizabeth Carlington Bostwick had a much better life as a viscountess than she would have had as his wife—countess or not.

"So I was able to continue enjoying the evening's entertainments in a rather comfortable pair of dance slippers," Lily continued, apparently unaware her brother had been temporarily lost to his remembrances of his last days as a bachelor.

"It was rather generous of Lady Morganfield to loan you the shoes," Sarah remarked, giving the butler another nod. Given her husband's reaction to Lily's tale, she doubted Gabriel would be of a mind to finish the main course. At least one of his dogs would enjoy what he could not.

"I thought so, too," Lily agreed with a nod, taking a bite of her beef and giving a moan of appreciation. "Your cook is excellent."

Sarah smiled. "She is, and rather agreeable, too. Not the least bit surly, as I've heard some can be," she claimed. Her curiosity got the best of her, though, and she was forced to ask, "What happened once you were wearing the shoes?"

Lily finished chewing and swallowed. "Oh. Well, I conversed with several people and danced with Lord Morganfield and Lord Torrington," she replied, remembering how nervous she felt until Milton Grandby, Earl of Torrington, asked if she had a godfather.

"I've really no idea if I do," she had replied to his query. "May I be so bold as to ask why you wondered?"

The earl had given her an arched eyebrow coupled with an expression that hinted at mischief. "I have one-and-twenty goddaughters," he claimed happily. "But I'm more than willing to take on another before I'm father to my own."

Lily had been so stunned by the comment, that she knew not how to reply at the time other than to say she would be honored. "Which, that reminds me. Lord Torrington—"

"*Grandby*," Gabriel interrupted. "He prefers to be called *Grandby*," he added when he noticed Lily staring at him.

"Oh. Grandby," she repeated, realizing she had heard the man's name in multiple conversations and had not realized his identity. At least, not until two nights later when she had dinner with the Grandbys and Wellinghams at Woodscastle.

She was about to ask why he would go by a moniker other than his titled name when Gabriel shook his head. "Don't try to understand, for it makes no sense. It goes back to his early days as an earl. His uncle called him Grandby by mistake at Boodle's, and he declared that he preferred it to Torrington. Only those who don't know him dare call him Torrington."

Lily blinked, wondering if she might have called him 'Lord Torrington' whilst they danced.

"What about him?" Gabriel pressed, suddenly interested in his main course. He lifted a bite of beef to his lips and was about to eat it when Lily shrugged.

"He would like to claim me as his goddaughter," she announced happily.

Gabriel dropped his fork to his plate, apparently stunned by the news. "Claim you as his goddaughter? Why, the man must already have a dozen or—"

"One-and-twenty," Lily said with a nod. "He would like another before his own daughter is born."

Gabriel blinked. Then he blinked again. "And he wants her to be *you?*" he whispered, wondering what the earl had in mind for his sister.

"Yes," Lily replied a bit defensively, tucking into her meat.

Sarah regarded her husband for a moment before leaning in his direction. "He has done well by his goddaughters," she whispered hoarsely. "He sees to suitable marital arrangements when necessary."

His eyes widening, Gabriel shook his head. "Does he think I cannot arrange a suitable marriage for my own sister?" he asked his wife in dismay.

Lily dropped her fork. "Of course not!" she said with some haste, realizing her brother had taken offense by the other earl's offer. "I do believe it's a sort of challenge for the man."

"Challenge?" Sarah repeated.

Taking a sudden breath, Lily sighed loudly. "Not a challenge so much as an *obligation*. To see how he can arrange the chess pieces of the *ton* on a board." At Gabriel's furrowed brows, she continued with some excitement. She and Samantha had put voice to just such a theory only the night before Samantha had left for Italy. "The goddaughters who have married are matched up with an interesting array of gentlemen. Very few of them were the expected matches, you see," she explained.

Sarah exchanged a glance with Gabriel, wondering where this was going. "For example?" she prompted.

Taking a deep breath and letting it out, Lily said, "Lady Clarinda Brotherton and Lord David Norwick."

"To whom she was betrothed," Gabriel said with a nod.

"But now she's married to his twin brother," Sarah interjected. "But apparently the man looks so much like his late brother, half the *ton* doesn't know or remember that the older twin died."

Lily nodded, familiar with the story from having heard it in Lady Torrington's parlor. She briefly wondered if the countess preferred being called Mrs. Grandby. If she did, she hadn't said anything to Lily.

She gave her head a shake as if to clear it, she continued her list. "Lady Charlotte Bingham and the Duke of Chichester."

"To whom she was betrothed," Gabriel spoke quickly.

Sarah straightened. "That's not quite true," she countered. "She was betrothed to his brother, who died in that awful fire."

Gabriel buried a tooth in his lower lip. "True," he agreed. He glanced over to his sister, who gave him a nod.

"Lady Hannah Slater and the Earl of Gisborn." Before either Sarah or Gabriel could interrupt, she added, "Apparently, he was betrothed to Lady Charlotte after his first betrothal ended when Lady Jennifer died in that awful fire."

The two nodded in agreement, but before either could say anything, Lily continued listing couples. "Olivia Waterford and Michael Cunningham. Lady Julia and Alistair Comber. Lady Evangeline and Lord Sommers. They're all married because Grandby did something to ensure it."

"But that doesn't mean he should be *your* godfather," Gabriel said.

"But I told him he could be my godfather," Lily murmured, avoiding eye contact with her brother. "I didn't see the harm, seeing as how I don't have one and he is—"

"You might have consulted me first," Gabriel countered, appearing rather hurt. "You should have consulted me. And how do you know you don't have one?"

Lily blinked. Her mother had never spoken of godparents, never mentioned who might take on the responsibility of raising Lily should she die. "I am quite sure I don't have another godparent," Lily replied. "Do you know otherwise?"

Gabriel seemed as if he were about to reply when the air seemed to rush out of him. "No," he admitted finally. Truth be told, he knew very little about Lily's circumstances before his secretary informed him of her existence—and her whereabouts. Even then, he only knew what his mother was willing to admit when it came to just why Lily was working in service at Fitzsimmons Manor. Not heartless enough to have the maid who was pregnant with her husband's child fired from her position at the Trenton townhouse in London, Charity Fitzsimmons Wellingham instead arranged for the woman to work in her brother's household. A gentleman first and foremost, Matthew Fitzsimmons, Viscount Chamberlain, was happy to take on the maid. He was about to marry and required the extra staff. As a result, Lily grew up at Fitzsimmons Manor, first working as a scullery maid and then later, when she was old enough, as Lady Samantha's maid.

Remembering the Earl of Torrington's comment about Gabriel, Lily was careful with her next words. "Anyway, seeing as how Lord Torrington is already your godfather, it seemed only fair that he also be mine."

Sarah inhaled sharply, holding her utensils in mid-air as she gazed at her husband. "Is Milton Grandby really your godfather?" she asked him, a grin lighting her face.

Adjusting himself in his carver, Gabriel gave a slight shrug as his face reddened. "He is," he finally admitted. "Seems Chichester beat me by about six months for the honor of being his first godson," he added, referring to Joshua Wainwright, the Duke of Chichester. "I was his second."

Lily regarded her brother for a moment. "Then, when father died, did Lord Torrington adopt you?" she asked, not sure how god-parenting worked with the aristocracy. Her only familiarity came from the fairy tales she had read as a child.

Gabriel allowed a chuckle. "He didn't need to since our father died after I was past my majority," he explained. "I'm quite sure he would have helped had I required assistance, though," he added, thinking it was rather sporting of Grandby to check up on him those first few months. The earl insisted he be contacted if Gabriel required help, or if his father's man of business didn't wish to continue his position with the Trenton earldom.

"But he must have been involved when you were searching for a wife," Lily insisted, remembering the talk in Mayfair parlors regarding Grandby's ability to see to it his goddaughters made suitable matches. Perhaps his involvement in marriages also extended to his godsons.

Gabriel exchanged glances with his wife. "He did not, but then, I don't believe I would have taken his advice had he provided any," he explained with a shrug.

Lily's eyes widened. "But, you did," she claimed, daring a glance at Sarah before she returned her attention to Gabriel.

Her brother regarded her with a quizzical expression. "How so?" he asked, an eyebrow arched.

Angling her head to one side, Lily replied, "When it comes to choosing a spouse, he said to be sure to follow your heart."

The Earl of Trenton allowed a wan smile and gave her a nod. "Then I suppose I did," he admitted, his gaze settling on his wife. "I suppose I did."

CHAPTER 18

MIDNIGHT MUSINGS

"She looks well, don't you think?" Gabriel whispered as he pulled the counterpane off the bed and began folding it.

Sarah regarded him from her dressing table looking glass as she drew a hair brush through her blonde locks. She was quite sure she had never before seen the earl do anything so domestic as folding a counterpane. "Did we scare away the maid this evening?" she asked, turning on the chair so she could look at him directly—and to ensure she wasn't imagining his act of domesticity.

Temporarily hidden by yards of velvet, Gabriel chuckled. "I told her to spend the night with her husband. And I told her not to wake us before nine o'clock. Figure we're due a late morning so we can sleep in," he explained, managing to capture a couple of corners of the plush fabric between his fingers.

Sarah joined him to take the opposite ends of the counterpane. "I rather doubt Gabe will allow us the luxury of sleeping in," she replied with a grin as she helped him finish the final fold. The toddler seemed to be the first one up in the morning, his squeals of delight waking the nurse—and the rest of the servants on the third floor. The subsequent *thump-thump-thump* of his bare feet running along the main hall usually woke up

Sarah, and the louder *thump-thump-thumps* of the nurse who had to run to catch him never failed to bring a smile to her face.

Gabriel allowed a knowing grin as he tossed the folded counterpane onto a nearby chair and turned to wrap his arms around his wife's shoulders. He pulled her into a hug. "You didn't answer my question," he murmured, his lips brushing her earlobe as he pushed her hair away from the tender flesh.

"She looks like an aristocrat," Sarah whispered, realizing he wanted an answer to his question about Lily. "All prim and proper and..." She sucked in a breath as his teeth nipped the lobe. "Worried."

Gabriel pulled away, his brows furrowing so a wrinkle appeared on his forehead. "Whatever do you mean?" he asked, his hands moving to the ties of her dressing gown. He undid the bow and spread open the edges of the satin fabric with his hands.

Sarah sucked in another breath as his palms skimmed over her breasts and around to her back. "She wants desperately to make the right decision regarding a husband, but she also wants to be sure you're in agreement with whomever she chooses," she managed to whisper as her hands fumbled for his robe's ties.

His lips trailed down her jaw-line to her neck. "I want her to be happy," Gabriel claimed in a hoarse whisper, "So even if she decides to marry a... a commoner, I'll support her decision, of course," he added between kisses.

Sarah yanked the robe's tie open and spread her hands on his bare chest. "Truly?" she whispered before her lips captured one of his nipples. One of her hands trailed down the front of his body, her fingers barely touching his warm skin until they delved down to his thighs and gently cupped his sac.

Gabriel groaned, and his body jerked as her forefinger trailed up the back of his manhood, following the pulsing vein to the tip. Before she had a chance to wrap her hand around his arousal, he released his hold on her and moved his arms to her back and behind her knees. She gasped as he lifted her against his body, her dressing gown falling from her body as he turned and placed her on the bed. Before he joined her there, he allowed his own robe to fall from his shoulders. "She can marry a cit, if she chooses," he stated as he held his body over Sarah's.

Her breaths coming in shallow gasps, Sarah nodded. "Or a... a clerk?" she managed to get out as her hands returned to his body, to his throbbing manhood.

Gabriel stilled his movements. "A clerk?" he repeated, just before his mouth took one of her breasts.

"Better than a tailor, I should think," she whispered frantically.

"True," Gabriel responded as his lips moved down the front of her body. Even before he had his head between her thighs, Sarah spread her legs and lifted her knees. Her fingers speared his blond curls, the nails scraping his scalp just as his tongue flicked across the swollen nub in the center of her feminine folds. She cried out his name just as he flicked the nub again.

"I do hope she's not considering a fisherman," he said suddenly.

Sarah stilled herself, momentarily lost to rational thought. "I promise, she is not considering a fisherman," she said on a frustrated sigh.

"Thank the gods," he replied. And with that, his lips took purchase on the swollen nub and suckled it until Sarah cried out once more, her hands pulling his head from between her thighs as a wave of pleasure crashed through her body, shook her, and crashed through her again.

Gabriel was up and over her body in an instant, his engorged manhood sliding along her glistening folds, rubbing against her womanhood until she whimpered for him. He plunged himself into her welcoming center, groaning as her sheath gripped him and pulled him deeper into her body.

He had thought he could delay his release for a moment or more, thought he could simply pull out of her and thrust himself in a time or two more, but his release had already taken hold, already sent the signal to spill his seed into her throbbing warmth. The spasms of pure pleasure gripped him, stilled him, passed through him until he simply gave up and slumped onto Sarah's body.

Sarah sighed as the wash of warmth filled her lower body. She sighed again as another wave of pleasure coursed through her lower body.

Could anything be so amazing as the sensations Gabriel could set off with a few simple flicks of his tongue? Then with a few simple kisses with his lips? Even after a few minutes, his throbbing manhood still filled her, still incited darts of pleasure. She clenched on him, delighting in his moans and the slight grin that appeared on his lips as his head finally settled between her neck and shoulder. "You minx," he murmured.

A chuckle burbled forth, and Sarah clenched on him again when she thought he would remove himself from atop her. "Stay. Just another moment," she whispered, hoping he would simply fall asleep atop her.

He never slept long after their couplings, merely a few minutes before he would remove himself from her body and settle himself onto the mattress next to her. He always pulled her body close to his, though, tucking her against him or settling her slightly atop him so her head lay in the small of his shoulder. She always found him still in the bed when the morning light filled the room.

He had only left their marriage bed on one occasion, when a head cold had him so uncomfortable, he moved to the study where he finally fell asleep in one of the upholstered chairs. She found him the following morning with the kitchen cat wrapped atop his head, her purring audible to anyone in the room. When his eyes opened as she kissed his cheek, he murmured, "My head feels as if it weighs two stones." Managing to suppress her giggle, Sarah had simply lifted the cat from his head and set her on the floor, eliciting a yowl of protest from the feline. "Oh, much better," Gabriel whispered as he fell back to sleep.

Sarah wondered if Gabriel had even been aware of the cat sleeping on his head.

"Mmm." Gabriel moved a hand to cup her breast, his forefinger circling the still-engorged nipple. "Thank you for being such a good mother to my little bastard," he whispered, reaching over to kiss the breast closest to his face.

Sarah smiled, one of her hands moving to his curls to tousle them. "You're welcome, I think," she murmured.

There was a pause before he asked, "Do you suppose we'll have another?"

Stilling herself, Sarah realized she had the perfect opening to tell him she was fairly sure she was expecting a baby. "Oh, yes," she replied with a nod, her fingers massaging his scalp. "In time for Christmas, I should think," she added, wondering if he had fallen asleep when he didn't immediately respond.

Several seconds passed before Gabriel lifted himself onto an elbow. "This Christmas?" he asked then, the hand on her breast moving to cup her face.

Sarah nodded in the pillow. "Maybe even in November. It's rather hard to determine since my monthly courses never actually resumed," she explained. "Little Gabe is still helping himself to an occasional luncheon, and until..."

Gabriel's lips were suddenly on hers, kissing her with an urgency that she felt in his entire body.

"You minx!" he cried out.

Sarah giggled. "I've wanted to tell you. It's just that I wasn't completely sure," she hedged before she kissed him lightly. "I do hope it's a boy. An heir for you," she murmured.

"I wouldn't mind a girl, truly," he said before pulling her on top of his body.

Sarah gave him a quelling look. "After everything you've gone through with your sister? You'd be willing to do it again with your own daughter?" she countered, her eyebrows arched up in surprise.

Gabriel blinked and then frowned. "I see your point," he replied. "Although, I think I would just send my daughter to a convent. Just save myself the grief," he whispered.

Sarah winced, not the least bit happy to think of her daughter spending her days locked away in a nunnery. "A boy it is, then," she whispered, settling her head into the small of his shoulder and hoping a boy was indeed on the way.

Sleep took both of them within a few moments.

CHAPTER 19

AN EARL AND A VISCOUNT
PLAY THEIR PARTS

The following week, Gabriel, Sarah and Lily took their seats in the dining room, their first opportunity to enjoy a formal dinner since the night of Lily's arrival. With duties having taken Gabriel away for several days, and Samantha in Stretton to oversee the Spread Eagle while members of the peerage were in residence, Lily had spent the time at Trenton Manor playing with Gabe.

Although she hadn't given any consideration to motherhood before meeting the young viscount, she found herself imagining having one of her own. She imagined one with blond curly hair and blue eyes, pudgy knees and plump cheeks, a dimple appearing every time he giggled.

Lily was thinking of dimples when her brother addressed her as the soup bowls were set in front of them. "I understand an earl may ask for your hand," he said. "Who, pray tell, might he be?" he asked.

Lily's eyes widened and she dared a glance at Sarah. The countess merely shrugged, giving her a glance that suggested she wasn't sure how Gabriel would know anything about the Earl of Montaine.

"Well, I do not think the Earl of Montaine would have shown me any consideration if it hadn't have been for the attention Viscount Fraley had been paying me at a *soirée* I attended,"

Lily countered, thinking this might be the perfect opportunity to tell her brother about the dueling lords.

Gabriel frowned. He wasn't familiar with Charles Castlereigh, Viscount Fraley, although he had heard the man was a poor gambler.

Now Graham Denberg, Earl of Montaine, was another matter altogether. Certainly he would make a suitable suitor for his sister. "Do share," he encouraged before taking a sip of wine.

Lily nodded, giving a nervous glance in Sarah's direction. "If you're sure," she replied. And with that bit of warning, she proceeded to tell the tale of Graham Denberg, Earl of Montaine, and Charlie Castlereigh, Viscount Fraley.

*G*raham Denberg angled his head and kept a passive expression on his face, telling himself he could safely take his leave of the Carlington household in another ten minutes or so. At *ton* events such as this more intimate soirée, he felt out of his element. At a ball he could abide, the crush of bodies providing him a level of anonymity. He could spend four hours among hundreds of people and never once have to say more than a word or two of greeting—*pleasantries,* his mother called them—or speak of the weather or how becoming a gown or color might be on a particular dance partner. Safe, predictable, pleasant courtesies a shy person could afford anyone with whom they came into contact.

Not that Graham was particularly shy, of course. But despite having grown up knowing he would one day be an earl didn't mean he was quite ready for what happened in Parliament. Although he had been an earl for only nine months, he could count the number of months he had attended sessions on one hand.

His father had died near the end of a Season, so Graham hadn't claimed his seat in Parliament until the beginning of the fall session. Like most lords, he took his leave of the capital at Christmastime, traveling to Dorchester, the seat of the

Montaine earldom, to spend the holiday with his mother, Elaine Denberg, Dowager Countess of Montaine.

Graham had only been back in London a fortnight before receiving the invitation from Lord and Lady Morganfield to attend their soirée. As the last small gathering of aristocrats before most would depart for the summer—there had also been a ball, although Graham hadn't been invited—he felt obliged to attend. He also felt a bit beholden to his host. Although he was still battling the discomfort of being the newest member of Parliament, he was fast becoming the most outspoken Lord in Parliament.

But he couldn't claim a level of comfort in putting voice to his thoughts, a level of comfort in being in the same room with aristocrats who had held their titles far longer than his nine months—the level of comfort David Carlington, Marquess of Morganfield, seemed to enjoy, and had for more than twenty years.

Despite Morganfield's early political scandal—the man had shared secrets with a mistress who turned out to be a spy for the French—he was one of the most powerful men in Parliament. And as one of its newest members, Graham Denberg, Earl of Montaine, was determined to follow in the marquess' steps.

Well, except for the scandal part, of course.

So it was a bit of a surprise when he found himself in the midst of what could be construed as a quarrel. A scandalous quarrel.

He wasn't quite sure what had happened to cause Miss Lily Harkins to take issue with Charlie Castlereigh, Viscount Fraley. It was rumored the young viscount had announced his intentions to ask for Miss Harkins' hand at some point during the Season. She had been the darling of last year's balls, her come-out at the Mayfield ball a success despite her having been sponsored by Lady Samantha Fitzsimmons, the very lady on whom Lily had waited as a maid for several years.

"Really now, Fraley. You must allow Miss Harkins a bit more space," he struggled to get out, alarmed at how little of it there appeared to be between the fronts of the two whose verbal sparring was increasing in both intensity and volume. Indeed, if either one took another step forward, Charlie would find himself leg-shackled if for no other reason than he could be accused of an impropriety worthy of an immediate wedding.

"Charlie Castlereigh, you are a rake!" Lily announced, her voice loud enough to be overheard by at least a few couples nearby.

Graham held his breath. Perhaps the viscount was already guilty of just such an impropriety.

"My lady, I am no such thing!" Charlie countered, his voice kept low but pitched so his impatience was quite evident.

"When my brother finds out what you've done, you'll be... you'll be... drawn and quartered!" Lily hurried on, oblivious to the sudden stares of those who stood within earshot.

"Whatever has he done?" Graham asked, moving so he stood just as close to Gabriel Wellingham's half-sister as Charlie did.

Jerking her head in surprise, apparently just then noticing the earl, Lily backed up a step. Her gaze took him in, her head lifting and lowering as she seemed to assess the identity of his tailor, the maker of his boots, the type of gemstone in his cravat, and the brand of chronometer that hung from his waistcoat pocket.

It was times such as this when Graham knew his passive expression would serve him well. No one would look at him and know his thoughts, guess which way he might be swayed in an argument, know if he were angry or annoyed or happy or simply bored. And when the expression wasn't quite enough, he could simply stare at the other person, hold their gaze until they gave up trying to figure out his motives, and redirect his attention to something else.

He used that stare to good effect. That stare had ensured he got his way when he most wanted it.

Graham was using it now, determined to unnerve Lily Harkins, to make her admit her mistake and take back her proclamation. To make her come to her senses and realize that with her announcement, she was setting up Charlie for scandal, and setting herself up for a summer of embarrassment and shame.

What was the girl thinking?

"I didn't mean for our *discussion* to be overheard," Lily said in a hoarse whisper, her words directed to Graham. "I was simply stunned he would do such a thing at a *soirée* is all," she added.

The viscount let out a huff. "Oh, please. It was merely a peck. And it would have been on your cheek had you not turned so quickly," he added, his comment clearly laying the blame for what was apparently an unwelcome kiss on Lily.

Graham witnessed how the chit seemed to puff up, her face reddening, not with a blush of embarrassment, but anger, pure and simple. Fraley's words clearly had her incensed. "Had you approached from in front of me, I wouldn't have had to turn my head to figure out whose face was looming next to mine," she argued, her voice kept low but still filled with venom. "Have you any idea how frightening your face can be, all…?" She moved her hands in front of her own face so the fingers were splayed wide as she exaggerated a hideous expression. "*Disgusting*," she finished with a huff.

Charlie Castlereigh rolled his eyes in response, his attention finally landing on Graham.

The earl was suddenly sorry he had ever moved into their sphere. He could have simply helped himself to a glass of champagne and occupied a corner with what appeared to be a rather lonely potted palm for the rest of the evening. Instead, he found himself as the third in an argument of some sort.

Was this a lovers' quarrel? Was it a spat between betrothed aristocrats? Or perhaps Fraley intended to force the poor girl to marry him by taking advantage! He had heard she had a dowry worth thousands. Was Fraley merely ensuring he would end up with the largesse?

The rake!

"So, what did you think of our charade?" Lily asked, her expectant expression forcing Graham to swallow. And blink in confusion.

"I beg your pardon?" he asked in response, feeling a bit lost. He glanced over at Fraley, surprised to see the viscount displaying a much happier countenance.

"We had you, right?" Fraley asked, his grin broadening and his eyes so bright, Graham blinked his own in shock.

Not sure how to respond to the odd comment, Graham shook his head. "I feel as if I have walked in on a discussion better left at Bedlam. What, pray tell, are you about?" he asked, his question directed to Lady Lily.

"We're rehearsing," she replied with a nod. "For the play we're to do later this evening," she added when the earl didn't seem to register her explanation.

"A play?" Graham repeated, his head shaking.

Charlie Castlereigh spread his hands out before him. "A parlor play, is all," he replied with a shrug, as if he were dismissing their involvement as minor to the overall production. "We've been tasked with playing a couple who is annoyed with one another," he added, pulling one of Lady Lily's hands onto the sleeve of his tailcoat as he gave her a glance that included a lifted eyebrow.

The move seemed rather forward to Graham, who felt a bit of annoyance at seeing the viscount appear to literally take possession of Lady Lily. "Your banter was so believable, I was certainly fooled," he admitted then. "But I suppose it comes easily when there is so much of you about which to be annoyed," he added, surprised to hear his own words spoken aloud.

Good grief! Had he really just spoken the offensive words so the viscount—and Lady Lily—could hear them?

It was Viscount Fraley's turn to blink. "Montaine!" he said *sotto voce*. "Do I detect a hint of jealousy in your rebuke?" he asked, his voice kept low. Unfortunately, with Lady Lily on his arm, she was able to hear everything the two of them were saying.

Graham Denberg's eyes narrowed. "Jealous?" he responded. "Of what? A viscount who is so destitute from gambling, he requires a wife's dowry in order to stay in London?" The words were out of his mouth so quickly, Graham realized too late he should have censored them. He should have kept them to himself entirely. He didn't really know if Fraley could afford a wife or not—and it was really none of his business. What had him putting voice to such uncharitable thoughts?

Lady Lily?

Good God. Where was a potted palm plant when you needed one?

A quick glance at the one in the corner showed it was already busy hiding their hosts, who seemed to think the fronds were providing cover as they displayed their fondness for one another.

Another wave of jealousy swept through Graham as he realized the Marquess of Morganfield truly loved his Italian wife. Why, if they continued as they were doing this very instant, he wondered how long it would be before the marquess had his wife's gown down past her shoulders and his lips on the tops of her breasts. On the front of her breasts and between her breasts...

But enough about their hosts.

A brittle silence had settled around him, for his words had Fraley's eyes widening so they appeared most frightful and Lady Lily lowering hers so her attention seemed to be on the patterned Axminster carpet beneath her slippers.

"I am not destitute, Montaine," Fraley ground out between clenched teeth. "I am far from it. And you would be wise to keep your jealousy reined in."

Lady Lily suddenly lifted her head, her eyes searching those of the Earl of Montaine's.

Jealousy?

But that couldn't be. The earl had never shown her any consideration. He had never requested a dance with her at the balls the Season before. He had never asked to escort her in the park during the fashionable hour. He had never paid a call on her at Fitzsimmons Manor.

So how could he be jealous?

Or was this just more rehearsal for the play that was to

begin once their hosts broke their lip-lock? Goodness. The palm in the corner must have paid witness to a good deal of clandestine meetings over the years. Why, already another couple was patiently waiting their turn to hide their amorous actions behind the plant's fronds.

"I do believe we'll be most believable in the play," Lily said then, thinking the Earl of Montaine was simply another player and her partner's banter with him was part of the script. "Why, you had me quite convinced you despise the viscount," she said, turning her attention on the Earl of Montaine.

The earl blinked as he turned his own attention onto Lily. He almost countered her claim with the words, "I do despise the viscount," but thought better of it. What good would it do to have the young lady thinking the worst of him? And, bless her heart, she had just given him the perfect out for his unforgivable behavior. "Was I truly believable?" he countered, giving both Lily and Fraley an expectant expression.

Fraley visibly swallowed. "Quite," he responded with a nod, apparently wondering if his reaction was in keeping with the spirit of the play or if he had been played.

Where was the script?

"I believe we are ready for the stage, my lady," he said, his attention still on the earl.

Lily gave him a brilliant smile. "Oh, good. Though I do think I am in need of a glass of champagne before we do this performance," she hinted, hoping Fraley might volunteer his services.

She wasn't disappointed.

The viscount gave a bow. "Allow me, my lady," he said. Even before he had returned to a standing position, a footman appeared with a tray of glasses, their bubbling contents sending out a spray of tiny droplets in a halo over the crystal flutes. Fraley helped himself to one and gave it to Lily and then took another for himself. "To a new thespian," he said as he held his glass aloft.

Lily's eyes widened.

Thespian?

Despite all the time Lady Samantha had spent teaching her the ways of the *ton*, the manners and verbiage and the rules and the do's and don'ts, Lily had no idea what the term 'thespian' meant.

Noticing how the earl raised his glass—had he grabbed one from the tray as well?—Lily simply raised hers in turn and joined them when they each took a short sip of the champagne.

Lily drained her glass, delighting in the sensations created on her tongue and in her throat as the bubbly liquid made its way down. Within moments, she felt giddy. Her knees seemed to take their leave of her body. Anything below them seemed to have disappeared as well. And her tongue seemed to belong to someone else.

"It's time," Lady Morganfield said when she suddenly appeared at the viscount's elbow and leaned into their group.

Lily blinked as she turned to find their hostess bestowing them with a brilliant smile and pointed looks. Despite the fact that her husband had had most of her bodice off her body only moments before, she seemed fully dressed and entirely appropriate. Other than her bee-stung lips, she didn't appear as if she had been the victim of her husband's amorous attentions only moments before.

"We're ready," Lily managed to say in response, although her tongue seemed to get in the way of the simple words.

"Indeed, we are," Fraley agreed, giving their hostess a deep bow. Montaine followed suit, apparently allowing the viscount to take the lead.

"There's a stage set up in the ballroom," Adele Carlington, Marchioness of Morganfield, replied before she left their group, apparently off to gather the rest of the players.

Where was the script?

Lily's eyes widened when she realized both Montaine's and Fraley's eyes were directed on her. "You heard Lady Morganfield," she said. "We should be making our way to the ballroom."

She found her arms on those of the viscount and the earl, her empty champagne glass no longer in her hand. A few minutes later, she was in the Carlington House ballroom, up on stage with Viscount Fraley and the Earl of Montaine sitting in a chair in the front row of spectators.

"Please, I beg you, do not take anything I say in the next few moments to heart, my lady," Fraley said as he positioned himself on the stage in front of her. "Except for the kiss, of course. That you may take to heart," he added before schooling his expression into one of dispassionate resolve.

Lily blinked.

The kiss?

Was she expected to allow the viscount to kiss her in front of an audience? In front of the Marquess of Morganfield's guests?

All of them?

When she glanced out from the stage, she found at least two score of people staring back at her. She blinked again as she returned her attention to the viscount. His gaze seemed fixed on her. On her lips, actually. And when Lady Morganfield clapped her hands and brought the audience from a dull roar to a silence so profound, Lily was quite sure everyone could hear her breathe, the marchioness said, "And now, we're proud to present, *The Kiss of a Viscount.*"

There was a moment of terror as Lady Lily registered Lady Morganfield's words.

The kiss of a viscount?

Oh, dear! She had thought she and the viscount were merely minor players in a much larger play! But the marchioness' words implied they were the only players. And Charlie Castlereigh, Viscount Fraley, seemed quite intent on playing his role as realistically as possible in his portrayal of the viscount whose kiss was supposedly the object of the play.

"My lady, I should like to kiss you this very instant," Fraley announced, his intentions directed as much to the audience as to her.

Several guffaws could be heard from those in attendance.

Lily froze. "In front of all these people?" she almost asked out loud. Instead, she remembered what they had rehearsed in the salon. "And if I do not wish to be kissed? What then, my lord?" she countered, relieved they had rehearsed this part.

"Why, I'll make it your wish," Fraley replied, one eyebrow cocking in a manner Lily found a bit offensive. She didn't have a line just then, so she didn't say anything. But she wouldn't have been able to, for the viscount's lips came down onto hers so suddenly and so possessively, she was left speechless.

The audience certainly wasn't left speechless. Their roars of approval were probably heard at both ends of Park Lane!

Lily lifted her hands to the viscount's shoulders and pushed as hard as she could until Lord Fraley was forced to disengage his lip lock. "Charlie Castlereigh, you are a rake!" Lily announced, her voice loud enough to be heard by everyone in the ballroom.

"My lady, I am no such thing!" Charlie countered, his voice kept low but pitched so his impatience was quite evident to the entire audience.

"When my brother finds out what you've done, you'll be... you'll be... drawn and quartered!" Lily hurried on, oblivious to the crowd beyond the stage. She could just imagine the reports in the gossip rags.

Earl's illegitimate sister kisses a viscount in front of a huge audience at Carlington House. Turn to page six for the whole sordid story!

I am ruined, Lily thought in dismay. Was this the viscount's way of assuring he would gain her dowry in a marriage of convenience? Why, of course it was!

"No, please, my lady," Charlie said as he took her two hands in his. "I love you too much. You cannot deny me what I have become to believe is true love betwixt us," he announced in a tone suggesting he truly believed the words he was saying. Either the viscount was an excellent actor, or he truly believed what he was saying!

Who knew what the audience believed?

Lily blinked. Then she blinked again. They hadn't rehearsed

these lines. The Earl of Montaine had interrupted them at this point.

"Perhaps I cannot," she replied, not sure what her lines were supposed to be. She had never been given a script. "But I know in my heart I cannot allow you such an impropriety. My brother will be most displeased," she added, not really sure if he would be displeased or joyous over learning she had been kissed by a viscount in front of an enthusiastic audience.

She dared a glance in the direction of the Earl of Montaine, thinking he must have missed his cue. Wasn't he supposed to save her from the viscount's unwelcome advances?

The viscount's eyes widened. "When I inform him of my love for you, he will be unable to deny me permission for your hand in marriage."

At the word 'marriage,' Graham Denberg, Earl of Montaine, straightened in his seat. His brows furrowed, and he wondered if the play was really the viscount's underhanded means to acquiring Lady Lily's hand in marriage instead of a mere parlor play. No one else seemed to be waiting in the wings to save Lily from a fate as bad as Viscount Fraley.

Sighing, Montaine stood and made his way to the stage, the audience cheering his appearance when he turned and addressed the crowd. "Really now, Fraley. You must allow Miss Harkins a bit more... space," he said in a most exaggerated manner.

When the audience let out a resounding sound of approval, he turned to Lily. "Whatever has he done?" Graham asked, moving so he stood just as close to Gabriel Wellingham's half-sister as Charlie did.

Lily regarded the earl with an expression that suggested she was most relieved at his unexpected intervention. "He... he kissed me," she said, her voice sounding breathless. A smattering of 'boo's and a few 'yay's sounded from the audience, which seemed to have gained in size.

Goodness. Were there this many people in attendance at the *soirée*? Or had Lord Morganfield sold tickets, too? Were theatre critics positioned in the back row, ready to report on her poor stage presence and breathy voice? At least she didn't have to sing!

In an exaggerated move, Graham turned to regard the viscount with an arched eyebrow. "I've a mind to call you out, Fraley," he announced, his serious comment drawing cries of agreement and titters from the crowd. "Pistols at dawn? Wimbledon Common?"

The roar of the audience was deafening. Lily stepped back, not sure what to do. None of this was part of the plan when Lady Carlington approached them about putting on a play of manners. She was quite sure the marchioness merely planned it as a way of giving Lady Lily another possible suitor.

The earl's reaction made it seem as if she might have yet another admirer besides the randy viscount, which was a bit of relief given Charlie's behavior. The man had insisted on a real kiss during their rehearsal. And then he had kissed her in front of the huge audience!

"We must make it as believable as possible, my sweeting," he had said, which had Lily's eyes wide and then blinking in surprise at his use of an endearment best said to a spouse. And then he had kissed her in a way suggesting he was as bad at kissing as her brother, Gabriel. That is, as bad as he had been at kissing before his marriage to Sarah Cumberbatch.

Goodness!

She hoped Sarah had been successful in teaching Gabriel how to kiss so his kisses wouldn't be compared with those of a dog. But the viscount had kissed as if his lessons had come from a rather large, friendly dog. All slobbery and wet and quite noisy. As if he were eating soup and slurping tea and kissing all at the same time.

Now, with the Earl of Montaine's unexpected appearance on their stage and his sudden nearness, she thought she had wandered into the wrong parlor.

Was the earl also interested in her? Was he interested in a romantic way?

Charlie took a step back, leaving Graham standing entirely too close to Lily. "Why, my lord, it is I who should call you out," the viscount said in a voice far more dramatic than it needed to be. Perhaps he was trying out for a part in the penny opera. Or was he hoping for a good review by whatever theatre critics might be in the back row?

"Name your weapon, Fraley," Graham responded, his chin thrust forward, "For this beautiful creature has already promised her heart to me."

A chorus of gasps and cheers erupted from the audience. Fraley stared at the earl as if he had suddenly realized the entire matter was off-script. "Well then," he replied with a shrug. "She's all yours." With that pronouncement, the viscount left the stage as the audience clapped and a few let out sounds of disappointment.

Graham dared a glance at Lily, one eyebrow going up in apology. He took one of her hands in his and kissed the back of it before turning to face the crowd, her hand still firmly grasped in his. He bowed to their cheers. Nervous, Lily curtsied and gave a smile, hoping she wasn't betrothed to either gentleman by reason of public spectacle.

"Brava!" Lady Carlington called out as she joined them. "Thank you to all three of you for your interpretation of *Two Gentleman of Verona*."

Lily frowned. Weren't they doing an interpretation of the *The Kiss of a Viscount?*

G raham had to still his features to keep from reacting. He hoped he hadn't just become betrothed to Lady Lily by reason of insanity. "Just follow their lead," Lady Carlington had said just before her husband whisked her off to the potted palm and a few minutes of surreptitious kissing. He had agreed only because, well, how could he refuse? Lady Lily was a comely blonde with a dowry said to be more than five times his annual income. Perhaps he should be hoping he was betrothed by reason of unexpected matchmaking.

"Charades will commence in the parlor in five minutes," the marchioness called out, moving to take Viscount Fraley's arm so she could lead him out of the ballroom, presumedly to make him the first actor in the parlor game.

Just as quickly as the crowd had assembled in the ballroom, it now dispersed, some to the parlor, some to the card room, and others to the retiring rooms.

*L*ady Lily was left with the Earl of Montaine hovering next to her, his hand still holding hers in a grip that suggested she might be forced to go home with the man. It was as if he didn't intend to let go!

"My lord," Lily said as she indicated her hand. "I was hoping I might have use of that limb again," she hinted, feeling the telltale pins-and-needles sensation of having slept on it. "That is, unless you require it for some clandestine purpose to benefit King and country," she added, one eyebrow arching up with her cheeky query.

Graham couldn't help but allow a chuckle. Then he laughed out loud. He lessened his hold on Lily's hand by placing it on his arm and taking her other to lift it to his lips. "You are a gem, aren't you?" he asked rhetorically. "Truth be told, I thought you would be..." He stopped speaking, his eyes darting about as if he'd caught himself about to say something entirely inappropriate. He reluctantly let go of her gloved hand.

"Uncouth? Common? Beneath you?" Lily finished for him, her manner serious as she clasped her hands together in front of her. A sense of disappointment fell over her just then. She rather wished he had kept hold of her hand. She thought the earl had come to her rescue of his own accord since what he had said and done didn't seem to be part of the script—nor what had been rehearsed in the salon.

"Hardly," Graham responded. "Vain, unapproachable,

haughty," he said, countering her words. At her look of surprise, he added, "You are the Earl of Trenton's sister, are you not?"

Lily wondered if the earl had been present for her brother's first days in Parliament. Gabriel had been far too vocal with his dissatisfaction of the lords and their laws back then. Perhaps the earl thought she would be as unlikable as her brother had been. "I am," she affirmed with a nod.

Graham shrugged. "And yet, I find you entirely agreeable. And beautiful, too," he continued. "Your father, Graydon Wellingham, may have been a disagreeable..." He stopped again, aware he was about to say 'ass' in the presence of a lady. She might have been the daughter of a maid, but Lady Lily was still a lady. There was no call to be gauche when describing her father. So imagine his surprise when she did it for him.

"Ass?" she said quietly. "Or perhaps rake, rogue, bastard, libertine—?"

"Rogue will do," Graham said, holding up a hand in surrender. He allowed a grin. "You are a breath of fresh air in an otherwise airless room, my lady," he said with a grin. "And where are my manners? I do not believe we have been properly introduced. Graham Denberg, Earl of Montaine, at your service," he said as he gave her a deep bow.

Lily curtsied. "Lily Harkins. Or Wellingham, I suppose," she corrected herself. "'Tis very good to meet you. And thank you for saving me from Viscount Fraley. I have reason to think he may have been about to propose marriage," she said with an arched eyebrow.

The earl allowed another grin. "The fact that you would not have welcomed such a proposal says much, my lady," he said, offering his arm. Lily rested her own on it, and they made their way out of the ballroom.

"How so?" she asked, deciding she rather liked the earl. He lacked the pretentious snobbery she encountered with most of those of his rank.

Which had included her brother.

CHAPTER 20

INTERMISSION

"You think me snobbish?" Gabriel interrupted, his fork and knife poised to cut his venison medallions in gravy.

Pulled out of her recitation of the story, Lily had to remember what she had just said. "Well, not now, of course," she replied with a shake of her head. "But back then, well…" She paused a moment, giving Sarah a glance in the hopes her sister-in-law would help her out of the awkward situation. Sarah's attention was on her plate, however, so Lily was forced to continue. "Yes, I thought you were a snob."

Gabriel gave a shrug. "Oh. All right, just as long as you no longer feel that way," he replied, returning his attention to his venison.

Lily released the breath she was holding and gave a nod. She considered where she was in the story and continued.

"Viscount Fraley is beneath you," the Earl of Montaine answered simply. "Anyone can tell you require a man of means at your side. You need a man of appropriate rank, and nothing less than an earl will do for you," he added in a serious manner. The playfulness he had displayed in the ballroom was gone.

Lily's eyebrows arched. "And yet, I would be satisfied with a commoner, I am sure," she countered, curious as to what the earl would do with that tidbit of information.

"Nonsense," he replied, not the least bit surprised by her comment. "Even though you have only been a lady a bit over a... a year is it?" he asked as they made their way down the wide hall.

Lily nodded. Had the earl indeed been keeping track of her time as the acknowledged daughter of an earl? "Two Seasons, my lord," she replied.

"You have grown accustomed to your new station. I believe you would miss the little luxuries you enjoy should you return to a life in service," the earl stated, his words sounding as if he knew her too well.

Bristling at having the earl presume what she would and wouldn't miss should she decide to renounce her brother, Lily was about to counter his claim when he added, "Or would you really? Perhaps my assumption is presumptuous."

Lily slowed her steps so that the earl was forced to follow suit. "I have not given a thought to returning to service, my lord. I gave only a mere thought to wedding a commoner. I fail to see how marriage to a commoner can be equivalent to life in service."

Graham stared at Lily for a moment, apparently stunned by her words. There was more in the pretty blonde's head than he had given her credit for, it seemed. But why would she be considering marriage to a commoner?

Had one made his intentions known? Did the Earl of Trenton know his sister was considering someone other than a lord as a husband?

"If your commoner is in possession of some fortune, I suppose you would be spared from further work," he remarked, although not with any conviction.

Lily stared at the earl for a moment. What difference did it make to him if she chose to marry a commoner? The man had never danced with her at a ball. In fact, prior to this evening, she couldn't recall ever having seen the earl at any *ton* events.

"Have you ever considered that marriage to a lord might entail far more work on a wife's part than marriage to a commoner?" she countered, feeling a bit of satisfaction that she had thought of a rebuttal so quickly.

Graham Denberg blinked. He then blinked again as he considered Lily's words. Goodness! She was quite bold for one so young. And then he remembered why she might have mentioned marriage to a commoner.

Her brother had married a commoner.

Despite having the opportunity to marry just about any eligible young lady from two or three Seasons ago, the Earl of Trenton had instead opted to marry the manager of a posting inn. Certainly the Countess of Trenton wasn't still overseeing the Spread Eagle in Staffordshire?

Or, perhaps she was.

No wonder Lady Lily seemed to think an aristocrat's wife worked! "You should know that most lords, and especially their wives, aren't expected to run a business, my lady," he replied. "Although I hear tell your sister-in-law does a fine job with her inn."

Lily tried hard to suppress a look of surprise, but she couldn't keep her eyes from widening at the earl's comment. Obviously, the Earl of Montaine was familiar with the Trenton earldom. "Indeed, she does," Lily said with a nod, wondering if the earl intended a cut indirect with his comment. "But even when she passes the responsibilities to the new manager, she will still be in charge of a rather large household in Bilston. She will also be in charge of overseeing dozens of servants in three different houses. As well as keeping the books, and managing the governess and tutors for her children."

She was about to amend that last to 'child', but she had a sneaking suspicion Sarah was expecting a baby. The countess' latest missive hinted little Gabe would not be the lone babe in the Bilston manor much longer. "All the while she will be bearing heirs and spares."

Nodding his head, as if to admit he had misspoken, Graham reached for the gloved hand that had returned to rest on his arm and lifted it to his lips. "Forgive me for my ignorance, my lady," he replied in a hoarse whisper, brushing his lips over her knuckles.

Lily regarded him for a moment, her brows furrowing. "You are forgiven, of course, although I hardly think it an offense to know so little of what it is women do when you are an unmarried man and can have no knowledge of it."

Straightening, Graham shook his head. "I have a mother who still lives," he replied. "I could have asked her. I... I should have asked her," he murmured, his attention no longer on his companion but rather on one of the marble statues gracing an alcove in the hall wall.

Lily allowed the earl a moment of introspection before she glanced down the hallway. It was empty, all the *soirée* guests apparently in the parlor for the game of charades or in the card room. Would her absence be noted? If she wasn't careful, not only would a review of their parlor play appear in *The Times*, but an accounting of her escapades would appear in tomorrow's *The Morning Chronicle!*

"My lord, I do believe I should be—"

"I should like to court you, my lady," Graham stated. "That is, if you haven't already accepted another's suit?"

Lily blinked, her eyes widening when she comprehended the earl's declaration. "I have not, but—"

"Then, I shall call on you on the morrow. Perhaps a ride in the park is in order?" he suggested, his enthusiasm running away with him.

Staring at the earl in surprise, Lily shook her head. "Sir Tristan has already claimed tomorrow's ride in the park," she said in an apologetic tone. She glanced again toward the parlor, fearing her absence was already being discussed among those who weren't actively participating in charades.

The earl frowned. "He's a mere baron," he countered, obviously offended she would keep an appointment with someone of lower rank than he.

"True," Lily replied. "But I accepted his invitation when he last called on me."

Graham frowned. He was disappointed to learn the chit was under consideration by others, but he couldn't be surprised by the news. "The next day, then," he said with a nod.

Lily shook her head. "Lord Fraley has already asked me to join him for a tour of the British Museum," she said with a sigh.

A sense of melancholy settled over the earl just then. Goodness! How had he missed his opportunity with the lovely lady? *I don't attend enough balls*, he reasoned. *Nor do I attend enough soirées.*

"But I could ride with you the day after that," Lily offered, not wanting the earl to think she was being unreasonable.

Graham lowered his head as he considered the timing. "I will be on my way to Dorchester," he said quietly. *Without a wife.* Which was to be expected when he hadn't seen to courting a single daughter of the aristocracy for the entire Season.

A sense of relief settled over Lily just then. "Perhaps when you return to London?" she offered, hoping the earl wasn't upset with her. Did he expect he would court her in one day and marry her the next? Take her with him when he left for Dorchester?

"Perhaps," he replied with a nod. "My lady." He reached down and lifted her hand to his lips again. "When next we meet." He bowed over her hand and took his leave.

Instead of making his way into the parlor, he instead continued down the wide hall to the vestibule, where a footman saw to his coat and top hat.

· · ·

*L*ily watched as the earl took his leave of Carlington House, wondering if the man was truly disappointed or if he realized he might have dodged a bullet.

A bullet?" Gabriel Wellingham suddenly interjected, his brows drawn together. "Whatever makes you think he dodged a bullet?" he asked as he gripped his knife in one fist.

From the expression on his face, Lily thought perhaps the Earl of Trenton might be capable of flaying Graham Denberg, Earl of Montaine, with said knife, although if it was anything like the knife she had on her plate, it wouldn't do much damage to the earl other than a light scratch.

Lily sighed and took a quick glance in the direction of Sarah, who merely rolled her eyes. "I do not believe the earl was truly interested in marrying me," she replied. "He wasn't to be in London more than another day," she reasoned. "Hardly enough time to court and marry someone."

Gabriel relaxed in his carver and regarded his sister for a moment before scrubbing the side of his face with an open palm. He finally leaned forward, one of his elbows coming to rest on the edge of the table. "The Earl of Montaine is in desperate need of a wife," he claimed in a low voice, as if he didn't want any of the servants to overhear his remark. "He has obviously put off courting as long as possible and now finds himself in the untenable position of having to marry without benefit of a suitable amount of time to court someone."

Sarah straightened, giving a wave toward the footman nearest the kitchen. The man disappeared through the door, apparently to fetch the next dinner course. Once he was out of earshot, she said, "He is said to be courting a baron's daughter in Dorchester. One of the papers that arrived this morning has an article about it," she added, giving Lily an apologetic glance.

Lily couldn't help but feel a stab of disappointment at hearing Graham Denberg was courting another.

Although she hadn't been particularly attracted to the man

nor his manner that night at Morganfield's *soirée*, she still felt a bit of a thrill knowing he was interested in her in that way. He probably didn't need to marry for money, as he had implied Viscount Fraley needed to.

"His man of business will be relieved to hear it," Gabriel said as he straightened in his carver. "Montaine owes money to every gaming hell in London."

Lily gasped, stunned to hear her brother's comment. Then she remembered the earl's comment about the viscount needing to marry for a dowry.

How would the Earl of Montaine know of the viscount's gambling habit unless he had a gambling habit of his own? Or unless he frequented the same gaming hells?

Relief settled over her sense of disappointment, the heady mix leaving her confused. Goodness! Had she been able to ride with the earl, he might have proposed. She might have accepted.

She probably *would* have accepted.

And now she would find herself betrothed to a man who planned to use her dowry to pay off gambling debts!

Several footmen appeared, each bearing a plate of dessert. The confections were placed before the three of them, and all but one of the footmen disappeared through the door to the kitchen. "So, I suppose it's a good thing I was otherwise promised to Lord Fraley for a ride in the park the next day," she said with a wan smile.

Gabriel gave her a quelling glance. "A story you shall tell us during tomorrow's dinner," he said as he stabbed his spoon into his bread pudding.

Lily straightened in her chair. "But, I didn't go for the ride with Lord Fraley," she said. "After what happened up on stage, I suppose he thought he wasn't welcome to escort me. Or perhaps he thought my affections were transferred to Lord Montaine. Either way, he didn't appear to take me for a ride the next day."

Gabriel rolled his eyes. "What are my fellow lords about if they don't honor their invitations?" he asked. "I, for one, do not wish to hear anything more about my despicable peers for the rest of the night."

Sarah suppressed a grin until she had Lily's attention. "I am quite in agreement," she said with a nod. "And all that much more thankful that I ended up with one who is not the least bit despicable." She gave a wink in Gabriel's direction.

Her husband's complexion took on a reddish cast as a slow smile spread over his face. "Why, thank you, my lady. I shall remember your words when—"

"When I am next in need of a few coins from your purse," Sarah interrupted, one of her eyebrows arching up suggestively.

Gabriel's smile faltered and then reappeared as he realized what she was suggesting. A *tumble*! "Then, too, I suppose," he agreed, one of his own eyebrows arching to match hers.

Lily angled her head to one side, amused at how her brother and Sarah teased one another. Perhaps she could find a husband with whom she could find humor now and again. She rather doubted she would have with the Earl of Montaine. The man seemed far too serious. But then, it hardly mattered if the man was courting someone else.

Two down, two to go.

CHAPTER 21

A HEART-TO-HEART IN THE GAZEBO

"Are you ashamed of me?" Lily asked quietly, her fingers pleating the fabric of her overskirt. Other than the watered silk of her newest white ball gown, the yellow muslin of her round gown was the finest fabric she had ever worn. The delicate gathers at the empire waist fell into soft folds that seemed to flutter when she walked. She thought of the last time she had worn the gown. She wore it on the day she had paid a call on the Wellinghams at her cousin's import business. That was the day she had met Thomas and Emma. The same day she had become reacquainted with Billy Overby.

William, she corrected herself.

She remembered how his eyes had widened when he recognized her, or perhaps merely thought he had when he realized she was dressed far too well to be the servant he had spent time with so many years ago.

He probably thought she couldn't possibly be the same girl, or else he knew she was and merely thought he was seeing a ghost. After all, his last look at her had been when she was dressed in a plain gray gown and threadbare spencer. Why he had given her a second look that night, she knew not, but his gaze had held hers as his golden brown eyes turned almost smoky.

A slight shiver passed through her body as she remembered

how he had looked at her. How she had felt powerless to move and was unwilling to even try.

A hand waved in front of her eyes and she was forced to blink. "Oh!" she let out as she straightened on the gazebo bench and turned her attention back to her brother. Her cheeks flamed when she found herself wondering how long she had been daydreaming.

"No, I am not ashamed of you," Gabriel repeated. "And however could you think such a thing?" He was leaning against one of the gazebo supports, one knee bent with his foot resting on the decorative wall.

Lily was about to admonish him when she noticed his expression suddenly change. Her eyes widened in response.

"Have you done something to be ashamed of?" he asked then, his foot dropping to the floor and his stance suddenly making him appear as if he might pounce.

"No!" Lily replied with a shake of her head. "I was referring to Lady Morganfield's soirée, which reminds me. I think you should know I've been volunteering at Lady Bostwick's charity."

Gabriel frowned, wondering why being kissed would remind her of volunteering before he remembered Lady Elizabeth Bostwick was Lady Morganfield's daughter. "Lady E's Finding Work for the Wounded'?" he finally replied. "That's certainly nothing to be ashamed of," he added.

Lily gave him a quelling glance. "You're not *angry* I would work there? Given your past with Elizabeth Bennett-Jones?" she asked quietly.

A snore erupted from the direction of the floor, where little Gabe slept on a blanket. Both Lily and Gabriel turned to regard the toddler for a moment before they grinned.

Sobering, the earl inhaled and let the breath out slowly. "Lady Bostwick did me a favor when she sent me away that day I intended to propose," he said, absently patting his son on his back. "I hold no grudges against her, and certainly none against her charity. It's a very worthy cause," he added.

"Thank you," Lily replied. She thought of their earlier

discussion. "I may have spoken too soon when I told you I didn't have anything to be ashamed of."

Gabriel's eyebrows lifted. "Did you now?" he countered.

"Well, not really. As long as you don't count being kissed by Lord Fraley in front of all the guests at the Carlington House soirée as well as in the salon during our rehearsal. Such as it was," she added, her head dropping to one side. Despite the number of witnesses, nothing had been said about the kiss in any of the articles in the news rags the following week. It was as if Lady Morganfield had seen to it her soirée was mentioned but without any of the salacious details from their parlor play or the cheeky game of charades that followed.

An involuntary shiver seemed to grip Gabriel just then. "Eww," he responded, allowing a broad grin to show his amusement. The grin faded though and he took a seat next to her on the bench that lined the interior of the gazebo. "Promise me you won't accept his offer," he said quietly.

Shocked by his plea, Lily turned to regard her brother. "I promise, I will not accept Lord Fraley's offer," she said with a quick shake of her head. "Besides, I rather doubt the viscount will propose. Not after what the Earl of Montaine said to him," she added.

Gabriel's brows furrowed. "You think he was embarrassed?" he queried.

Lily gave a slight shrug. "Wouldn't you be if an earl announced to a roomful of the peerage that you were an inveterate gambler and you were only after a chit for her dowry?"

Leaning back so his head rested against the wall, Gabriel acted as if he was giving careful consideration to the question. "Back then, I wouldn't have known to be embarrassed," he murmured.

The temptation to giggle in response to her brother's initial response was quickly tamped down as Lily considered his confession. "But now?" she ventured.

Gabriel shook his head. "Now I know better than to make a spectacle of myself in front of the *ton*."

Lily sighed. "I think there are times..." She allowed the

sentence to trail off. When Gabriel turned to regard her, she gave another shrug. "There are times I wonder if this is all worth it," she said as she spread out her hands, apparently to indicate her new life.

The sight of little Gabe, finally sound asleep on a blanket spread out in the middle of the gazebo floor with his knees tucked beneath him and his bottom up in the air had her attempting to suppress a sudden chuckle.

"I don't know how he does it," Gabriel said in a whisper. "Although, my mother claims I slept the very same way." He reached up with the flat of his hand to push one cheek up in an exaggerated version of his son's flattened cheek. "She said I used to wake up with one cheek up over an ear."

No longer able to suppress her amusement, Lily let out a giggle. "I slept the very same way," she admitted. "It's a wonder we didn't suffocate."

"Exactly!" Gabriel agreed with a matching grin. "Or perhaps we lacked air for too long and it's made us a bit queer."

Lily nodded in agreement. "Perhaps."

Gabriel leaned over his son and picked him up, the toddler readjusting himself in Gabriel's arms so his head rested on his father's shoulder. The earl returned to the bench and lowered himself to sit next to Lily. "I only want what's best for you," he whispered. "You do know that, I hope."

Turning to watch her nephew sleep, Lily nodded. "Even if I may not want the best?" she countered in a hushed voice.

Gabriel gave a shrug, which readjusted his son's head on his shoulder so the boy's soft snores were more audible. "I suppose we can negotiate," he conceded.

Lily's face brightened. "Thank you, brother," she murmured. "I'll tell you all about Sir Tobias Fulton during another dinner," she offered.

Gabriel frowned. "Who?"

Lily inhaled to respond and instead shook her head. "He's a baronet," she replied with a shrug.

"As I said, 'who'?" Gabriel replied with a grin. "You can tell me about him during another dinner. In the meantime, I do believe this young man's mother will wonder what I've done with him," he added as he indicated the sleeping toddler he held. "I'm going to head back to the house."

Lily nodded her understanding, wondering if whomever she married would be such an attentive father. "I'd like to stay here for a while if you don't mind," she replied, indicating the gazebo and surrounding gardens.

Her brother shook his head. "Just don't get lost in the maze," he said as he took his leave of her.

Lily's eyes widened. *Maze?*

Although she had no desire to wander about a hedgerow maze all afternoon, Lily gave her brother a look that suggested she might just attempt the puzzle. Instead, she remained in the gazebo and pondered her future.

CHAPTER 22

A PICNIC IS A PRELUDE TO ANOTHER TALE

The weather was grand for a picnic by the pond. Should rain decide to fall, they could always move their meal into the folly. At least, that's what Lily said as she talked her brother into the midday repast. "Oh, please. It will be divine," she had pleaded, rather shocked to learn they didn't do picnics at Wellingham Manor.

"Mother thought them the meals of peasants," Gabriel replied with a shrug. "But since she is not in residence, I will be happy to oblige your request," he said with a good deal of aplomb. "Provided you share the details of your courtship with the Marquess of Reading."

Lily stilled herself, trying rather hard not to appear too terribly surprised by her brother's condition. "Oh, must I?" she replied with a roll of her eyes, exaggerating her response as if she were a recalcitrant child.

Gabriel raised an eyebrow. "If not during the picnic, then you must over dinner," he countered, hoping the Marquess of Reading hadn't done something completely scandalous and quite within his nature. He was better known as the Rake of Reading, but he was also in desperate need of a wife. Perhaps his days as a rake were over.

Nodding, Lily said, "Then over dinner." *Hopefully another night*, she thought. "I would prefer to tell you about Sir Tobias

Fulton instead," she offered, "Seeing as how I met him in the park and we'll be out-of-doors."

The earl seemed to give her words some thought before he nodded. "Then you'll need to let the kitchen staff know of our plans," he said, thinking she would know better than anyone in the household what a picnic might entail.

Smiling, Lily gave her brother a curtsy and took her leave, hurrying off to the kitchens to make the arrangements. Happy to help the few servants she found below stairs, she recited the ingredients to the cook and her assistant, who frequently glanced at one another as if they weren't quite sure they should follow the former maid's instructions.

Once the fruits, cheeses and meats were set out onto the butcher block, Lily assembled them in a wooden crate, a bit sorry there wasn't a large basket available. Once the container was filled, another servant appeared with a small basket for the plates, napkins and utensils as well as a bottle of wine. Lily was about to take the basket and head upstairs when she remembered little Gabe. The toddler would require something to eat and water to drink.

The scullery maid grinned as she added a lidded jar of water and some biscuits to the basket. "The tyke will eat anything," the maid assured her when Lily gave her a questioning glance.

Satisfied they had packed everything necessary for a midday meal, Lily headed upstairs with the basket and found Sarah and little Gabe in the study with Gabriel.

"Are we ready?" Gabriel asked, his words causing Sarah to do a double-take and to finally stare at Lily.

"Ready for what?" she asked, pulling Gabe into her arms.

"You didn't tell her?" Lily admonished her brother.

"I haven't had a chance. She's only just arrived."

"Gabe was napping," Sarah said in her own defense. "And what is it we should be ready for? It's nearly time for luncheon."

Lily grinned as she lifted the basket and pulled back the cloth that covered the bottle of wine. "We're having a picnic at the pond."

Lily knew she would never forget the look of joy that

appeared on Sarah's face at that moment, or the squeal of delight Gabe made when he saw his mother smile.

"That's a capital idea!" Sarah replied. "And if it should rain, we can always finish our picnic in the folly. I rather doubt we'll need shawls," she added as she stood up. "My bonnet is still in the vestibule..."

Gabriel dared a quick glance at Lily, wondering if she had spoken with Sarah before she brought him her idea.

"... And Gabe is wearing a fresh nappy," she continued, as if she hadn't noticed the siblings' quick glance at one another.

"Then let us be off," Gabriel said as he stood up. He allowed the ladies to proceed him into the hall and to the vestibule.

Fitzroy, the butler, didn't blink an eye as the four left Wellingham Manor and headed across the clipped lawn.

"I've never picnicked with your brother," Sarah said as she walked arm-in-arm with Lily. Gabriel, one arm filled with little Gabe and the other carrying the small basket—a footman had been dispatched with the main meal in the wooden crate a few minutes earlier—followed behind, his attention squarely on the gently swaying hips of his countess.

"Which implies you picnicked with someone before me," Gabriel said, a frown forming as he reluctantly tore his gaze from Sarah's bottom.

Sarah turned her head to regard her husband. "I've only ever picnicked with other women," she said, realizing that to admit to anything else would only put Gabriel in a sour mood for a few hours. "Whilst I was at the Spread Eagle. Once the beds were made and the public room was cleaned after luncheon." She turned her attention back to Lily. "I must admit, I do not miss all the cleaning and the bed making and pounding carpets and the complaints," she claimed with a sigh.

"Complaints?" Lily repeated. "I cannot imagine anyone would complain about the accommodations at the Spread Eagle."

Sarah gave her a quelling glance and then turned to look back at her husband. "Your brother did," she replied, a teasing grin belying her statement.

"But, why?" Lily asked, turning to regard her brother with a frown.

Gabriel shook his head and hurried to walk abreast with the women. "The kidney pie was cold," he stated firmly. Before Lily could respond, he added, "This was before Sarah was managing the inn, of course, for it would have been piping hot had she been in charge back then."

Sarah gave her husband a wink. "But he wouldn't have said a word to me if he hadn't had a reason to complain," she whispered loudly enough for her husband to hear.

"Which is how I came to be acquainted with your sister-in-law," Gabriel continued, ignoring his wife's comment as he set the basket onto a large blanket that had been spread out near the bank of the pond.

Thinking the rest of their evening at the Spread Eagle should remain private—he had accompanied Sarah to her room and enjoyed a rather boisterous tumble and an interesting conversation that would set him on a collision course with his destiny in London—Gabriel changed the subject. "And now it's your turn, my sister. I wish to know all about Sir Tobias Fulton and his intentions toward you," he said. He lowered Gabe to the blanket and assisted both Sarah and Lily to sit down before settling himself.

"Sir Tobias Fulton?" Sarah repeated, her attention bobbing between her husband and Lily. "But I haven't read anything about a knight in the newspapers," she claimed.

Lily angled her head to one side as she opened the wooden crate and pulled out some of the food. "That's because he's a baronet," she said with a shrug.

In the middle of unwrapping the slices of ham, Sarah paused to stare at her sister-in-law for a long moment. "Oh," she whispered. She sat back and tried to remember what she had read of baronets in deBrett's. "A commoner, then," she murmured, wondering if Gabriel had ever met the man. Or if he had heard of him. She was oblivious as little Gabe helped himself to a slice of ham and a piece of the cheese Lily had offered him.

"He is," Lily agreed. "And, a bit odd."

Intrigued, Sarah leaned on one arm and regarded her sister-in-law. "Odd, hmm? Then do tell us all about him," she encouraged.

Lily was more than happy to oblige.

CHAPTER 23

A BARONET IN THE PARK

On a day such as this, when the sun was barely over the horizon and the fog hadn't yet lifted, Sir Tobias Fulton, would normally be asleep in the only bedchamber in his bachelor's quarters in Golden Square.

Today was not a normal day. But then, neither were most of the days of the past month.

As a relative newcomer to London, Tobias was still trying to set a routine, one that would accommodate his new responsibilities as a baronet as well as his continuing work in the field of botany.

He had awakened in the bed of his mistress, a one Madeline Pendleton, who had recently come under his employ at the urging of his new friend, Alistair Comber.

"You're almost an aristocrat," the son of an earl chided him. In reality, he was a commoner with a hereditary title, but Tobias was not about to argue with Alistair. "And if you're not looking to marry,"—and he was not, at least, not yet—"Then it's best you hire yourself a mistress or risk contracting some disease from a London lightskirt."

When Tobias inquired as to just how Alistair knew about Madeline and her skills in bed, Alistair claimed he didn't have personal experience with the woman but knew of her from a fellow member of Boodle's, the men's club. "The man recently married and has cut his ties with the woman," he explained as he pointed to a horse he thought would be perfect for Tobias.

The two were at Tattersall's, and the next auction was about to begin when Tobias agreed to seek out the mistress—and bid on the horse.

An introduction was arranged, a contract was drawn up, and within the following week, relative newcomer Tobias found himself with a mistress, a horse, and a townhouse he could almost call a second home. Almost, because Miss Pendleton explained that he wasn't to spend the entire night there. Despite the fact that she expected to sleep until at least noon, she expected him to be out of her bed before dawn.

Having been taught by his mother to never argue with a woman—"You'll never win, no matter what you say," she had warned with a finger pointed into his chest—Tobias knew to simply take his mistress at her word.

Tobias dressed himself as he had done for all his days as an adult (and most of those of his childhood). He hadn't the benefit of a valet because, well, he didn't need one.

His mother, well-versed in the ways of the aristocracy (she was the daughter of a viscount), saw to it he was tutored, educated at Eton and Cambridge, and introduced to several members of the Royal Society. He could copy the mode of dress of any and all he met.

When he was ready take his leave of his mistress, Tobias leaned over the bed, bussed her on the cheek, and bade her farewell.

"Good day," she murmured, never opening her eyes.

Sighing, Tobias let himself out of the townhouse and was about to make his way back to Golden Square when he thought instead to visit Hyde Park. At this time of the morning, surely no one would be about, and if he found some plant to study, he wouldn't have to be concerned about being seen plucking it from the ground.

A few wisps of fog circled his legs, and the lawns were still wet with dew as he made his way along a crushed granite path, his gaze aimed at the ground just ahead of him as his umbrella swayed with each step he took. With so much to study, so much to see, it was no wonder he was entirely unaware he wasn't alone in his perusal of the park's plant life.

That is, until he collided with the only other person who seemed to be in Hyde Park at the time.

"Oh!" she managed to get out before taking a step back to regain her balance.

"Damnation!" came out of his mouth before he had a chance to censor his response, and not just because he had run into a woman walking along a path perpendicular to his own. He had just spotted a rather rare flower—he was quite sure it was a pasque flower—nestled in a patch of lawn.

"Pardon me," the woman managed to get out, one kid gloved hand moving to her bosom, a reticule dangling from the wrist. "Are you unhurt?"

Tobias blinked, his gaze taking in the petite blonde who looked quite shocked. *Goodness!* He had just about been knocked over by a woman so slight, he doubted she weighed more than five stones dripping wet.

The image had him blinking again when he found the thought rather titillating. She was quite pretty with her wide-open cornflower blue eyes and a halo of curls apparent, despite the fashionable poke bonnet adorned with a spray of bright fabric flowers that nearly hid her entirely from view. Tobias was quite sure the flowers were intended to depict roses, but the shapes of the petals weren't quite round enough, nor did they curl over at their tops in quite the right shape of curve.

He had to blink again when he realized he was trying to reconcile his knowledge of roses with fabric reproductions that had never been intended to appear authentic. At least some attempt had been made at realism, though. He was fairly certain the petals were made from red velvet.

Redirecting his gaze, he noticed the girl's pelisse was probably of the latest fashion as well, although Tobias had been in London such a short time, he didn't yet know such things with any certainty. But the blue superfine was fitted to her figure so well, he rather doubted it mattered if it was from last week or the last century.

She looked stunning wearing it.

Perhaps it was because he had been pressed against a similar figure less than an hour ago, or perhaps because he wished he still were, Tobias felt his loins stir in response to the thought of her, unclothed and tucked into his bed at his Golden Square townhouse.

All thoughts of the pasque flower directly at his feet were forgotten as he stared at her.

What had she asked?

"I am unharmed," he managed to get out, giving his head a brief shake. "And you?"

*L*ily Harkins took a steadying breath, sure the handsome man had been studying the cut, quality and design of her pelisse to determine if it was of the latest fashion. Perhaps he was a tailor out for an early morning stroll. Either that, or he had been undressing her with is eyes to determine if she might make for a pleasant early morning tumble.

Either way, she was decidedly uncomfortable in his presence. "I am unharmed, as well," she said with a curt nod, her gaze taking in his close-cropped hair, finely tailored top coat, Nankeen breeches, and Hessians. He had to be a tailor, she sorted, *or an aristocrat.* But given aristocrats were rarely out of bed this early in the morning, she decided he was a tailor.

She was about to step around the man and continue on her stroll, rather sorry she wouldn't be able to take a closer look at the purple flower she had come to see.

Just yesterday, she had spotted the furry leaves and tiny blossoms amidst the expanse of lawn. Stopping a moment, she had bent to take a closer look, nearly plucking the bloom before deciding instead to leave it be. Now she was worried the poor plant would be trampled. The tailor was about to step on it!

"Excuse me, but could you...?" she reached out and tugged on the man's coat sleeve in an effort to make him take a step forward. "Could you please not step on that beautiful flower?" she pleaded, her attention on how close his boot was to the dark, velvety leaves surrounding the purple flowers.

"Oh!" Tobias managed to get out before he dutifully stutter-stepped away from the pasque flower. "I nearly forgot what I'd been looking at when you ran into me," he claimed as he turned to look down at the plant.

Lily blinked. Rather incensed he would think she was the one who had collided with him instead of the other way around, she managed a, "Well!" before she turned on her heel and made to walk in the opposite direction. She could return to Fitzsimmons Manor by way of a different path. There was no need to spend any more time in the presence of such an inconsiderate tailor.

"I didn't mean to make it sound as if *you* were the one who was at fault," Tobias replied, one of his gloved hands hitting his forehead. "It was entirely my fault for not paying attention to my surroundings. I'm dull like that," he said and then rolled his eyes. Did he have to admit it to a perfect stranger? A beautiful one, at that?

Lily turned around and regarded the man, rather amused at his claim. *I nearly forgot what I was looking at...* "So, you noticed the flower, too?" she half-asked. "I saw it yesterday and thought to come see it again today," she added as she moved toward the man. She put out her right hand. "Lily Harkins," she said, deciding not to add the 'Lady' in front of her name.

Tobias stared at her gloved hand a moment, as if he wasn't quite sure what to do with it. He finally reached for it and brought it to his lips, surprising Lily. "I apologize. Sir Tobias Fulton," he said before brushing his lips over her knuckles. "I'm rather new at all the pleasantries. And new in town, as well," he said, bowing his head before straightening.

Lily took back her hand, surprised by the man's introduction. "Are you a knight, then?" she asked, her head canted to one side.

"Baronet," he replied with another nod.

"Oh," Lily managed to say before nervousness had her

looking at the flower. *I had it half-right, I suppose.* She berated herself for guessing the man might be a tailor. "What kind do you suppose it is?" she asked as she indicated the bloom.

Tobias glanced about, apparently nervous. Had she been sent to tease him? Or to run into him just as he discovered a rare bloom in the grass? "Pasque flower, I believe," he said with some authority. "Or rather, I'm quite sure. It's rather rare here, but not unheard of."

Lily's eyes widened. Not ever hearing of such a flower, she was curious. "How is it you—?"

"Botany," he interrupted with a nod. "My avocation, I suppose one could say," he added, his head bobbing side to side.

Lily was reminded of Lady Pettigrew and how she tended to bob her head from side to side when she was faced with making a difficult decision. Or any decision, for that matter.

"Oh," Lily finally replied, remembering the term 'botany' had been used by Lady Samantha to describe the science of plants. Lady Evangeline Sommers' brother was a well-known explorer and seemed rather well-versed in all the natural sciences. She wondered then if Lord Everly could be considered a botanist. Or perhaps he was a naturalist.

She frowned, wondering if she dare ask Sir Tobias Fulton for an explanation when she remembered the poor plant.

"You won't pluck it from the ground and dissect it, I hope?" she asked with some alarm. The purple flower looked almost like a miniature tulip. To think, she had almost picked it the day before! Thank goodness she had decided to leave it, thinking perhaps more blooms would join the single flower in a few days, and there would be a patch of purple in this part of the park.

"Heavens, no!" he replied in equal alarm. "Although I must admit to the temptation to at least dig it out of the ground and transplant it to a more hospitable setting."

Although she was heartened to learn he wouldn't destroy the plant, she wasn't particularly pleased to hear the alternative, either. "Well, you must do what you must, I suppose," she said with a nod and made to take her leave of the man.

"Where is your maid... or chaperone?" Tobias asked as he tore his eyes from the pasque flower to take a quick look around where they stood. "Or companion?" he added, thinking perhaps he had underestimated her age.

Lily gave a small shake of her head. "I... I left without one," she finally answered, the comment leaving her lips slightly parted.

"Do you think that was wise?" Tobias asked, one eyebrow arching in judgement. *Good God! The woman is alone in Hyde Park at six-thirty in the morning!* Didn't she know she could be accosted by footpads or, worse, a ruffian hell-bent on taking advantage of just such a chit?

Although her eyes widened, the comely blonde lifted her head and angled it just a bit, a move that made her seem defiant. "Probably not. I just wanted to take a walk," she explained, lifting her head another fraction. "And see the flower, before the rest of the household was about." She lowered her head, her shoulders following suit. "Actually, I wished to be alone is all," she murmured then, her eyes downcast.

Tobias dared another look around, realizing this part of the park was rather open. There wasn't a suitable hiding place nearby where an unscrupulous man could lay in wait for one such as her.

At hearing her last words, he found he felt a bit sorry for her. Perhaps she was surrounded by people all the time and considered this time in the park a refuge. Or perhaps she had experienced a tragic event and wished to mourn or... well she wasn't exactly dressed for mourning. A pale yellow sprigged muslin gown showed below her blue pelisse, and her yellow poke bonnet allowed her gorgeous golden blonde hair to glow in the early morning sunlight.

Tobias glanced about, still wondering if perhaps one of his friends from Cambridge had arranged with the young lady to play a prank on him. Perhaps they had planted the flower. But there was no one about given this part of the park was generally abandoned at this time of the morning. The morning fog had barely lifted. The dew drops still clung to the tops of the blades of grass.

And then he wondered if perhaps he was still abed and dreaming the entire scenario.

Of course, that had to be it!

For when could such a ridiculous situation arise unless it was in his imagination? Probably brought to life by an especially long night of drinking and debauchery?

This last thought had him frowning as it wasn't really in his nature to practice such ungentlemanly pursuits. He had a mistress, after all. One he rather liked, even if she didn't allow him more than a peck on the cheek before he took comfort in her arms and in her bed. Which was a shame, really, given Madeline had such lush, kissable lips.

Come to think of it, the young lady who stood before him had such lips. They were moist, plump and the color of a pale strawberry.

I am dreaming, he decided, his frown slowing changing to a smile. *Which means I can kiss the chit as much as I'd like.*

*L*ily stared up at the baronet, rather surprised at just how far up she had to look. Although she was on the petite side, she found most men not much taller than she. This particular man was rather pleasant in appearance. Indeed, he was rather handsome despite his very short hair and angular features. And, at the moment, his eyes, no longer on the purple flower near his foot, were regarding her with a rather dreamy expression.

And then, quite suddenly, his lips came down onto hers.

CHAPTER 24

A KISS INTERRUPTED

"*H*e kissed you? Right there in the park?"

Lily blinked as she was suddenly pulled out of her story. Gabriel was staring at her, his blue eyes round. "I wouldn't call it a kiss," she replied. "A mere peck, actually."

Sarah pulled a napkin up to her lips and attempted to suppress a giggle, which had her husband glaring at her. "Sarah! My sister has just informed me she was kissed by a baronet!"

Shaking her head, Lily said, "Barely a baronet. He had only recently inherited his title," she reminded him.

"Then, what did you do? Scream, I hope," Gabriel countered, his knife stabbing a slice of cold beef in what appeared would be the manner in which he would skewer Sir Tobias Fulton should he find himself in the man's company.

Lily sighed. "Allow me to continue my tale, and I'll tell you," she replied.

Gabriel's frown deepened. "Proceed," he finally said, obviously not happy with the afternoon's story.

*L*ily should have taken a step back. Should have placed her hands on the man's shoulders and given him a hard push. However, had she done the first, the baronet's lips would have ended up in the middle of her bodice—a far more scandalous position for them to land than on her lips—and had she done the second, the man would have ended up taking a step back and crushing the pasque flower in the process.

Far better to just allow the peck and be done with it, for surely the baronet would realize his impropriety, lift his head, and apologize profusely.

Lily was counting on it.

However, he did not.

Although the kiss was short and rather pleasant—the baronet wore a sandalwood cologne, and his lips were firm and smooth and well suited to hers—the man seemed to act as if he were in a trance. As if he thought himself still abed and dreaming.

Dreaming of her.

Which suddenly had Lily's insides all aflutter. *Goodness! Did men often sleepwalk in the park in the mornings?*

Curious, she decided to ask him. "Do you often sleepwalk in the park?"

*S*ir Tobias Fulton was contemplating a second kiss—the first was far too short but really rather pleasant—when the young woman's question brought him up short. "I beg your pardon?" he asked, his eyes blinking as if he had to bring them into focus.

Lily angled her head to one side. "I asked if you often sleep-walk in the park, which can be the only explanation for why you would do what you just did, Sir Tobias."

The baronet stared at her as his eyebrows furrowed. *How did she know I was dreaming? Was she dreaming, too?* Dreaming of him at the very same time as he was dreaming of her?

Faith!

"I am merely dreaming, my lady, as are you," he answered, quite proud of his powers of deduction. "I am still abed with my arms around my mistress," he added with a nod.

· · ·

*A*mused by the man's response—did he think she was a dunderhead?—Lily gave a nod. "Actually, I am wide awake. You, sir, are the one dreaming," she countered, an eyebrow arching with her accusation. "And if you believe you have your arms around your mistress..." Lily took a look around, relieved to see there were no mistresses—or anyone else, for that matter—in the park, "Then *where*, pray tell, is she?" Lily asked, rather proud of her rejoinder.

Sir Tobias Fulton did his own survey of the park, practically turning around in a circle before he suddenly swallowed, hard. "Still in her bed," he answered carefully. A rain drop fell on his nose, and his eyes crossed to bring it into focus before it dripped off the end of it.

Noticing the impending storm—gray clouds were moving swiftly from the west—Lily realized she needed to be on her way. "You should join her there, sir. I, on the other hand, am going to head for home," she said as she gave him a quick curtsy and headed off toward Park Lane.

Tobias was about to allow the young lady take her leave, but he found he rather liked the young lady. She had the ability to deduce. She was pleasant to gaze upon, and she had good taste in plants. And she obviously had an excellent sense of humor. "I'll escort you," he called out, hurrying after her. He managed to reopen his umbrella, holding it out to cover her more than himself.

"Is it raining in your dream?" Lily asked once they had settled into a hurried gait across the lawn.

"No, actually, I don't allow inclement weather in my dreams, my lady," he answered, his voice sounding almost cross.

Lily gave him a sideways glance, catching the quirk of his lips just before he hid it. "Just your mistress, then," she teased, deciding she rather liked the odd baronet. He had good taste in plants. He had a sense of humor. And he had an umbrella.

Sir Tobias nearly tripped on an exposed tree root. "Apparently not," he countered. This time, he didn't try to hide his amusement. "Or she would be here, complaining, no doubt."

Curious about mistresses, Lily asked, "Are they allowed to? Complain, I mean?"

Tobias shrugged. "I really don't wot. Madeline is my first," he replied, apparently unaware he was discussing mistresses with a lady of quality.

"Well, she must have come recommended by someone," Lily guessed. How else did men find their mistresses? It wasn't as if there was a mistress shop in Oxford Street. But if there were such a shop as a mistress shop, it would probably be in St. James Street, she considered, right next door to White's.

"She came highly recommended," Tobias agreed. "My friend, Alistair, encouraged me to employ her at the same time he found me a horse..."

The baronet stopped in his tracks, suddenly aware his companion had stopped walking several steps ago. He spun around to find her staring at him. "What is it?" he asked. "And don't tell me it's time to wake up. I'm having one of the best mornings—"

"Alistair?" Lily had repeated, her eyes wide. "Alistair Comber?" she added, her head feeling a bit light and her stomach, well, truth be told, she was starving, so it didn't feel as heavy as it should have just then.

The baronet frowned, apparently realizing Lily knew his friend. Which meant she could be his... "Are you his wife?" he asked. "Because, if you are, I can assure you, Mr. Comber has never availed himself of Madeline's charms," he quickly stated, moving to hold the umbrella over Lily's head. "He merely recommended her because a friend of his had employed her, but the friend recently married, which—"

"Which meant Madeline was out of a position unless she landed a new protector," Lily finished, a sense of relief washing through her.

"Yes, exactly!" Tobias agreed, pleased with her perceptiveness.

Lily allowed a sigh of relief. Alistair Comber was married to Lady Samantha's best friend, Julia Harrington. Despite his background as an officer in the British Army and his frequent trips to Tattersall's to appraise the horseflesh, Alistair always seemed to hold his wife in high regard. Lily couldn't imagine the man keeping a mistress on the side. Julia wouldn't have allowed it!

Relieved there was a reasonable explanation for Alistair's involvement with Tobias' mistress, Lily resumed the trek toward Fitzsimmons Manor.

The two walked along in companionable silence until they reached the crushed granite path leading to Park Lane. "Tell me, Miss Harkins. Is your opinion of me lessened because you know I employ a mistress?" Tobias asked in a low voice.

Surprised by the question, Lily gave it some thought before she countered with, "The more important question, Sir Tobias, is your opinion of yourself lessened because you have hired Madeline?"

She wondered how the baronet would reply. He had spent the entire morning sleepwalking in Hyde Park. Who knew if he really employed a mistress or if he merely dreamed he did?

Frowning at her response—she had deftly dodged his question—Tobias sighed. "I am led to believe employing a mistress is a must for an aristocrat, my lady."

"But you're not," Lily replied. "An aristocrat, that is," she clarified. Baronets were commoners who simply inherited their titles.

Tobias took in a deep breath and let it out in a whoosh. "True." He paused a moment. "Truth be told, I would probably fair better with a wife, given she probably wouldn't cost me so much, and she would probably allow me to bed her more often than does Madeline."

Lily was about to ask how much he paid Madeline for her services, but the baronet volunteered the information.

"You see, I'm required to provide a townhouse as well as pay her modiste bills and give her pin money every week to spend as she sees fit."

Stunned at this bit of news, Lily had to use every bit of facial control she possessed not to boggle at the man's words. "And I suppose you're not allowed to live at the townhouse," she guessed.

"I'm not even allowed to spend the entire night there," he agreed. "Which is why you ran into me here in the park. I just left her house—"

"*Your* house," Lily corrected him.

Tobias stopped. Lily had gone several more steps before she realized the top of her bonnet was becoming drenched. She hurried back to stand under the umbrella. "What is it, sir?" she asked gently, seeing his look of consternation.

"You are right, of course. It is *my* house. I should be the one to set the rules. I should be the one to say if I can spend the entire night there."

"Was there a contract? Terms you had to meet?" Lily interrupted.

Tobias' face fell. "There is, of course," he managed to get out, deciding Madeline had probably covered all the contingencies. She had been a mistress for several years. By now she knew every clause that needed to be included in such a contract. Tobias had been so eager to sign, he simply did so without having his solicitor look over the agreement.

Lily shrugged. "So, you'll know better for the next one," she offered, not sure what else to say.

Tobias shook his head. "Oh, no, milady," he replied quickly. "There won't be another. I'll take a wife before I take another mistress," he claimed.

Her eye's widening with his assertive response, Lily turned her attention on him. "Do you have a lady in mind then?" she asked, thinking he probably had his eye on a bluestocking. A bluestocking would suit him well, she thought, given his avocation.

"Yes. Yes, I do," Tobias replied with a nod. "*You*, my lady. I should like you to be my wife."

Rather glad they had just made it to the front door of Fitzsimmons Manor, Lily angled her head and regarded the baronet for a moment, wondering if perhaps the man was teasing. Or if perhaps he was still sleepwalking. But no, his expression was anything but humorous. Indeed, he looked as if he had eaten a sour lemon. "Then I look forward to meeting you in the park again, Sir Tobias. It's so very good to have met you." With that, Lily curtsied and hurried through the front door.

Her back against the vestibule wall, her eyes closed as if doing so would help her to forget the baronet's parting words, Lily sighed and slowly slid down the wall.

"*Y*ou are not marrying that man."

Lily looked up from her plate, startled at the words. Her brother hadn't been the one to say them, but rather his wife.

Sarah repeated her edict. "You are *not* marrying that man."

Lily nodded and shook her head all at the same time. *How did one agree to a negative?* "I hadn't thought I would," she agreed. She dared a glanced in the direction of her brother. Both of his hands were against the sides of his face, scrubbing his cheeks. Low moaning sounds were emanating from him, which had her thinking he might be suffering from indigestion.

Or perhaps he was choking!

She was about to crawl over to him, to stand behind him and pound him on his back until he coughed up whatever had him choking, but Gabriel suddenly inhaled deeply. "What is this fascination you women have with a man's *mistress?*" he asked, keeping his voice low.

Little Gabe had fallen asleep, his chubby legs tucked beneath him so his bottom was up while his face rested on the blanket.

Lily stared at her brother for a long time, rather stunned by his question. She straightened out the blanket, giving Sarah a glance before she said, "There are some who say that lords love their mistresses and only marry so they might have legitimate heirs."

Gabriel gave a slight nod. "For some, that is true," he agreed. It would have been for him if Lady Elizabeth hadn't spurned him.

"It would seem to me, then, that to be a mistress might be a far better fate than being the wife of an aristocrat," Lily continued, her voice nearly a whisper. "If one wants to be loved, I mean," she added.

Her brother shook his head, unable to come up with a suitable response. When he glanced over at Sarah, he found her staring at Lily.

"Or you can simply marry for love," Sarah said quietly. "Like I did."

Lily stared back at her sister-in-law, well aware her brother was doing the same. At any moment, he would move from his place at the edge of the blanket and plant a well-deserved kiss on his wife's lips, apologize for his impropriety, and then take his leave of the ladies, claiming the need for a glass of port and a cheroot. Lily was sure of it. So sure, in fact, she held Sarah's gaze a moment longer and then allowed a brilliant smile.

As if on queue, Gabriel stood up and moved to where Sarah lounged. Instead of simply leaning over to kiss her, however, he placed his hands beneath her arms and pulled her up to face him.

Sarah let out a sound of surprise before Gabriel had her pulled against the front of his body, his lips taking hers in what appeared to be the most romantic kiss Lily had ever imagined.

She was sure her face was bright pink. She should look away, and yet she couldn't. She dared a quick glance at the only other adult in the area—the single footman who was still sitting on the wooden crate—noting his attention was clearly directed in a different direction. And little Gabe was no help. He was still sound asleep!

She should look away. She should pretend she wasn't seeing such a blatant display of affection. She should be thinking of what it would be like to be kissed like that by one of her suitors. A flutterby seemed to take up residence inside her stomach.

But even as she tried to imagine being kissed like that by the baron or the earl or the baronet or the...

Her eyes closed a moment.

The rake.

She hadn't even told that story yet, but the thought of him kissing her had her entire body shivering.

She was about to contemplate how she might *initiate* a kiss with a suitor when she was suddenly aware of Gabriel lifting Sarah into his arms and carrying her off of the blanket and up to the folly. The two seemed oblivious to her. And to the footman who seemed to have a great deal of difficulty in pretending to ignore their move to the folly since he was sitting right next to it.

Well. She supposed she could make her way to her brother's study and simply help herself to a glass of port and a cheroot. Or she could stay where she was and continue to think about being kissed.

And about kissing someone.

William, she thought with a sigh.

In the end, she scooped up little Gabe and made her way back to the house. She allowed a smile when she realized the footman was doing his best to quickly pick up the picnic items and remove himself from earshot of the folly.

CHAPTER 25

PARLOR APOLOGIES

"I apologize for my public display of affection yesterday," Gabriel murmured, his fingers laced together as he rested his elbows on his knees. "It was—"

"Rather romantic, I thought," Lily interrupted him, a grin splitting her face. "And certainly not unexpected given what Sarah said to me," she added. She blushed anyway, reminded of how happy she had felt to see her brother show his love for his countess.

Would any man ever be so moved as to sweep her into his arms and kiss her senseless in the middle of the day? Or place gentle kisses upon her lips next to a pond? Or in front of a footman, no less?

Gabriel shook his head. "Still, it was hardly appropriate for you to have seen—"

"I once watched a fellow maid being tumbled when she was out-of-doors," Lily claimed with an exaggerated sigh, her voice rather calm for the words she was saying. "I have seen a man's naked bottom. I paid witness to a lady being tupped as she was bent over the edge of a library table in the middle of a *musicale* at Lady Torrington's home. I hardly think kissing your wife in broad daylight is *scandalous*."

Rolling his eyes, Gabriel sighed. "I forget sometimes that

you haven't been sheltered from the vices in London as most of the ladies in the *ton* are," he replied, his brows furrowing. "I wish I would have known about you sooner. Found you sooner. Perhaps I could have protected you from—"

"I still would have seen—and heard—Lady Fitzwilliam in the library," she countered. She was about to imitate the sounds the woman had made during her encounter with a rather randy—and much younger—viscount, but decided she had better not. It was bad enough her brother felt pity for her.

Gabriel rolled his eyes again, not about to admit that two years before, he might have been the randy man with Lady Fitzwilliam. How very different lovemaking was with Sarah compared to when he had employed mistresses!

"Anyway, I appreciate you seeing to Gabe whilst we were otherwise engaged. I take it he gave you no trouble?" he asked, thinking his son seemed rather comfortable in the presence of his aunt.

Lily's smile widened. "He was sound asleep," she replied. "And quite the little gentleman when he awoke." After a pause, she asked, "When he's grown up, do you think he'll behave like a spoiled aristocrat?"

Gabriel let out a snort. "Hardly," he replied with a shake of his head. "Sarah won't allow it to happen."

Sighing, Lily leaned back and regarded her brother for a long time. He was so unlike what she had expected when he had first appeared at Fitzsimmons Manor, claiming he wished to recognize her as his sister. Although he could be arrogant and his temper flared up on occasion, he was really a rather pleasant fellow. And not at all like the stories that she occasionally overheard during tea time in Lady Torrington's parlor.

Sarah entered the parlor and gave the two a suspicious glance. "Something tells me I've missed an important conversation."

Lily shook her head. "Hardly," she said, saying it exactly as her brother had only moments before. "We've only talked of scandalous behavior and your son," she said with a teasing grin.

Her eyes widening in alarm, Sarah glanced over at Gabriel. "He's only two! What has he gone and done now?"

Lily and Gabriel chuckled until Sarah relaxed and finally took the chair across from her husband. "I've ordered the tea cart, and the nurse will be bringing little Gabe down to join us," she said. "So, before she gets here, what kind of scandalous behavior are you discussing?"

Gabriel leaned forward and lowered his voice. "That of my sister's suitors, one in particular," he said, angling his head toward Lily.

Lily gasped. "We were not!" she countered, giving her head a shake.

"But we will. I insist you tell me all about your time with your fourth suitor."

Allowing a sigh, Lily nodded. "At dinner then," she agreed, secretly relieved she didn't have to tell the two about the Marquess of Reading right then and there. The three hours until dinner would give her enough time to come up with a story that fit the facts but allowed her out of what she was quite sure would be a forced marriage.

Later that night

Several footmen had just departed the dining room when Gabriel asked Lily about Lord Reading.

"Reading?" Sarah repeated, her attention bobbing between her husband and Lily. "But I haven't read anything about a man named 'Reading' in the gossip sheets," she claimed.

Lily pretended to study her soup. Steam was curling into ribbons above the bowl, forming a rather interesting pattern. When she used her spoon to stir the liquid, the steam followed and swirled before disappearing. "No, but you've probably heard of the Rake of Reading," she said. At seeing Sarah's sudden look of recognition—and horror—she added, "They are one and the same."

Sarah seemed to turn pale before her eyes. "Oh, my God," she whispered, swallowing before she dared a glance at her husband. "Is there a duel in your future?" she asked, as she displayed an expression of concern.

Blinking at his wife's fright, Gabriel straightened in his carver. "I suppose we're about to find out," he replied, nodding to his sister.

Recognizing her cue for what it was, Lily took a deep breath and began her tale of her time with the Rake of Reading.

CHAPTER 26

THE RAKE OF READING

April 1817
A light rain fell as Randall Roderick, Marquess of Reading, made his way on horseback to Lord Weatherstone's residence in Park Lane. Although he could have made the trip from his mansion in Cavendish Square in a well-sprung coach or a high-perch phaeton, he preferred the company of his horse, Zeus. The black bay was huge—sixteen hands tall—and never failed to negotiate the busy streets of London with anything but a proud gait and a prouder countenance.

A groom ran up to take the horse from Reading as he dismounted. The marquess tossed the boy a crown. "See to it he gets some oats," he ordered as he gave the reins to the surprised groom.

"Aye, guv'nor," the boy replied with a nod, his eyes huge when he realized the denomination of the coin.

Although he could have protested being put into the care of a boy half the size of his master, Zeus fell into step behind the groom, apparently aware a bucket of oats was in his future.

Reading watched the two as they made their way to the mews behind the house, never taking his eyes off his horse until it disappeared into the stables.

Once he was sure the bay wouldn't bolt, Reading made his way to the brightly lit double-doors of the Weatherstone mansion. He grinned as he considered what the evening might hold.

The Weatherstone gardens were renown for the number of marriage proposals that had taken place among their rose bushes, the number of first kisses that had been exchanged behind the hedgerows, the illicit activities that even Reading himself had enjoyed amidst the flowers that surrounded the fountain.

The statue of Cupid had probably paid witness to the creation of half of a generation of the *ton* given its location next to a rather roomy bench that had served more than its intended purpose a number of times.

Reading had to resist smiling at the thought of how quickly last year's lover, the widow Barbara Fulton, had lifted her skirts at his mere cock of an eyebrow, his cock following suit only a moment later.

Too bad she had moved to Bath the following week.

Reading wondered who he might impale on this festive night. Although his hair was graying at the temples and he had overheard someone at Boodles claim he was developing a second chin, Randall Roderick was quite sure his reputation as the Rake of Reading, for good or bad, was intact. For this evening, he rather wished it weren't, for this was the night he needed to seriously pursue a wife.

The Marquess of Reading was in need of an heir.

A legitimate heir.

His four sons were all bastards. With his financial help, however, all were being raised in the very best households and would attend Eton and Oxford when they were old enough. Well, all except for Reginald. The youngest was showing an unnatural affinity for the studies offered at Cambridge. Reading resisted the urge to shiver at the thought.

"My lord," the butler greeted him with a bow as Reading removed his cape in a flourish and deposited it across the butler's waiting arms.

Having been at Weatherstone's balls for well over ten years, Reading knew exactly where to go for a glass of brandy and a balcony view of the assembled peerage. As he made his way to his destination, he kept his eyes peeled for possible contenders for the role of his marchioness.

His search didn't go unnoticed.

Reading took a sip from the crystal balloon as he surveyed the ballroom below, allowing a smile when he realized Lord Weatherstone had served him his very best brandy.

"This is the year, isn't it?" the ancient man asked as he poured the smoky elixir.

Reading frowned. "The year?" he repeated.

Lord Weatherstone angled his head, his snowy white hair forming a halo around his wrinkled face. "The year you need to take a wife," he clarified, one bushy eyebrow arched on his forehead. "Lucky for you there's a fresh batch of beauties in the ballroom." His attention was momentarily diverted by his wife, who was waving at him to join her.

The marquess stared at the earl for a moment, hiding his annoyance. "Indeed," was all he could think to say. Did others know he was on the lookout for a wife tonight? Did everyone think this was the year he had to find a wife? The year he had to marry and sire a legitimate heir?

Apparently so, for no fewer than three other peers made similar comments to him as he made his way up the stairs to the mezzanine level overlooking the ballroom.

Perhaps he could find a candidate from above. Simply stare down onto the colorful assemblage, close his eyes, and point down. Then, when he opened his eyes, whomever he was pointing at would receive his proposal.

After three tries, however, Reading was at a loss. Everyone he had pointed to was either a man, a married woman or a servant.

Perhaps he needed to take a different approach. He glanced down and considered the options.

Colors were the key, of course. Any woman wearing a brightly colored gown was either married or widowed or willing. Those in white were not. At least, most of those in white would not be willing to join him in the famed gardens.

Occasionally, one of two would make his acquaintance so they might give up their virtue—willingly, he hoped, for he claimed never to have taken a virgin against her will. Unfortunately, they usually did so in an attempt to gain a proposal—and a position as his marchioness.

He often wondered if it was because of his reputation—he was the Rake of Reading, after all—or because they found him handsome and charming and irresistible.

He rather hoped it was the latter, especially this year.

As he gazed at the whirling gowns below, he was struck by the sight of one blonde chit with curly hair. Although she wore a glittering band around her forehead—the gemstones were no doubt paste—

"*P*aste?" Gabriel interrupted suddenly, his fork clanking onto the fine porcelain plate on which his dinner was artfully arranged. "They are not *paste!*" he exclaimed, nearly spilling his glass of wine.

Sarah was quick to reach over and lay a hand on her husband's sleeve. She had moved to a chair across from Lily instead of at the opposite end of the table from Gabriel, making it possible for her to intervene should he get upset.

And perhaps play footsie with him.

"Darling, Lily may not have been referring to herself just then," she said with a soft voice, the soothing tone helping to calm the irate earl.

"Oh, but I was describing me," Lily countered with a nod, a bit annoyed her brother had interrupted her just as she was about to get to the good part of the story. "But I wasn't wearing the Trenton diamond headband that night," she added, understanding why her brother had put voice to his objection. "I had Lord Chamberlain put that particular piece in his safe. Truth be told, it makes me rather nervous to wear it. I'm always afraid someone will relieve me of it, or that one of the diamonds might pop off in the middle of a dance and land in someone's champagne glass, or that all of them will suddenly drop off in the oppressive heat of the ballroom."

Her face screwed up.

"Which I suppose is how they came up with the term, 'dripping with diamonds'," Lily said then, her blue eyes widening with her realization.

Gabriel blinked. Then blinked again as he imagined the scenarios his sister described. "Truly?" he replied, his brows furrowing.

"Truly," Lily agreed, finally understanding her brother's concern. "I know you meant well by entrusting me with it, but it's a bit more than my head can handle."

Gabriel gave a glance at his wife and the sapphire bracelet she wore, remembering how hard it had been to convince her to wear it every day.

Her gaze followed his. "Give her time, Gabriel. She's not yet used to being the sister of a rich man," she murmured. "And that diamond headband *is* probably far too large for her head. It certainly was for mine."

Gabriel finally nodded before kissing Sarah's hand. "So, my sister, do tell us what happened next," he encouraged. He gripped his fork and continued with his meal as Lily took up where she left off.

*T*he gel had done nothing to tame the unruly curls that surrounded her face. There didn't seem to be a single pin in her coiffure! *Why, what an unconventional lady she must be,* he thought as he felt a bit of excitement.

When her head suddenly lifted and her eyes met his, Reading gave a start.

She's gorgeous, he thought as he stared at her. The blonde quickly turned her gaze away though, as if she were searching the crowd for someone.

Leaving his brandy with a startled footman, Reading quickly took the steps down to the ballroom level, intent on finding the blonde.

. . .

"*D*id you notice him?" Sarah asked. "While he spied on you from above?" she added, thinking it was rather interesting Lily would know she was being watched.

Lily blinked, once again pulled out of her storytelling too soon. "Well, I was aware of someone staring at me. The hairs on the back of my neck were standing up, but I found out later that was because Lord Brougham was breathing on me. The ball was a crush, you see. Lady Weatherstone had to be pleased." She stopped when she noticed her brother staring at her, a look of impatience apparent. "Oh. I didn't know Lord Reading was staring directly at *me*, at first, of course. But I pretended to look elsewhere. And then I realized he had disappeared from the overlook."

Gabriel frowned, about to take a bite of his lobster. "Disappeared? What's that supposed to mean?" he asked in alarm, wondering if the rake had popped out of existence.

Sarah sighed. "He went on the prowl," the countess explained, placing a hand against her middle when she felt a bit queasy. Lily noticed her discomfort and motioned for the footman near the door to the kitchen.

"Would you remove that plate, please?" she whispered, pointing to the platter containing an entire fish with its head and tail still attached. "Perhaps you can serve it below stairs?" she suggested.

The footman gave a short bow, retrieved the platter from the table, and took his leave of the dining room just as Gabriel turned a quizzical stare onto his sister. "Was the fish bad?" he asked with some concern.

"The fish was rather delicious, actually," Lily replied, having helped herself to a large portion of it when it was first placed on the table. "But its odor, however, was offensive to her ladyship." She gave a nod in Sarah's direction, noting how the countess seemed most relieved to have the offending fish out of her sight even though she still looked a bit green.

"I didn't smell anything fishy about it," Gabriel countered, apparently upset the dish had been removed.

Sarah suddenly stood up and took her leave of the room, the back of one hand pressed against her mouth.

Lily sighed, loudly.

Having been caught off-guard by his wife's quick departure, Gabriel was barely out of his carver when Sarah disappeared through the door to the butler's pantry. He turned to stare at Lily. "What was that about?"

Rolling her eyes, Lily sighed again. "She cannot abide the odor of fish in her condition," she explained. "But she knows how much you like it, so she continues to include it on the dinner menus."

Gabriel blinked. "Her condition?" he repeated.

It was Lily's turn to blink. Hadn't Sarah told Gabriel she was expecting a baby? And if she hadn't, what was Lily to say now? "Uh, her... allergy... to... *cod*," she stammered, not quite sure what kind of fish had been so artfully displayed on the platter the footman had spirited away.

Gabriel understood almost immediately what Lily meant by her comment, but the fact that she hadn't come right out and say her sister-in-law was expecting a baby had Gabriel rather amused.

Does she think Sarah hasn't told me yet?

Even if she hadn't told him, he had noticed her rounding belly, noticed how her breasts were more full, her body softer and more willing. He would have to be a dunce not to recognize the signs of a woman who was eating too many cakes at tea time. "Why, she has never complained of such to me," he countered, deciding to have some fun at his sister's expense.

Lily paused in her effort to get a forkful of the offending fish to her lips. "I'm sure she doesn't wish to offend you, brother," she managed before stuffing the fish into her mouth. The thought of Sarah being sick in the butler's pantry had her suddenly a bit queasy. She placed a hand against her middle, wondering if she, too, should take her leave of the dining room.

Gabriel noticed the move on his sister's part, his first

thought was that she might feel sick. It had him wondering if she, too, was expecting a baby, which meant some rake—probably the Rake of Reading—had ruined her! But he hadn't noticed that she had eaten too make cakes at tea time. Indeed, if anything, Lily had thinned out some since her arrival at Trenton Manor. Perhaps the cakes at tea time didn't suit her. Perhaps her cravings were better satisfied by the fish she seemed to be eating with such urgency.

"When are you expecting to give birth?" he asked, deciding to put voice to his question while there were no footmen about.

Lily's eyes widened to the point that Gabriel thought they might pop out of her head.

His sister stood up and took her leave of the room, following the same path as Sarah had a moment ago. "Not for at least a year, my lord," she managed before she disappeared through the door to the butler's pantry.

Gabriel sat back down in his carver, stunned at his sister's sudden disappearance. *A year?* Why, that seemed an awfully long time for a pregnancy, he considered.

He was about to give the odd thought another go when Sarah reappeared in the doorway and calmly took her seat at the table. "I apologize for my sudden departure," she said with a sigh.

Gabriel shook his head. "If the fish doesn't suit you in your condition, please don't include it on the menu on my behalf," he said in a low voice. "I can live without it," he added, noting her expression of surprise.

"Are you sure? I don't wish to deny you what you like at dinner," Sarah said.

"Positive," he answered with a nod. "Now, you must tell me what kind of baby Lady Lily could be carrying that would require at least a year of gestation," he ordered, interlacing his fingers at the edge of the table.

Sarah blinked. And blinked again, thinking her husband was teasing her. But his expression was quite serious. "Baby?" she repeated, just as Lily reappeared in the room.

The young woman quietly returned to her seat and was

about to resume eating when she noticed both Sarah and Gabriel staring at her. "What?" she asked, her fork poised to stab a Brussels sprout.

"Sister, you have some explaining to do," Gabriel said with a pound of his fist on the table.

Confused by her brother's comment, Lily stared first at him and then at Sarah, who merely gave a shake of her head. "Well, Lord Reading didn't find me right away," she said, thinking her brother was waiting for her to continue her story about the Rake of Reading. "I went to the ladies' retiring room, thinking I could hide there until he had found some other chit to seduce," she explained.

Gabriel frowned. "You know about the marquess' reputation?" he asked, wondering how, if she knew, she still found herself with child. *Forewarned was supposed to be forearmed,* he thought.

Stunned by her brother's question, Lily stared at him for a moment. "Of course, I know," she responded. "Everyone in London knows of the Rake of Reading," she added. "So that is why I went to the retiring room. I thought to hide out for a fortnight. Or at least until Reading had secured a more willing woman," she said with a hint of humor in her voice.

Her brother's expression had her realizing he was in no mood for humor. She quickly sobered.

"And?" Gabriel prompted.

Lily sighed. "He was waiting outside the retiring room door when I finally took my leave."

Gabriel gasped. Sarah moaned. Lily allowed a shrug.

"What did you do?" Sarah asked in a whisper.

"I walked right past him and hooked my arm into that of Lord Bostwick's," she answered. "*Now,* may I continue the story?"

Gabriel stilled himself at hearing his sister had made her acquaintance with the man who had married the woman he might have married. "Is he the father?"

Lily frowned and blinked several times. "Father of what?" she countered, her head shaking as if she couldn't follow his line of reasoning.

"Are you... *enceinte?*" he finally asked outright.

Sarah's eyes widened as she turned them on Lily, wondering what she had missed when she was in the butler's pantry.

Shocked by her brother's question, Lily shook her head. "Of course not!" she insisted. "*Now* may I continue the story?"

Gabriel settled back in his carver and finally seemed to take a breath. "Please do," he replied with a hint of relief. "Please do".

"*M*ay I ask a favor, my lord?" Lily said, not turning to determine the identity of the man whose arm she had taken possession of when she hurried from the ladies' retiring room.

George Bennett-Jones, Viscount Bostwick, glanced back in the direction of his wife, one eyebrow arching up as if in apology. "Of course," he replied, thinking the young blonde woman was barely old enough to be in the Weatherstone's ballroom. "As long as it doesn't involve a tryst in the gardens," he added. "My wife rather adores me, and I should like to keep it that way."

Lily dared a glance to her right, realizing with a bit of relief that she had taken possession of George Bennett-Jones. "Perhaps a dance? Lord Reading seems intent on making me his next conquest."

The viscount nearly stopped in his tracks. He dared a glance behind him, pretending to survey the crowd before giving the gloved hand on his arm a pat. "Fear not, my lady. I shall save you from the Rake of Reading and see to it you have partners for every dance from now until the end of the ball."

Lily felt a bit of relief mixed with surprise. "Just the one dance should do," she replied. "I can take my leave right after that."

Bostwick angled his head. "Suit yourself," he said, bowing before her as they took their place in line for the quadrille. "By the way, I don't believe we've been properly introduced," he said from where he stood across from her. "George Bennett-Jones," he said before bowing.

Lily couldn't help but notice he didn't add his title. She didn't either. "Lily Harkins," she said as she curtsied. "It's very good to make your acquaintance."

She knew from the viscount's impassive response that he already knew who she was—otherwise, she expected he would have shown some kind of reaction to her being the sister of the man who had originally intended to make Elizabeth Carlington his wife. The man who had made such a fool of himself by being a horrible kisser. Lady Elizabeth had been the recipient of said kiss. And now she was Viscountess Bostwick.

The music started, and Lily was forced to remember the steps as she and the viscount danced. Throughout the entire twenty-minute set, she was aware of Lord Reading watching her. Indeed, the man didn't even try to hide the fact that he was staring at her.

At the end of the quadrille, when Bostwick moved to give her a bow while she gave him a curtsy, he angled his head toward the marquess. "Would you like me to engage him? Give you a chance to take your leave?" he offered.

Lily's eyes widened. *Engage him?* What did the man have in mind? Did he want a duel in Wimbledon Commons? That would certainly give her enough time to get all the way to Fitzsimmons Manor. "You're too kind," she said. "But I believe I can manage from here."

George walked up to Reading on his way to rejoin his wife. "Behave, or you will be challenged to pistols at dawn," he said in a low voice, the threatening tone unmistakable.

Reading frowned, unable to respond since the viscount had moved passed him so quickly. When he turned his attention back to where Lily had been, he found her gone. "Damnation!" he muttered under his breath.

"Are you looking for me, my lord?"

Reading whirled around to find the blonde chit regarding him with an arched eyebrow. A glass of champagne dangled between two of her fingers. "I was," he answered carefully.

"Looking for a tryst in the gardens, no doubt?" Lily half-questioned, deciding to be as direct with the marquess as possible. She took a sip of the champagne and held it on her tongue for a moment, secretly delighting in how the bubbles formed and dissipated before she swallowed.

A bit surprised by her frank comment, Reading blinked. "Well, only if my lady makes the request of me. I can be very obliging in that regard," he added, trying hard not to seem desperate.

"To what end, my lord?"

Reading blinked again. If the chit was going to be blunt with him, then he would be the same with her. "A proposal of marriage."

It was Lily's turn to blink. *That's not the answer I was expecting,* she thought with some alarm. He was teasing, she realized, or attempting to trap her. "Why, you're an amusing man, my lord," she finally said. "But I do hope you don't expect me to believe you would propose. Let alone, marry me."

Shaking his head, Reading wondered at the beautiful chit's words. "Oh, but I would," he said, his head dipping so his second chin appeared below his first. Aware his double chin had suddenly made an appearance, Reading quickly raised his first chin. "I am at a crossroads in my life, you see," he went on, managing to surreptitiously study the young woman before him as he made the claim. "I am of an age where I simply must take a wife and get a child on her—preferably an heir—as soon as possible." He didn't add that they could start that very night on the second part of his must-do's.

Lily heard what she was sure was sincerity in the marquess' words, but caution held her back from showing any empathy just then. "These crossroads... do you come upon them often, my lord?" she asked, pretending she was as vacuous as half the chits in the ballroom.

The marquess narrowed his eyes. Was the young woman teasing him? One minute she seemed far too smart for her age, and then next, she was... well, she was a conundrum. "Twice in my life, actually," he replied in all seriousness. "Once, when I went off to attend Cambridge instead of taking my seat in Parliament—my father died the week before classes started, you see—and then last week, when I discovered I had turned five-and-thirty, my hair had begun to gray and... well, let's just say I need a legitimate heir."

Lily took a sip of her champagne and regarded the Rake of Reading with new-found respect, but not a lot of it. "You've no intention of honoring your marriage vows once you do marry, though, do you?" she challenged.

His ire suddenly up, the marquess' brows furrowed until a crease formed between them. The evidence was in his eyes as they flashed daggers at her. "I've a mind to ruin you just so you'll *have* to marry me. Then I would prove my fidelity to you," he claimed. "For the rest of my life."

The words had come out so suddenly, so forcefully, Lily had to take a half-step back. "A moment ago, you were plotting how you were going to get me into the gardens for a tryst," she accused in a hoarse whisper.

Reading nodded. "Yes. Yes, I was. So I could ruin you. And then..." He allowed the sentence to trail off, his entire body seeming to slump as his anger seemed to disappear with his second chin.

Lily moved a bit closer, leaning in so that others wouldn't hear her words. "Why me?" she asked.

The marquess shook his head.

Why not?

Well, he couldn't very well respond with that. It would only make him sound as desperate as he felt just then. "You're gorgeous. You're clever, I think. A bit world weary it would seem. And I've just now realized that I have no idea who you are," he added, "which makes you that much more intriguing to me. I'm intrigued enough to want to spend my lifetime finding out all about you." He didn't add that the finding out all about her would be mostly done in bed with her clothes off.

Her eyes widening with the rake's words, Lily was half-tempted to invite the man to accompany her to the gardens. She was intrigued enough to want to find out if the earl could perform a suitable kiss. But his other words reminded her she had better introduce herself. Once he learned her identity, he would surely continue his pursuit of a wife with someone else in the ballroom. The man obviously didn't have time for a tryst in the gardens when he needed to be finding a wife. "I am Lily Harkins, illegitimate sister to the Earl of Trenton," she said with a curtsy.

The earl stared at her for a moment, his features impassive to the point that Lily realized she couldn't tell if he was surprised by her introduction or simply bored by it.

Until he bowed and took her hand.

"Randall Roderick, Marquess of Reading," he said. When he stood up to his full five-foot, ten-inch height, he added, "And I would be honored to take you as my wife."

Lily wasn't sure if it was the man's unexpected proposal, or the oppressive heat in the ballroom, or the fact that her maid had given her corset ties an extra hard tug when she dressed her for the ball, but Lily's vision suddenly grayed at the edges. *What is happening to me?* she wondered as the gray turned to black and Lord Reading's gaze went from one of adoration to one of concern.

Before Lily quite realized what was happening, the marquess was whisking her through the throngs of ball goers and out one of the sets of French doors leading to the gardens, her feet barely touching the floor in the process.

Once the cool night air filled her lungs—the rain had left behind the scent of wet grass and fresh air—Lily's eyes cleared and she was able to stand on her own.

"My lady, are you all right?" Reading asked, apparently for a second or third time.

Lily blinked and glanced around, realizing they were the only couple out on the stone flags leading to the gardens. *Goodness!* How many of those in attendance had seen her hasty retreat? And how had she even been able to take her leave of the ballroom?

She dared a glance at the marquess. "How did I get out here?" she asked, her voice sounding rather weak.

Reading shrugged. "I escorted you," he finally answered. "'Twas no trouble. You're rather petite and light on your feet. But I must say, I find myself wondering if I should be flattered or offended."

Her head clear and her eyes quite wide, Lily regarded the marquess for a moment. Was he writing poetry in her honor now? *How ridiculous!* And when she finally comprehended his words, she frowned. "Why ever would you be offended?" she asked. "Did I...?"

Reading allowed a grin, his head angling in a manner Lily found rather endearing. "I asked for your hand in marriage, and you *fainted*," he replied. "How am I to interpret such a response?"

Daring a glance back at the French doors to ensure no one was watching them, Lily placed a hand on his arm. Reading bent his arm and turned to lead them along the flagstone path, all the while keeping his eyes on Lily.

"The one did not beget the other, I assure you," Lily answered. "I merely found myself unable to breathe." Her other hand moved to press against her ribs. "Either because of the heat or because..." She stopped, not sure if she should say anything about her tight corset.

The marquess gave a nod. "Tight corset?" he offered, a twinkle appearing in one of his eyes.

Lily allowed a look of surprise, both at his comment and at how charming the man could be. "Indeed," she agreed with a nod.

"I would be a... a fool not to offer to help her ladyship in that regard, but something tells me my reputation precedes me. I would hate to make your opinion of me any worse than it already is," he said, his voice sounding sincere.

"Are you referring to your reputation as a rake?" she countered.

"Indeed," he agreed. After a moment of silence, he added, "I used to feel a bit of pride at being known as a rake, or a scoundrel."

Lily gave him a sideways glance. "You say that as if you no longer do."

Reading dipped his head. "I don't. I'm far too *old* to be out late, gambling and spending my nights with..." He allowed the sentence to trail off.

"Mistresses?" she guessed, thinking perhaps he was about to say 'whores' and then thought better of it.

"Widows, actually, but when all is said and done, there isn't much of a difference, I have found." At Lily's look of surprise, he added, "They all have the same expectations. They want jewels, usually. And although my coffers have allowed me to be generous, I find myself wishing I could see the damned baubles actually being *worn* by a woman under my own roof. In my bed, by the same woman, night after night." He swallowed and then cleared his throat, realizing he had probably scandalized the poor young woman who stood gazing at him. "Now I've gone and shocked you into silence, I see," he said.

Lily shook her head. "I used to be a maid. Nothing shocks me anymore, my lord."

They walked along in companionable silence, the path winding about the gardens beneath paper lanterns that occasionally bobbed in the slight breeze. When they reached the famed fountain, Reading came to a halt and moved to stand before Lily. "You say nothing shocks you, but what would you say if I told you I have four bastard sons?"

Had he been wanting to tell her the entire time in the garden and only now found the courage to do so? Or had he made some decision that required he admit the damning information?

Keeping her face as impassive as possible, Lily shrugged. "What would you say if I told you the oldest is my age?" she countered, having heard of the boys the marquess had sired with four different women from her days as a maid. Servants were the worst gossips!

"Gads!" the marquess replied. "Nothing like making a man feel really old, although I was rather young when he was born. Younger than you, I should think."

Lily angled her head to one side. "If it's any consolation, my lord, you do not comport yourself in the manner of an old man. You're quite the opposite, in fact."

Reading stared at her for a moment, as if he were experiencing a revelation. "I've a mind to kiss you right here and now. Kiss you until you succumb to my charms and agree to marry me. Tomorrow, if you'd like."

Despite her initial revulsion at learning the Marquess of Reading was in attendance at the Weatherstone's ball, Lily now found she had a completely different opinion of the man. She almost felt pity for him. "I beg you pardon my surprise. How is it you can even consider *me* for matrimony? You do know I'm *illegitimate*?" she whispered.

The marquess gave a shrug. "It matters not. Once we're married, you become my marchioness. You would be under my protection. And I assure you, there would be no further talk of your parentage in the *ton*," he said with a good deal of authority. As if he needed to provide additional incentive, he added, "The coronet is quite stunning, although it's been years since I saw my mother wear it."

Rather astonished by Reading's cavalier attitude about her status, Lily tried to imagine what life might be like with the marquess. "Why is it you're just now seeking a wife?" she asked as she faced him, the fronts of their bodies far closer than propriety allowed.

The marquess dipped his head. "I didn't intend to be a rake when I started out," he said quietly. "But I also didn't wish to be leg-shackled at a young age. I liked my freedom. I... I *liked* being in the company of women. The more beautiful, the better, of course. But to my credit, I found none of them were looking to be my wife. Not even the virgins," he added when he noted Lily's look of surprise.

"What were they looking for if not marriage?" she countered.

Reading angled his head to one side. "They were looking for the same thing I was. An evening's companionship and a pleasant tumble. A few words telling them how lovely they looked." He took a breath. "Even if they didn't."

Lily frowned when she heard the last bit, but at least he was being frank. "Again, I ask, why do you seek a wife?"

The marquess displayed a frown much like hers, as if he should have an answer to her question but just didn't know what it was. "Duty, first and foremost, I suppose. I need an heir. A legitimate heir," he said with a nod. "But..." He stopped, remembering where he was. He should be kissing the young lady. He should be ensuring someone would see them together so that she would be ruined. So ruined that she would be forced to marry him. "Truth be told, I want more than an evening's companionship, more than a pleasant tumble," he whispered. "I want someone to be at Reading Manor when I return from Parliament, someone with whom to eat dinner at night. Someone to be doing needlework or whatever it is you ladies do when you're in the parlor by the fire at night while I'm drinking a glass of port and reading the latest treatise on the failures of the French monarchy." His face screwed up at that last statement, but he went on. "I want someone to come to my bed with me, someone I can undress, and make love to, and sleep next to for the entire night, and I don't want to have to get up in the middle of the night because I'm not allowed to spend the entire night in the same bed with her."

This last had Lily blinking, remembering she had heard a similar complaint from Sir Tobias Fulton.

What was it about mistresses who refused to share their beds for the entire night?

The Marquess of Reading frowned, one eyebrow dipping so low, Lily thought it might become the top of his nose. "Good God," he said suddenly. "I do want a wife," he claimed.

Lily had to resist the urge to giggle, for the marquess' expression was almost comical. Poor man!

"You make a very compelling offer, my lord," she said with a nod. "Might I be allowed to think on it awhile?"

Randall Roderick regarded her for a moment before giving her a nod. "Of course. I would hope for an answer in the morning, but I can wait until the beginning of Parliament in the fall. But no longer," he warned. "I should like to be married in time for Christmas. So I have a wife with whom to share the holiday," he added. *And someone to warm my bed on those cold winter nights.*

Tempted to give the man an answer right then and there, Lily had to still herself. Only an hour ago, she had attempted to flee from Reading due to his reputation as a rake. Now she was seriously considering his offer of marriage!

Lifting her head, Lily gave him a nod. "I understand." And before she knew quite what she was doing, she found herself kissing Reading on the corner of his mouth, one of her hands resting against his cheek as she did so. She inhaled the scents of brandy on his breath and amber cologne on his cheek, wondering if the combination would always have her thinking of him.

The marquess stood very still as Lily slowly pulled her lips away, but one of his hands captured the one on his cheek and held it there, held it there while he slowly moved his mouth so that he could place a kiss in her palm. His eyes closed, he then turned her hand over and kissed the back of it. "Dance with me," he murmured.

Lily blinked and glanced around where they stood, wondering if they had an audience. Given the popularity of the Weatherstone gardens for trysts, she was surprised to find they still seemed to be alone. Perhaps the earlier rain was a deterrent. "Here?" she replied when he didn't make a move to return to the ballroom. The faint strains of a waltz reached her ears. "I don't yet have a voucher to dance the waltz," she whispered.

Reading hadn't yet released her hand, and now he simply held it up while his other hand moved to her waist. Before Lily understood quite what was happening, they were dancing around the fountain. His steps were measured, far smaller than they would have been inside, and their bodies were far closer to one another than they should have been. But Lily found she couldn't deny the marquess the dance. It seemed to give the man great joy, and his face lit up so he appeared much younger beneath the light of the paper lanterns.

"I shall never forget this night," Reading said in a low voice.

A frisson passed through Lily before she dared to speak. "Why, pray tell?" she whispered.

The marquess dipped his head. "You are the first woman ever to kiss me first," he replied. "And the reformed rake that I am is winning a battle with the old me, refusing to allow me to return the favor." This last was said on a sigh, as if he truly regretted his decision not to ruin her on the spot.

Lily allowed a smile as she regarded the marquess. "Thank you for the dance, my lord," she murmured.

Giving the man another kiss on his cheek, Lily took her leave of the marquess and of the Weatherstone's residence.

CHAPTER 27

A TALK IN THE FOLLY

"A penny for your thoughts."

Lily was startled enough by her brother's voice that she gave a start and whirled about. When she realized her interloper was merely Gabriel, she let out the air she had been about to use to scream and instead said, "You might feel a bit short-changed."

Gabriel gave her a grin and offered his arm. "You're up awfully early, but something tells me you are everyday." He certainly appreciated the mornings she was up with little Gabe, entertaining him with stories and playing with him on the floor of the nursery or taking him out on the lawns to run after a rubber ball before the rest of the household was up for the day. He knew the nurse was appreciative, as well. The woman was adequate when it came to caring for Gabe, but she was not a very sociable person until after she'd had her breakfast and a cup of coffee.

Gabriel had spied Lily from his bedchamber window as she made her way out of Wellingham Manor. She had been strolling on the north lawn toward the pond when he decided to don a top coat—he had barely finished dressing—and caught up to her. Breathless, he joined her on her walk. Given their direction, he figured she was making her way toward the folly next to the fishing pond.

"I am. Old habit from my days as a maid," she agreed to his comment about her being up early. "And morning is a good time to think."

Matching his pace to the one she set, Gabriel regarded his sister for a moment. "What, pray tell, has your attention this fine morning?"

Lily gave a one-shouldered shrug before sighing. "I have begun to wonder why the men of the *ton* do not seek more companionable wives," Lily murmured as she linked her arm with the one he offered.

"Some do," he countered. "I did."

Angling her head to one side, Lily regarded him for a moment before stepping up into the folly. "But the ones that do not. How can they expect to have a satisfying life with their spouse if they don't choose one they like?"

Gabriel took a deep breath, not sure how much he should say. At one time, he had followed the dictates of the peerage, intent on choosing a wife that would gain him political advantage. If she were beautiful, it would be a bonus. If she came from a wealthy family, it would be even more so, but given his wealth, he had no need of a dowry.

At one point, he thought he would love one of his mistresses, so he hadn't been seeking a wife to be anything more than a mother for his heirs. "They may never have a satisfying life with their spouse," he replied with a sigh. "Believe me. Even if they marry to gain a substantial dowry, they complain about their spoiled wives. Complain about how much they cost their little kingdoms," Gabriel murmured as he waited for Lily to take a seat on the padded bench along one wall of the folly. "All in the name of doing their duty." He sat down next to her, leaning back so his back rested against the stone wall. "I could have been one of them."

Lily gave a sigh. "The wives complain about their husbands, too, when Lady Samantha and I are having tea in their parlors. Some of them never seem satisfied. I don't wish to be one of those wives who complain," she added. "But I can hear myself saying some of the same things they say. I'm sure I would, too, if

I were married to a man who stayed out too late at his club, or who gambled all night, or who spent time in a brothel."

Wincing, Gabriel straightened. Although he had to admit he wouldn't have understood her comment a couple of years ago, he certainly understood it now. "I had such high hopes for you. That a worthy peer would realize how lucky he would be to have you as his wife. And not just because of your dowry, of course," Gabriel struggled to get out as he repositioned himself on the padded bench. "I thought that since you had spent so many years in service, you would be seen as desirable for all the things you already know how to do."

Lily shook her head. "What ever do you mean?"

Gabriel regarded her for a moment. "You already know how to run a household. You probably know how to put on a dinner party, how to host a ball," he explained. "You certainly know how to keep an heir entertained."

Her expression lightened at her brother's words. "I do know how to do those things," she agreed with a nod. "But I fear the circumstances of my birth will forever be a source of trouble. I am a bas—"

"Don't," Gabriel interrupted, his head shaking from side to side. "Don't say it. You are my sister, and that is all that matters."

Lily hung her head for a moment, touched by Gabriel's words. "I fear you'll wish I was not when I request that you please not make me accept any of those marriage proposals," she whispered.

Gabriel gave a bark of laughter. "*Make* you? I cannot..." Gabriel paused a moment. "I will not dictate whom you should marry," he said, the words obviously difficult to say.

Lily's eyes widened, the blue irises darkening with his words. "But if you could..."

His own eyes lifting to the ceiling of the folly, Gabriel shook his head. "Are you looking for a recommendation?" he countered.

Managing a small nod, Lily replied, "Yes. Of course."

Gabriel inhaled and held his breath for a moment. "Well, if

his courtship doesn't pan out in Dorchester, the Earl of Montaine. He is honorable. He has vast holdings and can probably afford his gambling habit. I also believe he's rather fond of you."

Lily frowned, a crease appearing between her blonde brows. "How can you know that?" At no point in her tale about Graham Denberg had she hinted the earl might feel affection for her.

"I received a letter from Montaine a few days after the Morganfield *soirée*."

If she hadn't already been sitting down, Lily was quite sure she would have fallen down upon hearing her brother's news.

Why hadn't Gabriel said anything over dinner that night when she had first recounted her evening with the earl and Viscount Fraley? And what had the earl said in his letter that might differ from what she had described in her tale?

"His description of the evening's events were similar to yours," he said, choosing his words carefully, "But he felt a need to inform me of what had happened. In case I heard any gossip. In case I needed to prevail upon him to offer for your hand in order to save you from ruination."

Lily let out a squeak and then sighed rather loudly. "And did you? Hear anything, I mean," she asked, rather alarmed at the news.

Gabriel shook his head. "Not a word from that night, which would normally be a bit of a surprise, except we're speaking of an event that happened at Carlington House." At Lily's look of confusion, he continued. "You see, Morganfield's marchioness has quite a unique relationship with the newspapers in London. If she wants something printed, it gets printed. If she does not..." He allowed the sentence to trail off, realizing his last visit to the marquess' residence could have been documented in great detail in *The Morning Chronicle* had Adeline Carlington wished it.

Thank the gods he was allowed to enter and leave without anyone but the Carlingtons and a couple of servants knowing about his failure!

That was the day he intended to ask Lady Elizabeth for her hand in marriage. Instead, the young lady had berated him for having mistresses. Too many mistresses. He shuddered as he remembered his thoughts as he left Carlington House, sure the three women he employed as mistresses were spies intent on seeing to his downfall in Parliament.

Ending those liaisons—it was expensive, but necessary—made it possible for him to concentrate on becoming the best earl he could be for his earldom as well as open to the possibility of taking Sarah as his wife instead of some aristocrat's spoiled daughter. "I have reason to believe Adeline Carlington's influence also includes the topic of discussion in Mayfair parlors," he added with a cocked eyebrow.

Allowing a grin, Lily nodded. "Not a word was said about the play. About Viscount Fraley kissing me in front of all those people," she agreed, rather happy to know Lady Morganfield had protected her from certain scandal. "So, did you inform the Earl of Montaine know you weren't holding him to his offer?"

Gabriel nodded. "I also let him know that if he truly wanted you as his wife, he would have to make you an offer. Has he done so?"

Lily swallowed and then shook her head. "I have not seen the Earl of Montaine since the morning after the Morganfield's *soirée*," she replied, her voice almost a whisper. "He came to Fitzsimmons Manor. He said he wanted to ensure I had arrived home safely the night before." At Gabriel's look of confusion, she added, "There seems to be something terribly wrong about walking a few houses down in Park Lane to attend a *soirée*."

After a pause, she continued. "But I think Montaine also called on me to determine my interest in him. I could tell he wasn't particularly pleased with the idea of marrying a former maid, though," she explained, remembering that night as if it had happened yesterday. "If we didn't live in London, and he didn't have to answer to every aristocrat who wondered why he would marry beneath him, he probably would have proposed that morning."

A look of sadness crossed Gabriel's face just then. "I suppose you have your answer then," he whispered.

A combination of relief and disappointment settled over Lily. "I do," she agreed with a nod.

They sat in companionable silence for several minutes, the songs of birds and the chirps of crickets the only sounds around them.

"Truth be told, brother, I came thinking I might adopt spinsterhood for my future—"

"What?" Gabriel's face showed as much surprise as she had ever seen him display.

"As a maid, I couldn't expect to marry, to have children," Lily countered. "But now that I've had an opportunity to see what a marriage is like, what spending time with a child is like, I find I want that kind of life now."

The idea of spinsterhood was suddenly a frightening prospect. Lady Samantha had nearly resigned herself to that fate, claiming she rather liked the idea of the independence she would have to live her life how she saw fit.

The idea had appealed to Lily as well, until she had paid witness to what life was like at Trenton Manor. Now... now she couldn't imagine living in a townhouse with a small staff, a paid companion attending Society events with her. Could she ever hope to be invited to a dinner party? To the theatre? Or would her evenings be spent in her home, alone by the fire?

"You can have another Season if you'd like," Gabriel offered. "When you return to London, there's no need to decide on a husband right away if you'd rather not," he added.

Lily angled her head to one side. "I thank you for the offer," she replied, imagining having to attend another Season of balls and *musicales* and *soirées* with the intent of finding a husband. She countered it with the image of spending her evenings sitting by the fireplace reading a book or doing needlework whilst a husband enjoyed a glass of port and a book of his own. Or perhaps she would be down on the floor, playing with a baby, or lying in bed, being held by a husband whilst she held a baby.

"I want a family," she said quietly. "I want a life like you and

Sarah and little Gabe have," she continued. "With a man who will value my opinions like you value Sarah's."

Gabriel raised his eyebrows and allowed a wan smile. "You just like the idea of being able to tease your husband and not suffer a spanking because of it," he countered, a bit of mischief showing in his eyes.

Lily's own eyes widened. "Well, that, too, perhaps," she agreed, wondering if Gabriel had ever spanked Sarah. She rather doubted the woman would have allowed it. After a pause, she added, "You do love her. Don't you?"

His grin broadening into a brilliant smile and his face reddening with embarrassment, Gabriel nodded. "More than I ever thought possible. Honest to God, Lily, I don't know what I would do without her." He paused a moment. "But I do know I would still be a horrible kisser."

S arah stilled herself upon overhearing the simple words Gabriel spoke, her heart clenching so it felt tight in her chest.

Once she had seen to it little Gabe was eating his breakfast, she had gone in search of the siblings. She had made her way down to the folly in the hopes of joining them for a pleasant morning next to the pond. But at overhearing Lily's words about wanting a family, she had paused and instead leaned against the outside of the folly, out of sight of the two whose conversation was as serious as any they had shared over dinners or the picnic.

She was relieved to learn Lily still wanted all the trappings of a family despite having spent so many weeks with them—she might have instead decided she preferred a life without a husband, without children—and returned to London to live the life of a spinster.

Sarah was pondering the thought when she heard Lily reply to Gabriel's admission of love.

"I am glad to hear it, brother. And happy to know I will soon have another nephew, or a niece." Lily couldn't help but notice Gabriel's chest puff out at the comment while she paused a moment. "Which are you hoping it will be? A son or a daughter?"

Having given it a good deal of consideration since the night he had learned Sarah would bear him another child by Christmas, Gabriel shook his head. "I will welcome either equally. It matters not. Truly," he added when he saw Lily's look of doubt.

"But, don't you want a boy? An heir?" she countered, surprised he would claim to welcome a daughter.

Gabriel gave a shrug. "As I said, it matters not. If she only ever gives me daughters, then the Trenton earldom will end up with our cousin. And, truth be told, Thomas would probably be better at running the earldom than I am," he claimed.

"*Thomas?*" Lily repeated, shocked to hear their cousin was next in line for the earldom. She shook her head. "But... but that will never do," she said, her head still shaking.

"Why ever not?" Gabriel asked, straightening on the bench. "He's certainly capable. Good God, the man has built himself his own little empire. His business covers nearly all of England and Scotland. He's got overland coaches and ships and..."

"It's not that," Lily replied as she sat up straighter. "If the Earl of Torrington's wife doesn't bear him an heir when she gives birth in a month or so, and given her age, it's unlikely she'll have the chance to try again, then Grandby's earldom will be inherited by Gregory Grandby."

Gabriel frowned before he gave a shake of his head. "So?"

Lily sighed. "Well, I can't imagine Gregory would move to a different household if he inherits. Gregory and Thomas own their home, Woodscastle, equally. Can you imagine two earls living under the same roof?" she asked, her grin giving away the humor she felt at the thought. She almost giggled.

Gabriel laughed out loud. He continued to chuckle until Sarah appeared, a smile indicating she had heard the comment about Thomas and Gregory.

When Sarah stepped up into the folly to join their conversation, Gabriel stood up and hurried to her, bestowing her with a kiss and a quick hug. "I did not intend to be away so long," he said as he saw her to a seat next to Lily. "But Lily and I have been discussing her options."

Sarah glanced over at Lily. "Are there any left?" she asked, thinking the four that had been discussed—five if they included Viscount Fraley—were out of consideration.

Lily shrugged. "One or two, I suppose," she said.

The earl angled his head. "I have no intention of seeing you wed to a man who does not deserve you." *Or your dowry,* he almost added. "Which means we must decide who is *worthy* of you." He pulled a note from his waistcoat pocket and carefully unfolded the corners.

Lily's attention went to the missive as she considered who might have sent it. Given its worn and somewhat wrinkled appearance, she realized her brother had been carrying around the parchment for some time. Perhaps he had opened and closed it several times. Or perhaps he had forgotten to remove it from his pocket before it was last laundered.

Had someone sent him news from London? Bad news?

She leaned forward, her hands clasped together on her lap. "What have you there?" she finally asked when curiosity got the better of her.

A passing thought had her wondering if it was further word of Lady Samantha. Based on the latest news from Fitzsimmons Manor and the occasional article in the newspapers that made their way to Wellingham Manor, Samantha's betrothed didn't sound any better than any of Lily's suitors!

Gabriel reread the note before giving her an answer. "A request for permission to court you," he said quietly. "The only one I have received—other than Montaine's query—in fact."

Lily's eyes widened as she wondered which of her suitors had followed the correct protocol in requesting her brother's permission. "From whom?" Her hand went to Sarah's, and she gripped it as if needing the older woman's support. She couldn't imagine the baron or the viscount taking the time to pen a note. Perhaps the baronet, but even he seemed so distracted at times, Lily wondered how he accomplished anything beyond his avocation.

"Mr. William Overby."

Lily allowed an, "Oh!" and stood up so fast, Gabriel was caught unawares. Sarah was forced to stand as well given her hand was still held tight by Lily.

Gabriel struggled to get to his feet, curious of his sister's reaction. Her face displayed happiness, though. She wore a smile that had the clouds parting above and the sun lighting the entire countryside. She even twirled around, once she had given up her hold on Sarah, and her arms wrapped about her middle as her skirts billowed out.

When Lily noticed Gabriel's expression of confusion, she knew her reaction might land her in Bedlam and she stopped. She quickly sat down.

"You didn't tell us about Mr. Overby during any of our dinners," Gabriel accused, returning to his seat far more carefully than his sister had.

Her face taking on a blush, Lily gave her brother a suitably guilty expression. "I did not," she agreed.

"But, something tells me you told Sarah about him," Gabriel accused, giving his wife a quick glance. Indeed, Sarah hadn't shown the least bit of surprise at hearing of William Overby.

The statement wasn't a question, so Lily simply nodded. "I didn't tell you because... because I didn't want you to be disappointed in me."

Shocked by her words, Gabriel stood up and regarded Lily for a long moment. "I rather doubt I could be disappointed in you. Even if you... even if you tell me you're in love with a tailor," he managed to get out, although his face had taken on the look of someone eating a lemon straight from the rind.

Lily's eyes widened. "Oh, please. I do have some scruples," she countered, her voice rising with her displeasure.

Gabriel took a breath as if he was about to say something else, but he slowly let it out and returned to the bench. He raked his fingers through his unruly curls. "Do you fancy yourself in *love* with Mr. Overby?" he asked in a whisper.

Pleating the fabric of her skirt with her thumb and forefinger, Lily gave a slight shrug. "I think so. At least, I am if being in love means thinking about him all the time."

Gabriel leaned his back against the wall of the folly, thinking perhaps his sister might be exaggerating. "Is he the first person you think of when you wake up in the morning?"

Lily squirmed a bit. "I suppose," she hedged.

"And the last person you think of before you go to sleep at night?"

Lily sighed, tears brightening her eyes. "Yes," she whispered, her face displaying a rather deep pink blush. "I think of him when I'm doing needlework, when I'm eating breakfast. I think of greeting him when he returns home every night from his work. I imagine myself round with his child. When I'm playing with your son, I imagine he's my son and Mr. Overby is his father. I think about how it would be to grow old together—"

"You're doomed," Gabriel stated, his manner not displaying the least bit of humor.

Sarah let out a sound of surprise and rolled her eyes in response to his comment.

Lily lifted her head and stared at the ceiling of the folly. She groaned. *I've said entirely too much. Now he'll send me to a nunnery,* she thought with some despair. "What did Mr. Overby write in the note?"

Gabriel gave her a glance before he shook out the parchment, took a deep breath, and began to read.

Dear Lord Trenton,

 Several years ago, when your sister, Lady Lily, was still a maid, it was my pleasure to make her acquaintance whilst attending the festivities at Vauxhall Gardens. The pleasure was short-lived, though, when I was forced to send her running for her own safety from a rake in whose company I had the misfortune of being that evening.

 I shall never forgive myself for not accompanying her home that night, for not seeing to her safe arrival at her home. Instead, I stayed behind in the hopes I could save her friend and fellow maid from ruination. However, attempting to save a chit from something she has already suffered and merely wishes to experience again is, what I discovered that night, a lost cause.

I tried in vain to forget about the events of that night. I severed ties to my friend. I was promoted to my current position at Wellingham Imports, and I immersed myself in work. But despite my best efforts, I could not put thoughts of your sister out of my mind.

So last June, when she appeared before me all yellow and golden like the rays of the sun, her blue eyes once again mesmerizing me so that I might no longer have control of my faculties, she bid me to take her to your cousin, Thomas Wellingham, and I did so. The following day, your cousin's wife, Mrs. Wellingham, ordered that I escort Lady Lily to the park for her morning walks until such time as your coach arrived to take her to Staffordshire and your protection for the summer.

I, of course, followed Mrs. Wellingham's direction, for I would have welcomed any excuse to spend time in your sister's presence. It was with a heavy heart that I had to bid her farewell when your coach appeared the very first day I was to escort Lady Lily to the park.

I believe that during that walk, I would have mustered the courage to share my feelings, to ask if I might be allowed to court her with the hope she would one day agree to be my wife.

For you see, my lord, I can no longer imagine my life without your sister in it. I think of her when I wake in the morning, and she is who I dream of when I sleep at night. I think of her when I am eating my breakfast. I think of her whilst doing my work at Wellingham Imports. I imagine her waiting for me when I get home at night, round with my babe. I imagine us playing with our children, and I think fondly of the two of us growing old together.

What I cannot imagine is a life without Lily, for I do not believe it would be a life worth living.

Despite my lack of relation to anyone in the peerage, I am writing to ask your permission to court your sister when she returns to London. Should you require a character, I have been assured by my employers, the Wellinghams, that either one would

be happy to oblige such a request.
    I look forward to your favorable reply.
    Sincerely yours, William Overby.

Sarah sighed and allowed a heartfelt, "Ohhh," when her husband finished reading.

Lily stared at the back of the note and then at her brother, stunned to hear William's words spoken aloud. "I would not have thought him capable of such eloquence," she murmured. *Nor that he would have the same thoughts of me as I have of him.*

What I cannot imagine is a life without Lily, for I do not believe it would be a life worth living.

Gabriel allowed a snort. "So, this is the man you might be in love with," he said, the words more a statement than a question.

Sighing, Lily nodded.

"Not a bad note for a man who claims to be a clerk," he allowed.

"He's a clerk for our cousin, Thomas," Lily reminded him. "At Wellingham Imports."

Gabriel nodded, realizing he need only send a note to Thomas and ask about William to learn the truth of the young man. "How is it you can be so sure you have feelings for this boy when you spent only a few hours in his company?" Gabriel asked, his passive expression giving her no idea what he thought of her would-be suitor.

Lily glanced at Sarah, as if needing her help, before she turned and regarded her brother for a moment. His query rather surprised her. "How is it you knew you had feelings for Sarah when you spent only an hour in her company?" she countered, just then understanding why Sarah thought it important that Lily knew how she had come to know the earl. "And Mr. Overby is three-and-twenty. Hardly a boy."

Gabriel stared at Sarah for a moment, his brows furrowing. "You told her how we... the circumstances of how we met?" He seemed rather surprised by this bit of information, and perhaps a little embarrassed.

Sarah gave a slight shrug with her nod. "I did."

Lily willed herself not to blush, not to feel embarrassment on her brother's behalf. "She did. But not because she wanted to put a bad light on you, brother."

Gabriel shook his head. "The only bad light on me would have been due to my stubbornness in not renewing my acquaintance with her more quickly once I realized she was the woman I wanted... the woman I *needed* to make my countess," he countered quietly, giving Sarah an apologetic glance.

"I think she told me so as to make you a bit more human to me."

His frown deepening, Gabriel regarded Lily for a moment. "I hardly think you would see me as—"

"I was frightfully afraid of you, Gabriel. You're an earl. A wealthy earl. With power to make things go your way." Gabriel's sudden snort had Lily pausing. "What? Are you denying you have power?"

Shaking his head, the earl allowed a chuckle. "Power over whom, do you suppose?" he asked, his quick grin fading a bit. "I am powerless when it comes to Sarah and to my son." When he thought Lily was about to protest, he continued. "I have power to protect them, of course, which I promise you, I will use until my dying breath. I have power to see to it my earldom is the best it can be for those who serve me, for those who work the fields and tend the sheep and run the businesses. I have some power in Parliament, although not much.

"But I do not believe I have the power to say who you should or should not love. Nor do I have the power to tell Mr. Overby he cannot love you."

Lily's inhaled sharply. She held the breath for a long moment, waiting for Gabriel's next words.

"Therefore, I shall write to Mr. Overby and tell him he has my permission to court you."

Lily exhaled, her hands reaching for her brother's. "Thank you," she whispered.

"However," Gabriel added, his manner now more serious than Lily had ever seen it. "He will accept your dowry without protest and use it to provide an acceptable house for you and your children. He will not gamble—"

"He does not."

"—nor will he take a mistress—"

"I would not allow it," Lily said, shaking her head, annoyed her brother would even think William capable of the thought of employing a mistress.

"Nor will he frequent brothels."

"He wouldn't dare," she countered, her head still shaking. "I would leave him. Kill him first, and then leave him," she corrected herself.

"And he shall continue his employment with Wellingham Imports until such time as he secures a promotion in a position elsewhere or is too old or infirm to continue working there."

Lily blinked. "But... but what if I require his presence at home?" she asked, thinking there would be days when she wanted his company, when she required him for some reason.

Gabriel considered the question for a moment, thinking of the times Sarah begged him to forego seeing to some menial task in favor of spending the day with her. She usually had a good reason and had made it worth his while to reschedule, in fact.

Thinking of those times had him feeling aroused, and he had to direct his thoughts back to the clerk who wanted his sister as a wife. "I suppose, should Thomas see fit to allow him a day off now and then, it would be acceptable for him to take a holiday."

Allowing a grin, Lily leaned over and hugged her brother. "Thank you."

Gabriel returned the hug, hoping he had made the right decision. When he pulled away from his sister, he allowed a sigh. "I need to make my way back to the house. Seems I have a letter of permission to write to Mr. Overby," he said.

Sarah grinned. "And now that Lady Samantha has an offer of marriage from the Marquess of Plymouth—"

"*What?*" Lily exclaimed, turning about on the bench to give Sarah her attention. "The marquess she was with on that island?" she asked, stunned to hear the man had proposed when Samantha had already accepted an offer from a baronet. "When did this happen?"

Sarah placed a hand on Lily's shoulder. "Just a few days ago, and I received a letter from Lady Chamberlain this morning with the news. Seems the marquess missed Samantha as much as she missed him after their ordeal in the Mediterranean," she explained. "She'll be a marchioness in Yorkshire," she added, exchanging glances with Gabriel.

As Lily took in the good news, she realized her brother was regarding her with a frown. "What is it?"

Gabriel dipped his head. "I think it's about time you returned to London. Another Season will start shortly. Perhaps Mr. Overby will realize he'll have to take the opportunity to court you before then, or he'll be competing for your affections with another herd of young bucks." He gave a bow and took his leave of the folly.

Lily turned and hugged Sarah, knowing her whispered "thank you" wasn't nearly enough. Somehow, Sarah had convinced her brother it would be acceptable for Lily to be wed to a commoner. "Whatever you said to him was enough," she said in awe. "What *did* you say to him?"

Sarah grinned. "I merely had to remind him that *he* married a commoner," she replied.

Buoyed by her brother's edict and Sarah's words, Lily nodded her understanding, hoping she would be spared from attending too many social events during the coming Season. Until she was betrothed, she would be seen as an available chit, which meant she needed to renew her acquaintance with William Overby at her earliest convenience.

She and Sarah returned to the house with thoughts of packing foremost in their minds.

CHAPTER 28

A BROTHER AND A SISTER
REUNITE

"*Y*our apartment is beautiful."

The words were said as if the young woman who spoke them couldn't quite believe what she was seeing.

"Thank you. I think," William replied as a smirk replaced the look of nervousness he had displayed as he escorted his sister through his four-room home. For some reason, he wanted her approval. Wanted her to affirm his choices in the furnishings and decor, for if she liked them, chances were good Lady Lily would as well.

Despite having lived in the apartment for nearly a year, William hadn't hosted his sister there before today. They had spent the afternoon in Berkeley Square so he could treat her to an ice at Gunter's Tea Shop in honor of her birthday. When she requested he also show her where he lived, he had nervously agreed to do so, deciding it was ready for a female's inspection.

Katie Overby regarded her brother for a moment. "Goodness. I don't see you for months on end, and when I finally do, it's as if we've spent all of our yesterdays together," she said, a smile appearing. "I suppose you don't miss us much, since you haven't been to visit Bingham House," she admonished, referring to the modest home she lived in with their step-parents, the Binghams.

William shook his head. "I see Mr. Bingham at the warehouse nearly every day, and I occasionally see Mrs. Bingham when she brings his luncheon," he claimed. "And you're always at school—"

"No longer," Katie interrupted. At his raised brow—she was sure he was about to ask if she had finally quit finishing school—she added, "I'm officially graduated from Warwick's."

Katie had attended the grammar and finishing school since she was fifteen years of age. Now nineteen, she could claim the abilities to speak French, dance, and do needlework as well as to draw, paint, speak proper English, and comport herself as if to the manor born. No one would ever guess she had begun her life in the slums of London.

William grinned. "Congratulations," he said, indicating she should take a seat. "A proper lady now, are you?"

Katie shook her head. "Don't congratulate me just yet," she countered. "I haven't yet made my come-out. Mother says I will next month, though."

Although William didn't refer to Livia Bingham as 'mother'—he still remembered his birth mother—he knew Katie had been too young when Madeline Overby died. Katie had only ever known the Binghams as their parents. "You'll be married by Christmas, I expect," William said as he made his way to the alcove that made up his kitchen. The teakettle was boiling, its hiss reminding him he had started to make tea upon their arrival from their afternoon trip.

Katie made a sound approximating a snort. "And how can that be when I haven't a single suitor?" she asked.

William returned with a tea tray. He set it down on the low table in front of the settee. "I'll let you do the honors since I'm sure I would make a cake of it," he said, not entirely teasing. He had practiced several times by serving himself, following the example Lady Lily had displayed when he had visited her at Fitzsimmons Manor, right down to pouring the milk so it swirled into a spiral in the cup. "And as for suitors, you only need gaze into a looking glass. You look so much like our mother, it's uncanny," he claimed, fighting a lump in his throat.

He had always thought Katie resembled their mother. Now she could pass for her. "She was beautiful. You'll have multiple offers I'm sure, which means I'll need to—"

"Father will see to a proper match, I'm quite sure," Katie interrupted, grinning when she imagined her brother challenging all of her potential suitors. "You need a haircut," she stated, quickly changing the subject as she poured the tea.

William ran a hand through his hair, his fingers raking the thick locks to their shoulder-length ends. "I agree. Perhaps you can do the honors before I return you home," he suggested, remembering that the phaeton he had borrowed from the Binghams was still parked out front. He would either walk or take a hackney back to his apartment after he dropped off Katie.

"Rather trusting of you," Katie replied, holding out a teacup to him.

Taking the cup, William regarded his sister for a moment. "I need to tell you something," he said quietly.

Katie looked up from pouring her own tea, rather alarmed at his quiet statement. "Oh?" They had spent the entire afternoon together, teasing one another and catching up one another on their lives, so she was rather surprised at his sudden seriousness. "What is it?"

"I found our uncle. Augustus Overby."

Blinking, Katie set the teapot down onto the tray and regarded William with a shake of her head. "Uncle?" she repeated. "We have an uncle?"

"I know," William said with a nod. "I was just as surprised. When I was told about the man, I was rather hoping it was Father, but still, it was so good to meet him."

Katie continued to shake her head. "How? Where?" she asked, her tea forgotten.

"The young woman I told you about—Lady Lily—she mentioned there was a Mr. Overby working at a charity in Oxford Street. Claimed I looked like him, so I stopped in and it was Augustus."

Her skepticism evident, Katie shook her head. "How can

you be sure he's a relation?" she asked, once again displaying alarm.

William hung his head a moment. "He knows about us. Apparently looked for us when he returned from the Continent, but we weren't at the apartment in the Seven Dials, and he didn't know where else to look. Thought perhaps Mother had taken us to live in the country. Hoped she had taken us from the city, in fact," he added with a sigh. "He wasn't exactly in a position to take on children since he was wounded in the Battle of Talavera and didn't have employment. Until Lady Bostwick hired him to work in her office, that is," he added.

Katie lifted her teacup and took a sip. "Is he agreeable?" she asked, her manner still rather guarded.

William allowed a grin. "Very. And if I'm to believe Lady Bostwick and Lady Lily and the man who works with him at the charity, we are very similar in appearance," he explained. "You'll like him, I expect. He is agreeable and rather humble."

"Then I look forward to meeting the man," Katie said with a nod.

"There's something else," William said quietly. "Our father —our *real* father—he was in the army. All those years, he was on the Continent, fighting. He died in the Battle of Talavera."

Katie sighed and allowed a nod. "I don't remember him. I know I should feel sorrow, but I cannot," she replied.

At the sound of light footsteps, their *tap-tap-taps* sounding as if they were just outside his door, Katie angled her head and arched an eyebrow, a smirk appearing. "Are you expecting a lady friend?" she asked, pretending to be scandalized.

William's eyes widened. "No," he replied. "The only other woman who has even been in my apartment is my housekeeper," he claimed, thinking the light footsteps were probably those of a lightskirt hired to visit one of his neighbors. Then there was a *tap-tap* on his door and he straightened in his chair.

Katie's teasing grin was replaced with one of curiosity. She stood up and quickly made her way to the door, intent on discovering her brother's visitor before he had a chance to send her away.

"Katie!" he said, getting up from his chair as quickly as he could.

But Katie beat him to the door, opening it with a flourish. She suddenly stilled herself. "How do?" she said, managing a curtsy when she realized the young blonde woman who stood staring at her was obviously a woman of quality. Her mantle, which was a deep blue velvet, made her blue eyes appear even more so.

*L*ily blinked and regarded the young brunette who stood staring at her. She appeared to be the same age as her, and she was dressed in a day gown befitting a woman of quality.

Do I have the wrong apartment? Lily wondered, thinking the footman might be pulling a prank. If so, the joke wasn't funny. She checked the number over the door just to be sure. "Does Mr. Overby live here?" she managed to get out, a rushing sound filling her ears as her nerves went on high alert and her heart raced.

"*Y*es, yes he does," Katie nodded. She turned just as her brother joined her at the door, noting how he stared at their visitor as if he were seeing a ghost. When he didn't immediately say anything, Katie decided he was unable to form a coherent greeting. About to admonish him, she noticed how the young woman's gaze went from uncertainty to anger. Fury, even.

Before Katie could say anything, the dainty blonde suddenly turned and hurried back down the hall to the front doors of the building, her footsteps barely audible.

"Lily!" William called out, his tongue finally untied enough to say her name.

"Lily?" Katie repeated. "Who is she?"

William nodded as he suddenly bolted out the door and

down the hall. "The woman I'm in love with!" he called back as he made it to the building's entrance.

Katie watched in awe as her brother sailed down the hall, pausing to allow the footman to reopen the door for him. He might have simply opened it himself except the shorter man would have been thrown aside in his haste to catch up to the young lady who had disappeared the moment before.

"Lily!" he called out again, coming to a halt and glancing both ways. Stunned when he didn't see her—*how could she have disappeared so quickly?*—William stilled himself and took a deep breath. She had to be close. "Which way did she go?" he asked of the footman, who merely shrugged.

"I didn't see since I was opening the door, sir," the short man responded.

William threw his head back and cursed. Lily no doubt thought the worst of him, thought he was entertaining a young woman in his apartment.

Why had he been so tongue-tied? He had been so surprised at seeing Lady Lily at his door, looking even more beautiful than the last time he had seen her, he couldn't think what to say. Much like that day when he had first laid eyes upon her at Wellingham Imports. Or that day at Fitzsimmons Manor. That day her brother's coach had come to take her away for the summer.

Cursing under his breath and taking one more look up and down the street, William turned and found his sister watching him from the front of the building.

"She's gone?" Katie asked as she moved to join him in the street. At Williams's nod, she shook her head. "I'm so sorry. This is all my fault. She thought me..." Her face reddened and she quieted her voice. "She thought I was your—"

"Yes, I think she did," William said with a sigh, not wanting his sister to say the word, whether it be 'mistress' or 'paramour' or 'ladybird'.

Katie took his arm with both her hands. "Take me to... to... where does she live?" she asked.

William fought back the tears that threatened. "Fitzsimmons Manor," he managed to get out.

"Take me there. I'll explain everything to her," Katie begged.

William shook his head. "You needn't."

"Please. I want to make it right. I shouldn't have answered your door."

Tempted to allow his sudden hurt and anger to get the best of him, William could only shake his head or risk hurting his sister with unkind words. It would be easy to blame the misunderstanding on her.

How could he have been so tongue-tied? So unable to form a coherent greeting? And an introduction? He closed his eyes in an effort to tamp down his sorrow. "I rather doubt she had good news for me anyway," he said in a whisper. "Come, let's get our coats, and I'll take you home."

CHAPTER 29

A LADY RETURNS HOME

*H*ot tears streamed down her face as Lily pressed herself into the squabs of the Wellingham coach. She had thought to visit William in person, anxious to let him know of her return to London even before she had the coach return her to Fitzsimmons Manor. Perhaps she was also hoping he might propose.

How silly of me!

The young woman who had opened the door to his apartment was obviously a courtesan—she was far better dressed than a prostitute would have been—and rather pretty.

This last thought had her sobbing uncontrollably, nearly unable to breathe as the tears flowed down her cheeks. *How often did she visit? How many other men did she visit? How often did William welcome her into his bed? Did she spend the entire night with him?*

My bed! she found herself thinking as a stab of jealousy had her straightening on her seat. She managed to take a gulp of air, and her body shuddered before another round of tears dripped off her cheeks.

Aware that anyone walking past the coach might see her, she quickly pulled shut the curtains over the windows. *Goodness! I must look a sight,* she thought as she dug for a hanky in her reticule. Before dabbing at her eyes, she allowed more tears to flow, hiccuping between sobs in order to take short breaths.

What if the young woman was really his *wife?* Someone he had met and married whilst she was in Staffordshire? While she was telling tall tales of her other suitors in order that her brother might choose William over all the others? She allowed a moan of pain as another round of sobs shook her entire body.

Before long, the hanky was drenched. She chided herself on becoming a watering pot over a man. Over a man who apparently didn't miss her one iota. Over a man who had met and married without even considering her!

This last thought had her tears subsiding, her hiccups calming. The Marquess of Reading might have claimed he would honor his vows, but she rather doubted a rake could change his ways. None of her other suitors were worthy enough or merely required her dowry to maintain their worth.

Spinsterhood suddenly appealed to her again, suddenly seemed the only way to live her life. She wouldn't have any children of her own, of course, but the Grandbys had plenty she could visit and play with should she require their company. Sarah would have another baby before Christmas. She could spend the holiday with them.

She didn't need a husband to have a satisfying life. *I'll be a spinster,* she thought, ignoring the pang she felt at making the silent claim.

When she was quite sure she could speak normally, she knocked on the trap door in the ceiling of the coach. The driver's face appeared, showing surprise at finding her back in the coach. "Yes, milady?" he asked, his Cockney accent evident.

"Fitzsimmons Manor, please," she called up.

"Yes, milady," he replied before closing the door. The coach jerked forward and rocked gently as it made its way east toward Park Lane.

The house was quiet when Porter opened one of the front doors for Lily. "Where is everyone?" she asked as she allowed the butler to take her mantle and bonnet. A footman passed her, hurrying through the doors to retrieve her trunk.

"The theatre, my lady. Lord Plymouth invited Lord and Lady Chamberlain and Lady Samantha to accompany him."

Lily had to swallow quickly in order to stave off another round of tears.

Lady Samantha had a fiancé. She was finally engaged to be married. To a marquess, no less. "I'll be in my room. Could you have tea delivered, please?" Tea always made everything seem better. She was half-tempted to ask for the brandy, as well.

Porter nodded and moved off toward the kitchens as Lily climbed the stairs. She found her bedchamber exactly as she had left it, taking a bit of comfort in knowing some things didn't change.

A pair of footman appeared with her trunk and valise and quickly took their leave, although one asked if he should send up a maid. She was about to decline the offer, but thought better of it. Bonnie would know what had happened in her absence. At the moment and after three days in a coach all alone, she decided she wanted to concentrate on someone else. "Yes, please do," she finally answered.

The two nodded and took their leave of her room, leaving her in the deepening gloom of twilight.

Lily sat on the edge of the bed for a moment before the knock came at the door. "Come," she called out.

The lady's maid appeared, her smile bringing a bit of cheer to the room. "It's so good to see you again, milady!" Bonnie said as she stepped into the room, well aware Lily had been crying. She immediately moved to the trunk, intending to unpack it. "Are you all right, milady?" she asked as she undid the latches and opened the leather-clad trunk.

"A bit road weary, I suppose," Lily answered. "I'm concerned about Lady Samantha."

The maid shook her head. "You needn't be. She's quite fine and rather happy, milady. I can tell you all about it if ye'd like," she offered.

Lily allowed a wan smile. "Please do."

Bonnie beamed, obviously glad to have the opportunity to share what she knew of the Fitzsimmons' summer.

Lady Samantha was indeed betrothed, and not to the baronet who had apparently proposed on the docks when her ship returned from Valencia. Instead, she was about to marry the Marquess of Plymouth, the man with whom she had been stranded on a desert island for a week. The man she claimed she loved because, well, she just did.

The newspapers had printed varying reports of what had happened to *The Fairweather* and to the two people who had been lost at sea. Lily knew it because she had secretly read the articles in *The Times* that suggested Lady Samantha had either jumped overboard or had been washed off of the sailing vessel, *The Fairweather,* by a giant wave.

Sarah had obviously read the articles, perhaps after Gabriel had done so, and then claimed the papers had already been discarded with the day's trash when Lily wondered as to their whereabouts.

When she recovered the newspapers—Lily had sneaked down to the kitchens after most of the household was asleep—she pored over every article, wondering what news might have driven her sister-in-law to hide the papers from her.

Lily expected to find gossip suggesting *she* had done something wrong, something scandalous. Expected to find an article claiming she had accepted someone's offer of marriage, or an entry in the Society pages saying she wouldn't be granted a voucher to waltz by the patronesses at Almack's because Sir Tristan had fallen face first onto her bosom during a musicale. Or because she had been kissed by a viscount in front of all the guests at the Marquess of Morganfield's soirée, or because she had been spied in Hyde Park in the company of a baronet at seven o'clock in the morning. Or because she had been seen kissing the Rake of Reading in Lord Weatherstone's garden.

She was quite prepared to be angry by what she read and quite prepared to write a letter to the editor in an effort to set the record straight as to her character.

However, she could find no such article about her. Instead, she found one questioning the character of Lady Samantha, her best friend and confidante.

Who knew, though, if the incident described in the sensational news piece had really occurred or if the ship's owner was simply a gossip monger intent on sullying Samantha's reputation by suggesting she had deliberately jumped ship with another passenger? A male passenger?

How likely was it that Samantha would jump overboard of her own volition? Lily couldn't imagine a situation that would drive Samantha to do anything so rash, unless the ship had been set on fire or she was attempting to save another passenger who had fallen overboard. Either way, the fact that Viscount Chamberlain had left almost immediately for the Mediterranean suggested the situation was serious.

"Oh, she didn't jump overboard," Bonnie said, pulling out several gowns and smoothing the fabric as she did so. "She was caught in a wave and washed overboard. It's a wonder she survived. She nearly drowned!"

Lily nodded her understanding, but she also knew Samantha could swim. "But she survived," she said with a grin. "And has made it home safe?" she half-questioned.

The maid confirmed that Samantha was home, as were Matthew and Caroline Fitzsimmons. They had all returned from the Mediterranean on *The Fairweather*—the very ship from which Samantha and the Marquess of Plymouth had been washed overboard by a rogue wave. And despite a brief betrothal to a baronet who had apparently proposed only moments after the ship docked in Wapping, Samantha was now engaged to marry the marquess, a man she apparently loved and a man who apparently loved her.

Once married, Samantha would become the mistress of Castle Keys in Yorkshire.

Lily could feel nothing but relief and happiness for Samantha. The woman deserved a husband. Deserved a good life, although, truth be told, Lily could hardly imagine Samantha as a marchioness. A viscountess or baroness, yes, but a marchioness? Lily had to smile at the thought of seeing Samantha wearing a coronet during formal occasions.

When Bonnie pulled out the yellow gown decorated with

embroidered flutterbies, Lily inhaled. "I'd like to wear that this evening," she said, realizing she needed to change from her traveling clothes. Perhaps the yellow would help to stave off the sorrow she still felt at seeing William with another woman, the thought leaving her on the verge of tears again.

"Of course, milady," Bonnie replied, hurrying to help dress Lily. She barely had the gown buttoned up the back when there was a knock at the door.

"Come!" Lily called out, a sob escaping despite her attempt to swallow it.

Porter appeared, acting as if he hadn't noticed she'd had a good cry at some point during the afternoon. "There's a Miss Overby here to see you, milady. Are you seeing callers?"

Lily blinked. Miss Overby? *Miss?*

"Are you sure she said 'Miss' and not 'Mrs.'?" she countered, thinking perhaps the butler had misheard the woman's title.

As if he was a bit offended by her question, Porter straightened, a difficult proposition for a man as old as he. "I, in fact, confirmed the title she used, my lady. Miss Katie Overby."

Lily gave a start as she stared at the butler. *Katie?* Wasn't that the name of William's sister? *Why is* she *here?*

Or did her brother dispatch her to argue on his behalf?

A fresh sense of rage had Lily motivated to move. "See her to the parlor, please. And bring the tea there," she ordered as she moved to the window, half-tempted to ask that a bottle of brandy be included on the tea tray. She gave a nod to Bonnie, who resumed unpacking her trunk.

There was no longer enough light to see by, but Porter handed the maid a lit candle so she could light the lamps on the dressing table and nightstand.

Appalled at her red-rimmed eyes and tear-stained cheeks, Lily sighed. With Bonnie's help and some cool water from the pitcher, her face and hair were put to rights. She couldn't do much more about her appearance without a good night's sleep.

Smoothing out the skirts of her gown, she took her leave of her room and headed for the parlor, her back ramrod straight and her head held high.

CHAPTER 30

A SISTER SHARES A SECRET

*N*ervous, Katie Overby stood in the middle of the Fitzsimmons Manor parlor and decided she was suddenly rather glad she had attended Warwick's, if for no other reason than she knew what to do in an aristocrat's parlor. Knew what was expected of her. Until Lady Lily joined her, she could surreptitiously examine the room.

Although everything was dust-free, the furnishings were a bit on the worn side, as if the Fitzsimmons used the room on a regular basis and never replaced the upholstery. A fresh floral arrangement made up of roses and daisies decorated one of the side tables while the lamps and fireplace had been lit, enveloping the parlor in a golden glow. *Where was everyone?* She expected to find a family in residence and a staff of servants. Since her arrival nearly a half-hour ago, she had only seen the butler and one footman.

"Miss Overby?"

Her name had Katie nearly jumping where she stood. She turned toward the door to find Lily Harkins staring at her with a look of confusion on her face. "Yes," she said as she managed a curtsy. "Katie Overby."

Lily stared at the young woman, much as she had done when the door to William's apartment had opened. Indeed, this woman was the same woman who was at William's apartment! "You are William's sister?" she ventured, thinking it made more sense if she were his wife. Why else would she be here unless she intended to inform Lily she wasn't to pay any more calls on William?

Katie nodded. "It's very good to meet the woman who has my brother so..." She allowed the sentence to trail off when she realized she didn't quite know how much she was allowed to say.

Had William admitted his love for Lady Lily? Had they made some sort of arrangements for their future? Or was her brother merely hoping to court the woman who looked as if she could be Cupid's sister.

Well, if her aim was as good as her brother's, then Katie supposed it explained why William was so enamored with the blonde woman who stood before her.

Lily moved into the room, managing a curtsy before indicating a chair. Katie quickly moved to it, thankful she could get off her quivering legs.

"I've ordered tea," Lily said as she sat in the middle of the settee, her yellow skirts spread wide. She had seen Lady Chamberlain do the same, making the viscountess appear as if she sat on a throne. Suddenly feeling ridiculous, though, Lily smoothed her skirts closer to her body and regarded her visitor. *Sister? This is Williams's sister?* Her head felt as it were suddenly stuffed with cotton. "Did you come at his bidding?" she asked, not sure where to start with her questions.

At that moment, Porter appeared on the threshold with the tea service, pausing a moment. "Here on the table, please," Lily said without looking in his direction. Her gaze was fixed on her guest.

The butler placed the tray on the low table in front of the settee and gave a bow. He was about to ask if she required anything else, but Lily cut him off with, "That will be all, Porter."

The old man bowed again and took his leave, pulling the doors shut as he left the room.

Once the doors were closed, Katie shook her head. "I did not come at his bidding, my lady. In fact, I offered to do so, but he told me... he said it wasn't necessary. That he was fairly sure you didn't have good news for him anyway."

"Good news?" Lily repeated as she poured a cup of tea. "Milk? Sugar?"

Her shoulders slumping, Katie regarded her hostess for a moment. "Both. Yes," she replied with a nod. She tried to keep her attention on Lily but found it hard when she noticed how Lily poured the tea, how when she poured the dollop of milk, it swirled inside the cup to form a perfect spiral. She reached for the teacup when Lily held it out in her direction. "My brother served me tea just like this earlier today," she murmured in wonder.

Lily held her breath a moment, remembering how fascinated William had been with the swirling milk, wanting her to explain how she managed to achieve the effect.

Apparently, he had been practicing.

Shaking her head as if to clear it, Lily remembered her last query. "You said he was expecting good news. Or not," she said as she poured a cup for herself, repeating the swirling milk trick.

Katie dipped her head. "I wish to speak freely, but I do not want my words to incriminate my brother in any way," she said carefully. "I cannot help but think my presence in his apartment was somehow... upsetting to you."

"Oh, my," Lily murmured when she comprehended Katie's earlier words. "You're not his... courtesan," she whispered.

Katie's eyes widened in alarm. "No, my lady, and I can assure you, he does not associate with women of that ilk. I was only at his apartment because it's my birthday, you see, and he took me to Gunter's Tea Shop for an ice, and he's never shown me his apartment before, and I thought it was because he was ashamed of where he lives, so in his defense, he agreed to take me there.

"And now that I've been there, I find I'm rather envious, for it's a very beautiful apartment, you see. Very nicely appointed, which I suppose only makes sense since he has very good taste and is able to acquire such nice things because of his position at Wellingham Imports. I think the woman who agrees to be his wife will adore living there, although I don't know if wives are really welcome in that particular building since it is supposed to be bachelor quarters. But his things will be beautiful no matter where his wife chooses to be settled." She paused a moment and rolled her eyes. "And I'm prattling, aren't I?"

Lily blinked, rather glad the young woman had done so. She had certainly provided a good deal of information with her words. "I appreciate that you would speak on your brother's behalf," she finally answered. "I did, indeed, go there with the intention of informing him in person of my recent return to London. You see, I've been gone these past couple of months, but Mr. Overby was the last visitor I had before I took my leave, and I couldn't help but think we had so much more to discuss about so many topics, and I suppose I found myself wanting to continue that conversation and hoping that he might once again come to my rescue." She took a deep breath and let it out in a sigh. "And now I'm the one prattling, aren't I?"

Katie allowed a grin. "I appreciate that you regard my brother so highly. He is a good man. He's a hard worker. He has strived to become educated, and he has everything he wants in the world except..." She shook her head just then. "Except you."

Lily stared at Katie, tears pricking the corners of her eyes. "Me?" she asked, stunned at the other woman's words.

Nodding, Katie leaned forward. "I truly believe he loves you, my lady," she whispered. "He says he does. But I do not believe he thinks his feelings are reciprocated."

Blinking quickly in an attempt to stave off the tears that threatened to spill over her lashes, Lily took a deep breath. *He loves me.* She took another breath. "And if his feelings are... reciprocated?" she ventured before sniffling. "Do you suppose that would be the *good news* he was hoping for?"

Katie angled her head to one side as a brilliant smile appeared. "Oh, yes, milady," she said with a nod. "I'm quite sure of it."

Lily allowed the tears to flow, deciding she could do nothing to stop them. And although she could do nothing to stop her tears, she could at least provide someone with a bit of good news.

CHAPTER 31

A CLERK RECEIVES
PERMISSION

William returned to his building after having seen to the delivery of his sister to Bingham House and of the phaeton to the mews behind the house. Instead of employing a hackney, he had opted to walk the two miles, deciding he needed to clear his head and decide how to proceed with his life.

He was contemplating writing a letter to Lady Lily when he stepped up to his building and the footman presented him with a missive.

"Two pennies?" William asked, thinking a two-penny postman had delivered the elegantly folded note. He worked to fish the coins from his pockets.

"No, sir. It was delivered by a courier," the footman replied, shaking his head. "About an hour ago."

William blinked. *A courier?* He turned the note over in his hand and studied the wax seal. Although he didn't recognize the symbol embossed in the dark red wax, he could tell it was important. Absently, he handed the two pence to the footman and made his way to his apartment.

He waited until he was in his study and had lit a candle lamp before he slid his thumb beneath the wax and popped the seal loose. Unfolding the missive, he angled it toward the light and read the short sentence.

Dear Mr. Overby, You have my permission. Now get on with it. Gabriel Wellingham, Earl of Trenton.

William stared at the words and reread the missive three times before lifting his head. *I can court Lady Lily*, he realized, his breaths suddenly labored. *Which means I can marry her!*

He stared toward the door to his bedchamber, his mind's eye imagining Lady Lily in his bed, her blond curls splayed out on the pillow, her face displaying a pretty blush and a come-hither expression, one hand gripping the edge of the bed linens so they covered her bare breasts. Desire overwhelmed him, the subsequent lust hardening his manhood so it strained the placket of his breeches.

If he could court Lily, he could ask for her hand in marriage. And if she agreed to marry him, she would one day be in his bed.

His ardor was short-lived, however, when he remembered how she had fled from his door mere hours before, obviously convinced his sister was in his employ as a harlot.

Well, if Lady Lily believed he would engage a prostitute, then she certainly didn't know him well enough to be courted by him. How could she have come to his door—a door in a building of bachelor's apartments—and then flee so quickly without waiting for an explanation as to why a woman had answered his door?

Besides, how many other suitors had been given permission by the Earl of Trenton to court Lady Lily? And how many of those suitors were aristocrats? *Probably all of them*, he thought.

William Overby rather doubted Lily would consider his suit if she had other more suitable suitors vying for her hand.

Why would she?

He was merely a low-born clerk.

Sighing, William dropped the missive onto his desk and made his way to his bedchamber.

CHAPTER 32

A LATE NIGHT VISITOR

William regarded the ceiling, wondering if the woman who cleaned his apartment ever looked up to see the cobwebs that crisscrossed the ornate coffers. Perhaps Mrs. Greenleaf had done so, but simply couldn't reach that high to clean them. Or perhaps she hadn't noticed them, and only had eyes for what was around her, below her. Perhaps the cobwebs weren't even in evidence during the daylight hours and only appeared when the sun was setting, when its rays pierced through the west window and lit the farthest reaches of his beautifully appointed bedchamber.

Long past sunset now, the light had been swallowed up by the night, and the cobwebs had disappeared with the light.

Rolling over onto his side, William sighed and considered getting up. He had no intention of falling asleep in his clothes, but the overwhelming sense of melancholy had him wondering what he had to look forward to in life.

He thought he had done everything right, using his resources to outfit his apartment to his liking and fill his wardrobe with clothes befitting a man of a higher station than himself. He thought surrounding himself with the trappings of a richer man would bring him happiness. A sense of satisfaction. A sense of accomplishment. After all, how many men who had started out life in the Seven Dials could claim to have respectable employment as a clerk?

But without someone to share in his success, he felt no sense of satisfaction. No sense of accomplishment. No happiness.

He simply felt empty.

Sleep would be a welcome respite. Sleep offered an escape from thinking of what couldn't be. Of what might have been had he said more to the girl he had allowed to slip away from him that night in Vauxhall Gardens.

Allowed to slip away from him this afternoon!

She didn't slip away. She ran away. At my bidding, he remembered. At least, she had that night in Vauxhall Gardens. But today? She had taken one look at Katie and assumed the worst.

Run!

The mix of anger and betrayal he had felt toward Zachary had him now wishing he had run with Lily Harkins back then, run away from her friend and Zachary, leaving them to their illicit activities. At least he would have been assured Lily was safe, that she was returned to the household where she was employed.

He had worried about her for days after that incident, wondered if she had made it back to wherever she worked without being accosted by footpads or by men too drunk to know better.

Well, he now knew she had made it home that night. Made it home to eventually discover her existence was known to her half-brother. Known and valued.

Who would have ever guessed the Earl of Trenton would seek her out and recognize her as his sister and arrange for her life to change so completely? That she would turn out to be his employer's cousin? The one woman for whom he could claim to feel affection!

Stranger things had happened, he supposed. Back then, they would have been seen as equals, she as a maid and he as a laborer in a warehouse. Despite his promotion to the position of inventory clerk, William could hardly expect the Earl of

Trenton to allow Lily to marry below her new station, even if he had given his permission to allow him to court her.

Others with titles and who were far richer had already put voice to their intentions to ask for her hand—if they hadn't already done so. *The Morning Chronicle* might not have printed her name and the names of those who courted her, but anyone who knew of her existence knew who the editors meant when they wrote of her popularity at *ton* events.

Sleep... well, he wasn't yet ready to sleep, so it wouldn't do him any good to try.

He was about to sit up on his ornate bed when he became aware of light footsteps in the hall leading to his apartment. *Tap-tap-tap*. Normally, he ignored the feel of footsteps outside his front door, their vibrations through the floor indicative of whomever it was making their way to their apartment.

Mr. Peabody, who lived next door, was a rather short man who walked with a slight limp, his footsteps rather uneven. *Thump. Thump-thump. Thump.*

Mr. Avery, who lived in the unit across the hall, was on the heavier side, his gait slower but more even. *Thump. Thump. Thump.*

And then there was the Baron Brookstone, whose quick steps made it sound as if he hurried everywhere, which was usually the case. *Thump-thump-thump-thump*. The man seemed to be late for everything, including getting home in the wee hours of the morning from whatever club he had spent the night gambling.

The footsteps William felt at the moment were too light to be those of any of his neighbors. They were light and uncertain, as if their owner couldn't decide how to proceed. *Tap. Tap tap tap. Tap.*

So it was a surprise when a knock sounded at his door. It was a muffled knock, which indicated someone wearing gloves, but not a knock with any kind of force behind it. A knock that was as tentative as the footsteps that brought the someone to his front door.

Had his sister returned? But why would she?

She should be at Bingham House!

Alarmed, William angled his head but heard nothing else. Hurrying to the door, he paused before turning the handle and pulling the carved wooden door inward.

Through the six-inch wide opening, he boggled at who he found standing there. Lady Lily Harkins—or was she Lady Lily Wellingham now?—was staring at him with her large blue eyes, bright with what might have been unshed tears.

She was wearing what could only be described as a shroud, a mantle with a deep hood pulled over a poke bonnet that hid all her other features. But it didn't hide her identity, at least not from William.

He knew those eyes better than he knew his own. He had pictured those eyes in his mind's eyes before he fell asleep nearly every night since that night in Vauxhall Gardens. Blue eyes, so beautiful, and he was about to drown in their depths when the apparition before him spoke.

"Please, may I come in, Mr. Overby?"

The words were a whisper, their soft sounds permeating Williams's brain in what could have been a caress. Their meaning took a bit longer to comprehend, given his gaze was still fixed on those eyes. He was quite certain he was drowning in them. That he had drowned. And he wasn't making the least bit of effort to resurface for air.

He had a passing thought of how easy it had been to conjure her into existence. When she left earlier that afternoon, he had never thought to see her again. And yet, just imagining her had the young woman appearing at his door!

When the young woman turned to look down the hall, William blinked.

May I come in?

Why, of course, she could come in! She could come in whenever she wanted and whatever the time of day. Lady Lily was always welcome in his life whenever she deigned to grace him with her presence!

William blinked again when she turned her attention back to him and angled her head, as if she feared he was going to deny her entrance to his home. "Of course," he murmured, stepping aside to open the door wider. He gave a bow out of habit. "You're always welcome, my lady," he whispered, realizing he was allowing another woman into his apartment. No women other than his sister and housekeeper had ever been in his apartment. Not even a lightskirt had crossed his threshold.

Lily gathered the mantle close around her body and slipped through the door, her movements suggesting she was hiding from someone. But as soon as William had the door latched, she dropped a small valise to the floor and reached up with both hands to shove the hood from her around her bonnet. She just as quickly removed the poke bonnet from her blonde curls.

Bobbing a curtsy, she looked for some sign in William's expression. "I apologize for calling on you at such a late hour," she said in a quiet voice. "I thought of sending a note, but given a footman would have had to be dispatched, and I couldn't afford anyone wondering what I was up to, I would have had to be the one to deliver it.

"I had to see you."

William swallowed. *Note?* "You need never apologize to me, my lady. Truly," he murmured, staring at her as if he were seeing a ghost, for at the moment, he still didn't quite believe what he was seeing. "Welcome back to London," he managed, his earlier uncharitable thoughts of her gone from his brain.

She looked as if she had been crying. Had he been responsible for her tears? Or had she learned some horrible news when she finally arrived at Fitzsimmons Manor?

Was Lady Lily truly in his apartment? Nearly leaning against the plaster wall as if she needed it for support? Or had he simply conjured a vision of her as he lay on his bed imagining what life might be like with her as his wife?

Faith! There it was again! The thought that Lady Lily could be his wife. Which was ridiculous, for the earl's sister would never deign to marry him. She had her pick of at least four members of the *ton* who had expressed their intentions of asking for her hand in marriage. He might have come to the conclusion *she* would be his first choice should he decide to marry—

his only choice, actually—but he rather doubted *he* was her first choice.

*L*ily's eyes widened at William's comment. *I need never apologize?*

Well, there is hope yet, then, she thought. "May I prevail upon you for a moment of your time?" she asked then. She rolled her eyes. "What am I saying? Two moments, at least. Perhaps five?"

All night?

William stared at her, finally closing his mouth. He waved her toward the settee in the middle of the room, momentarily pleased when her appreciative gaze swept the room and seemed to take in his elegant surroundings all at once. "You are welcome to stay the entire night..." *The rest of your life.* "Should you wish to, my lady," he murmured, not even aware of how his words might be interpreted.

Lily returned her attention to him and shook her head, deciding to ignore his comment in favor of putting voice to her first impression of his living quarters. His sister was right in saying his apartment was beautifully appointed. "Your apartment is gorgeous," she said meekly as she removed her mantle.

William reached for the cape and saw that she wore the yellow gown beneath, the gown she had been wearing the day he had met her at Wellingham Imports. He moved to hang up the mantle and said, "Thank you, my lady. Please, do have a seat. May I...?" He paused, realizing he had never entertained anyone other than his sister in his living quarters before. "Would you like tea, perhaps?" he asked, thinking he should probably help himself to a glass of wine. Or a brandy. Scotch would do quite fine if he had any.

He didn't have any.

Lily nodded. "Tea would be most welcome," she replied. "With a spot of... brandy, perhaps? May I help?" she queried, her gaze sweeping the room, as if she were looking for something. Or someone.

"I can manage," William replied. Thinking she was in search of a servant, perhaps to act as a chaperone, he added, "I don't yet employ a full-time servant. Just a part-time housekeeper and laundress," he explained as he moved to the tiny alcove that made up his kitchen.

"What about your valet?" Lily asked as her attention drifted from one beautiful object to the next. She was sure he had to have a valet. She had thought that the day she met him at Wellingham Imports.

"I am my own, my lady," he replied with a smirk, his attention focused on making tea. It had been so easy when his sister was here earlier. Now, it seemed almost impossible.

Although his teapot had a small chip in the top, its spout was intact. He made a mental note to acquire a silver tea set. Wellingham Imports rarely imported silver products, but he supposed he could simply buy a set at a silversmith's shop in Ludgate Hill. Perhaps Lady Lily would provide some guidance as to an acceptable pattern.

Measuring the tea into the pot, he was glad to find there was more than enough hot water to make the pot of tea. He pulled the last two teacups from the cupboard above the water pump and arranged the creamer and sugar-pot on the small tray he used when he ate breakfast at home. Adding his only silver spoons to the tray along with the last two biscuits Mrs. Greenleaf had brought him when she last cleaned his apartment, William frowned as he examined his second attempt to serve tea to a visitor.

Something was missing.

The brandy.

The bottle was among his meager collection of spirits on the sideboard in the parlor. Hurrying to the sideboard, he grabbed the brandy and added it to the collection on the tray.

Satisfied he had everything arranged correctly, he carried the tray to the low table in front of where Lily had taken a seat on the velvet-clad settee. "Will my lady serve the tea? I fear I might make a cake of it," he murmured. He *would* make a cake of it. His nervousness would have the hot tea spilling all over the table, the sugar lumps disintegrating into grains that would be scattered the length and breadth of the table. The milk? Well, it would end up in a white puddle in the middle of it all, and not at all swirled into a perfect spiral pattern like the ones Lily created when she poured.

Lily glanced up at him, apparently impressed he was delivering the tea on a tray. She was even more impressed as she took in the arrangement on the tray. "You needn't have gone to so much trouble," she said. "I didn't intend to be such a bother."

William sighed as he took the upholstered chair across from the settee. "You are not a bother. And it was no trouble, my lady," he replied. "I am, in fact, rather honored by your presence."

Lily regarded him for a moment before reaching for the teapot. "Honored?" she repeated. "I hardly think you should feel honored," she added as she poured the tea. "Sugar? Milk? Brandy?" she asked as she raised her eyes to meet his. Except his eyes were aimed at the teapot, or her hands. She couldn't be sure which.

"Yes," he replied with a nod, his eyes still on the gloved hand that held the teapot handle.

Lily giggled, her nervousness finally dissipating.

From the time she had left Fitzsimmons Manor via the servants' entrance and managed to hail a hackney, she had questioned her sanity and wondered if she might be a candidate for Bedlam. Now she knew otherwise, for if she could just convince William Overby of her affection for him, perhaps he would renew his affection for her. And having tea was a good place to start.

CHAPTER 33

REFLECTIONS ON AN AFTERNOON AND HONORABLE MEN

*L*ily had only just returned from Staffordshire late that afternoon. She hadn't even gone straight to Fitzsimmons Manor but had stopped at William's apartment with the intention of telling him... well, she wasn't exactly sure what she would have said to him when she showed up at his door.

Discovering a young woman in his apartment had made two things quite clear to her. She couldn't abide the idea of a husband who employed a mistress or was otherwise unfaithful. And she realized she couldn't feel as hurt or as betrayed as she had felt unless she was truly in love with the man who now sat before her.

Returning her attention to the teacup in front of her, Lily dropped a lump of sugar into it before adding a dollop of milk and a splash of the brandy. "I've never added brandy to tea before. You'll have to let me know if I've done it correctly," she said as she held out the cup and saucer to William.

He nodded. "I'm sure it's perfect, my lady," he said as he took the dish of tea.

One eyebrow arching, Lily regarded her host with a look suggesting she doubted his words. "You're a bounder, Mr. Overby," she said with an arched eyebrow, daring him to contradict her statement.

Stunned by her accusation, William stared at Lily for a moment. "I am not a dishonorable man," he argued. "But if I were, I would still be better than a scoundrel, I should think," he countered. "Or a rake."

Lily's eyes widened, wondering if he referred to the men who had claimed to court her. She had only meant to tease the clerk. "True," she replied.

She finished pouring her own tea and raised the cup to her lips, well aware that her host's eyes followed her every movement. Although the tea had been hot—the man obviously kept his teakettle boiling—the addition of the milk and brandy allowed her to take a satisfying sip. "'Tis delicious, Mr. Overby," she remarked, daring a glance at him over the rim of her cup.

"William," he said. "You should call me William," he repeated before he took another sip of his own brandy-spiked tea. The alcohol burned his throat but seemed to help settle his nerves.

Lily stared at her host for a moment. Although the brandy felt warm going down, she wondered how long it might be before it dulled her worry. How long it might be before she felt comfortable enough to broach her reason for having come to the clerk's apartment.

Even though William Overby wasn't a member of the *ton*, he would know her presence in his quarters was entirely inappropriate. Especially at nine o'clock at night!

She downed the rest of the liquid in her cup and set it down atop its saucer. "You're probably curious as to why I'm paying a call on you at such a late hour," she ventured.

William set his teacup into its saucer and shook his head. "Truth be told, I am wondering why you would grace me with your presence at any time of the day, my lady," he responded, rather glad the brandy was doing its magic. His nervousness had subsided, and he felt a warm glow permeate his body. "Especially after your hasty departure this afternoon."

Lily giggled, the sound a rather pleasant tinkling that had him grinning in response. "I misunderstood what I saw," she said, angling her head to one side. "I like you, William," she claimed with a nod. "Better than I have liked any other man in my acquaintance," she added, attempting to suppress a hiccup. The sound escaped, though, and she quickly moved a gloved hand in front of her mouth.

"I like you, as well, my lady," William replied, relieved he could put voice to his attraction.

"You do?"

William blinked, her response unexpected. "I do. I... I have since that night in Vauxhall Gardens," he admitted with a shrug. "I shall forever regret having sent you away without seeing to your safe arrival at Fitzsimmons Manor," he added, his eyes closing for a moment. "I apologize for not accompanying you that night."

Lily stared at William for several moments, remembering the last time before today that they had seen one another, the last time they had shared tea in the parlor at Fitzsimmons Manor. "I rather wish I had stayed with you that night," she said, her voice quiet. "But you were so insistent. So I ran. I ran all the way until I reached the people watching the fireworks, and when I didn't see Mary or you, I ran all the way to a hackney and then to the back door of Fitzsimmons Manor.

"I didn't even wait up for Mary to return. I went straight to my quarters and tried to sleep. Of course, I couldn't. Not until I heard Mary come up the back stairs." She paused then, her expression darkening. "The housekeeper was waiting for her at the top of the stairs and dismissed her as soon as she reached the landing," she said, her words so quiet, William had to strain to hear them.

When Lily didn't say anything else, William angled his head. "Where did she go?"

Lily finally raised her head, but didn't make eye contact with him. "She went to work for Mrs. Gibbons in Covent Gardens," she replied, her face displaying a blush of embarrassment.

Stilling himself, William resisted the urge to groan. Lucy Gibbons, proprietor of one of the more popular brothels in Covent Gardens, was not a particularly well-liked madame. "Is she still there?" he asked, hoping beyond hope the maid had managed to find a way out of prostitution and had returned to working in service in a household.

"I've no idea," Lily replied. "I never heard from her after that first week." She sighed. "I promised myself I would never do anything so foolish again as to go to a pleasure gardens with someone who merely wanted to be... to be *tumbled*."

Wincing, William poured a dram of brandy into his cup and held out the bottle to Lily. "I don't intend to take advantage, my lady. Truly," he said when he saw her look of confusion.

Lily shook her head. "No, but thank you for offering," she replied as she poured another cup of tea for herself. William held out his cup and she refilled it, well aware of the scent of brandy that wafted from it. "Would you ever, do you suppose?" she queried, lifting the cup to her lips.

William blinked. "Would I ever what?"

Lily regarded him for a long moment, wondering if she could feel safe with him. Could she feel comfortable in his presence? *But, of course I can!* she thought, knowing she had never felt safer than she did right then, sitting across from him in his bachelor's quarters in Golden Square. "Take advantage," she finally replied. "Of me. Of the situation."

Wondering if she were baiting him, William leaned back in his chair and finished off his brandy-spiked tea. "Never, my lady," he answered. When she didn't respond right away, William frowned. "Something else has you vexed," he said in a whisper. "Pray tell, what is it?"

Lily raised her eyes to him, surprised he was perceptive enough to recognize her concern. "What have you heard of Lady Samantha?" she asked. "What are they saying in the papers now?" The last article she had read had been from more than a week ago, and although Samantha seemed ever so pleased with the prospect of her new life as a marchioness, Lily still worried about her ordeal.

William reached over to take one of her gloved hands, squeezing it. "In late June, Mr. Wellingham's courier delivered word that she and the marquess had been found on an island, apparently unharmed." Except for Lady Samantha's reputation, of course. "They were back on English shores the following week."

Lily nodded. "And this marquess?" she asked. "Do you know anything about him? About his character? I ask only because I do not want Lady Samantha to ever be *disappointed*. I don't ever want her to wonder if she made the right decision," she added.

William allowed a nod before taking a breath. "Ethan Range, Marquess of Plymouth," he said quietly. "According to Mr. Wellingham, he rarely leaves Yorkshire, so he is rarely in London. Has rather lucrative holdings up north. Coal mines." He paused as he regarded her for a moment. "He's apparently a very honorable man. If you're concerned for Lady Samantha—"

"I am, mostly because I thought she might have drowned," Lily interjected. She closed her eyes a moment. *An island?* She should be so lucky as to be on an island with a marquess who was like...

Well, she had no idea what the marquess was like. Perhaps he was an ogre. Or an old fart of a man. *Or a molly!* She opened her eyes. Plymouth was probably a rather handsome man who realized just how agreeable life with Samantha could be after spending so much time with her.

Lily could feel nothing but happiness for her former mistress. She had been Samantha's lady's maid for several years, after all. Samantha deserved better than to live her life as a spinster.

"Apparently, she was very brave and had nothing but praise for Plymouth. Said he was a rather honorable man," William said quickly, thinking he needed to assuage any concerns Lily might have had about Samantha's ordeal and her reputation.

Lily sighed. *Honorable?* Well, the man would certainly prove his honor when he took Samantha as his wife. In the meantime, there were four men who had claimed they would ask for her hand. Only one had done so, although she wondered if the Marquess of Reading would even remember his proposal.

Were the other three dishonorable then? Surely not Lord

Montaine, for he had paid a call the morning after the *soirée* to ensure she had arrived home safely. Sir Tobias and Sir Tristan Nesbit were another matter entirely.

To be fair, she had been away from London for two months, but there were no letters for her on the silver salver when she returned to Fitzsimmons Manor earlier that afternoon. No offers of marriage or promises of rides in the park or requests for dances at the first ball of the Little Season. Only the Earl of Montaine had exchanged letters with her brother. And the other three hadn't requested her brother's permission to court her.

But William had. And then he had sent her a letter so eloquent, it made her cry. She had to smile at the thought of his missive, the wrinkled parchment suggesting he had crumpled it up and thrown it away and then had second thoughts about sending it. She continued to smile at the thought of his heartfelt words, describing how they had first met all those years ago, of his regrets at not having seen to her safety.

Of his affection for her.

"And you, Mr. Overby?" she murmured.

"William," he replied in an attempt to remind her of how he wanted her to address him. "And am I what?"

Giving a slight shrug, Lily regarded William for a moment. "Are you an honorable man?"

Straightening in his chair, William was almost offended by her question. She had come to him, after all. Taken the Fitzsimmons coach and come to his door at nine o'clock at night and requested entrance into his apartment— with no chaperone in sight.

"I am and always have been an honorable man, my lady," he replied before his eyes darkened with desire. "Although to be honest, I want nothing more than to kiss you right now and to… to hold you. To share my bed with you every night for the rest of my life," he murmured, the words coming so easily, he wondered why he hadn't put voice to them when she had first appeared at his door.

Brandy was certainly a powerful elixir!

•　•　•

*L*ily stared at William for several moments, stunned by his words. "You want me as your mistress?" she countered, her brows furrowed as if in confusion. *He claims to be an honorable man in one sentence, and then suggests a dishonorable arrangement in the next!*

William frowned. He shook his head.

How had she come to that conclusion?

"Mistress?" he repeated. "Of course not. I want you as my *wife*," he stated as he sat up straighter.

Sitting up so she was level with him, Lily stared at her host. "Truly?" she countered, a look of surprise apparent on her face. "So, you did receive word from my brother, did you not?" she asked, one eyebrow furrowing. "With his permission?" Gabriel had assured her he would write to William to let him know of his decision.

William stood up and quickly made his way to his study, where he retrieved the note he had received only the hour before. He dropped it onto the side table next to where she sat, landing so it remained open and ready for her perusal. "I did," William replied with a wave toward the note. "Just today, in fact."

Lily dared a glance at the short missive. "He certainly used an economy of words," she murmured, noting how little writing appeared on the page.

"As did I. In the query I sent him," he claimed.

Her eyes widening, Lily shook her head. "Your query to me was far more verbose. And rather eloquent, I thought," she countered. "I do hope it was all right that I shared it with the countess," she added, curious as to the surprise in his expression.

William shook his head. The note he had sent to Lily was short and to the point.

> *Dear Lady Lily,*
> *I miss you.*
> *Terribly.*
> *Yours truly, William Overby.*

Nothing more. "I can hardly believe the two sentences I wrote could be considered eloquent," he replied.

It was Lily's turn to widen her eyes. "Oh, but it was. I thought it quite right that you told of our first meeting, and how you had thought of me over the years. Truth be told, until I read that missive, I wasn't sure you were interested in courting me." She paused a moment as she watched William shake his head. "Do tell me. Why was it so wrinkled? Did you change your mind about sending it? And then changed your mind again?"

When William continued to stare at her, much the way he had done that day they had met at Wellingham Imports, Lily shrugged. "Or perhaps it was simply crumpled in the post," she suggested then, realizing her words had him perplexed.

"*I* didn't send that letter," William whispered.

Which meant someone else had.

Someone who had found it in the wastebasket next to Mrs. Wellingham's desk.

Had Emma Wellingham discovered it and sent it on his behalf? He couldn't believe she would do such a thing.

But Thomas Wellingham *would* do such a thing, he reasoned. His boss knew exactly where to send such a missive.

I should like to have at least one success at matchmaking, he had said, the very day Lily appeared at Wellingham Imports.

Well, it appeared the man had finally succeeded.

Lily considered his denial and then glanced again at the simple words on her brother's note, rather surprised he had been so succinct with his response.

You have my permission.

Well, apparently Gabriel was a man of few words.

And at the moment, William knew he had to be as well. "Yes, my lady. I truly wish you to be my wife."

William stood up and leaned forward, capturing one of her

cheeks with his open hand, pulling her toward him as his lips took purchase on hers. Moving his body around the table, he was soon sitting next to her on the settee, continuing the light kiss, his tongue darting against her closed lips until they finally parted to allow him to taste and tease her mouth.

Her inhalation of breath was more an invitation than an expression of her surprise, allowing his tongue to explore her mouth and tangle with her tongue. When her fingers speared his hair, their fingernails scraping his scalp, William moved his lips to her jaw, to her neck and down to her collarbones, their slight pressure leaving a trail of moisture in their wake.

"Truly," he murmured again. "I have thought of you nearly every night since that night in Vauxhall Gardens," he whispered, knowing he could think of her without remembering the rest of that night. "You have haunted my dreams," he accused.

"I didn't mean to," she countered, her hand pulling his head away from her shoulder where his latest kisses had been pressed. "I had no idea," she whispered, allowing his head to return to its place in the small of her shoulder. It felt so right tucked there, his warm breath washing over her collarbones.

"I should have told you years ago. I should have found you and claimed you as my own long before your brother found you and elevated you to a station I cannot hope to achieve."

Lily's hands moved to either side of his head. "I will never be a true aristocrat," she whispered, finally resting her head against his forehead. "I will always be half a maid and half an earl's sister, and always a bastard," she continued, her explanation so quiet he barely heard her words despite how close he held her to him.

William closed his eyes, remembering the words on the missive.

You have my permission.

"And I shall always be half a street urchin and half a clerk," he replied, kissing her nose. "And never an aristocrat, but I will always be devoted to you. Will you marry me, Lily Harkins?"

Her eyes widening with his words, Lily finally allowed a grin. "I will," she replied, her forehead nodding against his. "I will."

William's lips were on hers in an instant, taking purchase on the soft pillows and suckling them until she finally pulled away to inhale sharply and giggle quietly.

"What is it?" he whispered, not wanting to break the spell that seemed to hold them in the moment.

"I thought that very night of how I wanted you to put voice to a vow. To tell me you wanted me. That you pined for no other," she whispered. "I never dreamed I would have to wait so long," she added with a quirked lip.

William chuckled, his forehead still pressed against hers. "You minx," he accused. He gave her another quick kiss and then allowed a long sigh. "Given how honorable I am, I believe it's high time I saw to your safe return to Fitzsimmons Manor," he murmured.

Lily pulled her forehead from his and angled her head. "That won't be necessary," she whispered. "Besides, I sent the coach on its way. I am spending the night with a friend, you see," she continued, her lips skimming over his cheekbones.

Swallowing hard, William regarded Lily for a long time. "What friend?" he countered, his brows furrowing in confusion.

A wanton smile replaced the teasing grin she had displayed only a moment ago. "You, of course," she whispered.

William blinked. "Your first night back in London? Won't the Fitzsimmons think that rather *odd*?" he countered. He didn't know whether to feel blessed by her intentions or annoyed with her wanton behavior!

"They're at the theatre with the Marquess of Plymouth. I rather doubt they will even know I returned to London," she murmured, rather glad she had been able to sneak out the back door and make her way down the alley to hail a hackney.

Pulling her into another kiss, William wondered how he was expected to remain an honorable man with Lady Lily spending the night. "You'll spend the night in my bedchamber, of course, while I sleep out here..."

Lily's lips were back on his, silencing his directive. When she pulled away, she shook her head. "We'll both spend the night in your bedchamber, where you will ruin me so thoroughly, there can be no question we will marry," she stated, her forehead pressed against his. "I am not letting you send me away again, William Overby," she whispered.

William nodded. "Yes, of course, my lady. Whatever you wish," he said as he moved to stand up, lifting her so she stood before him. "But know this. I... I love you. And we shall marry at our earliest convenience..."

His words were once again cut off as Lily kissed him. When she pulled away, she regarded him through lowered lashes. "I love you as well, William, but when I next open my eyes, I had better be in your bed."

CHAPTER 34

TAKING A HOLIDAY

August 17, 1817

"Where are we going?" Emma asked when she realized they had been traveling in the Wellingham Import coach far longer than it normally took to get to Woodscastle. She had apparently fallen asleep and couldn't tell if the darkness in the coach was due to the drawn curtains or if night had fallen.

She and Thomas rarely used one of the company coaches, only doing so if it happened to leave the warehouse the same time they did, had enough room for two people and happened to be passing by Chiswick on its way south.

Thomas wrapped an arm around the back of her shoulders and pulled her so her head ended up on his shoulder. "Go back to sleep, my sweeting. We'll be there soon," he murmured, sounding as sleepy as she felt.

Emma closed her eyes, finding it rather comfortable riding with her husband's arms wrapped around her. *Perhaps he'll be kind enough to carry me into the house and put me into bed*, she thought before sleep took her again.

Thomas allowed a chuckle to burble forth once he knew his wife was once again sound asleep. He rather hoped Emma would be pleasantly surprised when she awoke and discovered she wasn't in their bedchamber at Woodscastle. He also hoped she wouldn't awake until they were in Dunstable, where the driver was scheduled to stop at a coaching inn for the rest of the night. Rooms were arranged for them and for the driver of the coach while the team of horses would be switched out with four others belonging to Wellingham Imports.

Two months of clandestine planning with Gregory and Christiana was finally culminating in a much-delayed holiday to the Grandby country estate, Cherrywood, in Derbyshire. Given the travel time there and back, they would have but seven or eight days at Cherrywood as it was. But those seven or eight days would be their first holiday in a long time, and Thomas looked forward to the time he and Emma could spend by themselves.

Christiana had been rather helpful in seeing to it that a trunk and a valise were packed with Emma's clothing and toiletries. She even managed to coerce Gregory to deliver them to the warehouse that morning after Thomas and Emma had left Woodscastle.

"There are enough clothes in there for three weeks," Christiana said when Thomas spoke with her the night before. "Just in case you decide to stay longer."

Thomas nodded his understanding. "Do you suppose she suspects anything?" he asked in a whisper. He wanted to surprise Emma—had wanted to surprise her with the trip ever since the day his cousin Lily had come to visit for the first time. With Todd Vandermeer back from his holiday and Stephen Bingham seeing to the warehouse, Thomas figured it was as good a time as any to spirit Emma away for two weeks.

His sister shook her head. "Not as long as she doesn't look in her wardrobe and discover all her gowns are missing," she countered with a whisper. "I had the laundress leave one out for her to wear, so she shouldn't have any need to open it." She arched a brow at Thomas, a signal he realized meant he had to keep Emma occupied so she wouldn't go near the wardrobe.

He found the task rather easy to achieve both at bedtime as well as when they awoke that morning.

With any luck, he would be doing the very same with her for the next couple of weeks.

His head resting atop Emma's, Thomas fell asleep, a satisfied smile still on his lips.

CHAPTER 35

YOUNG LOVERS AT PLAY

William blinked as he watched Lily's eyes close completely, the blue irises hidden by delicate eyelids lined with a curled fringe of dark lashes.

Desire raged in him, his manhood having hardened so it strained against the placket of his doeskin breeches. "Lord have mercy," he whispered as he lifted Lily into his arms and made his way into his bedchamber. He managed to nudge the door shut with one elbow before he lowered her to the bed's counterpane.

Lily sighed as she settled into the soft mattress, a grin forming before she slowly opened her eyes. Her attention immediately went to the ceiling, to the ornate coffers—the bed didn't have a canopy or curtains that could be closed to provide privacy—before she sat up and her gaze slowly took in the room around her. Finally, she regarded William with a wan smile. "How is it you have such a beautiful bedchamber?" she asked in a whisper.

William lowered his head so that he could kiss her, a quick kiss to acknowledge her compliment. "I think because I made it for you," he replied, his voice nearly a whisper to match hers.

Had he decorated his apartment for the sole purpose of impressing Lily Harkins? To prove that he was worthy of her, even before she was an earl's sister?

Perhaps. Until this moment, he had never truly believed she would visit the bedchamber, let alone lie in his bed.

"That was rather thoughtful of you," Lily whispered, one hand moving to pull his head down so she could kiss him. She hesitated, her lips barely touching his. "Thank you," she whispered as her hand moved to his neck, across his shoulder to his arm.

William kissed her then, his lips taking possession of hers as her hands gripped his arms, her fingers pressing into the fabric of his coat. Soon, he climbed atop the bed, sitting himself just behind her so he could undo the buttons of her gown. "This is my favorite gown," he murmured, his fingers carefully working loose the fastenings. "And I shouldn't wish to see it wrinkled because I allowed you to wear it to bed," he said.

"I hadn't planned to," Lily replied as she turned her head, her chin resting on her shoulder.

William leaned over and kissed her eyelid. "You minx," he murmured, stepping off the bed. He turned around and lifted her from the bed, ensuring her slippered feet were touching the carpet before he slid the pads of his fingers beneath the edges of the open fabric and spread them so the gown's sleeves slid down her arms. Holding onto the gown as it fell down her body, he carefully held it by the shoulders before arranging it over the back of chair. When he turned around, it was to find her wearing only a corset, pantaloons, stockings, and a rather nervous expression.

"My turn," she said in a hoarse whisper, reaching out to touch the buttons of his topcoat. She could blame the brandy, she thought, amazed at how brazen she was behaving.

His breathing a bit labored, William allowed her fingers to deftly undo each button of his top coat and those of his waist-coat. Her hands spread open the coats and continued to hold onto them as they slid down his arms, forcing her to press her torso against the front of his body until the garments were free of his arms. She couldn't help but notice his eyes close and his breath hitch before she let go of one edge of the coats so she could bring them around his body. Like he had done, she held them by the shoulders and carefully hung them over the arm of the chair.

When she moved to pull his shirt from his breeches, William quickly took a step back. "My turn, my lady," he whispered.

"Oh," she breathed. Before she could protest, he moved his hands beneath her arms and lifted her until she was sitting on the edge of the bed. He knelt down and reached for one of her legs, his warm hand sliding up the silk stocking that covered her calf until it was beneath the hem of her pantaloons. When he found the ribbon that held her stocking in place, he pulled apart the bow. Sliding the ink-stained fingers of his other hand up the stocking, he slowly peeled the fabric from her leg, eliciting a gasp from Lily when he touched her bare flesh. Pausing, he dared a glance up, one eyebrow arched as if to request permission to continue.

Her eyes wide—he was being ever so careful, as if he knew he might snag the silk—Lily shook her head. "Why did you stop?" she whispered.

William blinked and quickly returned his attention to her calves. He pulled down the first stocking to her toes before moving to the other, his movements just as careful as they had been with the first stocking, his ink-stained fingers barely touching the fabric. When the two stockings dribbled to the carpet, he draped them onto the chair cushion, his attention going back to her bare feet for a moment. He was tempted to reach out and stroke his fingers over the pale flesh, to lean over and kiss her toes one after the other, but he thought better of it when she suddenly tried to hide one foot behind the other.

William moved to stand up, but Lily reached out with a hand to his shoulder. "My turn," she said as she moved her fingers to the knot at his neck, undoing the ends of the cravat and then unwinding the length of silk from around his neck.

When it was completely loose, she allowed it to drape from the edge of the bed. "Your turn," she murmured, her words coming out on a breath she hadn't realized she had been holding. Although the room was warm, her body shivered, very nearly vibrating with excitement.

"Are you cold?" William asked suddenly, quickly rising to his feet to reach for his dressing robe.

"No," Lily replied with a shake of her head. "Quite the opposite, in fact," she murmured as she grabbed at the fabric of his shirt and pulled it from his breeches. William hissed as her warm palms pushed the linen up the sides of his body, but he was quick to shed the garment, tossing it toward the chair with no regard for how wrinkled it might become. He had no valet to scold him, after all.

"I've a mind to scold you," Lily said, her lips displaying a pout. "I wanted to do that."

William couldn't suppress his amusement. "You can do it tomorrow night," he offered, which had Lily's pout disappearing and a pink blush covering her cheeks. He held his hands so they hovered just above her shoulders, as if he were afraid to touch her. "You're so beautiful," he whispered, his lips once again settling onto hers. His kiss was feather light, his touch so tentative against her bare skin, Lily shivered, and her lips suddenly grinned against his.

"What has you so amused?" he asked as his lips worked their way from her lips along her jaw and to the soft lobes of her ears, his tongue reaching out to touch the soft flesh. Her soft inhalation of breath had him remembering his vow to be an honorable gentleman. Perhaps her definition of an honorable gentleman was different from his. *Honorable, I am not.*

"Tickles," she whispered, her hands taking purchase on the sides of his body so she could touch him the same way he was caressing her.

William suppressed a chuckle at her teasing touches. "My turn," he whispered, his hands moving to where the ties of her corset were fastened in the middle of her back. He had the laces untied and loosened in a only a moment, rather happy to feel her sigh of relief as he spread apart the edges in the back enough to pull the corset up and over her arms. Even before he had a chance to toss it off toward the chair, Lily had the front of her body pressed against his, her chemise-covered breasts nestled into the crisp, dark hairs on his bare chest.

Aroused and a bit concerned he might not be able to hold off his release, William had to suppress the urge to cup her breasts with his hands and instead slid them down the sides of her body to the top edge of her pantaloons. His fingers undid the tapes. When he slipped his hands beneath the fabric, the pantaloons fell to the floor, and his hands moved under the short chemise to smooth over the globes of her bottom. He felt her sudden tenseness, felt her body go rigid against his, and he sought to discover why when he pulled away so he could see her face.

"It was *my* turn," she scolded, her eyes wide with her admonishment.

"Oh, I apologize," he said, about to reach down and pull the pantaloons back up onto her body. But Lily had her fingers at the placket of his breeches, working to unfasten the leathern buttons. She struggled for a moment before letting out a sigh of frustration.

"Allow me, my lady," he whispered. He paused a moment, not wanting to leave her standing nearly naked next to his bed. God, he wanted her so badly!

Reaching around her, he pulled down the counterpane and layers of blankets to expose the indigo-dyed bed linens. Before Lily realized quite what was happening, he had her chemise pulled up and over her head. Then he scooped her up in his arms and placed her onto the dark linens, her pale skin a stark contrast.

Suddenly exposed to his gaze, Lily quickly covered her breasts with one arm as she let out a squeak. "But it was my turn," she whispered, her protest silenced when she noticed how he regarded her.

William couldn't help but stare at what he could see of her. Smooth silken skin outlined the slight curves from her ankles to her knees and around her thighs. The inward curves at her waist and the ones she held covered with one arm. The sharp curves of her shoulders and neck, of her cheeks and lips and brows. And then there were the curves of her golden curls splayed out on his dark pillow, and those of her blue eyes as they opened wider with his gaze.

Unable to stop himself, William leaned down and kissed her as he worked to remove his boots with his feet. Realizing he needed his hands, he finally lifted his head and said, "Pardon me a moment." He captured the ends of the blankets and tossed them over Lily before he leaned over to remove his boots and stockings. Once he had his breeches loose, he was about to push them down when he suddenly stopped.

Lily pushed herself onto her elbows, the top edge of the blankets barely covering her breasts. "What is it?" she asked in a hoarse whisper.

William took a breath and considered how to answer. "I don't wish to frighten you," he answered, his manhood's arousal outlined in the doeskin breeches.

Blinking, Lily dared a glance over the part of his body she could see, reminding herself she had seen a man's naked bum before. And she had paid witness to a tupping, although not a lot of flesh had been visible. "You won't," she murmured, giving her head a shake. Her breaths were shallow, and she felt far too warm, her insides a bit molten. The space at the apex of her thighs seemed to be throbbing as moisture collected there. "Hurry," she pleaded, her face and throat coloring up as she made the demand.

Stunned by her simple word and concerned Lily was about to faint—she seemed to be breathing in awfully shorts pants—William pushed the breeches off his body and climbed onto the bed.

His lips covered hers as her hands moved to his shoulders, her fingers gripping them so their nails left crescents in his bare skin. Although he desperately wished to simply impale her, to thrust himself into her soft flesh and allow his release, he also remembered his comment about being an honorable man. He would see to her pleasure first, and if she still wanted him to take her maidenhead, he would.

William pulled his lips from hers so he could move them

down the front of her body, pulling down the blankets as he did so, exposing more and more of her heated skin to his lips and tongue.

Her quiet moans and inhalations of breath spurred him on. When his lips captured one of her nipples, her chest arched up, and she cried out when his tongue flicked over the ruched bud. Barely touching her with the tip of his nose, he slowly moved his mouth to her other breast, eliciting another series of gasps and quiet whimpers.

Moving one of his hands down the side of her body to a thigh, he smoothed it around the milky white skin and down to her knee, gently lifting it from the bed. Positioning himself between her legs, he moved his other hand down to her other knee and did the same, his mouth continuing its assault on her flesh.

No longer able to reach his shoulders with her hands, Lily was forced to simply allow him to do whatever it was he was doing to cause such amazing sparks of pleasure—like miniature fireworks—beneath the surface of her skin.

Light-headed from breathing too quickly, she struggled to slow her breaths, to pay attention to what he was doing—and where. She knew her knees were bent, her thighs spread apart, his hands suddenly beneath her bottom and lifting it up so her knees fell farther apart.

About to protest, about to attempt to regain control of her body, she found she could not, for a burst of pleasure so intense, so sharp and so satisfying seemed to grip her entire body. Even before she could catch her breath, before she could sort quite what had happened, the sensation gripped her again. She cried out, cried out again as the quick waves of pleasure crested over and over again.

She dared a glance down the front of her body, realizing William had to be using his tongue and perhaps his lips to incite the sensations. Perhaps he knew she saw him or perhaps he had realized she could take no more—her vision had begun to gray at the edges, and she thought she might faint—he suddenly moved his entire body atop hers.

"I don't wish to hurt you," he whispered, "But I do not think I can…" He paused and leaned down to kiss her on the mouth, his lips tasting of *her* as he nudged the tip of his manhood into her wet haven.

She felt his intrusion, her reaction to clench down and prevent his entrance. But when he stilled his movements and lowered his lips to one of her breasts, she slowly relaxed, slowly allowed him to continue pushing into her.

Still throbbing from the pleasure he had set off only moments before, her wet sheath took him in, slowly unfurling to allow him entrance. She was aware of the moment he breached her maidenhead, the sting forcing a hiss from her.

William stilled himself, cursing when he realized what had happened. He had half expected she was no longer a virgin. He had thought perhaps the master of Fitzsimmons Manor or another lord might have taken her virtue at some point in the past. He thought it common for lords to use their maids for quick tumbles. "I'm so sorry," he whispered against her breast.

One of her hands moved to the side of his face. "I am yours, William," she replied, a wan smile appearing.

William swallowed. "And I am yours," he countered, his lips moving up to take hers for a thorough kiss.

"Tell me what to do," Lily whispered, her hand still cupping one of his cheeks.

Momentarily confused by her words, William shook his head. "You say that as if you think I know, but… I do not," he said, his breaths still short.

He knew what to do, of course, but he wondered if he should continue. Wondered until he felt Lily's hands travel down the sides of his torso, until he felt her knees lift so his manhood was forced deeper inside her welcoming cocoon. And then he wondered no more as he pushed himself into her as far as he could go. Pulling himself out a bit, he gently pushed into her again, grinning as Lily pushed against him. When she did it again on his next thrust, he reached down and kissed her. "Yes," he murmured. His thrusts increasing with both speed and intensity, William struggled to breathe.

Lily inhaled sharply as her counter thrusts seemed to excite William, seemed to spur him to quicken his movements. Needing something to hang onto, something to anchor her to him, she moved her hands to his buttocks and gripped the hardened muscles.

William suddenly stilled himself, a growl forced from his throat as Lily felt a rush of warmth fill her lower abdomen. He thrust once more, setting off a shiver of pleasure that had Lily gasping in surprise, gasping and clenching on him so he jerked and growled once again.

His head landing on the pillow between her head and shoulder, William allowed a long groan. "Lily," he sighed, his breathing labored. "I do hope you feel thoroughly ruined, because I certainly do," he managed to get out, a soft chuckle following his words. He stilled himself, curious as to her silence. "Are you all right?" he asked then, concern evident in his voice.

Lily replied with a nod, her arms wrapping around his back in an effort to stay as close to him as possible.

Was she all right? Lily hardly knew just then, the darts of pleasure occasionally reminding her that he was still inside her. She held on, not sure what else to do. When she heard his breathing slow and felt his heartbeat subside from its staccato rhythm from only moments before, she allowed a sigh and closed her eyes.

When she awoke, Lily found William watching her, his head supported by a hand and his elbow pressed into the featherbed. He held one of her hands in his, and he kissed the back of it. "Good morning, my beautiful," he whispered.

Blinking at the words, Lily glanced around. "Good morning," she replied. "Is it?" She moved to sit up, but William leaned over and kissed her mouth, forcing her to lay back into the soft mattress.

"It's still early," he said when he finally came up for air. "Still dark, in fact."

"Do you have to leave?" she asked, trying hard to remember what day of the week it was.

"No," he replied. "It's Sunday, actually," he added. "Did you wish to go for a walk in the park?"

Lily closed her eyes and rolled so she was pressed against most of the front of his body. "Later," she murmured. "Much later. After I give you a haircut."

William groaned as he wrapped his arm around her, pulling her so she ended up atop his body. "Agreed." After a pause while he caressed one of her arms with the back of a finger, he asked, "Do you suppose we could walk to Berkeley Square instead of the park?"

Her eyes widening, Lily regarded William with a brilliant smile. "I suppose. Did you have a particular destination in mind?" she asked, hoping he was suggesting what he had said they would do when she returned from Staffordshire.

"Why, Gunter's Tea Shop, of course," he answered. "For an ice. Or a sorb—" The last word was cut off by Lily's kiss, one William returned when he realized what was happening.

"I love you, William Overby," she said when she finally pulled away.

Chuckling, William allowed his head to fall back into the pillow. "Had I known then what I know now, I would have taken you there the first day I met you," he murmured. He regarded her for a long moment, once again lost in her blue eyes until she slowly closed them. "You minx."

Lily felt his kiss on her forehead and smiled as sleep took her once more.

EPILOGUE

month later
Despite the four aristocrats who might have thought they were destined to marry Lady Lily, who might have put voice to their objections during the reading of the banns over the course of the three weeks following William's proposal, William Overby prevailed in his quest to marry the love of his life. He did so in St. James' Cathedral in Piccadilly, not far from his bachelor quarters in Golden Square.

He no longer lived there, of course, since his new brother-in-law had insisted his wife's dowry be used to purchase a house. Or rather, part of her dowry. A rather small part, it turned out, for Gabriel Wellingham, Earl of Trenton, was far more generous than he had led his sister Lily to believe that day he had given her his permission to marry the clerk.

William couldn't help but feel tempted to give up his position at Wellingham Imports—Lily's dowry would allow them to live quite comfortably for the rest of their days. His comparatively meager salary would be but a drop into his suddenly oceanic bank account at Barrings.

But he did not give notice at his place of employment for two reasons. Thomas Wellingham threatened him with bodily harm should he quit the firm, and Lady Lily insisted he needed to be gone at least part of the day so that she might have the opportunity to miss him, to imagine him coming home so she could meet him at the front door with a kiss and questions about his day.

Who was he to argue?

Although he rather doubted Thomas would do him any harm, he was more afraid of Emma Wellingham's retribution. She had trained him in how to be an inventory clerk and didn't wish to have to do it again with some other poor bastard from the warehouse. Besides, Lily had returned to her volunteer duties at 'Lady E's Finding Work for the Wounded'. She rather liked the opportunity to spend time with William's uncle, Augustus. Especially when the man shared stories of William's early childhood.

Fitzsimmons Manor might have been a beehive of activity, given two weddings were to take place. However, the Marquess of Plymouth had obtained a special license, the document allowing him to forgo the reading of the banns and the three weeks they would have required. He married Lady Samantha in a small ceremony attended by close family and friends and then promptly swept her off to his home, Castle Keys, in Yorkshire.

Samantha's latest missive from Castle Keys mentioned her joy at having her own studio in which to paint landscapes and new vistas to use as her subjects. She was also rather pleased to learn she had a sister in Emma Fitzsimmons. Although she had felt anger toward her real mother for having withheld the information from her for so long, she found she could not when she learned just why Caroline had kept the information secret from her and the rest of the world. At least her new husband had known the secret and no longer held her illegitimacy against her.

Oh, and given she was expecting a baby in seven months' time, Samantha was also looking forward to impending motherhood. The marquess was said to be cautiously optimistic about fatherhood.

Although William considered following the marquess' example by acquiring a special license, his thriftiness prevented him from paying out a tenth of his annual salary for the extravagance. He instead opted for the more traditional marriage license. The downside, he found, was having to wait more than three weeks before being allowed to marry Lily. Given the Fitzsimmons were in residence at Fitzsimmons Manor, it also meant he had to wait until after he and Lily were married before he could share his bed with her again.

Why, he had half a mind to take her on a drive to Vauxhall Gardens and have his way with her in the most remote part of the gardens! And he might have mentioned the ploy to his fiancée, but he was quite sure she would readily agree to the scandalous suggestion.

Better she behave. Better he be patient. Better he head off to work every day as he always did. On the days he was allowed to spend more time with Lily, he made sure to take her to Gunter's Tea Shop for a sorbet, treating her maid to an ice as well.

Given Lily's status as an affianced woman absent from the public eye for more than two months, the newspapers lost interest in her and her supposed suitors, turning their gossip printing presses to the new crop of young gels making their debut during the Little Season. The Earl of Montaine married the baron's daughter from Dorchester and was, according to the last account of his whereabouts, taking her on a wedding trip to the Lake District.

Lily sent a note to the Marquess of Reading, thanking him for his offer but informing him she had made the choice to marry a commoner. His reply was gracious, but Lily couldn't help but think the man was rather disappointed by the news of her betrothal. If the man was truly serious about taking a wife, he would need to reform his rakish behavior, but she doubted he was capable.

Her other two suitors were apparently no longer in the market for a wife. Sir Tristan Nisbet had a rather successful night at The Jack of Spades and won enough money to replenish his depleted bank account the night before his mother announced she planned to marry a wealthy cit, which he considered a double windfall. He was able to sell both her old townhouse as well as her new one.

Sir Tobias Fulton, on the other hand, discovered his mistress was bedding a duchess during the days. At first rather appalled, he was about to declare their contract void and have her removed from the house he let on her behalf when she countered with an offer he found he couldn't refuse. Seems a menage â trois was the perfect solution to their problem.

The week before his own wedding, William purchased a tony townhouse in Curzon Street—just a street over from Park Lane and only a few from Fitzsimmons Manor—and arranged to have all his belongings moved there. Three days before the wedding, several trunks belonging to Lily were delivered by a footman. A day before the wedding, her maid, Bonnie, appeared to put away her ladyship's clothes and prepare the mistress suite.

The witnesses, the Earl and Countess of Trenton, the Viscount and Viscountess Chamberlain, and Mr. and Mrs. Thomas Wellingham, assembled at St. James' Cathedral on the appointed day, dressed in their Sunday best. By the time William and Lily were married at eleven o'clock, the groom was desperate to spend the rest of his life with his bride. However, a wedding breakfast at the Trenton townhouse had to be attended and well-wishers had to be allowed to wish the happy couple well.

It was nearly seven o'clock in the evening when the Trenton coach delivered Mr. and Lady Overby to their townhouse. In keeping with the custom of carrying a bride over the threshold, William did so with Lily, although he carried her all the way from the coach to the front door and beyond.

"Would you like a tour of your new home?" William asked as he lowered her so her feet touched the Axminster carpet.

Spellbound by the elegance of the vestibule, Lily's attention was captured by the domed ceiling and its painting of clouds and cherubs. When William followed her gaze to one particular cherub, he grinned. "I thought she looked like you," he murmured.

Lily smiled. "Did you have it specially painted?" she asked, her back leaning against the front of William as she continued to study the artwork.

He allowed a chuckle. "I cannot take credit," he replied, wrapping his arms around her waist and turning her around so she faced him. "It was already here. As were the servants, although I have given them the night off so that we might have the evening to ourselves."

Lily's eyes widened. "That was rather generous of you," she murmured, a small smile appearing as she considered what lay ahead for the evening. "And in answer to your question, I should love a tour, Mr. Overby."

William frowned at her use of his formal name. "Does this mean I must address you as Lady Overby?" he asked as he placed one of her arms on his.

Lily gave him a startled look. "As much as it has a certain ring to it, I should think not," she replied as she walked with him down the central hallway.

"Lily, then," he said as he escorted her around the first floor of their new residence. He made sure to show her every room before he led her up the stairs to show her even more rooms on the second.

The very last room he took her to was the bedchamber.

*G*abriel, Sarah and Little Gabe had made the trip to London not only for Lily's wedding, but also to take up residence in the Trenton townhouse. The autumn sessions of Parliament were about to resume.

Having stayed in the townhouse for only a few days when they were last in London, Sarah didn't realize its close proximity to Park Lane and to Lily and William's townhouse until she watched the Trenton coach deliver its occupants from her vantage of a west facing window in the mistress suite.

Despite the thick carpet below her slippers, she could feel the vibrations in the floor as the earl climbed the stairs to the second story. *Thump-thump-thump-thump*. When they stopped, she had to suppress a grin, realizing he was probably watching her from the hallway.

"Did you have something to do with Mr. Overby's selection

of that particular townhouse?" Sarah asked as she turned to find her husband watching her from where he leaned against the door jamb, his arms crossed over his chest.

Gabriel angled his head before he moved to join her at the window. "I've no idea what you're talking about," he claimed as he followed her line of sight. The Overby's residence was, indeed, merely one street up and across the street from the Trenton townhouse.

Sarah gave him a quelling glance. "What did you do?" she asked, her voice filled with suspicion.

His eyes wide, Gabriel shook his head. "Nothing, I assure you. Well, I... I might have seen to it the agent showed him a couple of... poor choices to start with, but William's selection of that particular property was entirely up to him," he said with a shrug. He was struck quiet as he watched his new brother-in-law lift his sister from the coach and carry her up to the front door. In another moment, the two disappeared into the house. Reminded of when he had carried Sarah into Trenton Manor for the first time—Little Gabe held in her arms as he held her in his—Gabriel felt a tightening in his chest. "I wanted her to be close," he said with a shrug.

Turning to face Gabriel, Sarah gave her head a shake. "You're incorrigible," she accused, her face lighting up in delight as Gabriel suddenly took her into his arms.

"I am," he agreed, his moment of introspection over. "And I expect to be handsomely rewarded on this fine evening," he added as one of his eyebrows arched up. "And many more to come."

Sarah pretended to search the pockets of her gown for some money. "Well, kind sir, I seem to be short of coin," she teased when she pulled her empty hands from the pockets.

Unable to suppress his grin, Gabriel replied, "Thank the gods! I'll take my payment in your bed."

His lips covered hers before she could giggle in response.

• • •

"*D*id you know Trenton House was so close when you bought this townhouse?" Lily asked as she lay in William's arms, her body still trembling from how he had worshipped it only moments ago. The long, drawn out foreplay and tender coupling had her satiated but thinking she could do it all over again should he wish it.

Would do it all over again.

Perhaps she could entice him to do it again. And again.

Her fingers travelled down his arm, their tips inciting ticklish sensations under his skin as she felt the beating of his heart beneath her ear. *Thump-thump, thump-thump.*

"I did not," he whispered, moving his head so he could kiss Lily's forehead and bury his nose in her rose-scented hair. "I chose it so we would be close to the park. So we could go for walks in the morning before the rest of Mayfair is up and about." He suddenly opened his eyes. "Does it bother you that we live so close to him?" he asked. Truth be told, he hadn't really noticed where Trenton House was located with respect to the townhouse they now called home.

Lily allowed a soft giggle. "Not especially, since it means I can see Sarah and Little Gabe whilst you and Gabriel are off working," she murmured.

"Just how close *is* Trenton House?" he asked, raising himself on his elbow.

Her eyes widening at her husband's query, she gave a slight shrug. "Down Curzon about four, maybe five houses and across the street," she replied matter-of-factly.

A street away, he considered. Well, that wasn't so bad, he supposed. It wasn't as if they could spy on Lily and him from that distance.

He gave a glance toward the east-facing window and was suddenly out of the bed, drawing the velvet drapes across the sheers that hung over the entire expanse of glass. Climbing back into the bed, he settled himself next to his wife and finally allowed a grin of embarrassment. "Now, where were we?" he whispered.

Recognizing her opportunity, Lily allowed a wan smile and murmured, "Making up for lost time," as she leaned over and kissed William.

"You minx," he whispered, happy to do her bidding. Life would certainly be worth living now that Lily was in his life.

Thank you for taking the time to read The Desire of a Lady. If you enjoyed it, please consider telling your friends or posting a short review. Word of mouth is an author's best friend.

Thank you,
Linda Rae Sande

EXCERPT

Read on for an excerpt from Linda Rae Sande's
Book 1 in "The Sons of the Aristocracy" series
The Love of a Rake

September 16, 2017

While he waited for his wife to join him in the breakfast parlor, Milton Grandby, Earl of Torrington, read that day's edition of *The Times*. He was rather pleased to see the notice of the marriage of Lady Lily Wellingham to Mr. William Overby, the union effectively ending any speculation as to whom the young lady would choose to marry during the Little Season. Although he had to admit to a bit of surprise at learning she had married a clerk—four aristocrats had been rumored to want her hand in marriage or her dowry—Grandby thought her choice of a commoner a better fit. She would probably never be accepted in the *ton* given she was an illegitimate daughter of an earl.

If Lady Lily hadn't made a decision as to a spouse, Grandby was quite prepared to arrange a suitable one on her behalf. Given how his life would be changing any day now, though, he was rather relieved the matter was out of his hands.

He glanced at his chronometer, surprised that his countess, Adele Slater Worthington Grandby, hadn't yet appeared for breakfast. About to summon a footman to check on her, he was rather startled when one suddenly appeared, breathless, in the doorway.

"My lord. The countess says to beg your forgiveness, but she won't be joining you for breakfast this morning," the young man managed to get out.

Grandby blinked. "Oh. Did she say why?" he asked, hoping she wasn't feeling any worse than she had the night before. She had complained of back aches and swollen ankles, conditions he found he could help alleviate with a bit of sexual intercourse and by rubbing her feet. Despite her repeated admonishment of his advances—"I'm as big as a house, Milton. Honestly, how can you stand to be in the same *room* with me?"—Grandby found he rather liked his wife in her current condition, all soft and round and ready for his arousal no matter the time of day or night. He had to admit to feeling a bit exhausted, however; he had never engaged in this much intercourse even when he was an unmarried earl bedding a different widow every Season.

The footman colored up and stammered a bit before he said, "She's going to have a baby, my lord."

Grandby set aside his newspaper and nodded. "I'm well aware of Lady Torrington's condition," he replied with a grin. *Have been since March*, he nearly added.

Swallowing, the footman nodded. "Today, my lord."

Having taken a drink of his coffee, Grandby nearly choked as he comprehended the words. "*Now?*" he countered, rising quickly from the table. "Send for the midwife—"

"The butler is seeing to it," the footman interrupted.

"Then see to it word gets to Lady Norwick," Grandby ordered, knowing Adele would want Clarinda Fitzwilliam at her bedside. The Countess of Norwick was Adele's best friend and confidante, and she had just delivered twins a few weeks ago.

"Another footman has already been dispatched to Norwick House, my lord," the tall man countered.

Grandby frowned. "What? Am I the last to know?" he asked in alarm.

The footman, realizing he didn't know if he should attempt to answer the question, simply bowed and took his leave of the breakfast parlor.

The earl wasn't far behind, making his way to the stairs just as Clarinda Fitzwilliam appeared in the vestibule of Worthington House. She cradled a blanket-wrapped baby in one arm.

"Clare!" Grandby called out, changing his direction of travel in order to make his way to greet her.

"Grandby. So good to see you," the new mother said as she held out the baby. "Here. Take her so I can get out of my pelisse, won't you?"

Blinking, Grandby was suddenly in possession of a three-week-old girl. Although he was the godfather to twenty-one—no, make that twenty-two—women of various ages, Milton Grandby hadn't held a baby in his arms in over twenty years. He had seen this one before, as well as her twin sister, but both were in their perambulator and snoozing on their morning walk with their parents.

The baby, although awake, didn't seem the least bit bothered at being handed off to a man who was probably old enough to be her grandfather. "Which one is she?" Grandby asked as he adjusted his arm so her head was better supported. *This isn't so hard*, he thought, rather pleased with himself that the newborn wasn't howling at the sudden change in view. Perhaps his own baby, apparently on the way at any moment, would feel the same. He could only hope.

"That is Diana," Daniel Fitzwilliam said as he stood in the vestibule helping his wife remove her pelisse with one hand while he held another bundle in his other arm. Having helped deliver one of the twins—the midwife had assisted with the first and then left the room while Clarinda gave birth to the second, Daniel was a far more involved father than most aristocrats were. "And this is Dahlia," he said as he held out his bundle.

Rather surprised both girls were wide awake, Grandby was about to ask how the new parents were faring when a servant appeared at the top of the stairs. "Oh, milady, 'tis so good to see you. She's been asking for you. And the midwife still hasn't arrived."

Clare gave Grandby an arched brow, gathered up her skirts, and made her way up the stairs. "I trust you can entertain Diana for a while," she called out, knowing her husband would help if need be.

Having been at Worthington House many times in the past, Clare knew her way around and headed straight for the mistress suite. She hurried in without knocking, a bit startled to find Adele leaning up against a pile of pillows.

"Thank the gods!" the Countess of Torrington said as her lady's maid wiped her brow. "I was about to send for Milton to help, but I have a feeling he would faint," she managed as her face screwed into a grimace.

"I don't know how much help *I'll* be," Clare said just as Adele let out a rather unladylike howl. Alarmed, Clare moved to lift Adele's chemise. "How long has it been since your water broke?" she asked, her brows furrowing.

Adele dared a glance at the mantel clock. "A few hours now," she said, her voice weak. "I am too old for this, Clare," she added before her face took on an expression of pain.

"Nonsense. You're younger than Queen Charlotte was when she had her last. Do you feel like pushing?" she asked, remembering what she had been through with the quick birth of her twins.

"Anything to get this boy out," Adele countered.

Another servant appeared, this one apparently more familiar with childbirth than Adele's maid. She carried several linens and a bowl of water, setting them aside before seeing to Adele. "Twins, aye?" she said as she settled herself.

"Yes," Clare replied. "Three weeks ago," she added when the servant suddenly turned to regard her.

"Oh, congratulations, milady, but I was addressing Countess Torrington."

Clare stared at the servant for several seconds before

returning her attention to Adele. "Why didn't you tell me?" she asked in surprise. The two countesses were the best of friends, took frequent walks in the park together, and took turns hosting other Mayfair matrons for morning or afternoon tea.

Adele blinked. And blinked again as she shook her head. "No one said I was having *twins*," she replied just before another contraction had her crying out.

Wide-eyed, Clare looked to the servant. "You get the first. I'll get the second."

Within fifteen minutes, the Grandby twins made their debut.

"I have to think you're hoping for a boy," Daniel Fitzwilliam, Earl of Norwick, said as he settled into one of the leather chairs in Grandby's study. His niece, Dahlia, was alert and making bubbles as he held her in one arm. "I was hoping for a girl, I'll have you know. But at this point, I don't really care what it is as long as Adele..." Milton Grandby, Earl of Torrington, allowed the sentence to trail off, worry evident on his brow. "I don't know what I'll do if I lose her," he finally managed to get out, his attention turning to the Norwick twin baby he still held in his arms. "Geez, she's a heavy little—"

"Watch your language," Daniel interrupted, thinking Grandby was about to say 'bugger'.

"Lady," Grandby finished without missing a beat.

"The countess will be fine," Daniel said, aware one of his best friends was going through what he had gone through only a few weeks ago. At least he hadn't had a chance to be worried. Clarinda's labor had gone so fast, there was barely time to send for the midwife.

"We'll never have sexual intercourse again," the older earl announced suddenly.

Daniel blinked. "Yes, you will," he said with a nod. "And, please, my nieces do have ears," he added with a frown.

"Have *you?*" Grandby asked.

A bit confused by the question, Daniel had to think a

moment. "Well, not yet, but we will. In a few weeks," he ventured. "The Norwick earldom needs an heir, and my wife is willing to have as many babies as it takes. She's quite adamant when it comes to doing her duty," Daniel said as he raised Dahlia to his shoulder.

He wasn't about to get another child on Clare anytime in the next few months, but the Earl of Torrington didn't need to know that he had a supply of French letters on order. Thank the gods he had a discrete importer seeing to it. Wellingham Imports might be better known for the unusual products they imported from countries all over the world, but sometimes their most prized products were made in England. Thanks to sheep.

"Fuck duty," Grandby said suddenly.

"Grandby! Language!" Daniel nearly shouted, which had Dahlia suddenly fussing at his shoulder. He bounced her a bit, which seemed to settle the girl. Diana wasn't as easily assuaged when Grandby tried to bounce her, though, her face screwing into an expression of unhappiness. She let out a cry.

"I apologize," Grandby said to the baby held. "Please, don't cry," he added.

Diana blinked and stared at the man whose face filled her vision. She suddenly grinned, which had the man looking ever so startled.

"You'll do fine," Daniel murmured, rather amazed at how Grandby was doing with Diana. "In fact, Clarinda wondered if you would agree to be the godfather for these two," he said in a quiet voice.

The earl stared at him a moment. "Are you sure? I can't say as I did right by her when it came to *you*," he replied. Although Clarinda had been his first goddaughter, he had seen to it she married David Fitzwilliam, older twin brother of Daniel, even though she had been courted by Daniel. Given David and Daniel were identical twins and Clarinda was barely allowed in the company of Daniel for more than a few minutes at a time, she had accepted his suit and married David thinking he was Daniel. When David died in a horrible traffic accident earlier in the year, Daniel had stepped in as earl—he was the rightful heir—and taken Clare as his wife despite her mourning period having just begun. "No one will notice," Grandby had assured her. "The *ton* has a short memory, and the two look so much alike, most won't even realize David has perished," he said, knowing Clarinda was due to give birth in the late summer.

Daniel's head jerked up at Grandby's question and comment. "Whatever do you mean?" he asked.

Grandby gave a shrug, which had Diana studying him with a furrowed blonde brow. He watched the baby's face as he said, "I knew David was a rake. Knew he owned that brothel and gaming hell. But I also knew he needed to marry. He needed an heir—"

"Which turned out to be me," Daniel interrupted, his manner rather serious. Had Grandby undermined his attempt to marry Clarinda Brotherton, daughter of an earl? They had been in love back then—still were, in fact—which made her marriage to David cause a rift that would take years and their recent marriage to mend.

"True," Grandby agreed. "But I knew Clare's father wanted her settled with a titled man."

Daniel stared at the Earl of Torrington for a long time, anger passing through him as he considered the hell he had gone through when he learned Clarinda had married David instead of him. Instead of the man who had courted her with pink roses and walks in Kensington Gardens and soft words and softer kisses. "Then it's a good thing I still ended up with her," Daniel said with a hint of menace.

Milton Grandby regarded Daniel for a moment. "It is indeed," he said. "I made a mistake with my first goddaughter, but I promise you, I did not and will not make the same mistake with any of my other goddaughters," he vowed.

"And what of *your* daughter?" Clarinda asked as she stood in the threshold of the study, a blanket-wrapped baby held in her arms.

"Why, I plan to send her to a nunnery..."

Grandby was suddenly on his feet, staring at Clarinda, the

bundle in his own arms cooing in delight at the sound of her mother's voice.

"A girl?" Grandby whispered, his face splitting into a huge grin. "Let me trade with you," he said as he hurried to collect his daughter from Clare while she took her daughter Diana from him.

"Yes," Clare hedged before she motioned for the midwife to join her.

"And what of your heir?" she asked as she nodded to the bundle the midwife carried.

Daniel, who stood up upon his wife's entrance into the room, noted how pale the other earl appeared and was ready to retrieve the baby from him should the older man faint.

But Grandby's face continued to betray his joy. "A boy?" he whispered, readjusting his daughter so he could take the baby boy into his other arm. "Jesus, Joseph and Mother Mary," he murmured. He looked up to find Clarinda weeping. "Well, there will be none of that," he said. "Christ. I should take a trip to Ludgate Hill right now and buy every bauble in every jewelry store for my beloved wife, but I find I just want to be with her. Is she... is she well?" he asked in a whisper.

Clare nodded. "She's tired. Sleeping now, in fact, but I'm sure she wouldn't mind being awakened by you and your children," she added with a grin.

Grandby nodded and took his leave of the study. "Help yourself to the brandy. And the champagne and whatever else you want," he said as he made his way up the stairs with his prize possessions. "Hell, take everything!"

Daniel frowned as he stood in the threshold of the study. "Language!" he called out.

But the Earl of Torrington had disappeared into the mistress suite.

Daniel turned his attention to Clare. "How is it he is able to carry both babes in his arms like that?" he asked, his brows furrowed so a vertical line appeared between them. "It took me a *week* to be able to do that."

Clare reached up and kissed him on the cheek. "He's had far

more practice than you, my love. He has over twenty goddaughters, you know."

Daniel wasn't about to counter her comment, but he was quite sure Grandby had never held a baby in his arms before that day. At least, not recently.

ABOUT THE AUTHOR

A self-described nerd and lover of science, Linda Rae spent many years as a published technical writer specializing in 3D graphics workstations, software and 3D animation (her movie credits include SHREK and SHREK 2). An interest in genealogy led to years of research on the Regency era and a desire to write fiction based in that time.

A fan of action-adventure movies, she can frequently be found at the local cinema. Although she no longer has any tropical fish, she does follow the San Jose Sharks. She makes her home in Cody, Wyoming.

For more information:
www.lindaraesande.com

www.ingramcontent.com/pod-product-compliance
Lightning Source LLC
Chambersburg PA
CBHW031942130726
47905CB00002BA/444